Praise for Lucy Dillon

'Heartwarming, real and entertaining. You will love this book!'
Katie Fforde

'Warm and romantic.'

Elle

'Charming, heartwarming, entertaining.'

Glamour

'It's funny and charming ... a fabulous story that you won't want to put down, guaranteed to warm the heart of even the most devout *non-dog* person.'

Bookbag

'Heart-warming, fun and romantic. *Marley and Me* fans will love it.'

Closer

'A contemporary Bridget Jones, but with canines instead of chardonnay.'

Stylist

'A captivating book even if you don't like dogs.'

Daily Express

'A charming read.'

Star

'This heartwarming tale is sure to please.'

Take a Break

'I adored this juicy novel ... you'll be swept off your feet.'
Louise Bagshawe

'Essentially a feel-good novel, this has real subtlety and insight.'

Sydney Morning Herald

About the author

Lucy Dillon was born in Cumbria in 1974. She now divides her time between London and the Wye Valley, where she enjoys walking in the Malvern Hills with her Basset hounds, Violet and Bonham.

Also by Lucy Dillon

WALKING BACK TO HAPPINESS
LOST DOGS AND LONELY HEARTS
THE BALLROOM CLASS

LUCY DILLON
the
secret
of happy
ever after

HODDER

First published in Great Britain in 2011 by Hodder & Stoughton
An Hachette UK company

7

Copyright © Lucy Dillon 2011

The right of Lucy Dillon to be identified as the Author
of the Work has been asserted by her in accordance with
the Copyright, Designs and Patents Act 1988.

A CIP catalogue record for this title is
available from the British Library

Paperback ISBN 978 1 444 72703 6
Ebook ISBN 978 1 444 72704 3

Typeset in Plantin Light by Hewer Text UK Ltd, Edinburgh

Printed and bound in the UK by CPI Group (UK) Ltd, Croydon, CR0 4YY

Hodder & Stoughton policy is to use papers that are natural, renewable
and recyclable products and made from wood grown in sustainable
forests. The logging and manufacturing processes are expected to
conform to the environmental regulations of the country of origin.

Hodder & Stoughton Ltd
338 Euston Road
London NW1 3BH

www.hodder.co.uk

When I was seven, I broke my elbow and spent the whole summer in hospital. Missing the holidays was bad, but much worse was that with my left arm in a cast, I couldn't hold a book to read. I'd had my nose in a book virtually before I could walk, thanks to my mother's own passion for reading, and was halfway through a Hardy Boys mystery at the time of the accident. My strongest memory of that summer isn't the pain of the operations or the loneliness of the ward, but of my father sitting by my bed every night, patiently reading chapter after chapter of *Malory Towers* to me until I fell asleep. While his familiar voice was whispering Enid Blyton's words into the darkness, I was miles away from Whitehaven in a Cornish dorm with my friends Darrell and Alicia and their tuck-boxes and lacrosse sticks, sharing common-room dramas, planning pranks on scatty French teachers. Reading was the best medicine for a scared, bookwormish little girl, and I've never ever forgotten how magically effective it was, or how lovingly it was given.

This book is dedicated to everyone who reads aloud, and everyone who listens. But mainly to my daddy, who never once complained when I reminded him that he'd 'missed a bit out'.

Thank you to all the people who sent me long and hilarious emails describing their favourite children's books – I wish there had been room to use them all. You can tell a fair bit about someone from what their formative reading experiences were, and I'm happy to say that I seem to know a lot of Tiggers and Darrell Riverses. (As well as a Burglar Bill, a Very Hungry Caterpillar, and a book that I think is now outlawed in most public libraries in the UK.)

Special thanks, always, to my editor Isobel Akenhead and her assistant Harriet Bourton, who were patient and encouraging and never short of a brilliant suggestion, usually about Jilly Cooper; and to my inspiring agent Lizzy Kremer, who makes everything come right, like Mary Poppins but with better jokes. And to her lovely assistant Laura West, for reading Michael Morpurgo for me.

Thanks most of all, though, to my Mrs Pepperpot mother, for piling our house with books, and never telling me anything was too hard. And for reading, reading, reading.

Once upon a time . . .

Michelle stood in the middle of her new shop, trying to think of a name for it (Nightingale's? Home Sweet Home? Domestic Goddess?) whilst imagining the room filled with hand-sewn lavender bags and chunky beeswax candles, but, most of all, without the lingering aroma of smoked mackerel.

The sheer magnitude of what she was undertaking, all on her own, hit her for the fifth time that day, but she frowned and told herself – also for the fifth time that day – that she was doing the right thing. New start, new shop. New Michelle.

In an ideal world, she wouldn't be starting a homewares business in a fishmonger's, and certainly not on this high street, in a market town somewhere between Middle-of-Nowhere and Back-of-Beyond, but Michelle had a knack for selling, and she knew the most important things about this shop were right. Shabby Longhampton, with its red-brick terraces and depressing concrete precinct, was crying out for some prettiness. The premises were cheap (probably on account of the fishy smell), light and spacious, and located on the main street, right next to offices full of lunchtime browsers. Plus – and this was the main thing – this particular shop was 137 miles away from Harvey Stewart.

That bit had been the only part of her new life that Michelle had planned. Harvey's brain started to lose oxygen ten miles outside the M25, so out here, where even the dogs wore quilted jackets, she reckoned she'd be safe enough from him and his subtle ways of making her hate herself.

Thinking about Harvey made Michelle's armpits prickle. She distracted herself by tossing her big bunch of keys up and down and focusing on her new space, mentally sweeping away the plastic shelving, washing the walls with soft calico paint, and filling it with beautiful, clever things, until she felt in control again. If it hadn't been for the soothing powers of redecoration she doubted her marriage would have lasted the five years it had. Their house had been like the Forth Road Bridge; as soon as she finished it, she'd started again, just to take her mind off everything else.

Harvey had always said she had OCD. Obsessive Changing Disorder. That she'd never be happy until everything was perfect. '*If you had the faintest idea what that was.*'

For a second, Michelle wobbled on her high heels, as if she were standing on the crumbling lip of a cliff. Her head felt too light on her shoulders, unanchored to the rest of her. She hadn't let herself think too hard about what she was doing while it was happening, but panic had been flickering at the outside edge of her senses all the time. In the end, she'd left while she was still angry – no planning, no lists, none of her usual props – and now here she was, on her own in a town full of total strangers, but free. The rest of her worldly goods were coming in a van by Friday, but for now, she felt untethered, like a balloon accidentally released.

Her palm stung, and Michelle realised she was clutching the keys so hard the sharp metal wing of the Aston Martin key fob was cutting into her palm. Slowly, she opened her fingers and looked at the last remaining trace of her old life, already so far away it felt like someone else's.

Michelle's green Aston Martin DB9 Volante was now sitting on a Birmingham forecourt, sold to put down a deposit on the shop and on the run-down terraced cottage she'd moved into, but she'd kept the key fob to remind herself what she could do when she put her mind to it. Michelle had loved her Aston. Not just because it turned heads, especially with a small woman in shades behind the wheel instead of a middle-aged bloke, but because she'd bought it with the commission she'd earned as the top salesperson in her dad's dealership. There weren't many twenty-eight-year-olds determined enough to rack up sales like that. Especially when they didn't even like cars that much. As the pang of regret bloomed in her chest, Michelle reminded herself that some people didn't even get going properly until they were thirty, let alone start a whole new life. Loads of time to earn another car.

She looked around at the unpromising material she had to make that happen, and wobbled again. She didn't want to look at this much longer, but she didn't want to go back to the tatty canalside house, with its loud wallpaper and damp patches either. The shop was fishy and the high street was deserted, but it was still better than flinching every time the phone rang.

'Get a coffee, make a list,' she said aloud, her voice echoing in the empty shop, and she felt a little better.

Next door to the soon-to-be-ex-fishmonger's was a café and, unlike most of the shops nearby, it was open and doing a good Sunday afternoon trade.

Michelle ordered a double espresso and a piece of cake at the counter and settled down with her to-do list at a table near the window, where she could analyse her high street competition. Something about the place – the spotless cleanliness?

The homemade cakes? – relaxed her, but next to the chatting couples and families at the other tables, she felt self-conscious, as if her loneliness hung round her like a bad smell. How did you make friends as a grown-up if you didn't have an office, or a school run? Not business acquaintances like her new solicitor and the estate agent – that was easy, she knew the role to play there – but *friends*. Like . . .

Michelle frowned. Like who? Owen, her youngest brother, was the only person she really confided in; her female friends were really just the wives of Harvey's poker buddies. She'd slotted into his social life at twenty, just like she'd slotted into the family business at eighteen. No university mates, no exes, no schoolfriends . . .

Without warning, the door burst open and a huge Dalmatian barrelled in, black eyes gleaming and spotted ears pricked with excitement. The dog paused near the umbrella stand, tail whipping back and forth as it looked round the café, as if sizing up who was most deserving of attention, then its gaze fixed on Michelle and charged towards her.

To Michelle's surprise, no one else in the café reacted, and for a second, she wondered if she was the only one who could see it. The Dalmatian wagged its tail at her and Michelle felt touched, until she realised it was actually her slice of carrot cake that the dog wanted to make friends with. It already had its head angled to snaffle the cake, one paw on the chair next to her for better purchase, and she grabbed its red collar and pulled it back down.

'Sit!' she said sternly, and when the Dalmatian didn't respond beyond an amused loll of the tongue, she repeated it more firmly. 'Sit!'

The dog dropped obediently to the floor, its spotty tail thumping against the table legs as if Michelle was playing a game. Still no one around her seemed bothered by the dog's entrance. Michelle was amazed. The one time she'd tried to take her springer spaniel Flash into her local café, they'd acted as if she'd waltzed in scattering anthrax from a poo bag.

Flash. Flash and his melting gaze and big feathery feet. Her stomach clenched. Of all the things she'd left behind with Harvey – money, clothes, so-called eternity rings – the only thing she wished she'd packed in her car was Flashie. Was he wondering where she'd gone? Was he waiting by the door, pining for her? She'd only left him because taking him would have given Harvey the perfect excuse to turn up on her doorstep every other weekend, demanding 'access'. Playing the reasonable, bereft husband.

'Oh my God, I'm so sorry. Pongo! Stop it, no! He broke the lead!'

A blonde woman about Michelle's age and seemingly twice her height bumped into her table, struggling to wind in an extending lead with one hand while pulling the dog away from a nearby table with the other. She looked windblown and distressed, her authority undermined further by her clamping the handle of the lead between her knees while she tried to untangle it. As she yanked ineffectually at the knot, her wide-set blue eyes scanned the café nervously for signs of damage.

'Did he break anything? Did he spill your coffee? Let me get you another one. Please don't tell Natalie, he's already on a warning.' The words tumbled out of her mouth, and when Pongo stood up and – inevitably – his tail swished the sugar bowl off the table and into Michelle's big bag, showering it with granulated sugar, she covered her face with a hand. Michelle saw that it was chafed from the lead, with raw, chewed nails and scribbled notes in biro on the back of her hand.

Walk dog.

Ironing.

Treats/girls?

'Bollocks.' The voice behind the hand sounded close to tears. 'I'm so sorry. It's not his fault, it's mine.'

Michelle had been prepared to yell at her for not controlling her dog properly, but something about the woman's slumped shoulders reminded her of her own overwhelming weariness.

'It's fine,' she said instead. 'No harm done. Are *you* OK?'

The woman uncovered her eyes and tried to smile but the results were mixed. She had an open, peaches-and-cream sort of face; a primary school teacher, or a milkmaid from a child's book, thought Michelle. Simple and soft. Not suited to the kind of firm discipline required by Dalmatians.

The other customers were starting to turn around, peering at them with a special curiosity reserved for naughty dogs and toddlers.

'Oh no, your lovely bag . . .' the woman started, but Michelle pulled the chair out, trying not to nudge the Dalmatian who had already lain down at her feet, his head on her Marc Jacobs tote.

'Come on, sit down,' she said. 'Your dog already has. Get your breath back.'

Gratefully, the woman slid her slim frame into the chair and grimaced up from under long, golden lashes, her expression now more embarrassed than distressed. 'Is everyone staring at me?'

'Yes,' said Michelle. 'But it's fine. They were staring at me about five minutes ago.'

'Really? What embarrassing thing did your dog do?'

'Nothing. It was me they were staring at,' she added self-consciously. 'I've just moved here. New in town. Funny accent, probably.'

The woman smiled, and her face lit up from the inside. '*Nooo*. Don't think that! It's more likely because you don't have a dog with you. This is the dog café,' she went on, when Michelle looked non-plussed. 'People tend to come in here with their dogs because they're not allowed in anywhere else. Natalie gives them a Bonio if they behave themselves.'

Michelle turned round in her chair, and wondered why on earth she hadn't seen it before. Under the table opposite, where the elderly couple were sharing a pot of tea and a scone, was a black Scottish terrier curled around a West Highland White terrier in matching tartan jackets. Next to them was a family with a tubby chocolate Labrador sprawled over their feet, asleep. By the door were bowls on plastic mats, and the biscuits she'd seen in the big jars by the Gaggia were, on closer inspection, Bonios.

'That is what I call niche marketing,' she said. 'Smart. Very smart.'

When she turned back, the woman had pulled herself together, and was smiling in a warm, welcoming way.

'I'm Anna,' she said, holding out her hand over the table menu. 'This is Pongo. After the books, naturally. Well, after the film, in his case. I don't think his owners even know there's a book.' She looked cross with herself. 'Sorry, that was mean. Forget I said that.'

'I'm Michelle,' said Michelle. 'I've just bought the shop next door.'

'Really?' Anna seemed interested. 'You're a fishmonger?'

'God, no! No, it's going to be an interiors shop. Actually,'

Michelle went on, seizing the opportunity to get some inside info on her customer base, 'you can help me with some market research . . . Um, is she looking at us?'

The brunette who'd served Michelle at the counter was approaching them with pinched eyebrows, and immediately Pongo's tail started whipping back and forth again.

'His problem is that he loves everyone too much. Hello, Natalie!' said Anna. 'Sorry about Pongo. He'll be good this time, I promise.'

Natalie sighed and folded her arms over her frilled pinny. 'Anna, you know I love Pongo, but we have to have a "three strikes and you're out" policy. And some people would count stealing two lots of cake on one visit as two strikes.'

'But I've got his lead wrapped round my ankle. He'll be fine!'

'By all means come back when you've trained him to behave in public places,' she went on, 'but if he's disruptive to other customers . . .' She glanced at Michelle.

'It's OK,' said Michelle, feeling involved now. She didn't want to go back to Swan's Row yet – and Anna seemed happy to chat. 'Look, he's totally chilled out.'

The three women looked down at Pongo, who was lying beneath the table as if butter wouldn't melt. Michelle noticed, too late, that he had carrot cake crumbs round his muzzle. And her plate was empty.

'He's helping me with research,' Michelle went on, reverting to her confident sales voice. 'Can I have another cup of coffee, please? Anna? Coffee for you?'

Anna pulled off her crocheted beret and nodded, sending wisps of spun-gold hair floating round her flushed face. 'Um, yes. Lovely. If you're sure . . .'

Once Natalie was heading back to the counter, Anna leaned

across the table and whispered, 'That's so kind of you, but you should let me get the coffees. Please. After what Pongo's done . . .'

'Not at all, I need some local inside track, if you've got a minute.' Michelle finished off the dregs of her espresso. Already she felt more focused. 'So. Longhampton. Going by what I've seen so far, it seems to be a good place for dog owners and yummy mummies? Can you fill me in?'

Anna winced. 'I'm not sure I'm the best person to ask about either of those things.'

Michelle froze, her cup halfway to the saucer. Had she put her foot in it? Anna had the dog, didn't she? And she seemed about the right age to have kids – the hat she was wearing looked as if she'd borrowed it from a teenager.

To Michelle's horror, big fat tears were filling Anna's china blue eyes.

'Sorry,' said Anna, wiping her eyes with the back of her hand. 'This is so stupid. You must think you've found the town's mad dogwoman. Sorry!'

'No, I don't.' Michelle reached into her bag and pulled out a spotted cotton handkerchief. She had to shake the sugar off it first, which made Anna groan. 'I'm sorry, have I said something . . . ?' Michelle asked her.

Anna blew her nose automatically, then looked askance at the hanky.

'Keep it,' said Michelle. 'I've got lots.'

'You should stock these, they're nice.' Anna blinked hard and pulled her smile back on. 'Bit of a sore point, that's all. I'm only a mum at the weekends. My husband, Phil, has three girls from his first marriage, and they're round at our house now. We have them every other weekend and one weeknight.'

'Right,' said Michelle. Kids were out of her range of

experience. She didn't mind them, but then again she didn't mind zebras or Marmite. 'Are you here . . . because they're there?'

'Sort of. I'm giving them some dad time. As requested by their mother. We've only been married a year and a half, we're still kind of feeling our way through the whole stepmother thing.' Anna pressed her lips together. 'It's . . . challenging for everyone, but we're trying.'

'And the dog?'

'Is theirs. I think he was the final straw.' She glanced down at Pongo. 'It's not his fault no one bothered to train him. He sees the dog-walker more than he sees the girls, poor boy. I suggested we all went for a family walk this afternoon, but when I got to the front door, it turned out that only I was on it.'

'Do you prefer him to them?' Michelle wondered if that was the reason for the tears. Given the choice, she'd take a dog over three of someone else's resentful kids.

'No, no! I like all of them. I *love* children,' Anna insisted, apparently surprised at the question. 'It's easier for me to walk Pongo when they're not arguing about who holds his lead or throws the ball, but . . .' Her voice trailed off as Natalie reappeared and put two coffees and another slice of cake in front of them.

When she'd gone, Anna sighed. 'It's just not quite how I pictured it. But then things never are, are they?'

'What did you picture?' Michelle was skilful at asking questions so she didn't have to supply answers herself. She didn't want the subject to get round to her own marriage, which definitely hadn't lived up to expectations, hers or anyone else's.

'Something between *Mary Poppins* and *The Sound of Music*?'

Anna half laughed at herself. 'I mean, I'm an only child, I've wanted a big family since I was a kid. And when I married Phil, I read all the parenting books, you know, I wasn't going to be the wicked stepmother, I wasn't going to try to replace anyone, but in the end . . .' She shrugged and looked sad. 'If you could wave a magic wand and make people love you we'd all be at it, wouldn't we? Waving away.'

An unexpected lump filled Michelle's throat.

Anna stirred some sugar into her coffee, dissipating the froth. 'Sorry, that's too much information, isn't it? Boring! Tell me about this new shop. What are you calling it?'

'I haven't decided.' Michelle felt the warm beam of Anna's attention turned on her, and she started to feel excited about the place again. The fishy smell receded in her mind. 'I need something . . . comforting, and a bit magical. Happy. Any suggestions?'

'Home Sweet Home, then. Isn't that what we're all trying to create?' Anna grinned and pushed the cake plate towards her. 'Help me eat this,' she said. 'It'll be fifty per cent fat free if we share.'

The next morning, when Michelle arrived at the shop with her builder, her tape measure and her project file, there was a box on the step, tied roughly with raffia and bearing a label which read simply: 'Michelle'.

For a nauseating moment, Michelle wondered if Harvey had somehow found her, but it wasn't his style. He didn't do handwritten if gold-plated was available. She undid the raffia to find a packet of nice biscuits and a homemade Thank You card; in Anna's round handwriting was her address and phone number, and a request from Pongo to come over for a walk the following weekend, 'when I promise I'll behave myself'.

Anna had added her own note, inviting Michelle to drop in at the library where she worked so she could take her out for lunch and show her the high spots of Longhampton. 'A short lunch should do it!' Anna had added.

Michelle stood outside her new shop, and at that exact moment, the sun came out over Longhampton High Street. Already she felt better, and she hadn't even started decorating.

Two and a half years later . . .

I

'I loved the magical Christmas Eve in What Katy Did
*– wishes sent up the chimney, and families being Grateful
and Loving. Proper Christmas!'* Anna McQueen

Anna McQueen had planned her Christmas down to the last homemade gingerbread robin dangling from the tree, but her meticulously prepared vision of festive bonhomie certainly hadn't involved escaping from her own house using the dog as a getaway vehicle.

This isn't how it is in the books, she thought, letting a delighted Pongo lead her out of the wrought-iron park gates and down towards the canal, humiliation and resentment making her strides extra long. The wicked stepmother was supposed to cast her overworked stepdaughters out into the snow while she toasted her toes in front of a roaring fire, not the other way round.

Well, she amended, to be fair the girls weren't toasting their toes exactly. They were videochatting on Skype to their mum, Sarah, in her enormous new house in Westchester, NY. Sarah was probably toasting her toes. Or having them French pedicured by Santa's beauty elves.

That had been why Anna had ended up running herself ragged – trying to give them the best Christmas ever to make up for their mother taking a two-year job contract in the US back in July. Ironic, since Sarah still felt like more of a presence in the house than she did herself.

Anna blinked hard at the mental image of Chloe, Becca and Lily clustering round the laptop with squeals of delight at the exact moment she'd tried to start a new family tradition with a pan full of gold-leaf-topped mini mince pies that had given her a finger burn and stress-related indigestion. The mince pies – or the mass family ignoring of them – had been the final straw, sealed by a comment from Phil's mother, with her merciless timing.

'Did you make these?' Evelyn had enquired, her pencilled eyebrow arched to its fullest, most damning, extent. It was the first direct comment she'd addressed to Anna all morning, and when Anna had modestly nodded that yes, she had, Evelyn paused a beat, then said witheringly, 'Oh. In that case, I'll pass.'

Old witches, on the other hand, *weren't* in short supply.

Pongo bounded ahead of her on his new Christmas lead, thrilled to be getting the sort of energetic workout he normally only enjoyed when Michelle took him running. He was as glad to get out of the house as she was. If Anna hadn't texted Michelle from the loo where she'd hidden herself during the row about the iPad, she was fairly sure Pongo would have done it himself.

Anna's phone buzzed in her pocket, and she smiled when she read the message: 'Wine poured, chocs open, ears pinned back. Hurry hurry! M xxx'

At the end of the main road, Anna turned towards the grid of Victorian terraces that sloped gently down to Swan's Row, a line of small Georgian cottages facing the banks of the Longhampton canal. They'd been dingy for years, but were now quickly becoming the hottest properties in the area. Pongo practically towed her down to the bright red door at the end, which was garlanded with a generous holly-and-ivy wreath around the brass lion's-head knocker, and Anna felt a pang of decoration envy.

Michelle did Christmas properly. Magazine-properly. If she were being honest, Anna's own Christmas vision had been based on her 'What Would Michelle Do?' decorating principle. In addition to the splendid wreath, which Anna was pretty sure Michelle had made herself, she could see a perfectly symmetrical tree in the downstairs window, speckled with tiny candle lights and ruby-red glass baubles.

Her own tree was a bit wonky, because Phil had forgotten to go to the tree place until five minutes before they closed, then Chloe shut the car boot on the end of it, and the baubles were mainly on the bottom half, since she'd only managed to persuade her youngest stepdaughter, Lily, to help with the decorating. But it was loved, Anna told herself. That was the main thing.

She knocked, enjoying the satisfying weight of the knocker. Already her irritation was ebbing away. It always did when she called round at Michelle's. Michelle's house was like the room you were supposed to imagine when the hypnotherapist tells you to 'go to a calm place'.

The door swung open and a large glass of wine was thrust at her.

'Quick,' said Michelle, looking like a very businesslike elf in a pale sheepskin gilet and knee-high boots. 'Drink this. How long have I got to restore you to normal service?'

'Forty-five minutes? I can pretend Pongo ran away for a bit.'

'You've got your story straight already. I like it.' Michelle grinned and opened the door further. 'Come in, come in.'

Anna stepped forward, then paused. 'Even Pongo?'

Despite his deep love for Michelle and her grudging

fondness for him, Pongo was only ever allowed to wait with the coats and boots in the porch – the holding bay between the grubby outside world and her spotless home. Beyond the tiles it was a shoe- and paw-free zone.

'He's had Chloe trying to Sellotape her angel wings on him since eight this morning,' Anna went on, 'so she could use him as a prop when she called her mother. To sing at her. To *sing*, Michelle. She couldn't just say "Happy Christmas" like everyone else, she had to perform it.' She paused. 'She made us hum. Phil, humming.'

Michelle raised her hands. 'In that case, I'll have to make a seasonal exception. Hang on to him, I've got something he can try out for me . . .' She put Pongo into a 'sit' with a single pointed finger, then disappeared inside the house.

Anna sipped the wine, and was struck as she always was by a magical sense of going through a normal door that led to something unexpected. From the outside, 1 Swan's Row looked tiny. Only the twin box-tree balls on the steps were a clue to what was inside: an impossibly airy interior, with long views into ice-cream-coloured rooms filled with big glass vases of cloudy white flowers and pale sofas and enormous gilt-framed mirrors reflecting the light back and forth in an endless parade of beautiful things.

Since it was Christmas, Michelle had warmed up her colour scheme to include some tumbling pine garlands down the banister and deep berry throws over the chairs, but the overall effect was the same: clean, easy, calm, gently fragranced with unseen hyacinths and spicy candles. Anna loved it. Nothing was *too* precious or expensive; it was just the way she wished her own house would look, if she'd had time to do all the things style sections suggested. And if she had an eye for colour, an unflappable builder, perfect taste, a knack for finding stuff in auctions, and a homewares shop in the high street.

She gazed round. It was hard to believe that it was the same mildewed cottage Michelle had first invited her to for coffee nearly three years ago, after Pongo had dragged them both round the town's dog-walking lap. Well, no, Anna corrected herself – it was quite easy to believe, once you got to know Michelle. She was the most determined, organised person she'd ever met. Michelle had a daily list, a monthly list and a yearly list, and she calmly accomplished the lot, without any fuss. Once Michelle had written it down, it happened.

Anna felt a twitch of homework guilt: this year, Michelle had suggested that she made a list at the same time, 'to spur each other on' – by which Michelle meant, 'to spur *Anna* on'. She hadn't had time to start it. She'd been too busy falling behind with the current week's round of parenting chores, plus seasonal extras like in-law wrangling and mince pie failures.

Michelle reappeared with a large green bag and caught Anna staring at the latest addition to the hall table – a big reed-woven basket of paperwhites that Pongo would have smashed to the ground round at theirs within ten minutes.

'What's wrong?' she said at once, a frown creasing her smooth forehead. 'Too big? I'm thinking of stocking that for spring.'

'No. It's perfect. Perfect. The whole house is perfect.' Anna took a large gulp of wine and prised off her right boot with her left toe, not bothering to undo the zip. 'Even if I moved my husband, the three kids, the dog and every item of furniture out of ours, it wouldn't look like this.'

'Well, it helps not having a husband, three kids or a dog in the first place.' Michelle bent down and was doing something to Pongo with the bag, but Anna no longer cared. The wine and the paperwhites were spreading a festive goodwill-to-most-men through her system; the first glimmer of real Christmas spirit she'd had all day.

Christmas Eve had been quite festive, she thought wistfully. Before the girls had opened their presents. When she still thought she'd got them something brilliant and clever, something they would all bond over. Anna's skin crawled with embarrassment.

'There.'

She looked down to see Pongo encased in what looked like a babygro. He wagged his tail – or, at least something moved inside the bag.

'What on earth's that?' she demanded.

'Dog bag. I'm trialling them for the shop. If you've got carpets and you've got a dog, you need a dog bag,' Michelle went on, to Anna's amusement. 'What's so funny?'

'I don't let people take their shoes off in our house – their socks would end up a different colour from all the dog hair.'

'You can get an attachment for your Hoover that . . .' Michelle started, then good-naturedly accepted Anna's roar of 'not listening!'. She clicked her tongue and Pongo shuffled into the house after her, with a devoted display of attention he never bothered to bestow on any of his owners.

'Why don't you get your own dog?' Anna called, as the pair of them vanished into the kitchen. 'A non-shedding one? Something beige, to go with the decor?' She lined up her boots next to Michelle's running shoes on the wrought-iron boot rack. All storage accessories looked better when they weren't actually storing very much.

'It'd keep you company,' she added, not quite as loudly.

Anna and Phil had tried to set Michelle up with every single friend they had, only for each one to meet with a polite rebuff. Until the girls had moved in with them,

Michelle had been a regular fixture round at the McQueens' for dinner, but now diaries were harder to co-ordinate, the matchmaking dinners had fallen by the wayside, and Anna felt bad about it.

Phil didn't. 'Michelle's hardly lonely,' he'd insisted when Anna had suggested inviting her round for Christmas Day. 'She's got that big family of hers, and she's always jetting off for the weekend. Where was it last week? Paris? And Stockholm before that.'

'Those were buying trips,' said Anna. 'And you know what she thinks about her family.'

'Buying trips?' He'd seemed surprised. 'She told me it was a minibreak.'

Anna had marvelled, not for the first time lately, that a twice-married man with three daughters and a mother could understand women – and families – so badly.

'Company?' Michelle appeared at the kitchen door, her face defensive. 'Don't tell me. Phil has another freshly divorced mate who needs a woman to operate his washing machine? I haven't forgotten the Ewan incident.'

'Ewan wasn't . . . That was a misunderstanding.' Anna thought about backtracking; Michelle could get touchy about her singleness, and, now she thought about it – *stupid Anna* – this wasn't the best day to bring it up. But she hated the idea of funny, generous Michelle, here in her lovely house, all on her own.

'I just thought, you know, New Year's resolutions? You could adopt a rescue dog. Walk it with me and Pongo.' She tried a smile. 'It's been so hard to catch up with you now I'm on the school-run treadmill. And I need your conversation. You're my one connection with the non-Bieber world.'

Michelle's expression softened. 'I can still walk with you.

We need to make it a priority. Look, come through – I put some mince pies in to warm up.'

The kitchen–diner had been at least two poky back rooms before Michelle had worked her magic on the house. Layers of 80s rag-rolled wallpaper had been peeled away and replaced with dove grey Farrow & Ball paint, and handmade cupboards filled with Swedish porcelain. In a nod to the Christmas she wasn't celebrating on her own, big gold stars were propped between the plates. The plates hadn't been used for as long as Anna could remember; despite her gorgeous home, Michelle didn't go in for entertaining.

Anna sank down at the kitchen table and let the last of her tension go as she watched Michelle moving from cupboard to cupboard, assembling plates and knives. Her forty-five minutes were going too fast.

'Why didn't you tell me you'd be here on your own? I thought you'd be going to your parents' for Christmas Day,' she said, helping herself to a rose cream from the box of choc-olates opened, as promised, on the table. 'Don't they have a big get-together?'

'They do. That's exactly why I'm not there.' Michelle brought the bottle of wine over to top up their glasses. 'They get so competitive at Trivial Pursuit that if someone isn't crying by teatime they start an argument about who's got the best car so everyone gets a chance to be upset. I'll have to go at some point. Just . . . not today. Anyway, what on earth happened chez McQueen that you're hiding out here at half three? Did Phil fall out with his mum again?'

'Not yet. He may well be doing that now, though.' Anna put her elbows on the table and rested her eyes on her palms. 'It's me. I had to get out.'

'Well, you've been preparing this Christmas for the last three months . . .'

'No. It wasn't that.' She struggled to put her feelings in the right order, so she wouldn't sound selfish. 'I just feel like a bit of a spare part in my own home. I had a total disaster with the presents, for a start. I heard the girls laughing about them to Sarah.' Anna glanced up. 'Don't tell Phil that. He doesn't know.'

'What? I won't tell if you don't want me to, but he *should* know. That's so rude! What did you give them – Bobbi Brown brush kit for Chloe, like I said? And the driving course for Becca?'

Anna clamped her hands to the side of her face in a silent scream. 'No. I bought all three of them books. Books that I loved the most when I was their age.'

Michelle's mouth dropped open. 'Oh, no. You're serious.'

'Of course I'm serious. A year's worth of books! I'd have *loved* it. I thought I could read Lily's aloud to her at bedtime.' Anna felt her face go hot and red. 'I used to love bedtime stories with my mum. No one's ever read to those girls, it's such a shame, they're missing out on so many wonderful memories.'

'Anna, don't take this the wrong way, but you're thirty-one. And you're a librarian. Lily's eight. And Becca's doing her A-levels, so she probably doesn't want to see another book again in her life, and Chloe . . . Well, she's not exactly a big reader, is she?'

Anna took another swig of wine and tried not to think about the looks on the girls' faces when they'd unwrapped the big boxes. How come Michelle had guessed what their reactions would be, when she, who spent all day worrying about them, hadn't?

Becca had tried to be polite, but was obviously disappointed; Chloe, sneery; Lily, non-plussed. Luckily – or not – Phil had swept in with the enormous sack of presents he'd ordered from their many internet wishlists, and Anna had been left with Evelyn's condescending amusement and a lot of discarded wrapping paper. And thirty-six of her favourite childhood books, tracked down on the internet – first editions, signed copies, all special.

She swallowed, but humiliation was still filling her throat like cotton wool. 'Don't rub it in, I *get* that it wasn't what they wanted, and I know it's been difficult, adjusting to me as their stepmother, not someone they just see every other weekend, but . . .' Anna finally gave in to her pain. 'You're the only person I can say this to, Michelle, but what happened to *pretending* to be pleased with presents? Like I *pretended* to be pleased about the bloody Youth Restoring Serum?'

'Nice. I suppose you went overboard thanking them for that,' said Michelle dryly.

'Course I did.' Anna buried her nose in her wine glass. It actually said, 'for mature skin' on the box. She was only thirteen years older than Becca.

'I take it back – you *have* to talk to Phil about this,' said Michelle, yanking open the oven door to extract a baking tray. 'He needs to take some responsibility about how they treat you. You're not some housekeeper who happens to be married to their dad. You're their stepmother and they're living in your home. Here. Have one of these.'

Michelle pushed a plate of mince pies at her. Anna took one, and noted miserably that it was light and orangey and melt-in-her-mouth.

'From the deli,' said Michelle, seeing her woebegone expression. 'Short cuts are OK. Stop trying to be Superwoman.'

'Is it so freakish, though, to give books?' Anna asked, plaintively. 'I used to love spending Boxing Day reading. We all did. Me and Mum and Dad, sitting there reading our Christmas books with a chocolate orange and a pot of tea.'

'It depends which ones you tried to foist on them.'

'They weren't *worthy* ones, if that's what you mean. I gave Lily some books that she knows from her Disney DVDs, like *Mary Poppins* and *One Hundred and One Dalmatians* – I thought that would be a cunning way to get her interested. She has *got* a Dalmatian called Pongo.'

'As long as you don't go all "the book is so much better" on the poor child.' Michelle helped herself to a mince pie, cutting it in half. 'And what about Drama McQueen? What on earth did you give her? *Ballet Shoes*? That's about a stage school, isn't it?'

Anna lifted her chin. 'I gave Chloe all the Judy Blume stories I remember loving at fifteen. *Forever* and *Deenie*. And some *Malory Towers* . . .'

'*Malory Towers*?' Michelle's eyebrows vanished into her thick, dark fringe. 'What were you *thinking*?'

'I love *Malory Towers*,' she protested. 'I still read it now and then when I need cheering up. It's comforting.'

'It's only comforting because you read it when you were seven, and you thought all boarding schools had midnight feasts and gels who brought their ponies to class with them. And you gave that to the girl who can't decide whether she wants to audition for *The X Factor* or *American Idol* first?'

'Yes,' said Anna in a small voice.

'Dear God.' Michelle picked up her glass again. 'Is that what they're stocking in the teen reading section? No wonder kids aren't going to the library.'

Anna bridled. The library was a sore point. Her job as

Longhampton's Deputy Libraries Manager had vanished in a massacre of cuts three weeks before Sarah had left for the States. The pay-off wasn't bad, and Phil earned more than enough to cover the bills, but it had been more than a job to Anna. She'd run evening book groups, Reading Aloud sessions in old people's homes, Babes in Arms groups – anything to bring books into people's lives.

'I wasn't in charge of the Children's Library,' she said stiffly. 'That was a separate position. One that *hasn't* been merged.'

'Sorry,' said Michelle. 'But didn't we agree that it was time to think positive? Time to move on from that?' She made motivational fist gestures. 'Aren't we going to do that list? That list to focus your mind on the year ahead?'

'Do we have to?'

'Let's do it now,' said Michelle, pulling her ever-present notebook towards her. 'Come on.'

'I haven't got any paper.'

'I'll find you some. Call it an additional Christmas present.' Michelle went through to the sitting room, and Anna heard her opening up her desk to find one of her limitless supply of leatherbound notebooks.

Anna looked despondently at her glass. She'd half expected Chloe to be sneery, that went with the teenager territory; it had been Lily she'd hoped to please. Lily who looked so sad when she thought no one was watching, so lonely at the school gates with no mates to hang around with. Lily who tried so hard to make everyone think she was fine, when she obviously wasn't. Anna had never felt alone once she could read, and even if Lily refused the bedtime stories, Anna had hoped she might find a friend in Michael Morpurgo or Mr Gum.

'Cheer up, Anna,' said Michelle, dropping a notebook in front of her. 'They'll be off to New York tomorrow and you'll have a week to yourself with Phil, and when they come back they'll be full of stories about how Mum can't cook, and American chocolate tastes like vomit, and "where's my project you said you'd help with?".'

Anna stuffed another mince pie into her mouth and tried to ignore Pongo's begging face. 'They won't. Sarah's turned into one of those "my girls are my best friends" mums. They'll be in permanent shopping mode. She's working at head office now, not some backwater outpost in Longhampton, so it's power meetings and manicures. And lots of spare cash for treats, which we don't have any more.'

'So let her.' Michelle looked at Anna squarely. 'What are *you* doing while they're away? For *you*?'

She let out a long breath through her nose. 'Having a lie-in?'

Anna had never felt so exhausted. The first months after Sarah's departure had been one endless whirlwind – new schools, a new car to fit three extra people in, new clothes, new routine, new meals for three differently fussy eaters. In their mutual shock, they'd all rubbed along OK, mainly because Anna had done twice the running to cushion the shock for everyone else. It was only now the novelty had well and truly worn off that the real problems were starting to show through. Problems you weren't allowed to admit you had, like feeling you came a low sixth in the house, after the dog.

Michelle pushed the notebook at her. 'Come on. Do it now. Exam conditions – you've got twenty minutes to write down everything you want to achieve this year. Just you. Come on, I'll do it too.'

'You already know what you want,' protested Anna. 'You've probably got your list pre-written in your head.'

Michelle passed her a pen. 'Would you like me to write the

list for you? You can start with, "Give my husband a boot up the arse".'

'No.' Anna stared at the blank page in front of her. She didn't need that much paper; there was really only one main objective for this year, one she'd been waiting her whole adult life to get going with. Just thinking about it filled her with a glittering sort of excitement, but it was such a delicate goal. She didn't want to take away the magic by pinning it down, next to 'defrost the freezer' or 'make Chloe write a revision timetable'.

She looked up at Michelle who was scribbling away, making headings and sub-headings with brisk flow-chart arrows. Even though there'd been no one there to see it, Michelle had still done her full make-up, right down to her swooping black eyeliner. Maybe that should be a goal, learning to do eyeliner like that, thought Anna, admiring the staccato flicks at the edges of her round brown eyes. They were as neat and perfect as Lily's Bratz doll.

'Come on,' said Michelle, without looking up. 'Write it and it will come, that's my motto.'

Slowly, Anna wrote 'This year' at the top of the page, underlined it twice, and then wrote: 'Have a baby'.

Michelle looked up, halfway down her second page. 'Are you done? Already?'

Anna nodded.

'Let me see.'

She pushed the notebook across the table and watched Michelle's face, not sure how she would react.

Anna knew babies definitely weren't on Michelle's to-do list. Longhampton seemed to have the highest birth rate in the Midlands, and before Phil's girls had moved in, she and Michelle had spent hours moaning in Ferrari's, the local wine bar, about the 'you don't understand life until you have a child' born-again earth mothers who spent a fortune in Michelle's shop, bonding over the hundred and one reasons childbirth *didn't* make you instantly more valuable, understanding or wise.

For Michelle, the assumptions people made concerning her lack of children were annoying: the local businessmen insinuated that she was 'one of those strident career women', and the businesswomen thought she had it easy. Anna's grumbling, however, had been more of a defence. Being a mother-and-yet-not-a-mother was the worst of all worlds, when she longed for her own baby but instead felt she had to appear extra grateful for Phil's 'bonus children'.

'Wow,' said Michelle. 'That's your main focus for this year? I mean, it's a great one to have, but . . . nothing else? Not, find a new job? Or redecorate?'

Anna shook her head. 'I've been waiting long enough already. It's the only thing I've really wanted, since I was little, to have my own big family like the Waltons or the Marches. I used to nag my mum about when I'd get brothers and sisters.' She bit her lip. 'I once asked her whether they'd only wanted one child, and she said, no, they'd have loved to have had a houseful. It must have broken her heart hearing me playing with the cats and pretending they were babies.'

'Take it from me,' said Michelle, 'you wouldn't have wanted brothers.'

'I wouldn't have minded,' said Anna. 'I had imaginary brothers, imaginary sisters, horses, dogs . . . the lot. I don't think Chloe and Becca and Lily know how lucky they are.'

'So why didn't they have more?'

'They left it too late. Apparently there's a history of early menopause – not that Mum knew then. She basically told me to get on with it, so it's always been part of my plan.' Anna played with her wine glass. 'It was one of the things Phil and I agreed when we got married, that we'd give the girls time to get used to everything, but we'd definitely start trying for a baby of our own on our fourth anniversary – which is next month.'

'Blimey,' said Michelle. 'So I need to start stocking baby-gros with literary quotes on them for September, then?'

Anna grinned and raised her crossed fingers.

'Is Phil prepared for all this?' Michelle raised her eyebrow again, and Anna knew what was coming. 'If he's too knackered to walk Pongo, how's the poor man going to cope with baby-*making*, let alone the rest of it? He'll have to start pulling his weight. You're working harder now than you were when you had a full-time job.'

Michelle's typically generous Christmas present for her best friend had been a voucher for ten hours' ironing, five dog-walks and a whole spa day with her – but she'd made sure Phil had been there when Anna opened it. Phil had had the good grace to look shifty, and when Michelle had gone home, he'd offered to match all the hours. But that wasn't the point. He'd got her a new iron. The last few years it had been tissue-wrapped silk undies.

'Well, Sarah's contract's only for two years,' said Anna. 'She might even be back before the baby comes, so we might not have the girls living with us.'

'That wasn't what I asked.'

'Phil knows how important it is to me. It's important to him too. It's not that I don't love his kids, because I do, very much. But I'm not allowed to love them unconditionally, if you know what I mean. Our own baby will be as much part of me as—'

She stopped herself, and flinched awkwardly. 'Don't repeat

that. Actually, forget I even said it. It's one of the great unmentionables.'

'You can say anything to me, you know that,' said Michelle. 'Who am I going to tell?' she added, with a self-deprecating nod at her empty sitting room.

'Phil made a promise that we'd try for a baby this year,' said Anna, 'and one thing I have to say about Phil, is that he always keeps his promises. It's a dad thing, apparently.'

As she heard her own words, Anna felt a Christmassy glow in the pit of her stomach and it spread through her like a warm flame, burning away the last traces of resentment about Evelyn and the books. The last few years had been like an assault course, but she'd learned and bitten her tongue, and kept her side of the bargain, and now, finally, it was going to be her turn.

'What about you?' she asked, reaching for Michelle's notebook. 'What have you written . . . ? Wow. New shop? Double internet sales.' She glanced up. 'Michelle, don't you think *you* should be on this list somewhere?'

'I am.' Michelle pointed to 'Get elected to traders' council', under 'Personal targets'. 'And there.' It read: 'Run Longhampton Half-Marathon'.

'I don't mean that. I mean, what about you? What about your life away from work? I hate thinking of you on your own, night after night. This house is far too nice not to share with someone.'

Michelle's eyes widened in pretend horror. 'What? And have to tidy up after someone else? No thanks.'

'Forget the house. *You're* too nice not to share yourself with someone.' Anna reached out and grabbed her hand. She had to rein in her natural impulse to pat and hug when she was with Michelle – Michelle liked her personal space – but sometimes Anna couldn't stop herself. 'I know Harvey was a bastard, and Phil's mates aren't . . . your types, but that doesn't mean you should write off all men. There's someone out there for you, if you'd only look.'

Michelle squeezed her hand in return, then reached for her glass. 'I'm sure there is too, but I don't want to meet him just yet. I want to build up my pot of money, sell this house, then find some nice silver fox, early retired City hedgefunder with a yacht in Monaco.' She smiled, a quick, tight, red-lipped smile. 'Then we'll see how it goes.'

'Don't move to Monte Carlo,' said Anna glumly. 'I'd miss you.'

'You could come with me. You and your Von Trapp brood of little McQueens, all in matching T-shirts from Petit Bateau. Bring your guitar.'

Under the table, Pongo let out a heavy sigh and a suspicious fart.

'And on that note,' said Anna, 'I should be leaving. We need to take Evelyn back to the home, and I think I've drunk *just* enough to get out of driving her.' She pushed her chair back and ran her hands through her curly blond hair, pulling it up into a ponytail.

The landline rang and Anna automatically looked over to the telephone table, but Michelle ignored it, and poured herself another glass of wine.

'Aren't you going to get that?'

'Nope. You're here, so it can only be one of two people. My mother, calling to give me a guilt trip, or Harvey. I don't want to talk to either of them.'

'What? Haven't you spoken to your mother today?'

'Of course I have! What do you take me for? I called them this morning, before they all trooped off to church.' Michelle's forehead puckered faintly, between the eyes. 'I thanked them for the sheepskin slippers and car de-icing kit, and my mother moaned about the unsuitable presents I'd sent my brothers' kids, then dropped a few heavy hints about some lonely old unmarried aunt they'd had to do duty calls to yesterday. And then more or less told me I should get back with Harvey, or that'd be me.'

'But why him? You've been separated for over three years. It's not like he's the only man left in the world. You could have anyone.'

'Mum loves Harvey. And he's Dad's highest-performing salesman since I left. I think secretly they'd rather keep him than me.' Michelle looked away, and Anna thought she might be hiding a less flippant reaction. 'And . . . well, it's complicated. He was there for Christmas. I keep telling Mum she should just adopt him and get it over with.'

Anna tried to say something, but Michelle stopped her with a look. 'Anyway, I told them I was doing voluntary work in an old people's home. That Reading Aloud thing you do.'

Anna's jaw dropped; Michelle mirrored her exactly, and she looked so funny, her brown eyes cartoonishly wide in her heart-shaped face, that genuine laughter burst out of Anna for the first time that day. The idea of Michelle in the drab, cabbage-scented surroundings of Butterfields Residential Home – and reading a book, at that – was too outrageous.

'For that I'm going to make you come to the next session. Oh!' she said, her memory jogged. 'I meant to say – when we were collecting Evelyn this morning, who do you think we saw parked in the morning room?'

'Princess Anne? Terry Wogan?'

'Cyril Quentin. You know, from the bookshop. That'd explain why it's been closed for the last week.' Anna pulled on her duffle coat and started to wrap her scarf back round her neck.

'It's very hard to tell whether that bookshop is open or closed at the best of times.' Michelle pursed her lips.

'Oh, don't.' Anna's face creased with guilt. 'I tried to get half the books for the girls from his shop, but . . .'

'You got them off the internet instead. That's life. Bookshops are hard work these days. Especially when your window display still has Royal Wedding memorabilia in it – from Fergie's big day.'

Anna knew Michelle was right, but it still made her sad. 'It wasn't always like that. I used to love dropping in there for a browse, when Agnes Quentin was alive. She must have done most of the buying. Last time I was in I had to plough through piles of military history to find anything, and there was a weird smell of—'

Anna's phone buzzed, stopping her mid-sentence. 'Phil,' she sighed. 'His mother's woken up and the girls are fighting over the Wii. He wants Pongo back so he can take him out for a walk.'

At the sound of his name, Pongo emerged from under the table in his green babygro. 'Christmas really has come for you, my old mate,' observed Michelle. 'Twice as many walkies as normal.'

'Come on. Back to the fray,' said Anna.

'Keep the dog bag,' said Michelle, fondling his ears affectionately. 'Call it part of his Christmas present. Leave it on until you're outside, though.'

'Thanks.' Impulsively, Anna hugged Michelle, feeling her small but sturdy frame crushed against her own lankier one. 'Are you sure you don't want to come back with us? Christmas supper? I hate leaving you here on your own.'

'I'm fine. I've got a really expensive meal-for-one. Now let me go, you're smearing my make-up.' Michelle's voice was muffled against her coat, and when Anna pulled away, she saw that though her eyeliner was just as pristine as before, her eyes were wet.

'It's going to be a good year,' insisted Anna.

'I know,' said Michelle. 'Stop trying so hard and let it happen.'

Anna thought that was rich, coming from Michelle, but she let it go.

2

'I read the Narnia *series at the back of my
parents' wardrobe, hoping the oak walls would
become snowy branches.'*   Francine Toon

Physically, Michelle wasn't a typical runner – she was small,
and her legs were slightly shorter than she'd have liked – but
she had a determination that turned each circuit around the
town into a race with herself.

Just because it was Boxing Day – maybe because it was
Boxing Day – didn't mean she'd abandoned her routine: her
morning run, followed by a shower, a cafetiere of Kenyan coffee
and two glasses of water, porridge, to-do lists and then a sneaky
scan of the online gossip sites. Michelle liked to keep herself on
a rail-like schedule, but today she wanted to be up, about and
out in case her mother phoned back and tried to guilt-trip her
into driving down to Surrey, to be guilt-tripped some more.

She jogged down the deserted towpath, past the silvery-
grey waters of the canal where three brown ducks swished
along in silence, and turned left onto the footpath that led into
town. Her breath made puffs of white in the cold morning air,
and she felt the blood pumping around her body, fresh and
hot. A few dog-walkers were out, and she nodded at the ones
she recognised – Juliet, Anna's dog-sitter with the white terrier
and the chocolate Labrador, and an old couple with a grizzly
Dachshund, all of them wrapped up in waxed jackets.

Michelle's route took her down the two upwardly mobile rows of white Georgian villas towards the Victorian terraces nearer town, her eye ticking off the list of poet streets, Tennyson Avenue, Wordsworth Road, Donne Gardens. They were her ideal customer areas, and she liked to monitor what was going on. She glanced into people's front windows as she jogged past, and spotted a couple of her filigree silver stars and some of the outdoor tree lights that had sold out in one week. It gave her an extra burst of energy as she turned up the hill towards the main part of town.

At the top of Worcester Street, Michelle faced a choice: right, down and onto the high street, or left and round by the park. Normally, she wouldn't jog down the high street, but it was quiet and a thought had been niggling at her since Milton Grove, where every front-room window revealed a packed bookshelf, and in some cases, floor-to-ceiling books. Michelle wasn't a book person herself, unless you counted coffee-table art books, which she did love, especially arranged in height order on her footstool. But Anna's interest in Quentin's book-shop had made Michelle wonder if she might not be missing something that the poet streets might be interested in buying.

There were a few wandering souls escaping the morning after on the high street, but not many shops were open. Two women were gazing at the festive display in Home Sweet Home but they'd moved on before Michelle had gone past Boots. She slowed down outside the bookshop and peered in through the murky window, her heart still pounding in her chest as she stretched her burning hamstrings.

Inside the main room was gloomy, with stacks of books all over the place, and the mess alone made Michelle want to break in and tidy it up. It had been teetering on the edge of closure for weeks now; some days the open sign would never be turned round. Michelle had popped in a few times to say hello, but she hadn't been in for ages, mainly because Cyril Quentin was the sort of book maniac who could spot a 'non-reader' a mile off, and he made her feel thick. The impression she'd had the last time she went in was of a sort of clubby stillness that didn't, to Michelle's mind, fulfil a shop's only brief: to seduce and thrill the customer into parting with cash to take some of that thrill home with them.

A strange, forlorn feeling swept over her as she tried to make out where the front ended and the back room began. She wondered if the Quentins ever decorated. The shelves looked as if they'd been there since the shop was built, looming like ribs throughout the room. Michelle couldn't see where any light was coming from, it was so dark.

But the shop had potential. Massive potential. If you sanded the floorboards, she thought, and painted everything a soft oatmeal colour with bright accents, and put in some clever lighting, and took down those shadowy shelves, this could be the perfect bedlinen emporium. Home Sweet Home II.

Bedlinen was going to be the next big thing; Michelle knew it from her own obsessive browsing on the internet for featherbeds and baby-soft blankets. Her regulars complained that their gym membership and nights out had been crunched, but they still wanted to cosy up inside, especially in chilly Longhampton with its drizzly springs that never seemed to burst into flower until the last possible moment, and the damp, leafy autumns that started the day after Wimbledon finished.

Michelle gazed into the bookshop with her X-ray decoration vision, replacing the piles of paperbacks with brass-framed double beds made up with crisp white cotton and duck-down duvets, set on scrubbed floorboards with crimson-and-cream rag rugs dotted between. The shelves filled up with neatly folded blankets, Irish lambswool in sherbet stripes, lavender bags in the shape of hearts, and her signature purple ribbon tying up cleverly colour-coded bed sets.

Her heart beat faster, but not from the exercise. All she'd done was write down 'New Shop' and here it was – the shop right next door, Anna tipping her off before anyone else heard. It was meant to be. Someone up there had decided to throw her a chance, for once.

Michelle pulled out her phone, made a note to herself about tracking down the solicitors – she had a vague memory that Flint and Cook handled the older traders' businesses – then turned her music back on and jogged home, her mind full of paint charts, uplighters and soft mohair throws.

She was so busy planning her next move that she didn't even notice the man sitting on her step until he got up, and nearly made her swerve into the canal.

'Hello, Michelle,' said Owen, and flashed her the cheeky grin that worked on every woman with breath in her body – except her.

'OK, girls. Have you got everything?' asked Phil for the twentieth time.

Anna thought it was a pretty redundant question because, going by the huge bags piled up by the front door, there wasn't much the girls *hadn't* packed. She didn't say anything, though.

'Presents for your mum?' she asked instead, as neutrally as she could. Sarah, she knew, was getting a fabulous basket of gifts she'd helped Chloe and Lily to wrap. They'd spent hours on it.

'Yes,' said Becca.

'Presents for Jeff?'

Jeff was Sarah's boyfriend, although given he was nearly

fifty and a senior director at the management company she worked for, 'boyfriend' did seem to be pushing it. When Anna felt that she got the rough end of the girls' attitudes, she had to remind herself that she wasn't poor Jeff, the thoroughly pleasant American Sarah had met when he came over to restructure the UK operation, who'd committed the ultimate sin of being neither Phil, nor the George Clooney-a-like they felt their mother should have remarried, Phil no longer being available.

Chloe tossed her hair over her shoulder. She had beautiful hair, long and blond and naturally streaky like a tortoiseshell cat, and she used it as punctuation when she couldn't make her voice sarcastic enough. 'I still don't see why we have to give Jeff anything.'

'Yes,' said Becca firmly, speaking over her. 'English condiments. Mum says he misses English mustard.'

Chloe tossed her hair the other way and muttered, 'We should have got him breath mints.'

'Give it a rest, Chloe,' said Becca, checking her own bag.

Becca, at nearly eighteen, was only two years older than Chloe, but sometimes Anna thought she seemed to have accelerated straight out of her teens and into her thirties. She had long blond hair too, but wore it plaited and out of the way; for the last few months, it had been wrapped Heidi-style across the top of her head.

'Breath mints? Why?' As Phil looked up from his bag-balancing act, Anna caught the ghost of satisfaction that crossed Chloe's face, and she knew who the comment had been intended for.

'Oh my *God*, Dad, you know cheese and onion crisps? Well, Jeff's like the cheese and onion breath monster and he's—' Chloe's huge eyes looked ready to pop out of her face, so inexpressible was her revulsion.

'Jeff's all right,' Becca interrupted. 'And Mum clearly thinks he's all right and she's the one who has to smell his breath every morning. Can we hurry up, please? I don't want to be late.'

'Have you got . . . something to read on the plane?' Anna suggested tentatively. She hadn't wanted to shove the books into their bags, but the thought of an eight-hour flight without a good read was like torture to her. She'd put some flight-length books in her Christmas selection for that very reason.

'More than enough,' said Becca with a grimace, pointing to her leather satchel, which was bulging with revision. 'Passports, cash for the taxi, the internet check-in print-out, phone numbers, toothbrushes, hand sanitiser . . .' She looked worried for a second, then patted the bag. 'International charger adapters.'

'Are we missing someone?' Phil called loudly. 'Or shall we just go now?'

'No! Wait for me!' Lily came running into the hall, closely followed by Pongo. He was bouncing with excitement, and Anna wished she'd had time to walk him round to Michelle's in between all the packing. He was going to go nuts while they were out.

She checked her watch. Was there time to run him round the block now? No. Damn.

Anna couldn't remember the last time she'd just slung her bag over her shoulder, grabbed her keys and walked out of the door. It seemed like a whole different life. Leaving the house now involved dealing with nine other things first, three of which would change while you were dealing with the other six.

'Lily!' Phil pretended to look shocked. 'We nearly forgot you!'

'I was saying goodbye to Pongo. Why can't Pongo come?' Lily whined.

'Because he's banned,' said Chloe. 'They found out about

what happened with him and the daffodils in the park and they stamped his passport. He'd never get through immigration.'

Lily's brown eyes widened. 'How did they find out about that?' she whispered.

'I told them,' said Chloe. 'And I told them you helped him. So you'd better get your story straight when the man asks you at passport control.'

'Chloe!' Lily looked stricken. 'You didn't.'

'Of course she didn't,' said Becca, saving Anna the trouble. She shot a poisonous look at Chloe. 'Don't start her off now, or you can deal with the nightmares at Mum's.'

Of her three stepdaughters, Anna found Becca the easiest to get on with because she was more placid and pragmatic than the other two, but it was Lily that came closest to her secret dreams of how her family would be. Lily had an imagination – she worried, like Becca, but in a more creative, dramatic way. She wondered if Pongo didn't mind not being able to speak. She refused to eat bread for a while, after finding out that yeast was an organism that was 'baked to death'. And her face was like something from the *Flower Fairies* books: big brown eyes in a milk-pale face, a pointy nose and a small, expressive mouth that trembled sometimes, then broke into a melting smile.

'Seriously, can we go?' Becca begged. 'The roads are going to be mad round the airport. Dad, hurry *up*.'

'I hope you're going to be more polite to the porters at JFK,' muttered Phil, as he struggled under the weight of Chloe's bag.

It wasn't quite shut, and where the zip gaped open, Anna noticed a familiar splash of silver: her favourite Vivienne Westwood jersey top. The last stylish item of clothing she'd bought before the girls arrived, she lost her job and the New Budget Regime kicked in.

For a second, Anna struggled with the usual lose-lose dilemma – if she said something it would kick off an unwinnable fight, make them late, and leave a bad aftertaste for her time with Phil, as well as give Chloe something to whinge about to Sarah; but if she said nothing, Chloe would feel like she'd won, again. Doubly so, given the epic shopping trip she'd cajoled Anna into taking her on before Christmas.

Chloe specialised in petty but annoying incidents like this – mini tests of Anna's endurance that didn't mean anything on their own, but advanced the situation inexorably forward to one where Anna felt she couldn't say or do anything without looking like the wicked stepmother. The worst thing was, if Chloe had asked to borrow the top, Anna would probably have said yes – admittedly under some duress – whereas if she said that *now*, it'd look like she was only saying it to make Chloe feel bad.

Oh God, thought Anna in despair. Why did dealing with teenagers make you behave like one? At least birth mothers got a ten-year run-up to this sort of thing.

Becca caught her looking at the bag and pulled a sympathetic face. But she didn't reach in and pull out the top. Chloe's meltdowns were notorious, and conducted as if cameras were hidden around her.

'I thought we were going?' said Phil, back at the door, ready for another load of luggage. 'Tick tock.'

'We are,' said Anna. *Detach*, she told herself. *Focus*. The most important thing was to get them to the airport, not to satisfy Chloe's need to be the centre of everyone's attention, good or bad. 'Come on, Lily.'

She held out her hand, and Lily politely put her overnight bag in it.

★   ★   ★

At the airport the tearful goodbyes were halved, thanks to a combination of Christmas spending money and Duty Free shops. As usual, Phil was the one who looked most upset.

'Call me if you need anything,' he said, hugging them. 'Anything at all.'

'That's not what you said when I missed the last bus last weekend,' said Chloe into his shoulder.

'You weren't halfway round the world then.' Phil's worries about the children only seemed to apply when they were out of his reach, Anna noted; when they were at home, he was relatively blasé about abduction, drug-crazed rapists, WKDs, late homework, etc. She was the one who worried about all that.

Chloe wriggled out of his grasp. With a pair of shades wedged in her tawny hair, she already looked more like an extra from *Gossip Girl*, laden down with a bag of magazines, fruit she'd insisted on Phil buying but which she probably wouldn't eat, and the obligatory bottle of mineral water. 'Chill, Dad. We'll be fine.'

'Daddy, look after Pongo.' Lily lifted her face for a kiss. 'Tell him we miss him every day, in the morning and before bed.'

'I will. Becca, please don't spend the whole time revising, OK? Enjoy yourself too. Relax.'

'Relax?' Becca rolled her eyes. She looked tired already, even before the flight. 'With Mum and Chloe around? Chance'd be a fine thing.'

'I mean it,' he said. 'You've got your offer now. Have a few days off, OK? Plenty of time for stressing out when you're running your own chambers.'

Becca had wanted to be a barrister since she was Lily's age, something that Phil and Sarah were equally proud of, and, as of the first week in December, she had an offer to read Law at

King's College, Cambridge. Anna was proud too, but never quite knew how to express it, or whether she was 'entitled' to feel proud. She made lots of sandwiches instead, and left them outside Becca's room when the light was still on after midnight.

'Take care, Dad.' Becca hugged him, then after a tiny pause, hugged Anna too, sending a grateful shower of sparks into Anna's heart. 'Don't get used to the peace and quiet. We'll be back before you know it.'

She turned back to her sisters, and started to usher them towards the gate.

'Come on,' said Anna, patting Phil's arm. 'Don't watch them go through, we're not in some disaster movie. They'll be back in a week. And we're cutting it fine with the car park.'

He sighed. 'I know. It's just that . . . every time they go, I wonder if they're going to come back.'

Of course they're coming back, Anna wanted to scream. *Sarah's only got them for six days because she's going to Reno for a 'vital conference'.*

She took a deep breath. There was a lot she didn't say to Phil, in the name of peace-keeping. It was backing up inside her like uncollected recycling. If she didn't say it to Michelle, Anna suspected she'd end up doing a lot more talking to the dog.

'Well, if they don't come back,' said Anna, 'I'm definitely FedExing Pongo over to Sarah's, pet passport or not.'

He turned to her, his handsome face all hangdog. 'Do you think I'm a terrible father?' he asked, semi-rhetorically.

'No,' she said. 'I think you're a very good one. That's one of the reasons I married you.'

He slung an arm around her shoulders and hugged her to him, and Anna felt her own Christmas holiday start.

★　　★　　★

She retuned the car radio from Radio 1 to Radio 4 and, as they drove away from the airport without the sound of squabbling reverberating from the back seat, a weight lifted from her shoulders.

A whole week of just her and Phil, and no worrying about lists or bags, or putting her foot in it. And why wait for January to start the whole baby project? she thought, tingling with excitement. Why not get a few days' extra practice in? September babies were always furthest ahead in class.

'Phil,' she said seductively, at the same time as he said, 'Um . . .'

'You go first,' said Anna.

'I didn't want to discuss it in front of the girls, but I've been thinking about Mum,' he said.

Oh God, thought Anna. *No.*

'What about her?' she asked, as evenly as she could.

'I think she should stay in the home a bit longer. I'm not sure she's really well enough to go back to her house.'

Anna looked across the car at him, trying to read his face. He sounded matter-of-fact, but this was a big thing. It had taken the combined efforts of Phil, Evelyn's GP, a consultant and Becca, the favourite grandchild, to persuade Evelyn to move into Butterfields Residential Home while she recovered from a knee replacement. Anna knew the staff there from her reading programme, and, after she'd had a quiet word, they'd made a special fuss of Evelyn when she'd gone to 'view' the place – the reason she'd finally agreed to go. Evelyn responded well to a fuss.

'But the consultant says she's made a good recovery,' Anna pointed out. 'I can't see her wanting to stay longer than she has to with the "bunch of dribbling cabbages", as she calls most of them. I mean, whether she can manage the house on her own's a different thing, but we can get Magda to come in more often.'

'It's not that. I just . . .' Phil hesitated, as if he wasn't sure he should be saying what was on his mind.

'What?' said Anna.

'Yesterday she called me Ron. She looked straight at me, and said, "Ron, why are you wearing those awful slip-on shoes? You know I can't stand them." '

Ron was Phil's dad, a successful surveyor who'd died when Phil was a baby. Phil had no memories of him at all, but from what Anna had gathered or worked out for herself, Ron had married fairly late in life to Evelyn, his much younger secretary, a blonde bombshell with a golf handicap to match his. Golf aside, the strained photos in Evelyn's stuffy house suggested that the marriage hadn't been an entirely happy one. Phil had been born when Evelyn was forty, 'a complete shock', as she still put it, and Ron had died suddenly of a heart attack two years later.

'So she got your name wrong,' said Anna, trying to sound reassuring. 'She probably spent her whole married life starting every sentence with the words, "*Ron*, why on earth dot dot dot". Had she just woken up?'

'No, she was definitely awake. It was more the way she looked at me – spoiling for a fight.' Phil took a deep breath. 'It made me really uncomfortable. Like she was seeing him there, not me.'

'Well, old people get confused,' said Anna. 'Half of them up at Butterfields call me their daughter's name when I go in. They can remember the plots of romances they read half a century ago, but they can't remember what I'm called.'

'I didn't even know my dad wore slip-on shoes,' he added, with a very slight crack in his voice.

Anna could barely imagine how hard it must have been growing up without a father. She loved her dad, he was her source of warmth and love and companionable silences. She hated the way Evelyn refused to talk about Phil's dad, but occasionally threw out barbs like, 'You don't get your pig-headedness from me.'

'She's pretty hearty for nearly eighty,' she said. 'I'm sure it was just a temporary lapse of concentration.'

'That's what I'm worried about. I don't want her hale and hearty but losing her marbles. Setting the house on fire, or leaving doors open for burglars to walk in.' He gripped the steering wheel. 'Becca found the remote control in the fridge. We made a joke about it, but Mum must have put it there. That's a sign, isn't it? Of dementia? Putting things in the wrong place.'

Anna shook her head automatically. It was impossible to reconcile Evelyn, hair set in a candyfloss helmet, imperious and red-clawed, still capable of delivering a cutting remark just for the fun of it, with the dementia sufferers she read to, groping for some purchase on their surroundings like babies struggling to walk.

And, a smaller voice in her head added, was Evelyn going to be her responsibility too? As well as Phil's children?

'It might not be.' She reached out and caressed the back of his neck, where his hair, cut short for work, was growing out for the holidays. 'I'm going up there this week to do a Reading Aloud session – I'll have a word with Joyce. She sees this sort of thing all the time.'

'Would you?' He glanced over. His eyes were troubled, and she wanted to comfort the concern away.

'Course.'

'Thanks.' Phil managed a smile. 'Now, it's just you and me

for the next week. Just like old times, eh? Where do you want to go for lunch?'

'Home,' said Anna. 'Back to bed. I'll make you a sandwich later if you've worked up an appetite.'

'No, seriously. Simon from work says the Bridge Inn's been done up – he had a great steak there before Christmas. Fancy that?'

Anna's stomach tightened. 'It's Boxing Day, Phil. It'll be shut. Anyway, come on. We've got the house to ourselves! And you owe me a massage for all that cooking yesterday.'

'I know. But that's what afternoons are for, right? It's so long since we had a meal out, just you and me.' He wriggled his shoulders. 'I want to go somewhere that doesn't have swings outside, or a kids' menu. Somewhere with a dangerous pond. Don't you fancy that? Long lunch, the papers, no rush to get back for ballet?'

'Well . . .'

Phil looked at her sideways. 'It's not often I get to take my gorgeous wife out for a date. Don't deny me that small pleasure.'

Anna felt herself leaning towards his way of thinking. She couldn't remember the last meal they'd had, just the two of them. Lunch *à deux,* intelligent conversation, some wine . . . it might jump-start the afternoon anyway.

'OK,' she said, sinking back into her seat. 'But I'm having pudding. And we're out of there by three.'

'You're on.' Phil turned up the radio and started singing in a dad-like manner that Chloe would not have permitted, had she been there.

3

*'What if everything you drew and wished for
came to life?* Marianne Dreams *brilliantly taps
into every child's (and adult's) fear of waking
up in their own dream.'* Anna McQueen

'Merry Christmas!' said Owen, from behind the biggest bunch of white roses Michelle had seen outside a trade convention display.

'Are those from you?' she panted, still winded from her run. 'Because I'd rather . . . have had . . . a down payment on your . . . outstanding loans.'

'Nice! And a Merry Christmas to you too, Owen,' he said, pretending to look hurt.

Michelle responded by giving him a quick, sweaty hug, ruffling his dark curls with her free hand, then bent double to get the rest of her breath back while she tried to work out whether she should be pleased if he'd brought her roses when still he owed her three months' rent for his last house.

Owen was Michelle's youngest and by far her favourite brother. There was a seven-year gap between her and the two older ones, Ben and Jonathan, and it might as well have been a whole generation. Owen was twenty-four, the surprise baby and recipient of all the surplus charm, good looks and luck in the family. He got away with murder with everyone but Michelle, who'd spent her teenage years filling in the mothering that their mother had been too busy to deliver. As a result, she'd built up a certain immunity to his chat, while he'd learned a few valuable lessons about talking to girls – something he'd exploited at every opportunity since.

'This is a nice surprise,' she said, unlocking the door. 'Have you been waiting long?'

'Not really. Got a lift with a mate who was going to Birmingham. Here, take these off me?' he added, pushing the roses into her hand. 'I feel like a bridesmaid. And I cannot tell a lie – on this occasion they're not from me. They were on the step when I got here.'

Michelle pointed to his shoes and the rack by the door, and reluctantly he started to prise off his trendy trainers. While he was distracted, she ripped open the gift card and her throat, still raw from her run, constricted even further.

'Sorry not to see you on Christmas Day, babe,' said Harvey's smooth voice through the florist's innocuous handwriting. 'I miss you. Let's make 2012 our year. All my love, Harvey.'

Michelle shoved the card back into the flowers and dropped them on the table as if she'd found a snake in the heart of the bunch. She didn't even want to see them in her house: something about them was pure Harvey – the roses were pearly and perfect, but completely scentless, force-grown and flown in at the wrong time of year, delivered on a super-expensive day because if you paid enough, you could always get what you wanted. And yet on the surface it was a thoughtful gift that only a churlish, impossible-to-please cow would find fault with.

Poor Harvey. Always trying so hard. He didn't want Michelle to walk out on him, you know. He thought the world of her.

He wants to remind me that he knows where I live, she thought.

'From Harvey?' Owen asked.

She nodded. A paranoid voice in her head wondered if Harvey himself had been the 'mate who was going to Birmingham'. No, she told herself. Harvey would fly.

'He was asking after you yesterday at Mum's,' Owen went on, looking round her hall. 'I think he was hoping you'd be there. Oi! Why don't you have any photos of us in here?'

Carole Nightingale's hallway was proudly crammed with photographs of her children achieving things, or displaying their own offspring. In Owen's case, there were as many again of him just looking handsome and devilish. They made up for the pointed lack of graduation photos of Michelle, the only one without a degree.

'Because I don't like to scare my guests when they arrive. How come Harvey ended up having Christmas Day with you?' Michelle added, unlacing her own trainers so her brother wouldn't notice her shaking hands.

'He was all on his own, poor guy,' said Owen. 'Mum invited him over, the more the merrier. She likes him. We all do.'

'You don't know him, Owen.' Michelle had long since given up trying to explain to the rest of them, but Owen understood her a bit more than they did.

'Don't I?' Owen looked reproachfully at her. 'You can't blame Mum for inviting him round, Shell. He's been her son-in-law for years. Dad's just promoted him again. And you're still married to him . . .'

'Technically,' Michelle snapped. 'In another eighteen months, I won't be, whether he likes it or not. Separation without consent after five years. No one's fault.'

Owen raised his hands. He hadn't been at home when

Michelle had left Harvey; he'd been travelling round India, getting stoned and acquiring a tattoo Carole still didn't know about. He'd missed most of their marriage too, as he'd been away at college. 'You were the one who walked out, not Harvey. None of my business, I know, but—'

'Right. It's none of your business.' Michelle's voice was harsh, but she couldn't stop herself. Her heart rate was higher now than it had been powering up the hill. 'I know he's charming to Mum, and Dad thinks the sun shines out of his arse, but it's not the same when you're married to someone who won't even let you—'

'OK!' Owen looked a bit scared. 'OK! I get it. I didn't come here for an argument. Am I too late for breakfast?'

Michelle took a deep breath and tried to focus on her house. Her beautiful calm home, which was all hers. Her safe haven. No one weighed her here. Or checked her emails. Or her phone.

'No, you're not too late,' she said, forcing out a smile. 'Scrambled eggs?'

'To be honest, I'd rather have something you haven't cooked,' said Owen.

Owen arranged his lanky frame at Michelle's kitchen table while she moved around, trying to assemble her leftover deli pots into some form of breakfast acceptable to an overgrown student. He'd hoovered up half her loaf of bread before she'd even plunged the coffee maker, leaving trails of marmalade and clementine peel all over the clean cloth.

'Is this a flying visit on your way back to Dublin?' she asked. 'Or did you just need an excuse to get away from Mum's? Feet off the table, please.'

Owen swung his Converse off the table. 'I wanted to see my

big sister. It's been ages. I miss your bossy ways. And I wanted to check you hadn't been eaten by cats, living on your own.'

'Shut up.' Michelle hid the glow of affection beneath a mock-outraged glare. 'And what else did you need?'

'Do I need an excuse?' Owen pretended to look affronted, then dropped the act. 'Um, Shell, actually . . . I need to ask you a favour.'

It must be bad, Michelle thought, if he's asking me and not Mum. 'How much this time?'

'No, it's not cash. Although contributions are always welcome.' Owen looked up at her through his unfairly long black lashes. 'I actually need somewhere to crash for a few weeks.'

Michelle flinched involuntarily as she always did at the thought of anyone staying in her house, invading her perfectly arranged space. She knew it was irrational – and she loved Owen – but she couldn't help it. Invisible spiders crawled around her stomach.

'What happened to the job in Dublin?'

'Came to the end of the contract. I finished their website, and . . .' He shrugged. 'Well, I told Mum there was no more work out there, but, to tell the truth, it was kind of awkward.'

'Money, or a girl?'

'Both?' Again, the appealing, long-lashed look.

'You know that cuts no ice with me,' said Michelle. She folded her arms. 'You're twenty-four, Owen. Girls stop thinking that sort of carry-on's cute round about now. It just looks like you've got issues.'

'I know.' Owen prodded the omelette she'd cobbled together. 'I just . . . hate letting them down gently. I can't help being handsome. It's a cross I have to bear, like you have to clean everything in sight. What is this, exactly?'

'An omelette,' said Michelle. 'Why can't you stay with Mum? There's more work in London, surely?'

'She's redecorating again. And she said you've got loads of room, and you could do with the company.'

Michelle translated this in her head; Carole loved Owen, but not his habit of coming home at 3 a.m. without money for the cab. And the last time Owen had stayed with Ben, their oldest brother, their au pair had gone back to Latvia without warning, and Ben's youngest son, Hugo, had come out with a whole series of awkward questions and two new swear words.

'I had a look at your website on the way over,' Owen went on. 'It's rubbish. Might you be in need of an experienced and award-winning web designer to take a look at it and refresh your internet trade?'

'Fine,' said Michelle. It was typical of Owen's luck that 'redesign website' had been the third thing on her to-do list for the new year. 'But you can't stay here. The flat above the shop's empty at the moment – you can stay there while I work out whether to rent it out again. I've got my new season's stock in the main room, but there should be enough space for you.'

'Is that the equivalent of getting the stable with the manger and the donkeys? The flat with the storage boxes?'

'It's better,' said Michelle, pouring herself a cup of coffee. 'It has seagrass, and an en-suite bathroom.' She pushed a mug towards him with a warning look. 'But if there are any virgin births, Owen . . .'

'I have no idea what you mean,' he said, with a straight face.

Michelle had another look into Quentin's bookshop when she drove Owen round to the flat, and as soon as she got home, she started making phone calls.

Two days later, she was sitting in an empty office at Flint and Cook solicitors, dressed in her smartest suit, waiting to speak to the solicitor handling Cyril Quentin's affairs.

Sitting, and waiting. Michelle hated being kept waiting, especially when she had a sale to run, one which inspired a queue of impatient bargain-hunters.

She was crossly inspecting a Victorian map of Longhampton (many tanneries, a jam factory, more pubs than churches) when someone coughed behind her, and she spun round.

A tall, floppy-haired man in a tweed jacket with a green round-neck jumper underneath – three things that set Michelle's teeth on edge to begin with – was standing a bit too close to her.

Four things that set her teeth on edge.

'Hello,' he said, backing off a bit to extend a hand. His strawberry-blond fringe fell into his eyes and he pushed it back. 'Rory Stirling.'

The handshake was firm and the accent was Scottish, which created two positives, but then Michelle spotted crumbs on his jumper, which knocked him down again. She couldn't stand food debris. Beards made her want to heave.

'Michelle Nightingale,' she said. And, she added to herself, in semi-wonderment, how could a man reach the age of thirty-something and not know that you wore a *V-neck* with a tie? 'Thanks for seeing me at such short notice.'

'Not at all,' he said, gesturing towards the chair opposite as he sat down at his cluttered desk. 'It makes a change from drunk and disorderlies. And the usual rash of post-Christmas divorce consultations.'

'Good to be busy,' she said.

'Oh, it gets busier after New Year,' Rory replied darkly. 'That's when the *real* effects of a week with the in-laws kick in. Nearly always get a couple of wills rewritten, or people sneaking in to ask about conveyancing. And naturally it's the people who *don't* have happy families who get dragged in to deal with everyone else's fall-outs. Anyway, enough of my festive joys . . .'

Normally Michelle would have sympathised with that sentiment, being used to staffing her shop single-handed while her assistants went off to parents' meetings and birthday parties, but she was cold, and impatient.

'I understand that you're acting for Cyril Quentin,' she said. 'The bookshop on the high street?'

'We are indeed.'

Rory moved some papers from one messy pile to another. Michelle *hated* a messy desk.

Rory caught her eyeing a dead plant on the top of his in-tray, and pointedly moved it, dropping it in the bin behind him without looking. 'Have you spoken to Mr Quentin?' he went on.

'No, I noticed it was closed. I have the shop next door. Home Sweet Home, the interiors and homeware shop.'

'Ah! Yes, of course. The knick-knack shop. So how can I help you, Ms . . . ?' He patted the notes on his desk as if he were playing an invisible set of drums, then gave up when her details failed to spring up of their own accord.

With a tight smile, Michelle leaned over and moved the perfectly legible Post-it note with her name and details on from the top of his old-fashioned phone to the small clear space in front of him. 'Miss Nightingale. Michelle Nightingale. As in Florence.'

She made a mental note never to use Flint and Cook if they charged by the hour, and decided to take the meeting by the horns, as Rory Stirling clearly wasn't going to. 'I understand Mr Quentin's retiring, and I'd be very keen to lease the premises,' she said. 'Or, even buy them outright, if he's interested in selling?'

At the mention of selling, a light seemed to come on in the solicitor's eyes and he pushed his glasses up his nose with renewed focus.

At bloody last, thought Michelle.

'He owns the shop, yes, but I don't think he's intending to sell at the moment,' said Rory. 'He's instructed us quite specifically about finding a tenant.'

'In that case, I'd be very interesting in taking it on. I can give references, advance rent, whatever you need.' Michelle's smile became wider and warmer. 'I've been trading next door for nearly three years now.'

'People always need knick-knacks,' he said.

Was that supposed to be a joke? Michelle stared across the desk. Rory's long face didn't offer any clues, but then, going by his desk, he looked as if he was a stranger to storage solutions. And elegant stationery. And organic cleaning products – most of her range, in fact.

'They do if they're the right knick-knacks,' she said, lifting her sharp chin. 'I've got several exclusive deals with international suppliers, and I'm hoping to expand further this year.'

'Well, that's very commendable,' he said Scottishly. 'The high street needs some invigorating.'

'Best Neighbourhood Shop, 2010 and 2011,' she replied smartly. 'Did you see our hanging baskets this summer? We've won prizes for our window displays. I could do the same for next door.'

Rory leaned forward, resting one elbow on the desk. He had to move a file slightly to do it, which spoiled the casual effect, but he didn't take his eyes off Michelle's face. If she hadn't been struggling with her rising annoyance, she'd have taken more notice of their unusual grey colour. 'But – hanging baskets aside – what would you be bringing to the world of bookselling?'

'Bookselling?'

'Mmm.' He looked straight at her in a cool, assessing way and Michelle suddenly had the unsettling impression that Rory Stirling's brain wasn't as messy as his desk suggested. 'Bookselling.'

'But I wouldn't be . . .' Michelle stopped and readjusted her line of attack, seeing his eyebrows shift upwards as she spoke.

Oh, for God's sake, she thought crossly. He was obviously one of those 'books are the lifeblood of our civilisation' types, like Anna. Much as she liked Anna, she could be evangelical about the importance of literary heritage, and never seemed to notice how glazed Michelle's eyes went whenever she started raving on about how some television adaptation had missed the point of the novel. Rory Stirling had probably gone to protest at the library cuts – now that she looked at it, his was exactly the sort of jumper that library-goers wore. The two book group sessions she'd gone to with Anna, even the women had worn jumpers like that.

'It's a *very* difficult climate nationally for bookselling right now,' she said. 'As Mr Quentin himself must have realised. I think it would be tough for anyone to make books work on their own.'

'But not knick-knacks.' His face was straight, but his eyes were glinting with amusement. 'The knick-knack market is buoyant.'

Michelle clenched the hand he couldn't see until the nails dug into her palm. She could handle tough negotiators, but one thing she couldn't stand was having the mickey taken out of her. It had taken a long time to rebuild her confidence, after

Harvey's subtle chipping away. 'I'm committed to keeping a local shop open, to be run by local people, selling useful things that people want, instead of letting another of our high street outlets be swallowed up by a phone company, or a coffee chain.'

Rory leaned back in his chair and steepled his fingers like a lanky Bond villain. 'Well, don't we all, but Mr Quentin wants it run as a bookshop for at least a year. He dedicated his whole life to bookselling in Longhampton, and he's adamant that he'd rather see the place empty than let Longhampton lose such a vital cultural resource.'

'He'd rather see it *empty*?' Michelle couldn't stop her disbelief bursting out.

Rory actually looked proud of the old man's mad stance. 'As it happens, I fully agree with him. A town without a bookshop is a town without a soul.'

'Is that Shakespeare?' she enquired, more sarcastically than she meant to.

'Sir Walter Scott,' replied Rory, deadpan. 'No, of course not. It's just common sense.'

'I see.' She folded her arms, annoyed by his attitude. 'And have you had much interest so far, in running it as a bookshop?'

Rory Stirling paused, then twisted up the corner of his wide mouth. 'So far I haven't even advertised it as being available for rent. In fact, apart from me and Mr Quentin, I think you're the only person who's even noticed that it's closed. I'm impressed with your speed off the blocks, Miss Nightingale. No wonder your shop's such a success if you monitor the rest of the high street so carefully. Or do you have more time on your hands than you're letting on?'

Michelle kicked herself inwardly. She'd wanted to get in

straight away, having thought of nothing else since Anna had mentioned it, and now she looked far too keen. Still, if old Mr Quentin was going to make a big stand about only letting it to another bookseller, it wasn't as though he'd be inundated with offers.

Rory Stirling was still leaning back in his leather chair, watching her reaction in an annoyingly smug way. Was he teasing her, or was he serious? If Michelle hadn't wanted the shop so much, she'd have told him where to stick it.

Maybe if *I* talk to Mr Quentin, she thought. This guy's never going to put my case properly. Maybe I can persuade him. That nursing home can't be cheap. He's going to need all the income he can get.

'Well, that's a shame,' she said, gathering her things together to leave before her face could give her away. 'I don't believe it's viable as a bookshop, and to be honest with you, I doubt anyone with any retail experience will either. But I hope you find someone.'

She stood up, waiting for him to stand up to show her out. After a rude pause, he seemed to register what she was expecting and shoved his chair back, knocking over a stack of files.

'We'll find someone,' he said. 'It's a lovely old shop, lots of character. Lots of atmosphere. I'd hate to see Longhampton lose a gem like that. It's bad enough that the library's having to cut back.'

Ha, thought Michelle. I was right. Library protester. 'I suppose if more people had gone to Mr Quentin's and bought books instead of taking them out of the library, he'd still be open,' she said airily.

'That's not quite the same as . . .' Rory began, then realised she was joking, sort of. 'Oh. Touché.'

They stared over the desk, weighing each other up, and Michelle enjoyed a brief moment of triumph, which was lost as soon as she got outside and realised dust from Rory's filthy office was smeared over her freshly dry-cleaned suit.

The landline rang in the McQueen house just as the film – and Anna and Phil – were reaching an interesting part.

Phil's lips were nuzzling into the hollow of her neck, the exact spot that melted her insides to liquid, and Anna thought about ignoring the phone, but then she remembered the time she'd done just that and Chloe had spent ten minutes waiting at the bus stop with no bus money. The blame cloud had nearly engulfed the sun.

With a groan, she stretched out a bare arm behind her head and picked up the phone.

'Hello?' she said, in a tone that she could turn into a recorded message if needed.

'Hi, Anna, it's Michelle.'

Anna struggled into an upright position on the sofa and pulled the throw around herself. On top of her, Phil groaned and sank his forehead onto her bare shoulder.

'I'm not interrupting, am I?' Michelle enquired.

'Yes,' said Phil. 'Tell her, yes, she is interrupting our very rare mummy and daddy time.'

Anna covered the receiver and gave him her 'She's on her own, cut her some slack' glower.

'Phil and I were just . . . watching a film,' she said. 'I thought you might have been the girls phoning home.'

Although it was gone ten o'clock on the McQueen sofa, it was late afternoon in New York state – peak time for a call home. Chloe, Becca and Lily had only been gone two days – two heady, schedule-free days in which she and Phil had barely been out of bed, except to walk Pongo – but they still called the house at least once a day to make sure Dad was

OK. Or, as Chloe put it, 'to make sure he was missing them properly'.

Anna wondered if there was a time difference with Michelle too, because she sounded far too focused for a post-Christmas weeknight.

'Listen, when are you next going to see Phil's mum? At Butterfields?'

'What? I don't know. To be honest with you, Michelle, I'm not really thinking about Evelyn right now.'

'Tell Michelle to call you back in the morning.' Phil slipped his hand around her waist. 'Whatever it is can wait, and I can't.'

'I heard that,' said Michelle. 'Tell him I won't be long.'

'Neither will I.'

Anna glared at Phil to stop him, but couldn't prevent a laugh from curling around her mouth at the tragic face he pulled.

The first time Anna had seen Phil, he'd been wearing that same expression, and it had made her want to pull him into her arms. Ironically, he'd been with Pongo and all three girls – so she could hardly be accused of not knowing what she was taking on – being dragged unwillingly around Longhampton Town Fete on the hottest day of the year. It was difficult to tell who was enjoying it least, since Phil, Becca and Lily all had their faces painted as tigers. Chloe was a butterfly, with twice as much glitter as anyone else.

Anna had been running a cake stall for the library, and had watched the dark-haired, harassed man with the three young girls as they bickered their way over. While she was helping Becca choose the cookie with the most chocolate on, Lily plunged her baby hands right into the giant cupcakes, smearing pink buttercream icing over Pongo, who reared up in shock and knocked the whole table over, scattering cakes

everywhere and indirectly adding an extra 2 kg to the Guess
the Weight of the Labrador stand next door as Coco took
advantage of the early tea.

Phil had looked so helpless and horrified at the mess, and
even guiltier at the wailing that ensued, that she'd found herself
apologising to *him* as they tried to clear things up. It was hard
to be cross with a single father with a melty tiger face, especially when his eyes were so dark and beautiful she almost
forgot he had whiskers. The next lunchtime he appeared in
the library, looking grown-up and sexy in a suit and no face
paint, bearing flowers and a cash donation 'for the cakes we
squashed', and asked if he could buy her a coffee to say sorry.

She still saw the hangdog face now and again. Usually when
Michelle came round.

Anna pressed the mute button on the phone. 'Two seconds.
She doesn't have the same clocking on and off function as
normal people. She's spent all her holiday in the shop as it is.'

'Then she needs to get her love life sorted out.' Phil raised
an eyebrow. 'Just because she couldn't find a man tidy enough
to live with . . .'

Anna pointed a finger. 'That's not how it was.'

'No? You're her best friend and even you don't know why
she left.'

'Go and make us a cup of tea or something.'

With a grumble, Phil rolled off the sofa and padded away
to the kitchen.

Anna turned back to the phone. 'I'm going up there to do
the Reading Aloud group tomorrow,' she said. 'Eleven o'clock,
before they all nod off after lunch.'

'Can I come?'

Anna tried to keep the incredulity out of her voice and
failed. 'You want to volunteer to read Jean Plaidy to a room

full of oldies? Is this about getting your Christmas alibi straight for your mum?'

'No! It's my New Year's resolution, to put something back into the community. I thought I'd start with your volunteer Reading Aloud to grannies group.'

'Are you sure? I mean, I'd love it if you read – they really get so much out of it – but if you want to put something back you could donate some scented candles, or some flowers for the day room. A bit of Home Sweet Home would go a long way up there.'

'Well, we'll see,' said Michelle. 'Come round to the shop at quarter to. I'll give you a lift.'

'OK,' said Anna. Phil had appeared in the doorway with a bottle of champagne left over from Christmas and a couple of glasses. 'I have to—'

He crossed the room in a couple of strides and took the phone from her. 'She has to go now. Bye, Michelle.'

While Anna was still laughing, he took the phone off the hook again and shoved it behind a sofa cushion.

'You,' he said, pushing the bottle and the glasses into her hands, 'are coming with me. To bed.'

And with a groan, Phil picked Anna up, staggered slightly, then heaved her over his shoulder and carried her upstairs.

4

*'I still remember the goosebumps I felt when I read the
beautifully melancholy* Tom's Midnight Garden,
*and how sad I was that our newbuild house wasn't old
enough to have proper ghosts.'*   Becca McQueen

Anna knew it was a mistake, agreeing to meet Michelle at
Home Sweet Home instead of at her house. It was tempting
enough browsing there at the best of times, but with a hand-
printed 'Special Customer Sale Preview' postcard burning a
hole in her bag, she and her post-Christmas pull-our-belts-in
budget were doomed.

She pushed her purse firmly to the bottom of her handbag
as she approached the shop; it probably wouldn't stop her
wanting to buy everything in sight, but it might delay her for a
few vital, credit-card-saving seconds.

Home Sweet Home was generally agreed to be the reason
that Longhampton High Street was starting to pick up, a
strong green shoot of good times amidst the charity shops
and pound stores. The first thing Michelle had done was to
rip off the plastic fishmonger's signage and paint the
neglected exterior a soft honey-cream, picking out the
carved stone roses along the shop window in gold and
crimson paint. No one had noticed the stone roses for

decades. Within a month, three shops on the same side had refurbished.

Anna put her hand on the door handle, steeled herself by visualising the epic phone bill she'd got that morning and went in. Immediately her eye lit on a delicious pile of glass baubles in a basket, and her resistance melted like a chocolate Santa.

The shop was already packed out with shoppers carrying baskets loaded with filigree tree decorations and gingerbread hearts. Phil joked that Michelle pumped some kind of shopping nerve gas into the shop, but the truth was that she just had the knack of stocking what women wanted – the most beautiful, useful, unusual, pretty things; some expensive, some cheap, all presented as if they were precious, and just what you needed to make your home as welcoming as the shop. It didn't matter whether you were eight and obsessed with ribbons like Lily, or thirty-one and unable to resist an organic beeswax lip balm like Anna – there was something on every table that whispered, 'Buy me'.

She picked up the glass ball, imagining a cluster of them in Becca's room, hanging on gold ribbons around her window maybe, then put it down. They were on one income now, and the girls would be shopping it up in New York. But at half price they were such a bargain, and she'd seen Becca admiring them.

'Oh, aren't they gorgeous?' said a breathy voice. 'But, um, wouldn't you be worried about Pongo eating one? Not being funny, but they do look like tomatoes. I couldn't work out what was Christmassy about tomatoes till Michelle told me they were for the tree.'

Anna looked up to see Michelle's junior assistant, Kelsey, hovering by the table, and put the bauble down. Kelsey was lovely, like everything else in the shop, but about as useful as the glass baubles when it came to actual selling. She was mostly confined to dealing with internet orders, since she'd never managed to make the till work on her own, and had kindly talked Anna out of a couple of rash purchases – not, thankfully, while Michelle was around. Kelsey was like a golden-eyebrowed supermodel, or an angel whose wings had fallen off, and she drove Michelle insane with her unfortunate habit of missing shoplifters because she was unpicking her complicated love life on the phone to her friends.

If Gillian, queen of the window display, hadn't been so efficient, Kelsey would have been ruthlessly excised from Michelle's empire long ago, but like the green fig candles burning in high alcoves, and the Ella Fitzgerald soundtrack, she added a certain aspirational ambience to the place.

'Hi, Kelsey, is Michelle around?' Anna asked. 'She said she'd meet me here, at quarter to?'

'She's upstairs.' Kelsey dropped her voice conspiratorially. 'With a guy!'

'A *guy*?' Anna hadn't meant it to sound so loud, but the way Kelsey was winking at her made it hard not to.

'Yeah. A really good-looking guy. Bit young for her, if you ask me, but if you've got it, right?' She stopped winking and pulled a face to indicate that she felt Michelle did still have it.

'Are you sure he's not a rep?' asked Anna.

Kelsey snorted. 'Not unless he's selling sexy hair.'

'Michelle's upstairs sorting out the website,' called a voice from the room behind the main shop floor; a competent, older voice. 'It's gone down again, don't ask me how or why. And she's with her *brother*. She won't be a moment.'

'Her brother?' mouthed Kelsey, shocked.

'She's got three brothers,' said Anna, as Gillian appeared in her Christmas sale outfit: a red cardigan over her usual black shift dress, and an extra-rigid girdle flattening her Christmas excesses. There were no seasonal reindeer horns in here. 'Which one is it?'

'The hot one,' said Gillian. 'Pardon my French.'

Anna heard two sets of footsteps clattering down the stairs that led up to the flat, and before Kelsey had time to do more than fluff up her hair, Michelle and Owen were standing in front of a three-woman welcome committee.

'What?' said Michelle, seeing the blatant curiosity on their faces. 'Oh, I get it. Owen, let me introduce you properly. This is Gillian, who runs the shop. This is Kelsey, who posts out the website orders, and this is Anna, who stops me from going mad. Ladies, this is my little brother, Owen. He's our new website geek.'

'I prefer IT consultant,' said Owen, with a smile that reached his brown eyes, making them crinkle attractively.

Anna could see the family resemblance. Owen had the same dark chestnut hair as Michelle and the same sharp chin, but whereas her hair was cut into a geometric bob, his curled round his ears and over his collar. And his brown eyes flashed – she started to correct the Mills and Boon-ish word, then had to admit that actually, in this instance, it was fair enough – whereas Michelle's eyes were more guarded, noticing everything but giving nothing away.

Owen towered over his sister, with thin leather bracelets circling his wrists and long legs in skinny jeans. He looks as if he should be in a band, thought Anna, envying his long lashes. One of those ones that Becca likes, with a name that means something she was too out-of-touch to know about.

'Owen's going to be setting up the new spring web pages, and he's got a lot to be getting on with, so don't let him distract you,' Michelle went on, checking through her to-do list and crossing off a few things, while he beamed affably at them all. 'Owen, don't let Kelsey distract you either. She's got a lot to be getting on with down here.'

Kelsey looked thwarted and closed her mouth. Owen winked at her, and even though the wink wasn't directed her way, Anna felt a sort of passive flutter.

'OK.' Michelle clicked her pen. 'You, upstairs. You,' she pointed at Kelsey, 'serve those ladies over there. You,' she pointed at Anna, 'let's go and do some reading.'

'Are you sure you can spare the time?' Anna asked, as two more customers jangled the bell and made a beeline for the rack of handsewn cherry-print aprons.

'So long as I'm back for the afternoon rush,' said Michelle. She wound a scarf around her neck and pulled on her shearling jacket. It was buttery soft, and, like all her clothes, untouched by Dalmatian hair or accidental felt-tip pen marks. Anna envied the easy way Michelle made scarves hang right.

'Where are you going?' Kelsey asked.

'Butterfields.' Anna seized the chance to recruit some new volunteers. 'I don't suppose you'd like to volunteer a few hours a month, would you? All you have to do is read for about half an hour, and maybe discuss the book, share some stories about—'

'No, sorry. I'm not really a book person,' said Kelsey firmly. 'I prefer to wait for the film.'

'But reading's such a lovely thing to do. Very relaxing. You end up enjoying it as much as the people you're reading to,' Anna persisted. 'Don't you remember being read to at school? Or by your mum? What an amazing feeling it is letting the story come to life in your head?'

'No.' Kelsey looked horrified at the thought of anything coming to life anywhere near her head.

'Is it a council thing?' asked Gillian. She was a keen monitor of council expenditure.

'No, it's a volunteer group we started in the library to reach people who've lost touch with words and stories. Maybe they can't concentrate, or they can't read, or see . . . all sorts of reasons. I do the old people's home, my assistant Wendy ran sessions for the Learning Support Unit at the school, and there's another one at the hospital.'

'And you just . . . read?' asked Gillian.

Anna nodded. It was hard to explain how rewarding the reading scheme was without sounding holier-than-thou, but it made her feel she'd given something useful, which would last for hours after she'd left. 'Sometimes they read themselves, sometimes we stop and discuss a passage, or they talk about some memory it's brought back. I have to admit, I sometimes get a bit teary with the older folk. It's like they're waking up and you suddenly see their eyes look young again. All because of an idea someone had, then wrote down to share, and now that same idea is planted in memories all over the world, and it's as if it can turn back time. Isn't that amazing?'

Kelsey looked unconvinced but Anna thought she saw a glistening in Gillian's eyes. Next time she's coming too, Anna decided.

Michelle tapped her watch. 'We're cutting into their Jean Plaidy hour. Let's go!'

And with one backwards glance at a silk handbag covered in tiny chiffon butterflies, Anna let herself be swept out of the warm embrace of Home Sweet Home and onto the chilly high street.

Anna had reluctantly got rid of her sports car to pay for the bigger people carrier, but she had kept the same energetic driving style. Michelle was relieved when she finally indicated down the tree-lined drive to an Edwardian mansion with a sweeping turning circle and neat box hedges marking out the lawn. No croquet hoops, just a discreet sign saying, 'Butterfields Residential Home' and a wheelchair-adapted minibus outside.

'I didn't even know this was here,' said Michelle, admiring the ivy-covered frontage and long windows. 'It must have been quite a place in its day.'

'It used to belong to the town's one and only captain of industry,' said Anna, as she parked next to the only other car there. 'Some of the older residents can remember the family. Don't get them started on the Parrys. I've had to avoid any Catherine Cookson novels with servants in them, because some of the current residents' forebears were disgruntled parlourmaids.'

Michelle stood back from Anna as she marched across the gravel in her flat boots and announced their arrival via the security buzzer. She looked at them in the plate-glass of the entrance porch. They made a funny-looking couple, like a pair of comedians: sharp-edged Michelle in her jeans and leather boots, and graceful Anna in her long skirt, her blond hair stuffed under a knitted hat and her book bag slung over her shoulder.

Their reflections hovered on the glass, somewhere between the crisp winter air outside and the dingy institutional walls inside. Like ghosts, she thought. Michelle didn't want to say so to Anna, but old people's homes gave her the creeps. If she hadn't been set on charming Mr Quentin into changing his mind about the bookshop, there was no way she'd have got herself across the threshold.

As Anna pulled open the door and directed her into the once-imposing entrance hall, the majestic first impression of the exterior dissolved in a whiff of boiled vegetables and cleaning fluid. Michelle cast her eyes around urgently for any shreds of elegance that remained. There wasn't much to go on.

Everything's so grey, she thought – grey and thick. Where are the colours, the soothing smells, even some nice wallpaper?

Oblivious to her friend's reaction, Anna pushed open a heavy fire door and smiled at a helper in a nylon housecoat who was pushing a vacant-eyed man in a wheelchair down the corridor.

'That's Albert,' she said, under her breath. 'Only time I ever heard him speak was after we'd read some chapters of *Atonement*. At the end, without any warning, he said, "I met my Noreen in an air-raid shelter in Solihull, and I thought she was her sister. Had to marry her after that." The nurses nearly fell over.'

'And after that you couldn't stop him chattering away?'

'Well, no.' Anna stopped at another fire door and pulled it open to let Michelle through first. 'But it gave the carers something to think about when his family next came to visit.'

They'd reached the main day room, a grand, high-ceilinged reception room with chintzy winged chairs arranged in a circle, containing hunched-up old men and women, some of whom turned to see who'd come in. The others just carried on staring into space, their hands clawed around the arms of their chairs.

A chill went through Michelle at the solitude in the room, despite all the people in it. She loved living alone – couldn't bear the thought of sharing her beautiful house with anyone – but this, as her mother kept reminding her, was where it could all end up. Slow, featureless days in a room with other unloved people, forced into cells of single old folk, without even a horde of cats to eat you.

The fact that this house had once been loved too made it worse than one of those purpose-built retirement homes, she thought. Butterfields felt as abandoned as its residents. The plaster mouldings were partially boarded over, hiding what little decoration there was in the room. That marble fireplace would once have had invitation cards and photographs crammed on it. Those old ladies in their lumpy skirts once danced with hopeful boys, and wore seamed stockings, and had crushes, and told jokes. And now they were just sitting in their own closed-off worlds, waiting for what? Someone to come in and make them listen to bloody Jane Austen whether they liked it or not?

It was so quiet. No one spoke, there was no music, no television burbling away, no radio blurting out traffic reports . . . nothing. Just the faint ticking of the radiators and the occasional shuffle of polyester slacks against cushions.

Michelle pressed her lips together to stop herself saying something to Anna about the horrible mustard-yellow walls; she knew it sounded shallow, but she also knew it'd be the first thing that would drive her over the edge.

This could be me, she thought, sick with panic. Harvey was right. Mum was right. *This could be me.*

'Where's your mother-in-law?' she whispered instead.

Anna was fishing in her bag for her book. 'Not here yet. She'll make her grand entrance just before we start, to make sure everyone's looking at her.'

'And what about Mr Quentin?'

Michelle's cunning plan seemed pretty loopy now, even in her own mind. There were no books here, she thought. No bookshelves, no magazines, no papers. Mr Quentin must be going mad. He'd be even more determined to preserve his shop.

Anna looked around. 'I don't think he's here yet either. Why?'

'Oh, I thought I might have a word with him. About his shop.'

'Really?' Anna's eyes opened wide; she was too trusting to suspect any ulterior motive. 'Why?'

Before Michelle could think of an appropriate response, a middle-aged lady in a tunic and leggings bustled over to them with a clipboard and a pen suspended from her shelf-like bosom like a plumb line. She beamed with delight at Anna.

'Anna, my duck! Have you brought a helper today?'

'Yes, this is Michelle,' said Anna. 'Michelle, Joyce is the entertainments manager for Butterfields.'

'For my sins!' said Joyce, flapping her arm modestly. 'They keep me busy, this little lot.'

Michelle and Anna couldn't help looking in disbelief at the silent room of silent old people.

'So, what are we having this week?' enquired Joyce. She raised her voice so that the nearest residents could feel included. 'Something Christmassy?'

'I thought I'd read something from *Cranford.*'

'Ooh, lovely. That's been on telly quite recently, hasn't it?'

'Yes,' said Anna.

'It helps,' Joyce confided to Michelle. 'Though they sometimes get things confused with their families. Think they've had Joanna Lumley coming in to see them. They haven't.'

Joyce and Anna set about chivvying the residents gently, herding them like hens into a circle. Michelle felt awkward, but moved some chairs and sat down herself next to Anna, who introduced herself with an unselfconscious cheeriness, then began reading.

Anna's melodic voice easily filled the space around the chairs, and Michelle was surprised by how different it was from her usual conversational tone. She spoke more slowly and carefully, giving each phrase a rhythm that slid it directly into the imagination, building image on image, each character's voice distinct.

She'd read maybe a page when a white-haired lady appeared in the doorway, pushing a wheeled Zimmer frame with visible distaste. Unlike most of the others, she was wearing colours with a furious sort of defiance – a bright coral scarf round her neck and a pair of yellow trousers with plastic buttons. Her mouth was a horizontal slash of red lipstick, in a firm, unsmiling line.

'You started without me,' she said, glaring directly at Anna.

'No, Evelyn, we didn't,' lied Anna.

'Yes, you did,' she retorted. 'I've had a knee replacement, not a lobotomy. I could hear you down the hall. You can bloody well stop until I've sat down, thank you.'

So this was the mother-in-law from hell.

All eyes turned her way as she wheeled herself towards the empty chair furthest from the door. She might be an old bag, thought Michelle, but she knows how to work a room.

'I don't need a hand,' she said, waving away Joyce's attempts to help her into the seat. She took her time arranging herself, and Michelle saw Anna's composure wobble. She felt cross on her friend's behalf; no wonder she'd done a runner from her own Christmas Day if she'd had hours of this as well as the girls playing up.

'Anna,' she said in a bright voice, 'I think everyone's ready now.'

Anna turned the page, switched on a smile and started reading again.

When she began, a few of the more alert residents had their eyes fixed on her, hanging onto every word. Evelyn McQueen made a point of staring at the long windows, apparently intrigued by something in the garden. Apart from Anna's voice and the occasional flutter of a turning page, there was no sound in the day room, but it was a different sort of silence from the closed-off dullness that had blanketed the air before. Now there was a sort of tension springing between the chairs, and slowly more eyes turned Anna's way, then closed, then opened with interest.

Even Michelle found herself listening. It was as if there was someone else there in the room with them, someone comfortable and familiar. She felt herself relaxing into the chair, forgetting about its shabby covering as the story unfolded.

And then it came to her.

Anna. Anna could run the bookshop for a year.

The idea was so sharp it was as if some helpful guardian angel had actually spoken the words in her ear.

It was so obvious: Anna had loads of experience with books, and more importantly, she loved them. She came alive when she was talking about novels and words and the magic of storytelling blah blah blah. Her passion would make the shop sing, just like Michelle's own passion for her house had made Home Sweet Home work so well.

Michelle struggled to contain her excitement. She didn't need to persuade Mr Quentin to let her change the nature of the shop after all. That snotty solicitor had said it was just for a year; all she'd have to do would be to get Anna to sell what stock there was already, and there seemed to be a good bit of it. If the sums didn't add up in six months – and with the best will in the world, Anna wasn't a miracle worker – well, there was the argument. She'd tried; it hadn't worked out.

I should call Flint and Cook now, she thought. Before someone else does.

Michelle excused herself, but with Anna's voice rising and falling in the air, no one noticed her leave.

Slipping into a corridor, she got out her phone, dialled the solicitors and asked to be put through to Rory Stirling, trying not to read the notice about Type 2 Diabetes pinned to the wall while the hold music played.

Abruptly, 'Yesterday' stopped, and Rory came on the line.

'Ah, the Knick-Knack Queen of Longhampton High Street.' He sounded as if he was eating at his desk; Michelle struggled to contain her annoyance. 'How can I help?'

'Quentin's bookshop,' she said. 'Is it still available?'

'It is. I have the advert here in front of me, but as yet, there is no one in the ad department at the *Gazette* to take it.' He sounded amused. 'I thought we were quite efficient here, but you're putting us to shame.'

'Good. I'd like to take on the lease, please.'

'As a bookshop?'

'As a bookshop.' Michelle moved away from the posters and stared instead out of the window, at what had once been some kind of formal garden. A robin was hopping along the path towards a frozen bird bath. 'I've got a manager lined up who I think Mr Quentin would thoroughly approve of. Someone who's really passionate about books.'

'Of whom. Of whom Mr Quentin would approve.' Rory sounded amused, rather than suspicious, but she could tell he was dying to say, *Come on, this is a joke.*

'Whatever. I've been thinking about what you said,' Michelle went on, 'about every town needing a bookshop. You're right.'

There was a snort, then a surprised pause, then Rory recovered his professionalism.

'Well, that's great news,' he said. 'Would you like to come in to talk about paperwork?'

'I'll be in this afternoon,' said Michelle.

5

Anna stretched out her left leg under the duvet and wriggled her right toes under the dead weight of a snoring Pongo. She knew she should move him but she was as comfortable as he was. A pot of tea, some toast and the new Kate Atkinson hardback that Phil had bought her for Christmas – it was worth a dead leg for that sort of once-a-year indulgence. Anna had absolutely no intention of getting up before lunchtime, and she suspected Pongo wasn't too fussed either.

The phone rang and she leaned over to click it onto speaker so she didn't have to put the book down.

I bet that's Phil, she thought, checking to see I'm enjoying my breakfast in bed while he's back in the office. She'd tried to persuade him to go in a little late – so they could enjoy some rare morning privacy – but he'd insisted on being there by nine. He was a very dutiful boss.

'Hello?' she said, in her best Sybil Fawlty. 'McQueen Dog Sitters?'

'What?' said a voice that definitely wasn't Phil's.

'Oh, Michelle,' she said, nearly dropping the book onto her crumby plate, and getting marmalade on her fingers.

'Can you come over to the shop?' Michelle sounded excited. She also sounded very up and dressed.

Pongo's ears pricked up at the sound of Michelle's voice, though he didn't move. He wasn't usually allowed on beds, especially when Phil was around.

'When?' Anna asked, seeing her morning of reading vanishing. She grabbed the phone to stop Pongo reacting further to the invisible Michelle in the room. 'I haven't w-a-l-k-e-d the dog yet, and—'

'Come now! Bring him over.'

'Really? To your shop full of baskets and things to knock over?'

'Well, run him twice round the park first to wear him out a bit.'

Pongo's ears had detected action, and now he was nudging at Anna's knee with his nose, upgrading it to a paw when she didn't respond.

'What's this about?' Anna asked, giving up and putting her bookmark into the chapter she'd just started.

'Surprise,' said Michelle. 'Now hurry. Pongo!' she yelled. 'Walkies! Waaaaalkies!'

Pongo leaped off the bed in excitement and Anna resigned herself to getting up, fast.

When they reached the high street, Michelle was waiting for them outside the shop with a jute bag over her shoulder and a couple of takeaway coffees from Natalie's café in a paper tray.

'No, don't go in!' she said, guarding the door of Home Sweet Home from Pongo's curious nose. 'No, next door, Pongo!' Michelle waved a set of keys. 'The bookshop.'

Anna wrinkled her own nose, about to ask how on earth Michelle had a set of keys for the bookshop, but she was already letting herself in.

Pongo whined and strained after her. 'Can he come in?' Anna called.

'Sure.' Michelle's voice suggested she was already a long way into the shop.

With a warning look at Pongo to behave himself, Anna followed her inside.

The bookshop felt damp and chilly, but it was still an unsupervised bookshop, and Anna felt a frisson of excitement as she scanned the shelves with greedy eyes. Libraries weren't quite the same, she'd found; something about the prosaic smell of other people's houses and fingers seeping off the pages diluted that sense of magical worlds, but untouched, unread, unexplored books were something else.

She walked slowly, angling her head to read the titles that were left on the partially emptied shelves: Mr Quentin might have gone but his collection of military history titles still took the prime position by the door. It was strange seeing the shop without his mercurial presence behind the desk and without other customers browsing the shelves. It felt smaller than she remembered, and sadder.

Pongo was sniffing at the wastepaper bin by the desk. Anna checked there was nothing inside he could eat, then tied his extending lead to one of the desk's heavy legs and went off to find Michelle.

She was standing in the back room, where the shelves were obscured by piles of second-hand stock. Mr Quentin could never say no to a house clearer or a car boot sale. Books were scattered unceremoniously around Michelle's feet from where she'd dragged a shelf away from a wall, and she was looking critically at two slashes of buttercream paint applied over the faded magnolia.

'What do you think?' she asked, turning to see Anna's reaction. 'String or Matchstick?'

'They look the same to me. Are you allowed to do that to someone else's shop? Are you decorating this for someone?'

'No. And no.' Michelle took another paint pot out of the jute bag and started slapping on another patch below the squares of cream. This one was a rich red. 'Or what do you think about a real reading room feel? Too much like the inside of someone's liver?'

'Are you going to tell me what's going on?'

'In a minute.'

Anna couldn't bear to see scattered books. She bent down to pick them up and felt a tug of nostalgia as she recognised an old favourite: the same 70s edition of *Charlie and the Chocolate Factory* she'd had on her own shelves, complete with the magical chocolate machine gushing rainbow-coloured foam from a tangle of pipes. She opened the pages and the scratchy, busy illustrations immediately took her back to her small bedroom, her dad sitting like a giant on the half-size chair next to her bed in his shirt sleeves, reading 'just one more' chapter before she went to sleep. Roald Dahl was his favourite too; he did all the accents. Petulant Veruca and greedy Augustus, and with a surprising South American glee, the singing Oompa-Loompas.

The well-worn pages felt velvety as she turned them, and Anna's head filled up with memories of warm blankets, and Dad's after-work office smell, and his supper in the oven downstairs, and in her head, hot chocolate rivers and everlasting toffees and a feeling of being absolutely safe. Free to wander round fantastical worlds, into danger and battles and haunted houses, but with her dad right by her side, his familiar voice in her ear.

Anna had daydreamed about reading to her own children since she was a child herself and her heart expanded with impatient longing as she thought of the baby out there, waiting for her, waiting to start its journey into her life. When she and Phil had their own baby, she'd have a different life. A life where she'd feel needed, wanted, not just tolerated, like a competent temp.

Michelle's voice cut through her thoughts. '. . . coffee?'

She looked up. Michelle was offering her a takeaway cappuccino, and judging by the excitement radiating from her – and the new to-do list in her hand – it wasn't her first coffee of the day.

Michelle never had to worry about who she was, thought Anna with a stab of envy. She had a job. A thriving business. A life based on who she was, not who she wasn't.

'Anna? What's the matter?' Michelle turned to look at the wall, then back again. 'Is the colour really bad? Go on, you can tell me.'

'No, it's not that.' Anna took the coffee and told herself to get a grip. 'They're both . . . nice. But why are you painting?'

'I've rented the shop,' said Michelle, swinging her arm wide. 'Stage two of the Nightingale takeover of the high street.'

'Congratulations! Are you knocking through?' Anna made her face cheery, even though inside she felt sorry for the now-homeless books and Cyril's life's work, heading for the recycling to make way for witty cardboard stags' heads.

'Nope, it's going to be books.'

'Books?'

Michelle nodded. 'I'm going to run it as a bookshop.'

'But this is the worst *possible time* for bookshops,' said Anna, horrified. 'And I say that as Longhampton's sole remaining purchaser of books. I mean, it's great that you want to keep it open, but I don't want to see you ruined.'

'Well, we'll see. Tell me what you think about my ideas.' Michelle flipped over another page in her notebook, which was covered in her bold handwriting, arrows and bubbles springing in every direction. 'Redecoration and marketing are the key things. I was thinking about those presents you gave the girls. We could call them Book Bouquets, and offer it as a service – a stack of romances sent to a relative stuck in hospital, say? You can't have flowers in some hospital wards, apparently – I'm always sending silk flower bouquets up there.'

'Well, I'd buy that, obviously,' conceded Anna. 'Who's going to put them together, though? Kelsey?'

She didn't want to add, 'You?' because she knew she couldn't make the word come out politely. Michelle was the only person she knew who arranged her books in rainbow order.

But Michelle was still listing her ideas, clearly not in the mood for negatives.

'And I was thinking about organic book boxes, like veg boxes? For ten quid, we could send someone a mentally nutritious selection of titles, some new, some second-hand. Some easy "potato" books, some more challenging "turnip" ones. You know how you always make an effort to do something new when they send you a Savoy cabbage? Well, the book box would be like that. People would feel virtuous for trying a Swedish translation along with their new Marian Keyes, and it wouldn't cost us anything because – here's the clever bit – *it's here already.*'

Anna marvelled at how Michelle made everything sound so

possible. 'That's actually a really good idea. You'd need to put in a guide, though, get them interested in the turnip books. But who's going to . . . ?'

'Brilliant!' Michelle pointed her pen at her, and jotted the idea down in the notebook. 'And reading groups – during the day, not at night? I see the same faces in my shop during office hours – you know, the yummy mummies with babies and nothing else to do. They can't really get their buggies in next door, but they could in here, if we made the space between the tables good and big. I thought with some chairs in here . . . get the fire going . . . paint it the right colour . . .' She tapped her pen against her perfect white teeth. 'What else?'

'Pot of coffee brewing?' suggested Anna, half joking.

'Coffee, yes, good. And pastries. It's all about the extras in a place like this. I'll see if I can do a deal with the deli . . .'

Anna looked around and tried to see what Michelle was seeing, but she couldn't: the windowless room was stacked with boxes of second-hand stock Cyril Quentin had never got round to sorting, let alone shelving. The shelves themselves were tatty and the lino was torn, showing bare boards in some places. No one ever ventured into the back room. Even she'd only put her nose round the door once or twice before giving up, overwhelmed by the disordered stock.

'Children's books are good sellers,' she said, reaching down to pick up *James and the Giant Peach*, another old favourite. The downy, luscious peach dangling above the seething sea, strung up by thousands of seagulls. Anna had always been slightly scared of the gulls and had made her dad read it with the book flat, so she wouldn't let their sharp beaks into her dreams as she dozed off. 'Kids get through them so quickly, if they're fast readers,' she went on. 'You could maybe get the mums in to read to the smaller ones, like the Reading Aloud project? They had to cut back on that at the library, but it was always well attended.'

'Of course!' Michelle scribbled away, turning the page quickly.

'I don't want to sound interfering,' said Anna cautiously, 'but if you need some help with the books, I'd be happy to give you a hand.'

'I was hoping you'd do a bit more than that,' said Michelle. She looked up with a smile, and Anna could almost see the sparks of her enthusiasm prickling the dusty air. 'I was hoping I could hire you. To run the whole thing.'

'Me?'

Michelle nodded, as if it were too obvious to explain. 'I want to see the customers looking like those people at Butterfields.'

'What? Old?'

'No!' Michelle swatted her knee. '*Entranced*. Captivated by your storytelling. You've got library experience, you're not working at the moment . . . You can start at once, can't you?' She paused for the first time and gave Anna a searching look. 'I know you've been applying for jobs, but have you had any interviews?'

'No,' admitted Anna. 'To be honest, I'd stand more chance of getting into space travel than finding work in a library right now.'

She didn't know what to say: she was touched by Michelle's confidence in her, but also suddenly shy. Michelle was a mate, but she was serious about her business, and Anna didn't want to let her down. She hated letting anyone down.

But a bookshop. Her own bookshop.

A slow smile spread across her face. 'Honestly?'

'Honestly.' Michelle grinned. 'I can't think of anyone who'd do it better. You've got to believe in yourself a bit more. Didn't I tell you that when you wrote things down on a list they happened?'

She raised her cappuccino, and they chinked their paper cups of coffee, two friends setting off on an adventure together.

But even as she sipped, Anna's enthusiasm hit a cartoon brick wall. How was the girls' daily routine going to function if she was out during shop hours? The transporting, shopping, cooking, washing – it was like running a hotel.

And Pongo. There was another responsibility. He'd got used to having her around, and going out twice a day to meet his mates down the park. They'd have to get Juliet the dog-walker back – if she had any spaces.

She put down her coffee and shoved her hands into her hair. 'Michelle, I really want to do this, but I'm going to have to run it by Phil first.'

'Why?' Michelle tried to hide it, but Anna could tell she was irritated. 'Phil should be *thrilled*. You've spent the last year acting as a housekeeper for him, it's about time he let you get back to using your brain again. It'd do him good to realise how hard you work at home.'

'Well, it's not as simple as that,' she said. 'We've got routines, responsibilities. I can't just do my own thing any more. It's what you do when you're married.'

Too late, Anna realised that wasn't the most tactful thing to say.

Michelle flipped her notebook back so the cover snapped shut on itself, and looked at her with the cool, clear gaze that she sometimes found quite unsettling. Michelle's focus could sometimes verge on the superhuman; it was hard to imagine her worrying much about anything, once she'd set her mind to it. Anna wondered – very quietly, in case Michelle could read *her* mind – if that was a result of her divorce, or something that had contributed to it.

After three years, she still only knew the very vaguest of details about Michelle's failed marriage. Michelle knew Anna inside out, but there were areas of her own life that remained thoroughly fenced off.

'*Is* it what you do when you're married?' Michelle said. 'That's one of the reasons I decided I didn't want to be married any more. Having to run everything past someone else for approval, only to be told I couldn't do it.'

Pongo, having freed himself from his collar yet again, clicked over to her and pushed his head onto her knee.

'Get off, you hairy mutt,' she said, but stroked his velvety ears as she said it.

Anna felt torn, as she so often did. Phil wasn't like Harvey – as far as she could tell. He wasn't controlling or dismissive of her career, but without any real discussion, it had somehow become understood that the girls would come first. It was the lack of discussion that bothered her more.

'I'll talk to him,' she said.

Anna thought about the bookshop all afternoon as she powered round the house, shoving laundry into drawers, books onto shelves, magazines into piles, and hoovering the spaces in between.

She'd spent years daydreaming about her ideal book-shop – how she'd stock it, the quirky reps who'd nod at her interesting selections and gossip about new authors, the recommendation cards with unusual choices, the coffee always psch-psching in the background, the regular custom-ers who'd come back and say, 'Oh, Anna, this changed my life!' And now it might be a reality she wasn't really in a position to take it without causing disruption at home, just when things were calming down again.

She shoved the hoover under Chloe's dressing table, and her heart sank as she spotted something. All twelve of her present books were stacked in a corner, perilously close to the bin. Anna steeled herself and bent down to pick them up. So much for 'Oh, Anna, this changed my life!' She piled the scattered make-up back into the storage boxes she'd provided, put the books on the resulting space, and carried on tidying.

Detach, detach, detach.

The hoover whirred with a blockage and she yanked out a stray sock with more force than was strictly necessary, because it was slowly dawning on her that actually, she might have to turn Michelle down after all. Because whether Michelle approved or not, she did have responsibilities: the children she'd always dreamed about having, the ready-made family that had seemed like a gift, but which now had to come first.

That's parenthood, Anna told herself – but didn't kids love their parents? Didn't they put up with them with that affectionate 'Oh, *Mum*' love? She didn't get that. She got, 'You're *not* my mum!'

Anna stopped in front of Chloe's Hollywood-lit mirror and looked at herself in it, her hair sticking out of her collapsing bun, her nose shiny, her face pinched. Stop it, she told her reflection. You sound more like Chloe than an adult woman. Are you going to start *singing* about how shit everyone else is?

Her reflection glared back, the bags under her eyes more noticeable since the concealer had worn off. Anna realised the bad mood engulfing her chest was too heavy to jolly away. Time was ticking on. She'd been twenty-four when she met Phil. Now she was in her thirties. She had open pores and the beginnings of crow's feet. She'd be forty by the time Lily was leaving school.

Anna thought of the packet of contraceptive pills in the bathroom, one tiny pearl remaining in the mangled foil rectangle. She hadn't been to the surgery to get a repeat prescription. From now on, it was in the lap of the gods. And she'd written it down. It was going to happen.

With a new tingle in her stomach, Anna directed the Dyson into Lily's bedroom, the last room on her list, and the messiest.

Lily's bed, and most of the floor, was covered in soft toys. Being the youngest, she'd ended up with the teddies, tortoises and cats Becca and Chloe had discarded, as well as her own, all presided over by a regal pink creature called Mrs Piggle. After the divorce, Phil had overcompensated by giving her a new toy every visit, and now Sarah had started to do the same. The result was a herd of velour creatures that all had to be arranged in a comfortable position at night, since Lily was going through existentialist angst about whether they might have feelings, and thus, possible bad backs if left squashed up.

As Lily wasn't there to see her, Anna chucked them all unceremoniously on the bed and started making clean stripes on the carpet.

Lily was the easiest, in many ways. She had all Phil's affability, and a sense of humour, and she'd never blamed Anna for taking her dad away from her mum, because she had no real memory of her parents being together at all. Anna listened to Lily's endless narratives of Mrs Piggle's daily tribulations every bedtime, and she hoped she could turn that into shared reading time.

Ballet Shoes when she comes back, Anna thought, hoping Lily had started to read *One Hundred and One Dalmatians*, which she'd hidden in her flight bag. We'll start with *Ballet Shoes* if she's sick of dogs, and I'll let Pongo come up for bedtime stories as a special treat.

Her mood perked up, and she pushed the hoover under the bed with renewed energy. It met some resistance, and on bending down to see what it was, Anna made out a stack of book-shaped shadows, piled up against the wall.

She knelt and slowly removed them, her heart stinging.

Ballet Shoes.

What Katy Did.

Charlotte's Web.

Tom's Midnight Garden.

The Sheep-Pig.

One Hundred and One Dalmatians.

All twelve of the books she'd given Lily for Christmas, including the one Lily had evidently carefully removed from her hand luggage, the same way she carefully removed concealed peas from her casserole. Hidden, so as not to hurt Anna's feelings, but definitely left behind, unwanted.

Anna sat back on her heels and bit her lip, crushed. At least Lily had hidden them. At least she hadn't left them by the bin, like Chloe had.

You're failing them, said the voice in her head. *They've been here six months, and you still haven't got the first idea.*

Everyone said how well she was coping, but there was a difference between getting three girls off to school in the right clothes, and actually building a relationship with them. Anna had never tried to be the girls' mother – they had a mum, a very visible one who'd made it clear from the start that Anna was surplus to requirements – but she'd hoped by now they'd have made a space for her in their lives. A friendly, warm, big sister-ish space. But even that seemed to be naively optimistic.

I just want to be wanted, Anna thought, her heart aching. So often, when the girls were clinging to Phil, and he was pretending to be annoyed by their puppy-ish affection but secretly loving it, she felt as if she were completely invisible. Useful, but invisible in her own home.

She turned over the cover of *Charlotte's Web* and a whoosh of longing flooded her stomach. Her own baby would love reading. It would inherit her dreams of forests and pepperpots and magical gulls along with her DNA. Her own baby would love being tucked into bed by her – and her big sisters – and then they'd *all* sit there in the half-light, listening to Anna unfolding stories about giant peaches and magic carpets, like a proper family.

And that's going to happen, she told herself with a sudden fierceness. This year. *That's going to happen.*

Downstairs the door banged and Phil's car keys jangled onto the hall table, followed by his briefcase clunking on the floor.

'Anna? Anna?'

She rubbed her eyes with the back of her hand and stood up, still holding the books as Phil's feet ran up the stairs. Quickly, she looked round and put them on top of the dressing table. She'd think about where to put them back later.

'Hey!' Phil met her as she was coming out of Lily's room. He held out his arms to grab her for a kiss, then saw her struggling to hide her dismay. 'What's up?'

'Nothing! I just . . .' She racked her brains. 'I just found Mrs Piggle lying on her front. Very bad for her neck.'

'I'll phone Lily,' said Phil seriously. 'And let her know you've saved Mrs Piggle in the nick of time.'

'Don't tell her she was lying with Fat Duck, though.' Anna managed a twisted smile. 'Could cause ructions.'

Phil held her at arm's length and studied her face. 'Have you been crying, honeybun?' he asked gently. 'Your mascara's gone everywhere.'

He looked so tender that the words spilled out of her.

'They left their books,' she wailed. 'The books I gave them for Christmas. I packed one in Lily's bag but she took it out.'

'What books? Oh, those . . . Anna, don't take it so personally.' Phil pulled her in tight and stroked her hair, as he would stroke Chloe's after some histrionic fall-out with a friend. 'They're on holiday. They won't have time to read!'

'On the seven-hour plane trip?'

'They're *kids*. They'll be watching the film. Annoying the cabin crew. Even I don't read on planes, and I'm nearly forty.'

Phil always took their side, thought Anna. He didn't mean to contradict her, it was just an automatic dad-reaction, the way she defended Pongo's 'enthusiasm' to Michelle when she muttered about training classes. Was there any point pushing it? Trying to explain that it wasn't about the books, it was about *her*? Her constant panic that she wasn't giving them what they needed?

Phil was looking at her as if she was being irrational, and Anna realised she didn't want to leave it like that. They never really got time to talk uninterrupted any more.

'I should have explained the presents better. I wanted to . . . share some things I loved with them,' she tried. 'Something more meaningful than just ticking stuff off a wish list.'

He raised an eyebrow. 'Is this about Chloe's iPad?'

'No!' Except it was. Sort of. He'd overridden the promises they'd made about not replacing the last one, which she'd broken on a school trip. Anna didn't even have an iPhone.

Phil kissed the top of her head. 'Look, it was a lovely present, but not everyone's a big reader like you. I'm afraid you're going to have to learn to live with our Philistine ways. I'll talk to them when they get—'

'Oh my God, no,' Anna interrupted. 'Don't do that. "God. *Daaaad*. How to make things worse, or what?"'

She said it in Chloe's 'Zero-to-outraged in two seconds' voice, and he laughed again, quickly hugging her, then holding her at arm's length so he could scrutinise her expression. 'I take it back, you know us all too well already. How about a film tonight? Or dinner out?'

Phil's appetite for going out went into overdrive when the girls were away, as if he had to stuff a year's worth of activity into a week. Anna liked it too, normally, but she'd forgotten how exciting it was to be alone with him. She didn't want to share her freshly invigorated husband with a cinema audience.

'I'm tired,' she said. 'And I need a shower.'

Phil winked playfully. 'In that case, you get in the shower while I take this suit off. Tell me what you've been up to today. Did Pongo crash into anyone in the park?'

'Actually, I've been offered a job,' said Anna. She followed him through to their room and lingered as he pulled off his tie, then slung his suit jacket over the chair. Phil had broad shoulders. She loved the feel of them through a thin office shirt, his muscles firm under the cotton.

Phil stopped unbuttoning his shirt and turned round. 'I didn't even know you'd applied for anything recently.'

'I didn't. It's out of the blue. Michelle's taken over the bookshop on the high street, and she wants me to manage it for her.'

'Anna!' He widened his eyes. 'You'll be so good at that! Come here and let me show you how impressed I am.'

She grinned and let herself be pulled into his arms again.

'Mum's going to laugh when I tell her,' she said. 'Apparently when I was little, I used to get all my Ladybird books out and arrange them in our Wendy House, then sell them to my friends.'

'That's so you,' said Phil. 'What was your mark-up?'

'That's so *you*,' she said. 'You and Michelle both.'

'So when's all this happening?'

'Right now. The decorators are coming tomorrow – I'm supposed to be helping her sort out the stock. I haven't . . .' Anna hesitated. 'I haven't said yes, definitely. I wanted to run it by you first.'

Phil stopped, mid-belt-buckle. 'Why?'

'Well, who's going to take Lily to school and collect her, if I'm working shop hours? And get Chloe from dance class? And what about Pongo – he's going to need walking.'

'And my supper won't be on the table the way it used to be.'

'Well, that's hardly . . .' Anna realised he was winding her up. 'I'm serious, Phil. It's like running a taxi company *and* a hotel, keeping up with their social diaries. I'm assuming Michelle will want to have the same opening hours as her own shop and that's nine till six.'

'We'll work something out,' he said, slipping off his trousers and chucking them carelessly over the chair. 'I can take the kids to school half the week. Michelle can let you nip out to get Lily, bring her back with you. Might do her some good, hanging out in a bookshop for a few hours. Chloe too, for that matter.' He looked at her. 'It might give you something to talk to them about as well, if you want to share an experience. You know how interested Chloe is in the world of retail therapy. That might be an easier way to get her attention than books.'

'Maybe,' she conceded.

'Maybe? *Definitely*, if you can get her a discount at Michelle's. Now, are we having this shower or what?'

Michelle's right: he doesn't really have a clue, Anna thought, half amused, half despairing, as he sauntered into the bathroom. It all just happens, as far as Phil's concerned. It happens because I'm running myself ragged sorting things out so he doesn't have to worry about it, and the girls have no reason to whine to Sarah.

'So you don't mind paying for a dog-walker? And getting Magda back to do some cleaning?' she called through, just so it was on the record.

'Of course not.' There was a pause while he turned the shower on. 'I prefer Magda's ironing to yours, anyway. Come and get in here with me, Mrs McQueen. I've missed you today.'

Anna's stomach fluttered, and in her head, she pushed the abandoned books to one side. For once, reality was more tempting.

6

'The time-travelling adventures of Charlotte
Sometimes *taught me to be happy with who you are,
as you could be a lot worse off. Quite a few children's
books seem to have that message.'* Charlotte Allen

Anna thought it was impressive, but not surprising, that
Michelle had the power to raise a team of builders to refit a
shop at a time when most people couldn't even persuade
a plumber to leave his Yuletide sofa to unblock a U-bend.

She wasn't quite sure what *she* was doing herself, knee-
deep in Mills and Boons on New Year's Eve, but here she was,
nonetheless, taking orders from a bright-eyed Michelle while
Owen loitered in the background, waiting to do all the heavy
lifting they required.

He looked hungover already, his dark hair falling into his
face, dressed in an old college T-shirt and jeans that showed
off the top inch of his checked boxer shorts, but Michelle
insisted that he was ready to work. If he ever stopped texting.

'So, new stock in the front, second-hand in the back. And
junk about four-fifths of what we've got here?'

Michelle had to raise her voice over the sound of Lorcan
the builder's team of denim-clad decorators in the main area.
It was only just gone nine o'clock, and they were already

sanding, blasting, clunking, to the sound of Deep Purple – Anna didn't know exactly what they were doing, but Michelle had a checklist and several copies of her Action Plan, so presumably *she* did.

'Why not put new and second-hand together?' Anna suggested. 'Bring it out into the front, make it look vintage, not second-hand. It'd give the students a chance to get a cheaper copy of something, and some people like old editions.'

Michelle frowned dubiously. 'Really?'

'Yeah. They've got a bit of character to them. Like this.' Anna picked up an old Penguin edition of *Lady Chatterley's Lover*, its orange cover tattered round the edges. 'Look how lovely and soft these pages are. Don't you want to read that and imagine you're in some coffee bar in Swinging London? I *love* old books like this. It'll give the shelves an eclectic feel.'

The word 'eclectic' seemed to mollify Michelle; it was one of her favourites. 'OK. You're the expert. I want this shop to have that . . . pick-up-ability.' She rubbed her fingers in the air, trying to find the right words. 'I want . . .'

'Discovery. Adventure. Magic. I know.' Anna smiled. 'I get it. I saw your sketches for the shop sign.'

Michelle raised her eyebrows, stretching the cartoon flicks of her eyeliner into Betty Boop wideness. 'You like it?'

Owen had shaped Michelle's sketches into a neat image of a spotty dog leaping over a stack of novels, through a ribbon reading Longhampton Books.

'I do,' said Anna. 'Dogs and books – what's not to love? Pongo likes it even more. But you know people'll be disappointed when there isn't a Dalmatian in here?'

'They'll be relieved.' Michelle grinned. 'Owen, you could get going on clearing around the fireplace.' She pointed towards the corner. 'I want to get it unblocked and tidied up. The sweep's coming in at two to check it's safe to use.'

Owen pocketed his phone. 'Yes, miss. Do you want me to go up it as well, give it a clean?'

He was skinny enough, thought Anna. His heavy biker boots were the only thing that might stick in the flue.

She shook herself; Michelle was directing another stream of manager-instructions at her.

'Lorcan's got keys, so if you need to go out for lunch or whatever just give him an idea of when you'll be back. What else? Oh yes, I'm aiming to get the floorboards sanded in here by the end of tomorrow, so we need to shift some of these boxes. Not sure where yet.'

'Is there a flat upstairs like next door? Could you use that?'

'There is, but it's in use.' Michelle sank onto a crate and looked thwarted for the first time since she'd started this project. 'It'd be much easier to rent the whole building, but apparently it's not available. I'm working on that.' She flicked the pad, and Anna feared for both the solicitor and the tenant upstairs, whom they hadn't met – surprisingly, given the amount of noise the builders were making.

'I guess in the meantime we could use my flat,' Michelle went on.

'Er, no, we couldn't,' said Owen. 'I'm virtually sleeping on boxes up there as it is, thank you.'

'But you're not going to be there forever,' Michelle countered. 'Are you?'

'That depends on how long you make me do DIY instead of getting on with your website.'

'That depends on whether you spend as long texting your girlfriends and chatting up my staff when you're doing DIY as you do when you're supposedly doing my website.'

'Am I wrong, Michelle, or does DIY stand for Do It Yourself?'

'Shut up, Owen.'

Anna watched the pair of them bicker back and forth, and felt a sort of envy at the easy sibling grumpiness they had. It was something she'd noticed with the girls; their rows reached levels of hysteria that shocked Anna, but then they calmed right down again, because they knew underneath it all there was a bond bigger than any disagreement. Anna hated conflict; it made her tense up inside. She sometimes hadn't even been able to bring herself to charge the stroppier borrowers library fines.

'Should I be making coffee for the builders?' she asked, before Owen could retaliate.

'Not if you're busy. You can tell them there's coffee and biscuits in the back kitchen, so they'll have to come past you to have a coffee break. Which should keep *that* to a bare minimum.'

Michelle tapped her clipboard again, this time in a more final way. 'Right. I'm off next door, but if there's anything you need, give me a shout.' She beamed. 'If we get this sorted out, then I can get started on some actual decorating tomorrow!'

'Michelle, tomorrow's New Year's Day,' said Anna, surprised. 'You're not planning on working tomorrow, are you? Aren't you going to your parents'? Or having a hangover at least?'

Owen looked at her too. 'I'm not working New Year's Day,' he said. 'I'm going up to London tonight. I told you that. And Mum's having everyone over again for New Year's Day. Didn't you say you were going to come too?'

'That was before I decided to take the shop on.' Michelle looked a bit shifty. 'I'm definitely working tomorrow,' she said. 'This is my priority.'

'But Harvey's—' Owen started.

'I'm coming in tomorrow,' said Michelle firmly. 'If you two can't, that's fair enough.'

Anna glanced at Owen, who seemed genuinely surprised. If he hadn't been there, she might have pushed Michelle further, tried to persuade her to come over to theirs, rather than be on her own.

'Right then,' said Michelle brightly. 'If you'll excuse me, I've got a sale to run next door!'

Next door, in Home Sweet Home, a queue was forming at the cash register as Kelsey jabbed tentatively at the machine, and Michelle felt an unwelcome ripple of doubt that maybe trying to open a new shop at the same time as keeping her core business going wasn't a good idea, but she pushed it aside.

No doubts. From now on, it was all about looking forward. That was something her dad had drilled into her, ironically enough, way back when she'd started in his dealership instead of going to university. 'Don't worry about what you did yesterday,' he said, often, 'worry about what you haven't done yet today.'

Michelle could hear him saying it, his easy smile and funny tie hiding his sharp commercial brain. He'd said it to Harvey too, his main protégé, golf partner and co-wearer of funny ties. There were some similarities between her dad and Harvey – enough for Michelle to have persuaded herself that maybe dating him, then marrying him, wasn't such a bad idea – but kindness wasn't one of them. She'd realised soon enough that Harvey wasn't kind. He never did anything that didn't have a directly beneficial effect on himself, no matter how small or hidden.

Michelle felt her phone buzzing in her back pocket as she was persuading a customer to buy a set of holly-stamped espresso cups, and flinched when she saw who was calling.

Mum.

It would be a very loaded question about when she'd be arriving for New Year's Day lunch.

'Do you want to take that?' the customer enquired, and Michelle shook her head quickly.

'No, no. Now, did you see the matching cake plates? They're in the sale too.'

A couple of minutes later, Kelsey approached her with the cordless phone and a very apologetic expression. 'Your mum.' She waggled the phone as if it were red hot. Clearly she'd already had an earful.

'I'm busy,' said Michelle.

'She said you would say that. She says she wants to talk to you, because it's very urgent.'

Michelle started to ask Kelsey if she could hear sirens or the sound of the house burning down, but didn't have the energy to spare. Instead she held out her hand for the phone and went to click the mute button off, whereupon she found that Kelsey hadn't actually clicked it on in the first place.

Great.

'Hello, Mum.'

'Finally,' said Carole. 'I was beginning to think I'd have to come round to the shop to see my daughter.'

Michelle cleared her throat and forced herself to smile, so her voice would sound more cheerful. 'Well, it's a busy time. Are you OK? Kelsey said it was urgent.'

'It is urgent. I need to know if you're coming to us for lunch tomorrow. The boys are expecting you. We all are. You haven't even seen your new nephew yet. Is there some kind of problem, Michelle? Is that what it is?'

Michelle looked around; there were six customers in the shop, two engrossed in the half-price wrapping paper, one balancing too many fragile baubles in her hand, and three hovering around the jewellery cabinet. Impatiently, she caught Kelsey's eye and made a 'basket!' gesture towards the bauble shopper, then nodded to Gillian to open the case.

'Can we talk later? The thing is, Mum, it's not a brilliant time for me right now, the shop's heaving.'

'Some things are more important than work, Michelle. Like family. If you'd been here over Christmas . . .'

'Mum. I explained about Christmas. And I've taken over the shop next door too, so—'

'When?' There was a sharp intake of breath on the other end of the phone. 'You didn't mention this to me or your father. Is that a good idea, with the economy the way it is?'

'Actually, yes, I think so,' said Michelle. 'The rent was cheap, I've got plans, long-term plans for . . .' She gave up and stalked into the back office where she wouldn't be distracted by the need to tidy up or serve customers.

Carole was still talking. 'I really think you *should* have taken advice, Michelle. You rush into things without thinking properly. Why didn't you ask your father? Or Harvey?'

And Anna wonders why I don't want to go home.

'Because I'm an experienced business owner,' she said, 'who's perfectly capable of getting a loan and making a success of something. Mum, I've been doing this for a while now, I don't need to run things past Dad.'

She deliberately didn't mention Harvey. If anything, he'd probably been the one to drop the seeds of doubt into Carole's head about her abilities. He'd been good at that. 'No wonder you sold so many cars with legs like yours,' had been one of his favourites. No mention of her encyclopaedic knowledge of the range.

'But you're clearly not coping properly as it is with *one*

business if you can't even take a day off to come and see us,' said Carole. 'Can you put it on hold until you can show your dad your business plans and—'

'No, stop there, Mum. You don't tell Owen to phone home before he agrees to build a new website.' Michelle picked up the stress ball from her in-tray and started to squeeze. 'Did Ben ring you before he got Heather pregnant with their *fourth* child? I'd say that's much more risky in this current economic climate. Why is it just me who has to check in?'

Any mention of her grandchildren always tipped Carole over the edge.

'Don't take that attitude when all I'm doing is expressing some very justified concern,' she snapped. 'If you came home more often, we wouldn't have to have these conversations over the phone. And if it all goes wrong with this second shop, I suppose you'll just run away again? Leave someone else to pick up the pieces?'

The wind whistled out of Michelle's lungs, and she felt her skin shrink under her clothes. She knew her mother wasn't just talking about Harvey. Harvey was the end result of a much earlier problem, one they spoke about even less than her failed marriage, but which hung in the background, just out of sight, never referred to but never forgotten. A metallic taste coated the back of her throat, and slowly she released the stress ball, but it stuck to her damp palm.

When is this going to stop? she wondered bleakly. How long do you have to keep being reminded about mistakes you made when you were too young to even know they were mistakes?

'Poor Harvey,' said Carole finally, seeing Michelle wasn't going to rise to the bait. 'We had to have him here for Christmas, or else he'd have been spending it on his own with a microwave meal.'

The idea of Harvey sitting alone with a lasagne for one almost made Michelle laugh. Not when there were restaurants and old girlfriends, and the golf club.

'There's no *way* he'd have done that,' she scoffed. 'Whatever he told you, it was just to make you feel sorry for him so you'd invite him round.'

'He's still your husband, Michelle!' said Carole, clearly reaching the point of the phone call at last. 'And he's still my son-in-law. Harvey's a proud man, but I honestly believe he'd have you back if you just came home and said sorry. I think you should. Put whatever silly thing it was behind you and patch things up. You're not going to do any better than Harvey, if that's what you're imagining.'

'*I* should say sorry?' Michelle was so surprised by this that her voice came out in a squeak.

But why are you surprised? she asked herself. Mum thought the regulation haircuts were a sweet sign of his interest. She thought Harvey was being caring, never letting me out on my own, insisting on buying my clothes (always a size too small). And that's only the stuff she knows about. There was plenty more that Michelle was too ashamed to tell anyone.

'Of course you should! You should be saying sorry to that poor man until the day you die. I don't know many women who'd walk out on a kind, reliable provider like that, without so much as a backward glance. Not women with *brains*, anyway.'

'Mum,' said Michelle, and her voice was strangled with the effort of not slamming down the phone then and there. 'I'm not getting back with Harvey. Ever. And if he's now going to become a regular at yours, please tell him to stop sending me flowers. It makes me feel like I'm being stalked.'

'Flowers? You're *complaining* because someone's sending you flowers?' Her mother managed to sound amazed, with a loud top-note of disapproval. 'I wish I had your problems, Michelle, I really do!'

There, thought Michelle. That's exactly what Harvey wanted everyone to think. Me being unreasonable. Job done. And my own mother reckons I'm too thick to know when I'm on to a good thing. *Thanks*.

The tightness in her chest increased until she found it hard to breathe properly.

'I'm really busy,' she said, forcing the words out. 'I'm sorry. I'm not going to be able to get away tomorrow.' She knew she should have left it there, but the dutiful daughter in her couldn't stop adding, 'I'm paying the builders by the day, so, you know, the sooner I get the shop open, the sooner it can start earning money. I mean, maybe I can try to get away later in the month, when the sale's quietened down . . .'

Even as she was saying it, Michelle knew she didn't mean it. Her mother knew that too.

'Oh, come on, I've got Owen dossing in my flat because everyone else has clearly had enough of his carrying on,' she blurted out. 'Don't say I never do anything for the family.'

Carole let the pause stretch out as Michelle trailed off. The silence dripped with disdain. Then she sighed. 'Well, that's big of you, Michelle. Maybe he'll encourage you to think of someone else other than yourself, for a change.'

'What? *Owen* will? Owen's the most selfish of . . .' Michelle began, outraged, but Carole had already hung up.

I bet she's been rehearsing that in her head for days, she thought, trying to make light of it in her head, but inside she felt scalded with an old shame that never went away. Whatever Michelle achieved in her adult life – the sales awards, the marriage to her dad's golden boy, her business – it would never override the image she knew her mother kept in her mental gallery: the picture of a teenage Michelle arriving home in the back of her dad's Jaguar, mid-term, in silent disgrace, her father's face stony with confusion.

I don't care, Michelle told herself, clenching her fists. I am who I am *now*.

But she still felt small. Small and alone, as if she was at the wrong end of a telescope all of a sudden.

Someone knocked at the door and she pulled herself together as quickly as she could, blinking hard to get her bright and confident sales face back on.

Kelsey put her head round the door. 'Hiya.'

'Yeah, I'm coming,' said Michelle. 'Is there a rush?'

'What? Where? Oh, uh, yeah, it's a bit busy. These came for you.' She pulled her hand round and revealed another massive hand-tied bunch of flowers, multi-coloured roses this time. Kelsey's eyes popped in a silent 'Ta-da!'

'Ta-da!' she added, in case Michelle hadn't got it. 'Who are they from?'

Michelle's breakfast coffee reappeared in her throat and she had to swallow hard to stop herself retching.

They're only flowers. Just flowers.

'Thanks.' She reached out to take them, then said, 'Can you separate these into individual colours and put them into the milk bottle vases on the far set of shelves, and . . .'

She stopped. She didn't want Harvey's flowers in her shop. Every time she saw them it would feel as if he was inching back into her life. First her house, now her shop. A little toehold here, an 'Oh, you're so lucky, Michelle!' there. She could almost see him, his thick arms folded in that subtly aggressive way, the smile of triumph touching his face but not reaching his eyes. Eyes that never stopped assessing her, not for one second.

'Kelsey, do you want them?' she blurted out.

'Me?'

'Yes. Take them. Take them home. Thanks for all your hard work over the sales!' She shoved them into her hands.

'Wow, thanks!' Kelsey's eyes lit up and she nearly danced out of the back room.

It occurred to Michelle that now she'd have to find some present for Gillian, to avoid any staff fall-outs, but her brain was whirring round in circles.

Why now? Why was Harvey doing this now, after more than three years? She could imagine him starting his campaign with her mother, the sad expression over the drying-up he'd never done at home, the hints and whispers. She didn't even want to think about how Harvey would set her dad's concerns in motion, pulling the strings tighter until everyone was helping him haul her back. But why? Because he hated losing control of anything. Anyone.

Michelle grabbed her notebook, the one with her year's ambitions and to-dos, and opened it to her long-term goals.

'File for divorce'.

As the pen formed the F, Michelle's hand faltered. Harvey's face floated to the front of her mind. So handsome on the surface – bold cheekbones, wide mouth, blond hair – all apart from his eyes, which were small and cold, like little windows into his own smallness and coldness. But only she seemed to see that. Everyone else just saw the charming, sociable, easy-going salesman. He saved the smallness and coldness for her, his wife.

It was ironic that she'd decided to wait out the five years' separation rather than cite unreasonable behaviour. She'd had a lifetime's worth to choose from, but that was exactly why the thought of challenging him with it filled her with cold fear.

Harvey made out he was *so* reasonable – and was such a genius salesman – that he could convince anyone that she was the one with the problem. And he'd never stop.

I don't have to write it down, she thought, recapping her pen. But I'm going to do it. This year. I am.

7

*'The Mystery of the Green Ghost is the first
and only book so far I have read cover to cover
in one sitting – because I was too scared to put
it down and go to sleep.'*   Phil McQueen

'You're very quiet,' said Phil, as they passed the first sign for the airport. 'Was it that second bottle of wine last night? Can't you handle it any more?'

'No!' Anna swatted him on the knee. 'Speak for yourself. I was just . . . enjoying the peace and tranquillity.'

'Ah, the peace and tranquillity,' said Phil wisely. Then he grinned. 'And there I was thinking I'd finally worn you out. At least on honeymoon you insisted on spending four hours a day reading. I need another holiday to get over this one.'

'Well, now you are speaking for yourself.' Anna leaned back in her seat and smiled to herself. She wasn't counting any chickens, but if the websites were anything to go by, they already had a good to middling chance of a September baby being under way already. Just as well, since once they collected Becca, Chloe and Lily from the airport, they wouldn't have another private moment for weeks.

Phil took his eyes off the road for a moment to share a

cheeky glance with her, and Anna held his gaze. He still made her stomach flutter. If that *was* her stomach fluttering.

'I'm very lucky,' he said.

'I know. You are.'

'I mean, yes, I've missed the girls, but I'm glad we got this time to ourselves. Just us. I'd forgotten how nice it is to read the papers without being interrupted. And being able to open that second bottle of wine without wondering if one of us is going to be summoned to Bethany's house to collect Miss McQueen.'

'I know,' said Anna. 'I don't miss taxi duty. I don't even mind getting a hangover. It's nice to have one.'

'On Sunday morning, I just thought, how happy am I?' he went on. 'Being with you, walking the dog, getting coffee . . . I don't think getting old's too bad, do you?'

That brought Anna up short. 'What are you talking about?' she demanded. 'We're *not* getting old!'

Phil pointed at the radio. 'We're listening to Radio 2.'

'Young people love Radio 2. Becca listens to it sometimes.'

'Becca listens to it because she thinks it makes her look sophisticated. You know what? I found myself looking at one of those luxury sheds the other day. And I found myself thinking, mmm, I'd *like* one of those. I'd like to relax in it, with Pongo at my feet, and read my Jeremy Clarkson books. That's definitely old.'

Phil sounded a bit too pleased about this notion. It wasn't the first time he'd talked about feeling old, either. Anna hoped it wasn't a roundabout way of telling her something else – he had a habit of laughing her out of serious conversations, skimming witty little observations across the real matter in hand until the point of the conversation had passed.

'You're not even forty,' she pointed out.

'This year, though. And *slippers*. I wouldn't mind a pair of really good quality velvet slippers next Christmas. I saw some in Michelle's shop. Monogrammed. Or with something funky, like a skull and crossbones.'

'There's no way I'm giving you slippers for Christmas. Ever. Not even when you *are* old.'

'What about homebrew? Can I start doing homebrew? I don't have to grow the beard.'

Anna wanted to laugh, but she knew that if she did, she'd find herself agreeing with him. 'Will you stop making out that we're one step away from the Golden Moments Retirement Castle?'

'But we have a daughter who'll be able to vote this year. That's old.'

'You mean, *you* have a daughter,' said Anna, without thinking, then realised what she'd said and mentally slapped herself. 'I didn't mean . . . I meant, we have a daughter, but *I'm* too young to have an eighteen- . . . I mean, *you're* too young, really . . .'

But her first words hung between them. Silence fell, except in Anna's head, where all hell was being let loose.

The turn-off sign to the airport flashed past, like a warning.

'What?' he said, sensing her staring at him.

Had he noticed? Sometimes she was far more sensitive to these things than he was.

'What I meant was, I'm still too young to have an eighteen-year-old, and really, so are you. But that's the thing about being a bloke – it's perfectly possible to have a daughter who can vote,' she said carefully, 'and have a newborn baby all in the same year.'

'Now that does make me feel old,' said Phil, but his voice had changed and he didn't sound jokey any more.

'Why?'

'The thought of wet nappies, and broken nights, and sick, and feeling like a zombie for months, and did I mention nappies? If you think Pongo makes the house smell, you want to have a close encounter with twenty nappies a day.'

'You'd have your shed,' she tried, in a light tone.

'Oh, I see. *Now* the shed's acceptable.' He indicated into the left lane to take the airport turning and glanced at her as he moved into a space. His eyes seemed wary, and his fingers weren't tapping the steering wheel in time to the music any more.

Anna steeled herself. 'Phil, you haven't forgotten what we talked about when we got married, have you? About having a baby after we'd been married four years?'

'I haven't forgotten.'

That wasn't the answer she'd been hoping for.

'Well, it's this month!' Anna paused, trying to summon up some lightness so he wouldn't feel nagged. 'And I don't mean that you're getting past it, I mean I don't want you to get entrenched in the Radio 2, shed mentality, you old goat.'

The traffic had bunched up as the cars queued to get into the terminal lanes. Phil turned to her and put his hand on her knee, a last caressing ember of the intimacy they'd shared over the past days. 'Anna,' he said, then sighed.

Anna's chest contracted at the honesty in his face. He looked wary, but concerned, and his eyes searched hers as if he already knew his words weren't going to be what she wanted to hear.

'I'd love us to have a baby,' he said. 'But I'm not being flippant about how disruptive they are. It's amazing, obviously, and so rewarding, but your whole life completely changes. It's like being abducted by this tiny alien. Nothing is ever the same again.'

She flinched. 'I am aware of that, yes.'

If one more parent said this stuff to her – how you never understood love until you held your baby in your arms, how only a parent truly grasped the world's horrors, etc., etc. – she would throw Becca's violin case, the gym pile and bloody Pongo's basket at them. Her life had already changed completely, and if she ever breathed a word of how hard it had been, how stressful to have all the responsibility without the magic parent love drug, then she was branded a selfish, father-stealing homewrecker who should have known what she was getting into.

Phil didn't seem to notice the sudden whiteness of her lips. 'I know that. And you're doing a great job. But things have changed, haven't they? None of us were expecting Sarah to go off to the States. I don't want to unsettle Becca when she's stressing out about her A-levels, and Chloe . . .' Phil pretended to squeeze his forehead in despair. 'Every time she talks to me about this band I keep seeing the Pussycat Dolls in my head and I want to send her to a girls' boarding school. And Lily . . .'

'So what are you saying?' Anna asked. Her stomach roller-coastered. But he'd agreed! 'We can't have a baby now?'

'No.' Phil ran a hand through his hair. 'I'm not saying that. I'm saying that the playing field's changed. If you hadn't been here, there's no way I could have coped with all this. I had no idea how stressful those three could be. I just . . .' He took a deep breath. 'I'm just more wary about adding in a newborn to the mix than I was when we only had the girls for alternate weekends.'

'But Sarah's coming back next year,' Anna pointed out, trying to sound calm and rational even though inside she was howling with an unexpected, irrational fury. 'It could take a few months, the baby might not arrive until after she does.'

'That's true. Anna, is this really the best time to be discussing this? It's a big subject. I don't want to say the wrong thing and have you brooding on it for days, just because I used the wrong word because I was trying to change lanes.'

The traffic was starting to creep forward now, and she could almost see their time alone together slipping away like grains of sand in an egg timer.

'I don't know when else we'll discuss it,' she said, rushing to fit everything in before they arrived. 'I thought we were going to start this month. It's all I've been thinking about. I've been looking forward to . . .' She chose her words carefully, 'adding to our family.'

Phil reached across and took her hand. 'Anna. I love you. We'll work it out, I promise. It's just that I can remember what it's like to be a slave to nappies and green poo and to be honest, these last few days have been a window into how thoroughly enjoyable life might be once we pack Lily off to college. Just you and me. I don't want to share you.'

Anna looked at him. She didn't return the affable smile wreathing his face. Sod the bloody shed, she thought. And the bloody slippers. 'Are you saying you're looking forward to *not* being a parent, before I've even had the chance to *be* one?'

'There you go,' said Phil, withdrawing his hand to change gear. 'I've said the wrong thing.'

'Not if you meant it.'

'We've got loads of time. Aren't you always reminding me how you're only just thirty?'

He was joking now, but Anna wasn't going to let him skim this one away. Not with less than half a mile to go to the short-stay car park.

'I know I'm not old, but women reach menopause early in my family. You remember me telling you how my mum couldn't have any more children after me? She wasn't much older than I am now.'

'Science has moved on, though. And my mum was forty when she had me. That's another ten years.'

'But look how that turned out!' Anna bit her lip. Normally she'd have slunk under the seat in shame at saying something so tactless, but this was too important for her not to press on. 'I want you around for ages yet. I want us to run around the park together and do mum and dad stuff.'

'I don't know how stressed out my dad was, but I can't imagine he was any less stressed than me,' said Phil stiffly. 'And that was with just the one kid.'

There was an awkward pause. 'Sorry,' said Anna. She reached for his hand again. After a moment's hesitation, he let her curl her fingers around his.

'I can't wait to hear how *amaaaazing* New York was,' she offered, trying to bridge the gap that had opened up between them. 'Do you think Chloe's hair will be the same colour? Do you think they've missed us at all?'

'I bet they've missed you,' Phil said, as he indicated his way across to the short-stay car park lane. 'Sarah's a terrible cook.'

She shot a glance across the car and saw his eyes shining at the prospect of seeing his girls again. To her shame, Anna felt a twinge of jealousy on behalf of *their* baby, out there waiting for its half-sisters to budge up and make room for it.

The New York plane was late, and Anna watched as Phil paced and muttered. She took several deep breaths, trying to draw a line under the troubling conversation they'd just had. She told herself it would be great to see the girls again. Hearing Becca's dry footnotes to Chloe's melodramatic stories, listening to Lily's burbling narration of the world around her. She'd even got round to missing Chloe's habit of singing along to adverts as though talent scouts were hiding in the house.

But she knew they wouldn't have missed her for one second, and wouldn't bother to pretend they had, either. Well, Becca might. Becca was sensitive enough to spot the moments when Anna's smile slipped.

'I think this is them,' said Phil, bouncing on the balls of his feet to see over the crowd.

A couple of business travellers strode out of the gate, pulling wheelie hand luggage cases, already checking their phones and searching the assembled faces behind the rope for their drivers.

He moved a bit nearer the front – pointlessly, since there wasn't much of a crush. Anna had meant to tell him how good he looked today, in the Paul Smith jumper she'd bought him for Christmas, but she realised that while she'd nipped off to the loo, he'd taken it off, so the shirt Becca and Chloe had given him was visible under his jacket.

He glanced back and grinned at her, and Anna grinned back, quickly, tightly, seeing her husband disappear and their dad re-emerge. And inside, she felt utterly shabby for noticing.

This is why I want a baby, she thought, digging her nails into her palms. So I can *share* that feeling. So I can feel wanted, and missed, and loved too. Is that so unreasonable? It wasn't as if there was a finite amount of love to spread around the family, and that her baby would steal from the others.

Anna was standing at a different angle, further back, and she spotted Chloe first; it was hard not to – her mane of blond hair seemed bigger and blonder than when she'd left, and she seemed to be walking in her own spotlight. She was also wearing sunglasses and staring down at the floor, but as she rounded the corner and came into clear view, she shoved the sunglasses onto her head and a different expression crossed her face when she saw Phil standing in the crowd.

'Dad!' she yelled, and broke into an end-of-movie trot towards the barriers, one hand gripping her wheelie case, the other stretched out towards him. Phil stepped forward to meet her and pulled her into a big hug.

'Hello, Chloe-oey!' he said. 'We've missed you!'

'I've missed you too!' Chloe said, her voice muffled in his shoulder.

Anna moved firmly through the shifting crowd, back to Phil's side where she hovered awkwardly, waiting for the right moment to hug Chloe herself.

The hug went on and on. Anna wasn't going to step forward and risk crowding their moment, but neither did she want to look stand-offish. It was so hard.

Meanwhile, Becca's tall figure had appeared in the next batch of passengers; she was pulling a big case and holding Lily's hand. Lily looked small and worn out, and was rubbing her eye with a fist. Anna waved, directing Phil's attention to them, and grabbed the chance to open her arms to Chloe.

'Hi, Chloe!' she said with a big smile. 'Welcome back!'

Chloe had turned to look for her sisters, but glanced back at her. 'Hi, Anna.' Her accent had gone very mid-Atlantic in the short time they'd been away.

Embarrassed, Anna started to drop her outstretched arms, just as Chloe evidently decided she ought to make a gesture. The result was a semi-showbiz kiss on one side, and a half hug on the other.

Ouch, thought Anna. But she hitched her smile up again. 'How was the flight? Did you get any good films?'

'No. They were lame.' Chloe yelped and moved over to Phil

as he led Lily and Becca away from the gate, Lily on his shoulders, her hands in his hair and a beatific expression lighting up her tired face. Even with purple circles under her eyes she looked like a woodland fairy who'd lost her toadstool.

The couple behind Anna actually said, 'Ah, how lovely!' loud enough for them all to hear.

'Great! Do you want to go for a coffee before we go?' she asked, too keen. 'Or should I grab us one? A latte? Chloe? Becca?'

'Daddy, we went to the biggest shopping mall in the world, and it was full of cars that were so big they needed a step to get in them, and Mum's car is enormous. She says it wouldn't fit in our garage,' Lily was saying, at the same time as Chloe started to show Phil some new dance step she'd learned 'from Mum's personal trainer'.

Becca looked over towards Anna and gave her a sympathetic eye-roll. 'Happy New Year, Anna,' she said, and Anna could have hugged her with gratitude. 'But I don't think they need any more caffeine.'

Anna kicked herself. 'No, course not.' Another parenting error. Coffee was what you'd offer your best mate after a flight. Not kids. Even Becca knew that.

The talking continued without a break as they made their way to the car park, Phil wheeling the biggest cases, with Chloe and Lily hanging off him, and Becca and Anna following with the random jumble of extra carriers. Becca answered Anna's questions with her usual politeness, but she was monosyllabic with weariness – not surprising, Anna thought, if Chloe had been like that all the way back.

They piled into the car and Chloe insisted on plugging her iPod straight into the stereo, to listen to some new boy band album she'd downloaded while she was away.

The chattering from the back seat started up even before Phil had got out of the car park.

'Dad, I need to get a Saturday job,' Chloe announced over the top of Lily's interrogation about Pongo's exact movements while she'd been away.

'What for? You get pocket money.'

'I need hair extensions. Me and Bethany have got it all worked out – we're going to get Saturday jobs at Kit, and then if we save up enough by Easter, I can put my Easter money in as well and maybe get my teeth whitened too.'

'You've been talking to Bethany while you were in America?' said Phil, in panicky tones. 'Not on your mobile, I hope?'

'No. On Facebook.' Anna caught the muttered, 'Most of the time,' but she wasn't sure Phil did.

'Why hair extensions, Chloe?' she asked over her shoulder. 'You've got gorgeous hair.'

Chloe had formed a girl band called Apricotz with three of her friends from cheerleading. They sang to backing tracks on Spotify in the garage, while performing painstakingly precise choreography, and had a band logo that Bethany's dad had had printed onto stickers which now covered every available surface. Apart from Chloe's best friend Bethany, the other two members changed on a near-weekly basis.

Chloe's main career focus now, apart from winning the Lottery, was Breaking into Showbusiness.

'It's going to be our look. Tyra, she's our stylist, she says we need to have a distinctive thing, so we're each going to have a long plait, but with a different colour streak in it. Mine's going to be blue – don't freak out, Dad, that's why they're extensions, so we're not actually *dyeing* our hair.'

Anna looked in the rearview mirror: Lily had dropped off,

her head nodding like a heavy flower on a thin stem, but Becca was wide awake, staring out the window, her lips moving as she recited something to herself. Chloe's attention was fixed firmly on the back of Phil's head, but she was texting at the same time, without even looking at the phone.

It's like they've never been away, she thought.

'Who's Tyra?' asked Phil, going for the easiest question first. 'Do I know her?'

'Tyra from cheerleading,' said Anna. 'The one who got kicked out for not wearing her underskirt shorts for the Longhampton Leopards match, and bringing the school into disrepute.'

Phil's hands clenched the wheel.

Becca seemed to come back to life. 'Is Kit the one with the Perspex shoes in the window?' she asked suddenly. 'I didn't know there were so many strippers in Longhampton that they needed their own shop.'

'What?!'

'Shut up, Becca, like you'd know. You get your clothes from Oxfam because none of the real shops *stock* boring librarian clothes. No offence, Anna.'

'None taken,' said Anna, as mildly as she could.

'I don't know if I want you working in that shop,' said Phil. 'Isn't there anywhere else?'

'Imagine the staff uniform,' Becca went on. 'You'd end up wearing less than when you arrived, not more.'

'Shut *up*, Becca,' snapped Chloe, then whined, 'Daaaaad, it's really important for the band that we look distinctive, Mum says she knows someone who works on *American Idol* and she reckons we can get on the auditions for that too and they'd love us because we've got English accents and Bethany looks a bit like Kate Middleton.'

'But your exams start in—'

'And Mum says it would be good for us to have Saturday jobs. She said we need to start thinking about our university applications, and jobs show we're responsible and goal-focused.'

'And how did she square that with her last directive about you all working hard and using your weekends for revision?'

Chloe pouted. 'I knew you'd say that.'

'I'm not being a killjoy, I just don't want you spending your whole weekend in some tacky clothes shop,' Phil began, and Anna felt the atmosphere in the car charge with pre-argument static.

'Well, I know somewhere you might be able to get a Saturday job,' she said, before she had time to weigh it up properly.

'Where?' said Chloe and Phil at the same time.

'Well, Michelle's opening a new shop . . .'

'OMG!' squawked Chloe, clapping a hand to her chest. 'Michelle's opening Home Sweet Home Two? I totally heart that shop. It's literally my favourite place in the whole world.'

'Apart from the major mall,' said Lily. 'And that karaoke bar Mum took us to. And . . .'

Chloe ignored her. 'Why didn't you tell me?'

Becca also seemed interested now. 'Is she? Where?'

'It's not another Home Sweet Home,' said Anna. Her friendship with Michelle was one of the few brownie points she'd scored with the girls. 'It's a bookshop.'

'Oh,' said Chloe, sinking back in her seat.

'That I'm running,' Anna continued. 'And it's next door to Home Sweet Home, and it's going to be amazing. We've got lots of plans for it, author events and discussion groups, and I think we could do with a couple of keen and motivated Saturday girls to do a few hours at the weekend.'

'I'd rather work next door, if I've got to work at all,' said Chloe. 'Can't you get me a Saturday job there?'

'No,' said Anna. 'And anyway, you'd just spend your wages on more wings for the dog.'

'Not much chance of Chloe spending her wages in a book-shop,' Lily piped up, sounding so much like Becca that Anna did a double take in her mirror.

'Dad?' said Becca. 'I wouldn't mind doing that too. Having a Saturday job.'

'What about your revision?' Phil looked concerned. 'You're working so hard already. You've already given up orchestra, and five A-levels is a lot.'

'I can manage.' Becca stared out of the car window. 'I've been thinking about tuition fees and student loans, all that stuff. I think I should have an emergency fund built up. Just in case.'

Just in case was Becca's motto. Anna often wondered if she'd always been such a worrier, or if the divorce had made her look for disaster round every corner. Maybe wanting to be a barrister from an early age had skewed her expectations of life's random cruelties. Anna had thought for a while now that Becca worked a little bit too hard. The more Phil told her how proud he was of her, the later her bedroom light seemed to stay on.

'Becca, you don't have to worry about money,' said Phil. 'We've got that under control. You just concentrate on getting your grades.'

'But if you want to do it for a *break* from your revision, then I'm sure we could find you some useful stuff to do.' Anna tried to keep her voice non-committal. 'I find a bit of mindless stacking and selling and sweeping quite therapeutic.'

Phil turned to her, beetling his brows into a silent no. 'Do you think that's . . .'

Anna beetled her brows back. 'And you can keep an eye on Chloe.'

'Thanks, Anna,' said Becca. She turned away from the window and flashed a sudden, sunny smile at her. 'I'd like that.'

'How much will this gig pay?' demanded Chloe.

'Gig?' repeated Phil. 'Gig?'

'We can talk about it,' said Anna. 'You can come in and have a look round. Maybe even check out the stock?'

'Mmm!' said Becca, but Chloe didn't bother to answer. She was already texting and singing to herself. Probably Tyra the stylist, or Bethany the backing singer. 'I am back,' she sang under her breath. 'Back in my hood, back with my giiiiirls . . .'

'Give it a rest, Beyoncé,' said Lily, and Becca snorted.

8

*'I longed to be in the Famous Five as a child, to
the point where I constantly invented "mysteries",
just so I could solve them – and boss my sister
around in the "investigation".'* Louise Davies

Just ten days after she'd let herself and Anna into the grimy, unloved bookshop, Michelle pushed open the door and enjoyed a moment's pride that between them, she, Anna and Lorcan the builder had transformed the place into the vision she'd seen in her mind's eye.

Longhampton Books was now a shop customers would want to linger in. The cream-painted shelves made the room seem twice as big and the stock twice as inviting, and the newly sanded floorboards kept a touch of the old amongst the clean new decoration.

She'd fixed an old station clock between the front and back rooms, and hung up gold letters from a shopfront that spelled out the different sections on the simple whitewashed walls. The brass pendant lights that Lorcan's electrician had sourced and wired in for her last night already looked as if they'd been there forever, and Michelle made a mental note to see if he could get her any more to sell next door.

Also looking as though she'd been there forever was Anna,

leaning on the counter reading a hardback copy of *Little Women*. She was wearing her bookish glasses, instead of her contact lenses, and didn't look up until Michelle's boots had clicked halfway across the room towards her. When she did she looked so guilty her hair nearly fell out of the bun she'd improvised with a pencil.

'Sorry, Michelle, I was miles away.' She gestured to the book. 'It's *so* lovely. I must have read this a hundred times when I was little. I used to pretend I had three sisters too. And long hair to sell in an emergency.'

'Are there no kids' books about girls who grow up with annoying brothers?' Michelle got her notebook out and wrote '*4. Get jangly bell for bookshop to keep Anna focused*'.

'*The Famous Five*,' said Anna at once. 'Julian and Dick were Anne's brothers. And George wanted to be a boy. Who did you want to be out of the March sisters?' she went on. 'I always saw myself as Jo, loving books and being impulsive but fundamentally good-hearted.'

'I don't think I read it. Was it a film?'

'Michelle! You didn't read *Little Women*?' Anna looked shocked.

'No. I keep telling you, I didn't have a reading sort of childhood. I had brothers. The house was full of Airfix kits and *Shoot!* annuals.'

'You have to read it. You'll love it.' Anna thrust the book at her. 'Go on, I'll pay for it. Call it a present.'

'I don't have time to read,' said Michelle. 'I'm really not joking, Anna, I don't.'

'I can't believe that,' said Anna. 'I sometimes lock myself in the loo if I can't find ten minutes.'

'Remind me never to borrow any books from you, then,' said Michelle, turning her attention to the pen display on the desk. She knew there was no point trying to explain to a book lover why you didn't have the time or the inclination to sit down and wedge yourself into a fantasy world for hours at a time.

'So what do you *do* when you go home these days?' Anna demanded, as if it had never occurred to her to ask before. 'Now you're not walking my dog or being forced to have dinner with my husband's friends from work?'

'I . . .' Michelle hesitated. She was about to say, 'I do my accounts' but she realised how sad that sounded. Her next options were 'I do some cleaning or ironing' or 'I go for a run', neither of which were much better.

She shook her head, as if there were just too many things to list. 'I research new lines for the shop, I explore online boutiques, I check out design blogs, I make plans for the shop, and for this one too now . . .'

Anna was looking at her, and Michelle thought for one awful second there was a trace of sympathy behind her black-rimmed glasses.

That needed to be nipped in the bud. She didn't want Anna feeling sorry for her.

'We need to get on with our book bouquets.' Michelle reached into her bag and brought out her to-do list book and a bag of satin ribbons and bows from the wrapping table next door. 'I'm talking them up to the features ed on the paper. Choose me five books for someone in bed with some minor problem that you'd usually send flowers for. A woman, about our age. Nice big book to start.'

'What kind of big?' asked Anna. 'Big like a serious novel? Or big in the sense of covering a long period of time?'

'No. Just a big book. As in large.'

'Here.' Anna gave her *Little Women* again. 'I don't know a

woman who wouldn't love to read this. Sisters, tear-jerking deathbed scene, proposals . . .'

It wasn't quite as big as Michelle had hoped but it was a start. It would be a tall bouquet. 'OK, good. Next one. Slightly smaller. Comforting subject matter. Take me away from Longhampton.'

'Er . . . *Anne of Green Gables*? It takes you to the rural tranquillity of Prince Edward Island, Canada. Very cosy at this time of year.'

'OK.' Michelle took the book Anna passed her and frowned at the dust jacket: a red-headed girl in a pinny, laughing by an apple tree. 'Is this another kids' book?'

'Yes, but it's so lovely you can read it again as an adult and just feel . . . warmed through. It's about an orphan girl adopted by a brother and sister who really wanted a boy, and she melts their crustiness with her love of life and her eagerness to learn, and her freckly nose. I used to pretend that I was called Anne with an "e" because it was so distinguished.' Anna paused and narrowed her eyes at Michelle. 'You're *sure* you haven't read *Anne of Green Gables*?'

'Yes,' said Michelle. 'I spent most of my childhood dragging Owen out of trouble and getting make-up tips from *Just Seventeen*.' She stacked the book on top of the first and held out her hand. 'Another. Grown-up book, please.'

Anna looked around. The front desk, Michelle noticed, was littered with paperbacks, most of which were children's novels, going by the front covers. Anna's hand reached out for first one Dahl, then another, then withdrew under Michelle's warning gaze. Eventually she went over to the Humour section and grabbed a copy of *Cold Comfort Farm*.

'There,' she said. 'I gave this to Becca for Christmas, but she left it by her bed. I picked it because she's doing *Wuthering*

Heights for A-level, and it's such a funny parody of those sorts of brooding yokels novels. The heroine is a Bright Young Thing bossy-boots, another orphan who descends on a set of cousins and starts improving them whether they like it or not. I read it when I was about thirteen and re-read it now, whenever I need cheering up.'

'Cheering up? With all these orphans? Did you only read novels about dysfunctional families as a child?'

'Of course not!' said Anna, then paused. 'Although, I suppose *The Secret Garden*'s about an orphan, and so's *Ballet Shoes*, and *James and the Giant Peach*, and *Pippi Longstocking*, more or less, and . . .' She pulled a face, as if she'd only just made the connection. 'If they're not crippled with some disease, they do tend to be missing a parent or two.'

'And you don't think that's scary for kids?'

'A lot of children's fiction's scary, when you think about it,' said Anna. 'All those abandoned children coping with the world in their own way normalises the challenges of the adult world, and . . .' She trailed off.

'What's up?' said Michelle.

'I just . . . I just wonder if that's why Lily didn't read those books I gave her. If she thought I was making some kind of point about them not having a traditional family? Do you think she might? Or that Chloe might have said something?' She put a hand over her mouth and looked mortified.

Michelle wished Anna wouldn't take the blame for everything that happened in the McQueen household, as if she were the only one capable of making mistakes. 'Hardly. I bet Chloe didn't even bother to read the back copy of her own books, never mind Lily's. Anna, you've got to stop over-thinking this parenting thing.'

'Because I *wasn't* trying to make a point. I never even thought about it like that.'

'No one thinks you did. They just think you gave them boring presents,' said Michelle firmly. 'Look, you're the grown-up in this situation. If you want Lily to read a book with you, can't you just say to her, "Right, we're having a bedtime story tonight. It's *Ballet Shoes*. Pin your ears back."?'

'I can try,' said Anna uncertainly. 'I don't like to be too prescriptive about—'

'Kids need prescriptive. She's eight, not eighteen. Now, I need another book. Same size or smaller? Hey, come on. Focus!'

Anna shook herself. 'It's not going to be much smaller, *Cold Comfort Farm*'s a paperback.'

'Well, different colour then.'

Anna went over to the Humour shelf again and offered her another paperback, a jazzy Art Deco one this time. 'How about *Right Ho, Jeeves*? Oh.' She pulled the corners of her mouth down. 'Maybe not.'

'Why?'

'Orphan. Albeit rich orphan with omniscient butler.'

Michelle rolled her eyes. 'Give it here, it's a new book, we can charge full price. Last one, please. Short.'

'Michelle, you do realise that most fiction books only come in two sizes . . . *Peter Rabbit*?' Anna handed her a tiny Beatrix Potter hardback.

'Seriously? For a grown woman?'

'They're lovely. The drawings are so detailed and you can see the expressions in the little bunny faces. And it's all happy in the end. That's what you want when you've got a bad back. Happy rabbits.'

'You're the expert.' Michelle arranged the books with a deft movement and slid the wired ribbon underneath. With a few twists, she tied the stack up and fastened the lilac ribbon at the top, curling it into a rippling bow. She unrolled a silver ribbon, added an extra flourish and looked critically at the stack. 'What else can we put in with this? Make it look like thirty quid's worth of gift?'

'Some hankies for weeping into?' Anna held up a packet of delicate cherry-blossom print paper hankies from the bowl by the till, and a packet of organic chocolate buttons from another bowl by the cookery section.

They weren't the only things that had crept in from Home Sweet Home; dotted around the tables were all the book-related gift items Michelle could find. Pretty bookmarks, reading lights, bookends carved in the shape of owls . . . all designed to get customers in a buying frame of mind. And – although she hadn't said so to Anna – also to give them something to buy if they couldn't find the right book. It was Michelle's mission to ensure no customer left her shop empty-handed. She didn't trust the books to make it happen alone.

'There.' Michelle tweaked the ribbon and stepped back from the finished article. 'Our book bouquet. Better for you than sweets, lasts longer than a bunch of flowers.'

'Give the gift of nostalgia,' said Anna, picking up her marketing drift at once. 'Your childhood in an afternoon. Selected according to the preferences of the recipient and delivered by hand for . . . a fiver?'

'Seven quid. Make it worth Gillian getting her moped out.'

'I'll make some fliers to leave by the till.' Anna made a note in her book. 'It's a lovely present.'

'It is,' said Michelle, allowing herself a smile. She reached out and touched Anna's arm. 'Well done you, for coming up with it.'

'Well, *you* really . . .' Anna started, with typical modesty.

'No,' said Michelle emphatically. 'Your idea. Take the gold star.'

Anna looked pleased, and touched. 'Thanks,' she said. 'I'm really glad my useless gift-giving had some kind of happy ending.'

'Now, how about a coffee from that machine you said was so vital?'

Anna poured two cups of coffee from the jug, handed one to Michelle and smiled, her gentle face shining with enthusiasm. She looked younger suddenly, and Michelle realised she hadn't seen her look so relaxed in months. Since before the girls arrived in her house, in fact.

Anna sold the book bouquet within ten minutes of Michelle's departure, to a woman looking for something to give a friend who'd been ordered to bed for the last two weeks of her pregnancy.

'Lauren's not allowed to do anything other than read and go to the loo,' she said, falling on the display by the door with a delighted coo. 'And she's so sick of magazines, but she can't concentrate on anything too serious. This is absolutely perfect . . . Oh my God, *Anne of Green Gables*! Have you got any more?'

'I have,' said Anna, and sold her one, plus *What Katy Did*.

'I so wanted to be Clover,' the customer sighed, flipping through the book as Anna put the card payment through. 'Didn't you? I loved the bit where they were allowed long skirts and to put their hair up for the first time. I used to pin towels round me with kilt pins and swish around the house in my brother's boots, calling everyone ma'am.'

Anna nodded. 'Apart from the swing bit. It put me right off

swings. My dad had only just put one up in the garden and I wouldn't go near it for years.'

'Me too!' The customer widened her eyes. 'That bit where the pin comes out with the terrible crack . . .' She pulled a horrified face at exactly the same time as Anna did.

That was the nice thing about children's books, Anna thought as the woman left, promising to come back when she had 'more time for a proper browse'. They weren't like adult novels, where people pretended to have read the Booker short-list, but never did; everyone really *had* gobbled up the same Dahls and Blytons, and talking about them gave you that instant sense of something shared, that 'secret society' feeling that wasn't very secret at all because nearly everyone you knew had read the same things, had invited the same characters into their heads, and had woven secret scraps of themselves and their own feelings and fears into those imagined faces and voices.

She thought about what Michelle had said about *Ballet Shoes* and Lily, and decided she was right. There was no point waiting for other people; that was her motto for this year. And she would start the reading tonight.

Inspired by the sale and by the two customers who came in to inspect the new look and left with a vintage thriller and a *Complete Works of Shakespeare* respectively, Anna started to put together more bouquets – a Sunday afternoon Bunch of Detectives, with Miss Marple, Lord Peter Wimsey, Hercule Poirot and the Famous Five; a Romance Posy of pink and white novels by Georgette Heyer, Barbara Cartland and Jilly Cooper, topped off with *The Pursuit of Love* and a pack of Love Hearts, and tied with a silver ribbon.

She was threading a bag of toffee into the crime bouquet when a man in a suit entered the shop and marched straight to the front desk without bothering to browse.

Anna looked up, ready to smile, and stopped. He wasn't, as most customers did, pausing to gaze around the shop with an expression of admiration for Michelle's muted but welcoming colour scheme. Rather, he seemed annoyed.

'Can I help you?' she enquired, sizing him up. He seemed too young to be one of the 'Where did you put the tank books?' complainers, of which they'd had three so far, but his suit, now she looked more closely, was actually a tweed jacket. 'Are you looking for something in particular?'

He opened his mouth to speak, than glanced sideways as if he'd just noticed something. 'What happened to the military section?' he demanded. 'Used to be here, by the desk.'

'We moved it.' Anna smiled. 'It's in the side room.'

'Hmph. And the naval history?'

'Also in the side room. With the comfy chair. We thought it would be nicer for the history browsers to be able to sit down.'

He carried on looking round, in the proprietorial way many old customers had been doing. 'I like what you've done with the shelves,' he conceded. 'Nice clear labelling. You can see where you are. And you've restocked?'

'We've reorganised the old stock,' said Anna, pleased he'd noticed. 'There was quite a lot of it.'

'Good.' He started to step towards the local section for a browse, then pulled himself back. 'I'm looking for Ms Nightingale,' he said instead. 'Is she in today?'

'She's next door, in Home Sweet Home, but she's in and out with meetings.'

Anna racked her brains to think who this slightly pompous man might be – and what her best response should be. She assumed he was a rep, or maybe someone from the council: he was about her age, tall and good-looking, with an angular face and sandy-blond hair that fell into his eyes. He pushed it back now with an automatic sweeping gesture.

'Is it something I can help with?' she went on. 'I'm the shop manager.'

'Yes, in that case it is,' he said. 'It's about the pile of boxes in the communal hallway between the shop and the flat upstairs. They're blocking access.'

'I'm so sorry about that,' said Anna, half relieved but half guilty. 'They'll be moved by tonight. It's just that we're very short on storage space – the sealant on the floor in the back room hasn't dried as quickly as the builder hoped, so we couldn't put the last set of shelves back in, and so Michelle said if I stacked them there for a few days we'd be—'

'It's breaching fire regulations,' said the man. 'You can barely get a pushchair up those stairs anyway, plus it's a pain in the arse. I've got a massive scrape on my leg from trying to fold the bloody buggy small enough to get past.'

Anna reeled slightly. A pushchair? She hadn't noticed any children upstairs. She hadn't even noticed any adult occupants.

'I'm terribly sorry, Mr, um . . .' she said. 'I didn't get your name.'

'Rory Stirling.' He held out a hand. 'And yours is?'

'Anna McQueen. I'm sure we can sort this out very quickly for you,' she said, amazed that the baby hadn't been woken by the building work. Not that she wanted to bring that up if he hadn't noticed. 'It might be easier to pop in next door and grab Michelle now.'

He looked aghast at the thought. 'I've seen through the window. It's like a jumble sale in there. I don't want to get between those women and the last half-price scented candle.'

'I'll ring her,' said Anna, reaching for the phone. 'And I'm so sorry, it must be hard enough getting a buggy up those stairs to begin with.'

'It's a form of punishment.' Rory wiped a hand over his face, and when he revealed his eyes again, Anna noticed they were apologetic and bloodshot. 'Sorry, I didn't mean to shout,' he said. 'It's been a very long day or two. I'm not really an expert on buggies.'

'They're worse than deckchairs when you're not used to them,' said Anna.

'To be honest, I'd normally be fine about the books, so long as I got first dibs. Let me know if you're throwing any out. Especially any on Toddlers for Beginners.'

He added a tired smile at the end. It was a direct one, like a child's u-shaped grin. It sat endearingly at odds with his slightly fusty clothes.

'Why don't you take a seat?' said Anna, sensing a kindred book-ish spirit. 'Michelle won't be long. Coffee?'

'Milk, two sugars,' said Rory, looking round at where the machine was bubbling away. 'Now there's an improvement already.'

Michelle had long since perfected the art of serving three customers at once without making any of them feel neglected, which was vital at peak moments of sale chaos like this, with the lines jammed on the credit-card machine, a stress head-ache pounding at her temples, and now the phone ringing. A busy till was a happy one, as she told the staff, but today she didn't have the energy for it.

It didn't help that Owen kept sloping down from the office upstairs to photograph new items, causing an instant hiatus in service from Kelsey, and now – thanks to his kind fixing of her new phone – Gillian too. Michelle was less impressed. He'd returned from his New Year trip to London with a hangover, a love bite and a tiny new tattoo on his wrist in the shape of a single angel wing. Her new website was still only half done.

And she'd just noticed that Harvey had re-registered his details on the mailing list, after she'd blocked him from the old one. His shadow had appeared in her shop again.

'Kelsey, the phone!' she snapped, unable to bear the ringing, then checked herself. It wasn't fair to take it out on Kelsey. She grabbed it herself. 'Hello?'

'Michelle, I wonder if you could pop next door?' All she could hear behind Anna's voice was the gentle waft of a string quartet playing Bach. 'There's a man here who wants to see you.'

'Did he make an appointment?' Michelle smiled apologetically at her customer and put her credit card into the machine again. 'If it's a rep, tell him to come back next week.'

'He's called Rory Stirling. It's about the books in the hall upstairs. They're blocking access.'

Michelle's fingers slipped on the keypad and she accidentally charged the customer £9376.99 for her two Liberty silk scarves and silver-dipped egg box. The invisible metal band round her head tightened.

Rory Stirling. Great. That was all she needed: it was probably just an excuse to come round and tell her how she should be running the shop. She'd already had a few 'suggestions' from him via email about what she should be stocking. She'd deleted them all.

She jabbed at the cancel button. 'I'm so sorry . . . Let me do that again. Anna, just move the books and apologise. Tell him it was temporary. I'm rushed off my feet here.'

'Michelle, I think it'd be a good idea if you spoke to him yourself.'

'Fine, two minutes.' She redeployed her customers to Gillian and Kelsey, wove her way through the throng of people and out onto the high street.

The chilly air didn't help Michelle's head but the soothing atmosphere of the bookshop did. It was like walking into a hidden garden off the main street, with gentle music and the smell of coffee. However, when she saw Rory Stirling, irritation retightened its grip.

He was leaning by the big desk that doubled as the counter, chatting away to Anna with one lanky leg crossed over the other. Michelle noted he was wearing yellow socks. That made seven things about him that really annoyed her. She couldn't stand 'amusing' socks. Harvey had been a keen wearer of socks with motifs, which one solicitor told her was grounds enough for divorce in some parts of Surrey. Rory was also telling Anna something tedious about an author Michelle had never heard of, and Anna was smiling in an indulgent fashion.

'*Salve*, Ms Nightingale, *tandem*,' Rory said, turning round. When he stood up, she noticed that his shirt was un-ironed under his jacket.

'Tandem?'

'Latin. It means "at last". Anna and I were just talking about Latin A-level. How useful it is in everyday life.'

'If you're a gardener,' added Anna. 'Or a birdwatcher.'

Great, thought Michelle. Anna's finally found someone as daft as her about her bloody Latin A-level.

'Sorry to have kept you waiting, but I'm right in the middle of my busiest time,' she said. 'What's the Latin for "run off my feet"?'

'You've got me there,' said Rory. 'I can see you're busy. Looks as if the knick-knacks are flying off the shelves next door. Some of them have even flown in here.' He gestured towards a pile of soft woollen blankets Michelle had arranged by the romance section, right next to where she was standing.

'Yes,' she said. 'It's part of the reading experience. Cup of tea, warm blanket, romantic novel. Nothing wrong with that.'

Rory raised his eyebrow as if there *was* something wrong with that, and Michelle bridled. 'Cross-selling,' she said. 'It's how you make low-margin products like books work these days.'

'We've sold lots,' agreed Anna. 'I've got one. They're *so* cosy. Real one-more-chapter cosy.'

'Well, I hope you didn't move the military section to make room for blankets,' said Rory.

'What about spurs?' demanded Michelle. 'Would that have been OK? Or imitation pistols?'

'Rory was just saying how impressed he was by how much we've done in such a short time,' Anna said quickly, seeing Michelle's face darken. 'He's been away.'

'Indeed. When I left, it was a shell, and now it's the new Waterstone's. Mixed with Liberty.'

Michelle stared at him, trying to work out whether he was one of those men who'd been told that ladies like a bit of sparring, or if he was genuinely standing there, criticising her shop for making money. Rory Stirling was hard to read, especially behind his glasses. They were a bit like Anna's, square and tortoiseshell, only Anna's were ironically geeky, and Rory's seemed bona fide geek issue. Luckily for him, they didn't make his eyes look all weird and distorted, and she could see he had sandy lashes to match his hair.

'It looks like you've found a real book person here,' he added, and Anna beamed happily.

'Rory was just saying he was in the Puffin Club too.' She pointed to the ever-present pile of kids' books on the front desk.

'The Puffin Club?' Michelle pretended to look blank. 'No idea. Was that like the Tufty Club? Or the Pony Club?'

'Michelle! Don't tell me you weren't—' Anna began, but Michelle wasn't in the mood for more of Anna's rose-tinted nursery reminiscences.

'No, I wasn't in the Puffin Club. I went to *actual* clubs with *actual* friends,' she said. 'I didn't read about girls who had ponies, I *rode* ponies. I didn't read about tomboys who went on adventures, I *was* a tomboy who went on adventures. And boarding school is not like in Enid Blyton, let me tell you.'

Anna looked shocked by the force of her outburst, but Rory folded his arms, amused.

'I think the lady doth protest too much, don't you, Anna?' he said, tapping his long fingers on his sleeve. 'I think she's hiding a box set of *Worst Witch* stories.'

'Certainly not. Not everyone spent their childhood indoors with their nose in a book,' she retorted. 'That doesn't make me a Philistine, and it doesn't make me the wrong person to run a bookshop, if that's what you're getting at.'

A smaller, quieter voice pointed out that she might be over-reacting, but she couldn't stop herself.

'Of course it doesn't!' Anna started, in her conciliatory tone. 'No one's saying that.'

'On the contrary,' said Rory. 'You seem to have got the shop part perfect. It's looking . . .' He waved a long arm in the direction of her table displays.

He had arms like a spider, thought Michelle waspishly. She raised her eyebrow, waiting for his adjective.

'. . . More *shop-like* than I've ever seen it.'

'Have we moved the boxes?' she asked, turning to Anna.

'I'll give you a hand,' said Rory.

'No, there's no need.' Michelle pushed her sleeves back. 'My brother can do it. I'm sure you've got plenty of post-Christmas family break-ups to be sorting out.'

'Actually, I'm on holiday,' he said. 'Been doing family things for a few days, and I've got the rest of the week off.' He turned back to Anna. 'Luckily, the buggy's gone for the time being, but it'll probably be back sooner or later. And I need to be able to get my fishing stuff up there anyway.'

Michelle had started to walk over to the door to get Owen, but now she spun round. 'Hang on. You live up there?'

'With your . . . family?' Anna prompted innocently.

'No, it's just me most of the time,' said Rory.

Michelle wasn't interested, though; a big penny had just dropped. That *totally* explained why he was so adamant the place shouldn't be turned into some noisy café or busy phone shop. Talk about vested interests. It had less to do with Cyril Quentin's so-called legacy and more to do with Rory Stirling's lie-ins on a Saturday morning.

'Oh. *Now* I see why you're so keen on this staying a book-shop,' she said meaningfully.

'No, you don't,' he said, reading her cynical expression at once. 'My living here has got nothing to do with anything. I've been here a year or so, and yes, I came to be good friends with Cyril, being a book lover myself, and—'

'No need to go into the heart-rending details.' Michelle held up a hand. 'I'll shift the books and you can rest assured you won't have any more access problems.'

'Let me help.'

'No thanks. Don't want you suing me for personal injury.'

Michelle pulled her spine up to its full length and glared at him. She felt wrongfooted. Rory Stirling should have said something. It was *unethical*. Besides which, the thought that he was upstairs, keeping an eye on her, was very, very unsettling.

'It won't happen again,' said Anna quickly, eager as ever to smooth out any wrinkles. 'And come back soon and buy some books! We've got a whole box of old Puffin Club specials. Maybe you could get something for the baby?'

Rory shot an amused glance over to Michelle, then smiled more readily at Anna. 'Maybe. Thanks for the coffee,' he added, as he loped towards the door.

'You gave him coffee?' Michelle hissed, when it closed behind him.

'Yes! We got chatting and I'd just put the pot on . . . Why? Shouldn't I have done?' Anna squinted at her. 'Why were you so off with him? What's he done to you? I thought he was nice.' She looked pensive. 'Bit weird about the buggy, though, if he lives alone. Whose baby was it, do you think?'

'I don't care about the baby. He should have said he lived upstairs.'

'He did. Just then.'

Something niggled at Michelle. Hadn't he said he didn't have a family when she'd gone in to see him? That he was in the office because he didn't have family ties?

Anna looked at her more closely. 'Come on, Michelle, what's up? You were fine this morning. Rory's fine, honestly. I'm sure he won't make a big deal about it.'

Michelle knew it wasn't really Rory Stirling; it was Harvey. After three years of peace, suddenly Harvey was in the back of her head the whole time like a permanent stress headache. She was constantly wondering when the next unwanted floral reminder would appear, wondering what her mother was 'advising' him to do, wondering what he was saying to her mother about their marriage. It was worse than him just turning up on her doorstep.

'I'm feeling a bit stressed,' she admitted. 'Harvey's . . . Harvey's been talking to my mother. He wants to try again.'

'What?' Anna was instantly and gratifyingly outraged for her. 'He's got no right, you're divorced!'

Michelle took a deep breath. 'Actually, Anna, we're not. Not officially.'

'I thought you were?' Anna's brow creased. 'Why did I think that?'

'Because I never said. It's not something I'm very proud of,' she admitted.

'Then divorce him.' Anna turned her palms up, as if it was the easiest thing in the world. 'Get on with it.'

'It's not that easy,' said Michelle. 'Harvey refused to get divorced when I asked for one, even when I said I'd be the unreasonable party. He hates losing. I was going to wait out the five years' separation, then he has no choice. But now he's decided that's not going to happen either. And if my mum's behind him, too . . .'

Anna opened her mouth to argue back, but Michelle's hooded eyes obviously stopped her. She seemed shocked to see her so beaten.

'Don't say anything,' warned Michelle. 'There's nothing you can say I haven't already said to myself a million times.'

Anna grabbed her hand. 'You know what always cheers me up?'

'If you say *Winnie the Pooh*, I will have to kill you.'

'No! Once round the park and a big meringue from Natalie's café. I'll go halves if you want.'

Michelle managed a wintry smile. 'I prefer exercise. I'm going to shift those boxes for Rory myself.'

Moving the heavy boxes made Michelle's muscles ache, but it sapped the worst of her headache. What it didn't do, though, was distract her from the shifting sensation she felt inside, that her own neatly stacked life was starting to escape its storage.

9

'I wish I could give 101 Dalmatians *to all my new dog owning clients, so they'd know (a) how much exercise a Dalmatian needs, and (b) how much of a pickle humans can get their dogs into.'*   George Fenwick

Anna had never really thought of herself as an organiser, but the collection/delivery plans she'd put in place to keep Lily, Chloe and Becca's various schedules in the air at the same time as her new job and Pongo's exercise needs made FedEx look like a bunch of rank amateurs.

Michelle or Gillian covered the first hour so she could do the school run and walk Pongo, then Jack's mum walked Lily home to the bookshop on Mondays and Wednesdays, while Isabel's mum picked her up on Tuesdays. On Thursdays, Becca had a free study afternoon, so she covered for Anna in the shop for an hour while she went to get Lily, and on Fridays Phil finished work early to collect her, amidst coos of adoration and sympathy from the other mums, which he milked shamelessly.

Lily didn't seem to mind being passed around like a parcel; her main concern was how Pongo was taking to being 'abandoned' every day.

'Did he look sad when you left him this morning?' she asked Anna, as they walked down the high street towards the bookshop. Her bag was weighing down one shoulder, but she wouldn't let Anna carry it; it contained Mrs Piggle and her new all-American pig, Piggy-Jo, a gift from Sarah. 'How sad did he look, out of ten?'

'Two. He was fine,' said Anna. 'He'd got a busy day planned – trip to the park at lunchtime, film in front of the telly this afternoon, back to us for supper.'

'Does Pongo have his own bed at Juliet's? And who does he like most out of Minton and Coco? Does he have a best friend there?'

Minton and Coco were Juliet's own dogs; Pongo didn't express a preference for either, loving everyone enthusiastically, but Lily was obsessed with best friends. Anna was painfully aware that Lily didn't seem to have one herself.

'You're his best friend.' She wasn't sure she should be encouraging Lily's obsession with anthropomorphising everything from Pongo to Mrs Piggle but at least it got her talking. Any questions about school usually resulted in a worryingly unspecific answer.

'I know,' said Lily. 'But he's allowed to have one best *dog* friend too.'

'Maybe he has a girlfriend,' suggested Anna, 'like Missis Pongo?'

'No,' said Lily decisively. 'There aren't any other Dalmatians round here. He'd have to find one on the internet. A special internet Dalmatian dating site.'

'Perdita just arrived, didn't she? In the book.'

Lily wrinkled her nose. 'I don't remember that bit in the film.'

'Well, she was just wandering around when Pongo and Missis needed some help with the puppies. We could read that part together,' she suggested, then played a sneaky trump card. 'Maybe Pongo would like to join us? He could listen too.'

They were nearly at the shop now, and Lily stopped walking. Anna stopped too, thinking Lily had seen something pretty in the window of Home Sweet Home, but she hadn't. She just wanted to get Anna's attention.

'That would be nice for him,' Lily said very seriously. 'I think he probably misses us. He'd like to have some one-on-one time, and a story. Poor Pongo. Maybe he doesn't speak the same language as Coco and Minton. What if he speaks Dog French, and they speak Dog Italian?'

Anna's heart caught in her throat at the barely disguised sadness in the huge blue eyes, but Lily's acceptance of her suggestion to read together was a real leap. Her attempts to read *Ballet Shoes* had fallen on stony ground; Lily hadn't wanted to listen to girls 'showing off like Chloe' on stage.

'Then let's start tonight,' she said, trying not to sound too excited. 'We'll have a reading party! You, me, Mrs Piggle and Pongo.'

'Good,' said Lily, the sunshine returning to her face with the usual family speed that Anna found so disconcerting. 'Ooh, who's that boy talking to Becca?'

'Which boy?' Anna looked where Lily was looking – through the big plate-glass window of the bookshop – and saw Becca behind the counter, chatting animatedly to Michelle and Owen.

Becca looked a lot more awake than Anna had seen her recently, and kept twirling the end of her plait round and round as she spoke, glancing up and down shyly.

She must have come to discuss the Saturday job, she thought. Chloe had more or less dropped her nagging about it after Phil had caved in and increased her weekly allowance instead of risking her grades, but Becca seemed keen to help. She probably fancied the quiet atmosphere even more than the cash.

Anna squinted. She was looking very keen at the moment. Very keen indeed. Owen was flicking through a paperback and laughing, and Becca was laughing too, trying to make him stop and read the bits she was pointing at.

'That's not a boy, that's Michelle's brother, Owen,' she started to say, but Lily was already barging in through the door, pushing it hard to make the bell clang as loud as she could.

Michelle looked pleased to see her and Becca sprang up from the counter, blushing. Owen's demeanour didn't change. He carried on looking cool, skinny and relaxed.

'Ah, Anna, just the woman,' said Michelle. 'Meet your new Saturday girl.'

'Yay!' said Becca, half raising her hands in a self-conscious gesture of celebration. She shot a sideways glance at Owen as she did it, and Anna suddenly remembered the complex teenage formula to looking cool in front of cooler boys. It made her feel glad she didn't have to do it any more.

'Was that an interview I just missed?' she asked. 'Because I was going to ask some testing questions about whether she would keep the shop tidier than her room, and so on.'

'All done. I couldn't have picked a more ideal assistant. Becca's going to give Owen a hand with the website too, when things are quiet,' said Michelle. 'Home Sweet Home needs some copy and I thought we could put something online for this place, just to give it a marker, you know.'

'A marker? What, until we get a proper site going?' asked Anna. She was going to ask more, but there was a rustling behind her and Lily bustled forward.

'Hello,' she said, sticking out her hand towards Owen. 'I'm Lily Rose McQueen. Who are you?'

Anna felt a sudden surge of protectiveness; Lily was normally the shyest of the three, and Owen didn't seem the type to be used to talking to little girls. She held her breath, but to her surprise, Owen took Lily's hand solemnly and shook it, holding her gaze the entire time.

She looked transfixed.

'Hello, Lily,' he said. 'I'm Owen Bristol Nightingale. Don't laugh.'

'Bristol?' Becca spluttered. 'Was that where your parents—?'

'Becca,' warned Anna.

'No, it was not. My dad's a car dealer. Bristol's a make of car. Have you ever asked Michelle what her middle name is?'

Anna turned to Michelle. 'No?'

'It's private,' Michelle protested, turning red. 'Owen, don't . . .'

'Michelle Lotus Corniche,' Owen finished with relish.

'I never knew that.' Anna put her hands on her hips and added, only half joking, 'There's so much I don't know about you, Michelle.'

'For good reason,' she muttered.

'Most of the family only found out at her wedding,' said Owen. 'Good job Harvey's middle name was Neville. Balanced out the laughs.' He helped himself to the bowl of mints on the counter, ignoring his sister's furious glare. He winked at Becca, who blushed again.

'So, the website for the bookshop,' said Anna quickly. 'What can I do? How about putting some of the "We Love . . ." cards on the site? I've done quite a few myself, and I've been putting cards in with purchases, with a stamped envelope, so we're getting some back.'

She hoped Michelle had noticed how many there were,

dotted around the shelves. Anna loved pinning them up; she felt it was bringing the shop to life.

'I don't mind doing some more reviews,' said Becca.

'Me too!' said Lily.

'That'll mean reading some books first,' Becca reminded her.

'I don't mind.' Lily's eyes were wide with enthusiasm. 'Pongo and I are going to read one tonight, aren't we, Anna? We can do a review together, for the website?' She looked over to Owen, who nodded.

'I'll give it priority on the front page,' he said. 'How is Pongo's typing? Becca tells me he's a real klutz.'

Anna wondered how long Owen and Becca had been chatting for her to start filling him in on her dog. Getting conversation out of Becca was normally like getting blood out of a stone. But then something about the bookshop did seem to get people chatting, not just in the small reading group they'd started, but in the queue and the back room.

'I'll help him,' said Lily.

'Well, if you email them to me, I can put them into the beta site,' said Owen. 'Do you want to give me your email address?'

He was talking to Becca, and Anna saw a brief frown flash across Michelle's forehead as he reached for his phone to take down the details. Did she think Becca was going to distract him from the job in hand? It was more likely to be the other way round.

'Owen, just remember Anna's in charge in this shop,' Michelle said, pointing at her. 'Get everything from her so she has a chance to moderate it.'

'Oh, don't worry, I'm sure Becca's reviews will be perfect,' said Anna. 'Better than mine, probably. She's predicted a Grade A in English.'

Becca made a mumbling noise and stared at the pile of *Harry Potter* books on the counter.

'Impressive,' said Owen. He looked impressed, too. 'Are you off to university soon, then?'

'Becca's got a place to study Law at Cambridge,' said Michelle, again looking quite pointedly at Owen. 'She's got enough to do with her revision and her job here, so . . . no distracting.'

Becca did her usual eye-rolling display of embarrassment mixed with secret pride; Anna felt like hugging her.

'We can have a chat about the website now, if you want?' Anna suggested, moving towards the coffee machine. 'I'm here until six. We don't seem to be very busy and I've got lots of ideas.'

'That'd be great,' Owen started, but Michelle didn't give him a chance to finish.

'Tomorrow, maybe,' she said, steering him firmly towards the door. 'I want Owen to finish off the Home Sweet Home site first. Gillian's been setting up some Valentine's Day gift shots for us with the new season stock.'

'Gillian's setting up stock shots for you?' Anna raised her eyebrows. Normally Gillian ordered Kelsey to do menial tasks like that.

'Gillian's been very helpful,' said Owen. 'She says I remind her of her son.'

'Grandson,' said Anna. 'Darren. He did the website before you.'

'She's old enough to have grandchildren?' Owen said, astonished.

The studied immobility of Michelle's eyebrows told Anna that she was trying very hard to control her face. Clearly Owen had worked his charm magic on Gillian, too – a feat of some magnitude, since Gillian's 'all-time hero' was Cliff Richard and she thought men shouldn't wear any jewellery apart from wedding rings.

'Well, if you need anything,' said Anna, 'I'll be here till six.'

'And so will I,' said Becca casually.

'Great!' Owen raised a hand in farewell as Michelle escorted him from the shop with an apologetic backward glance.

'Can I have a biscuit from the special tin?' asked Lily, turning her attention from Owen and back onto food.

'Help yourself.' As Lily thundered through to the staff room biscuit tin, Anna watched Becca absent-mindedly stacking and restacking the books in front of her. 'Becca, you don't have to hang around here – go home if you want. I thought you were seeing Josh tonight?'

Josh was Becca's boyfriend, a red-headed scientist-to-be who'd run the gauntlet of a couple of dinners at the McQueens and still hadn't been put off trying to take Becca out to Longhampton's limited social venues. Phil had just about decided to trust him, on the grounds that he was too shy to get up to much and played the oboe in the school orchestra.

'I know what the football team's like,' Phil had muttered in her ear while they were washing up, 'and I don't remember there being any oboeists in it.'

Becca twisted the end of her plait. 'Um, probably not. I've got an essay to finish. Me and Josh are . . . You know.'

'Everything OK?' Anna asked. She didn't like to pry, but sometimes Becca would ask her things she didn't want to ask her mum, especially now Sarah had apparently gone into overshare mode in her new life.

'Fine,' said Becca. 'Well, no . . .' She sighed. 'I don't know. Sometimes Josh can be a bit . . .' Her voice trailed off again and she pulled a despairing face. 'Irritating?'

'They're all like that,' said Anna. 'They don't change. You just learn to manage them better.' She paused, thinking of the marked, somewhat martyred silence Phil had adopted about the baby issue. And the luxury shed brochures that had appeared on his bedside table. 'Although it takes a while.'

Becca picked up a book from the desk – *The Railway Children* – and as Anna poured herself a coffee from the filter jug, she thought how lucky she was that Becca was the oldest, and not Chloe. It could have been so much harder.

Becca did her best, at school and at home, because she wanted to please everyone. She bore the weight of Sarah and Phil's massive expectations without complaint. She put up with Chloe's self-narrating singing and sat through Lily's multi-toy productions of scenes from *Glee*. Her only real failing was her sneaky use of Anna's expensive skincare products, and an obsession with low-fat cottage cheese.

'Why don't you relax for a bit?' said Anna. 'Keep an eye on Lily in the back room and do me a review. Here, take this coffee.'

Becca took the mug with a smile and headed to the back of the shop, utterly unaware of how graceful she was, her plait swinging down her back as she walked. Then she turned and went back to Anna, putting down her coffee to give her a quick hug.

'Thanks, Anna,' she said. 'Thanks for the job, and thanks for talking Dad into letting me do it. I appreciate it.'

'My pleasure,' said Anna. It felt so sweet to do something for the girls that was all hers. 'Really.'

Later that evening, after baths and teeth-brushing, Anna took her copy of *One Hundred and One Dalmatians* into Lily's room, and let Pongo follow her in.

He was amazed to be allowed upstairs without a fight, and sniffed around Lily's room, investigating each fluffy toy individually. Anna's heart sank – if Lily decided to introduce him to each one, they could be there until the small hours – but instead Lily patted the space next to her on the bed.

'Come and listen, Pongo,' she said, as he curled round and round, trying to get comfy, while shooting nervous glances at Anna. 'Anna's going to read you a story about dogs.'

She looked at Anna, cueing her to join in with the dog conversation.

'Um, yes. Settle down, Pongo,' said Anna. 'Are you going to leave any space for me? Good. Now, the best way to let the pictures come into your head is if you both close your eyes and listen.'

'OK,' said Lily. She wriggled under the pink princess duvet and closed her eyes. Anna wasn't sure how long that would last, but she started reading anyway. Pongo put his head on his paws and went into standby mode.

In Anna's fond daydreams about reading to her imaginary children, they didn't interrupt quite as much as Lily did ('Why is he married to Missis, not Perdita?' 'Why doesn't Mrs Dearly have a job?' 'Where is Regent's Park? Is it bigger than the park here? Does it have ducks?' and so on) and it took a long time to get going.

But after a while, Lily stopped fidgeting and was drawn in by Anna's soft voice as it rose and fell in the semi-darkness. Anna also got lost in the story, wishing herself into the cherry-tree perfection of the Dearlys' household, with Nanny Cook and Nanny Butler and their intelligent pair of Dalmatians, who owned them with such love.

She was glad Lily's eyes were closed when she reached

the part about Missis's pups arriving, and poor starving Perdita being found on the road to help feed them. As an adult, Anna had never been able to get past that bit without dissolving into tears. She wasn't sure whether Lily was still awake or not, but she carried on reading anyway, about Perdita tentatively looking after two of Missis's pups as tenderly as if they were hers, and then she choked, too emotional to go on.

'Are you crying?' asked a small, sleepy voice.

'No,' said Anna. A fat tear fell off the end of her nose.

'Yes, you are. Why are you crying? Isn't it nice that Perdita got some puppies to look after?'

'Yes,' said Anna. 'It is.'

'Like you. You got to look after us.' Lily sounded pleased with that solution. She yawned, her mouth pink and wide like a puppy's.

'I think that's enough for tonight,' said Anna. 'Night night, Lily. See you in the morning.'

'Can Pongo stay here?'

'He'll be happier in his basket,' said Anna firmly, pointing to the floor as Pongo opened one eye. He slid off the bed and padded across to the door. 'Night night.'

Lily was asleep.

Anna pulled the door almost shut and nearly jumped when she saw Chloe on the landing behind her, slouching her way out of the bathroom in one of Phil's old dressing gowns, and Ugg boots. They didn't match her full make-up.

She'd obviously spent the evening perfecting her smoky eye technique rather than finishing her History essay, but Anna decided not to take it up with her. So far today, she was ahead with two McQueen children. That was a good record and she didn't want to spoil it.

'Anna,' groaned Chloe. 'I've got a headache and there's no Nurofen in the bathroom.' She clutched her forehead. 'I've got sooo much work to do tonight. I haven't even started.'

'Have you tried drinking a pint of water? And logging out of Facebook?'

Chloe made a teenage noise. 'I need drugs. Medicinal drugs.'

'Fine. There's some in my bathroom,' said Anna. 'I'll go and get them. Stay there.'

Chloe turned on the McQueen charm long enough for a sweet 'thank you' to emerge from the kohl-y murk, then she subsided into adolescent suffering again.

In her bedroom, Anna ignored the piles of clothes Phil had left by – not in – the laundry basket, and opened the cabinet in the en-suite bathroom. She reached in to get the paracetamol and her eye fell on the space where she normally tucked her Pill. The clinic had sent her a reminder letter, requesting that she come in for a check-up appointment, but following her earlier resolution, she had decided to ignore it.

Looking at the space in the medicine cabinet now, though, what she felt was a twinge of guilt. A voice in the back of her head said she should have discussed it again with Phil, but a louder voice, coming from somewhere less rational, insisted that, effectively, they *had* discussed it. They'd discussed it at length, and they'd come up with a decision they'd both agreed on. He'd grumbled a bit in the car at New Year, but he hadn't said categorically no. He *knew* what her plans were.

If Phil actively didn't want to have more children, she argued, he could deal with the contraception. His existing children and their punishing routines were doing a pretty good job on their own.

Anna closed the cabinet door and caught her own reflection in the mirror. Her eyes, still mascara-smeared from reading about Perdita's mothering of another dog's puppies, were shining with a determination that made her seem different, even to herself.

She blinked, and her expression changed to one she was more familiar with. Weariness.

'Anna,' moaned Chloe from inside her own room, loud enough to wake Lily. 'My head. Hurry *up*.'

At least when her baby finally did arrive, she'd be used to the endless wailing.

IO

*'Danny, Champion of the World is such a heart-
warming tale of a father and his son that you can
almost forgive the illegal poaching.'* Rory Stirling

Rory Stirling often dropped into the bookshop for a lunchtime
browse and although he was happy to chat to Anna about books
and Latin, he never mentioned his family or a girlfriend or the
mysterious buggy that he'd had so much trouble collapsing.
Anna let her imagination run wild around the solicitor; he had
the sort of face that would look good brooding, she thought.
The cheekbones and that hair that kept falling into his eyes.
When she was in the shop and he was upstairs, she kept an ear
cocked for baby-related sounds, but never heard a thing, apart
from the occasional burst of loud cricket commentary.

Kelsey, however, spotted Rory with a toddler when she'd
been covering for Anna one lunchtime, while Anna did her
Reading Aloud session at Butterfields.

'It was so sweet, he didn't know what he was doing with it,'
she reported, wide-eyed with 'Aww, bless' indulgence. 'He
looked like one of those dads who's just been handed the baby
to look after and he's all like, *Wooah! Which way up?!* Bless him.
And bless the little toddler. He was a cutie pie. Big pink cheeks
you wanted to smoosh.'

'Was it his toddler, do you think?' Anna was intrigued.

'He doesn't look the type to steal one,' said Kelsey, surprised.

'That's not what I meant,' said Anna. 'Did it look like he was looking after it for a friend, or was it his? You can tell.'

Rory hadn't struck Anna as having any of the new-dad vibes she picked up from other recent parents. Her brain now automatically divided the world around her into parents and non-parents – which was stupid, she knew, given that she herself was somewhere in between, but her broodiness was starting to do weird things to her head.

'Dunno. He came in here and was like, what book do I need for a child this big?' Kelsey mimed someone pointing in panic at a child one metre off the ground. 'I had no clue. He ended up getting one of those big army books with pictures in it. I have no idea what that poor child's going to grow up like.'

'It must be a godchild, or a nephew,' mused Anna. 'I wonder if he needs a bit of help?'

'To be fair, I'd say he needs all the help he can get,' said Kelsey. 'I don't know who looked more freaked out, him or the kid.'

A few days later, as if by synchronicity, Anna ran into Rory outside Butterfields, without any buggy or child in tow.

He was coming out as she was going in, his shoulders hunched up against the squally February wind, and his eyes fixed on the ground. He seemed lost in a world of his own, as Anna often was herself after a sobering hour with the lonely old souls.

'Rory!' said Anna, pushing back the furry hood of her jacket so he'd see it was her.

Rory's head bounced up, and he seemed surprised to see her there.

'Hello there,' he said, pushing back his hair with a familiar gesture, and Anna was struck by his rich Scottish accent. If you'd only heard him on the phone, she thought, you'd imagine he was some rugged, kilt-wearing Scottish nobleman, all tousled and handsome.

Not that he wasn't handsome. He had a certain angular charm, and clever eyes. Anna shuffled through her mental list of fictional heroes and slotted Rory into the Dr Who pigeon-hole. Scarves, and tinkering, and too clever to relate very well to people. Which made it even harder to imagine him with a toddler, but still. Stranger things happened

'What are you doing here?' she asked. 'If that's not a rude question?'

'Not a rude question at all. I had a consultation with a client about a will. And while I was here, I popped in to see Cyril Quentin, too – I had a few books for him.' He pointed at her as if he was making a connection. 'Are you here for this reading they're having?'

Anna nodded. 'I do it every week.'

'They're looking forward to it.' He grinned, scrunching his eyes up against the wind. 'Cyril was bagging his chair. Quite a rush to get seats. Well, as much as you can rush on a Zimmer frame. A slow shuffle to get seats.'

'Really? 'Anna was pleased. 'I'm always looking for other volunteers, if you're interested. It's just once a week, for an hour at most. Less, if you do it after lunch and they're all a bit sleepy.'

Rory thought about it for a second, then said, 'Why not? I drop in to see Cyril anyway, might as well entertain the troops.'

'You could do a breakaway group for the men. Bit of *Hornblower*, or some Len Deighton. They get a bit restless with Maeve Binchy.' She was half joking, but Rory nodded in agreement.

'I'm a big *Hornblower* fan. It'd be my pleasure. Do you choose the book, or is there some centralised list?'

'There are suggestions, but I tend to be led by what they want to hear. Most of them aren't backwards in coming forwards.' Anna grimaced. 'I'll point out my mother-in-law. She's one to watch.'

'Great,' he said. 'What solicitor doesn't like the sound of their own voice, eh?'

Anna grinned. Rory was a bit spiky, but anyone who had their own particular system for filing novels by mood, as he did, couldn't be all bad, despite what Michelle had been muttering. But then Michelle took strange instant dislikes to people, and Anna knew she hated being told what to do with her business.

'I don't mean to be nosy,' she said, pushing a strand of blond hair behind her ear, 'but was that your godson visiting the other day? I mean,' she added, casting around for a reason to ask such a personal question, 'we've started a bring-a-baby reading group in the back room, and if you wanted to bring him along, get some tips from our resident mums, I know they'd love to have you.'

She hoped he'd see it for the genuine offer it was, but he frowned, making two shallow grooves appear between his auburn eyebrows.

'Um, that was my son, actually,' he said.

'Really?' It came out too loud and too surprised, and the wind didn't carry it away in quite the way Anna hoped. Her surprise hung in the air between them.

'His name's Zachary.' Rory's lips made a thin line. 'He doesn't live with me, obviously. I only see him when his mother's down this end of the country, which isn't very often.'

'Oh.' Anna scrambled to make sense of those facts. Rory

didn't seem to want to offer any more details. 'I'm sorry, I didn't realise you were marr—' she started, then realised that wasn't right either.

'I'm not married. We were never married.' Rory raised one eyebrow. 'In fact, Esther and I split up a couple of months before Zachary was born.'

You split up while your girlfriend was pregnant? Anna pressed her own lips together now, to stop it spilling out. It seemed so unlikely. Wasn't that about the worst thing anyone could do? Rory didn't seem the girlfriend-abandoning type. He seemed so . . .

Well read?

'Any further questions?' he added defensively.

Anna shook her head. It wasn't any of her business, and yet she felt disappointed. How could you have a baby and then just walk away from it? Let it go like that?

Rory nodded a farewell and headed back to his car. Anna watched him, then turned quickly, before he spotted her watching him, and hurried out of the biting wind into the house.

People who like Wodehouse can be bastards too, she told herself, as Cyril Quentin caught her eye and smiled across the circle of chairs.

But she didn't like it when they were.

Chloe and the Apricotz had been rehearsing in the sound-proofed area of the cellar since Chloe got back from New York with her haul of CDs and new drugstore make-up, and with Chloe's friend Paige now replaced by Tyra's friend Ellie (who, crucially, had her own Wii with four controllers to play *Just Dance 2* in the cellar with them), the need to launch the Apricotz onto the unsuspecting public had become a driving force in Chloe's life.

Today the pleading had started in the car on the way to school, had continued as soon as Chloe's school bag hit the floor by the front door, and was reaching a crescendo over family supper, which Anna had instigated as a means of finding out what everyone had been up to at school, but which tonight was providing a useful platform for Chloe to rehearse her Cowell-bending 'You've got to let me go to Boot Camp, my rabbit only has three weeks to live, I'll give you 1937 per cent' speech.

'I *have* to go to the auditions,' said Chloe for the third time in ten minutes. 'They're in Birmingham next month. Oh, and I need you to sign the form.'

'No,' said Phil, for the third time. 'Now pass me the vegetables that I spent many minutes preparing in the microwave.'

'Sorry, Dad, I'm not asking you, I'm telling you.' Chloe gave him a perfectly pitched look of bafflement that made her look a lot older than fifteen. 'Everyone else's parents have agreed. It's next month. The twenty-first. Tyra's dad's taking us up there, but if you want to collect us, that would be great.'

'Didn't I just say no?' said Phil, but this time he sounded less convinced. 'I'm pretty sure I've been saying no. Becca, have you heard me saying no?'

Becca didn't look up from the History textbook she was reading alongside her plate. 'I heard no, Dad. But that's not what that sound means in Chloe's language.'

'What sound should I make to indicate no?'

'There isn't one. Have you tried sign language?' Becca turned a page.

Chloe smiled her cat-like smile and flicked her hair over her shoulder.

'Can we go back to shouting?' pleaded Phil. 'At least I knew then you were actually listening to me in order to disagree.'

'I'm *trying* to be mature about this,' countered Chloe. 'I thought that's what you wanted. Me acting like an adult. You're the one who's not engaging with the discussion.'

Anna had to admire Chloe's tactics, which she suspected she'd picked up from Sarah: repeating her requirements over and over again in calm, slightly patronising tones, as if negotiating holiday allocation with an entry-level employee, until the desired result was obtained. Anna hadn't been around for Phil and Sarah's divorce, but from the occasional conversations she'd heard between Phil and his solicitor during the early handovers, she got the impression that this was Sarah's tried-and-tested approach.

It was having a surprisingly successful effect against Phil's equally annoying tactic of being funny until the other person gave up. Not for the first time, Anna wondered how much of her husband's first marriage she saw reflected in the way his daughters behaved.

'I just don't think it's a good idea for you to be—' Phil started, but Chloe had moved on to her next phase.

'Anna, *you* could take me if Dad won't,' she said suddenly, just as Anna was helping herself to more vegetables. 'Dad, what if Anna took me? Would that get round whatever massive *issue* you've got with me doing this thing that I really, really want to do?'

'I . . .' Anna's brain froze as she tried to work out what she was supposed to say.

Phil glared at her, as if trying to transmit thoughts directly into her head, but it was too late. Seeing her hesitate, Chloe homed in instinctively for the kill.

'Maybe Anna's the best person to take us anyway. I mean, you're not going to get all weird and protective, are you? You're not my mum. Plus, you're young, you understand why it's, like, really important for me and the band to get this exposure.'

Becca and Lily were looking at her now, interested to see what her reaction would be. Anna knew it would be entered into the Great Database of Anna Responses, against which other future unreasonable requests would be weighed up and cross-referenced.

It was pretty bloody ironic, she thought, that somehow *not* caring about Chloe as much as Phil and Sarah did was now worth something to Chloe. While at the same time, favours like these – taxi-ing, cake baking, endless shopping trips – were demanded as proof that she *did* care. That she was prepared to make the extra effort, because she *didn't* have the genetic obligation. And when it was presented to her as a sort of special bonding treat, how could she say no?

'You can't just expect Anna to drop everything to suit you,' Phil said, seizing a fresh strand of argument. 'She's got to be in the bookshop at the weekend.'

'What's more important?' Chloe demanded, finally running out of niceness. 'Her job or her *stepdaughter*? Don't I mean anything to *either* of you? Do you want me to live in this dump all my life, and *die* here? In some boring job?'

'You'll have to *get* a job first,' Becca pointed out. 'I don't think anyone's hiring Christina Aguilera impersonators at the moment.'

'Shut up, Becca,' roared Chloe. 'Dad, tell her to shut up.'

Lily said nothing, but watched the argument with bug eyes, turning her head like a tennis spectator as the barbs whizzed from side to side.

'I bet Mum would take us.' Chloe tossed her hair and dared anyone to contradict her. 'She said, didn't she, Lily, that she'd

take me to *American Idol*? Anna *should* take us. It's her duty.
It's what a *real mother* would do for her—'

'Chloe!' snapped Phil, but not before everyone round the
table had winced in unison.

'Well, it's true,' she said defiantly.

Anna tried to hide the unexpected burning sensation in her
throat.

'We can talk about it,' she said, as calmly as she could. 'Why
don't you give me Tyra's mum's number and I'll see what the
plans are.'

'Anna! That's, like . . .' The sunny glow returned to Chloe's
face.

'It's not a no from me,' said Anna swiftly. 'But it's not a yes,
either.'

'It's a "We'll talk to Tyra's mum",' said Becca, translating
without looking up from her book. 'You should tell Louis
Walsh he can use that one.'

Chloe flicked her fringe and shoved her chair back. 'I'm
going to the cellar to practise,' she said. 'Don't disturb me,
OK?'

'We won't,' said Phil. He sounded conciliatory now, the
doting dad again. 'Text us if you need anything.'

Anna watched his expression as his eyes followed Chloe
out of the room, and she wished, just for once, that he'd tell
her to stop being such a brat. But he never did.

Phil had no trouble laying down the law with Lily and
Becca, but when it came to Chloe, he seemed scared of saying
no, and scared of saying yes. Anna wondered if it because she
was so like Sarah. Because she was, right down to the pointed
chin. Maybe it was because she'd been the most devastated by
her parents' divorce? Or maybe just because she was a teenager? Whatever Phil said, Chloe would want the opposite;

Anna's covert child-rearing reference books said fifteen was that sort of age.

Anna could only remember being fifteen by cross-referencing with *Now* albums and books. Fifteen for her was Douglas Adams, all the Brontës in a dramatic gulp, Pulp and Blur. Not arguing with her dad, flying to the States every three months to see her mum, and auditioning for talent shows. How was she supposed to give Chloe what she needed if she didn't know what it was? Phil knew her better. Why couldn't he do it?

Phil caught her looking at him and grimaced.

'That's what those cute little babies turn into,' he said. His tone was light, but his eyes were telling a different story.

She knew what he was thinking: 'Fancy handling that all over again, when I'm fifty-six?'

'Not necessarily,' said Becca, still engrossed in her book. 'Hello?'

'No,' said Anna. 'Not necessarily.'

Becca went off to do her homework, taking an apple with her, and Lily retreated to the corner of the sitting room where Pongo snuck onto the sofa next to her while she played her Nintendo DS on his back.

Anna cleared the plates from the table while Phil poured what was left of the custard into the remains of the apple crumble, and sat there picking at the serving dish with a forlorn expression.

'Can you get a move on?' she asked. 'I want the table to do some planning for the shop.'

He looked at her. 'You could have backed me up,' he muttered, rolling his eyes towards the cellar.

'I could have backed *you* up?' Anna carried on stacking the dishwasher. 'How? What was I supposed to say?'

'It's obvious, isn't it?' The cogs had obviously been whirring. 'I don't want my daughter prancing around half dressed in front of television cameras, letting them make her look ridiculous.'

Anna leaned on the table in front of him. She ignored the 'my daughter' bit. 'Come on, Phil, do you know how many weirdos audition for that programme?' she hissed. 'Thousands. She'd have to be very, *very* bad to get on to the part where they make them look ridiculous.'

His face twisted up and he dropped his voice. 'Do we know how bad she is?'

'Don't you mean how *good* she is?' Anna said. 'Have you listened to her recently? She sings for the whole of the school run. She *narrates* it. In song. And sometimes it even rhymes.'

Phil looked pained. 'Anna. I'm not into singing, you know that. I got the builders to soundproof that cellar for a reason. I love Chloe more than anything in the world, but even I realise she's no Mariah Carey. Apart from the mad demands. How bad are we talking?'

'She's . . . pretty good,' said Anna, trying to be fair. 'And she won't be on her own,' she added. 'There's the other three, whoever they are at the time.'

Phil clattered his spoon in the empty dish. 'It's not really the point, though, is it?' he said, looking thwarted. 'She acts as though she's twenty, but at the end of the day she's still my baby. If I go, I'll only wind up being on telly myself for lamping the judges when they don't let her win then and there. To be honest, I'd rather be the mean dad who wouldn't let her audition than have her upset. I couldn't bear it.'

Anna put her arms round him and kissed his head. 'You big

softy. It's not in any way a reluctance to spend all weekend in a queue with thousands of other Chloes?'

'Don't.' He closed his eyes and made a worryingly convincing 'soul-singer wobbly hand' gesture that made Anna wonder whether he'd been telling the truth about never watching talent shows.

She sank down onto the chair next to him. 'I don't want to see Chloe upset either, but it's literally all she talks about. If you don't let her go, she'll only demand to fly out for *American Idol*. Don't let it turn into "Mum loves me more than Dad" again, with a side order of "Dad thinks I'm a crap singer but Mum believes in me and my Journey".'

'It's typical of Sarah.' Phil rolled his eyes. 'Chloe's got her exams coming up. Sarah should be telling her to concentrate on those.'

'Then tell her she can go if her mocks are good. Or if she comes with me to read to her granny, or helps at the shop or something.'

'You are so sensible.'

'It's all relative.'

'Yeah, well, I bet Sarah's put her up to this. She was just like Chloe at that age, doing all the school musicals. She was Sandy in *Grease*. Spent all day walking round the school in her PVC trousers "to get into the part". All we boys thought about was how she got them on and off.' He paused and looked stricken. 'I hope Chloe's not wearing anything like that.'

Anna put the final plate in the dishwasher and said nothing.

It was hard to imagine Sarah in PVC trousers, or being fifteen, for that matter. Anna had only met her a handful of times, but she'd always been perfectly groomed, the ideal HR woman. That was the strange thing – Anna never felt jealous of Sarah and Phil's marriage. What gave her twinges were his references to their shared parenting, before the divorce. The births, the first steps, the tooth fairy. Stuff she'd never get to share, even though from now on, the girls would be in her life.

'I hope she can sing better than her mother,' said Phil, breaking into her thoughts. 'Sarah never hit one single note the entire concert, but no one noticed. She wore the PVC trousers for weeks. They got the part before she did.'

There wasn't much Anna could say to that, and she was struggling to come up with a response that wasn't nosy or jealous-sounding when Lily called through from the sitting room.

'Anna!'

'Yes?'

'Pongo wants his story now, please.'

'Tell him to get ready for bed first,' she called back. 'Then we'll have a chapter. Two if he makes sure you do your teeth properly.'

Phil looked at her, his mouth open. 'Pongo wants a story?' he repeated. 'You're kidding me. How did you manage to get Lily onto bedtime stories?'

'Not sure,' she admitted. 'But Pongo seems to love them.'

And Lily did too. They'd now nearly finished *One Hundred and One Dalmatians*, and Anna had even found Lily reading to herself one morning.

'Do you want to join us?' she asked.

Phil's mouth curved and she could tell he wanted to say yes. But he shook his head gently.

'No, it's all right,' he said. 'It's your thing. And I don't do voices as well as you do.'

Later on, upstairs, when she was reaching the end of the chapter and Lily's heavy eyelids were drooping while Pongo snored beside her, Anna looked up and caught Phil watching her from the half-closed door.

He smiled and put a finger to his lips so she wouldn't stop, and stood listening as Anna finished the part about the puppies rolling cleverly in soot to disguise their tell-tale spots. It always made her cry, so she was making a significant effort to keep it together.

Lily rewarded her performance with a loud snore.

Anna put the book down, turned Lily's nightlight on and tugged Pongo's collar to take him downstairs. She felt conscious of Phil's eyes on her, and hugged the moment to herself, hoping this would go some way to rebalancing Chloe's strop earlier.

See, she wanted to yell, and point at the tranquil scene. It could be like this!

Phil said nothing, but put his arms around her as she closed Lily's bedroom door to the exact inch-gap she insisted on. He pulled her to his chest and kissed her forehead with a tenderness that Anna found almost too painful to bear.

I I

'*A rescue pet, a champion race dog and a faithful
companion – Best Mate, Brighteyes, Paddywack
wherever he is, whatever his name – in* Born to
Run *teaches every reader that there is always
hope, just around the corner…*' Laura West

On a personal level, Michelle hated Valentine's Day – in her
opinion it was for teenagers and people in the first twelve
months of a relationship only – but from a sales point of view,
it was one of her favourite days of the year.

She bought plenty of ad space in the local paper for both
her shops, and the results were gratifying. Home Sweet Home
ran out of everything pink and heart-shaped a whole week
ahead of time, forcing her to bring out the new range of quilts
she'd been storing in the upstairs flat. They sold out too, which
only made her more excited about her bedlinen hunch.

But Anna had an even better Valentine's Day in the bookshop. 'Calorie-free' book bouquets sold out, as did the 'Read
Your Own Romantic Hero' kits for the single. She and
Michelle came up with a window display of chocolate hearts,
which customers could buy for their Valentine. Each one then
'led' to a special Valentine's gift in the shop – meaning they
were able to get rid of a lot of second-hand poetry, as well as a

number of *Guess How Much I Love You?* and *Winnie the Pooh* type kids' books, too.

All in all, it was a pretty good week for Michelle, marred only by a big padded card from 'an admirer' who didn't bother to change his handwriting or obscure the Kingston postmark. She had to trail over to the sorting office to collect it because it wouldn't go through the door, and then field a phone call from her mother enquiring as to whether she'd 'got any cards this year?'

Michelle thought about lying and saying no, but knew that would only result in the card being re-sent. She didn't dare say 'I got lots', either, in case that got back to Harvey too. Instead, she told her mother that yes, she'd got Harvey's card and that Owen had opened it, along with the stack of cards he got himself.

That bit was true. Owen received about seven, most of them purchased in Home Sweet Home.

After a brief burst of romantic spring sunshine, the weather turned gloomy, and the shadows seemed to return to the nooks and crannies. One morning, Kelsey refused to cover Anna's school-run hour in the afternoons, the hour when a new melancholy settled over the shop.

'There's something in there spooking me out,' she said, coming into the bookshop reluctantly. 'I've heard noises. In the back room.'

'What sort of noises?' Michelle stopped fixing silk flowers onto a pile of book bouquets and gave Kelsey her 'Don't mess with me' stare. Kelsey was prone to funny feelings, which usually came on when she sensed hard work approaching.

'I don't know. Like someone's in there. Watching me.'

'Are you sure it's not Rory moving around upstairs?' asked Anna, tidying up the coffee cups from the children's corner.

The gaggle of mummy friends had just left, but not before Anna had persuaded them to buy handfuls of Christine Pullein-Thompson books by arguing that it was cheaper than a real pony. 'It could be his son.'

'Yeah, he could be assembling a playpen,' said Michelle sardonically.

Anna gave her a reproachful look. Since Anna had come running back with the unexpected news that Rory the Bookworm was actually Rory the Love Rat, he'd become something of a talking point in quiet moments. As neither Michelle nor Kelsey would play Anna's 'what did the Famous Five grow up to be?' game, they'd taken instead to musing about what tragic or dramatic circumstances had led to an otherwise respectable man like Rory walking out on his pregnant girlfriend.

Michelle had no sympathy. She could tell Rory was the sort of man who'd read a book on breastfeeding then tell his wife she was doing it wrong. Kelsey had limited sympathy ('I saw this thing on telly about men who aren't ready to parent because they're still basically children themselves . . .'). Only Anna came up with more compassionate reasons why someone kind enough to visit an old man in a residential home might leave a pregnant woman, and even then, Michelle could tell she was only saying it because Anna was fundamentally incapable of being mean.

'It's the back room, it's definitely not upstairs,' Kelsey insisted. 'I've heard things, and I've gone in, and there's nothing there.'

'When was this?' asked Michelle, preparing to get forensic on her.

'The other afternoon, after you went to get Lily. I heard something move in there, but when I went in, there was no one there. Just a copy of *Tom's Midnight Garden* on the floor. Right in the middle of the floor.' Kelsey's eyes were round.

'No,' breathed Anna. '*Tom's Midnight Garden?*'

Michelle turned to Anna for clarification. 'Is the book significant?'

'You mean you haven't . . . ? No, of course you haven't read it. It's about a ghost,' said Anna. 'And a little boy who goes through a haunted garden and meets a little girl who . . . I don't want to spoil it,' she concluded. 'You should read it.'

'I'll put it on my list. Look, Kelsey,' said Michelle, 'if there is a ghost, it'd be Agnes Quentin, and she'd be leaving out books on How to Run a Bookshop.'

'I don't want to be in there on my own.' Kelsey's expression turned stubborn. 'Although I'll do it if Owen will sit in with me . . .'

'No,' said Michelle and Anna at the same time.

'I prefer Owen where I can see him,' added Michelle.

Kelsey folded her arms. 'Well, then, you'll have to ask Gillian, and she's been talking about getting her local priest in to spray it with water or whatever you're meant to do.'

Michelle sighed. 'Great.' What had she told Gillian? If Kelsey wasn't such a perfect dowsing rod for the 15–24 customer base, she'd think very hard about diva behaviour like this. Especially when Becca was turning out to be a very astute retail student.

'I've got to go, Michelle,' said Anna, checking her watch with a frown. 'I'm supposed to be taking Lily straight to a doctor's appointment and you know what they're like if you're late.'

'Go,' said Michelle. 'Don't worry about coming back. I'll close up here tonight. And you,' she said, pointing to Kelsey. 'You get back next door and sell some stuff.'

Kelsey grinned and tottered out on her jelly heels.

'See you later!' Anna grabbed her bag and dashed out.

'I'm expecting a headless horseman, at the very least!' Michelle called after them.

When they'd both gone, Michelle wandered around the bookshop, tweaking some of the displays and tidying the shelves here and there.

She didn't actually mind spending an hour or two in the bookshop. It was a nice space to be in now, of course, but the quiet time gave her a chance to spin her secret plans for its next incarnation – without any danger of being lectured about the sanctity of reading by Anna.

She'd been thinking about the bookshop all week. Michelle spent most Friday nights combing through her accounts, checking for fluctuations, fast sellers and dead wood, with the same fascination that she used to apply to the Top 40 at school, and although the bookshop figures were a lot better than she'd expected them to be, they were still only just nudging into the black. Not enough to justify keeping it going as a bookshop after the year was up, and maybe not even until then.

Anna's infectious enthusiasm was keeping the shop ticking over – her handmade posters, her impromptu book discussions, her recommendations – and some of it was down to basic local curiosity. But Michelle's instinct told her that she'd have to find some way of supporting the books if she wanted to keep hold of the shop. If it closed before then, Rory might decide to take the moral high ground and re-let it to someone else.

Michelle fluffed up the pile of mohair throws – 'reading blankets' – by the door, and chewed her lip. The blankets were providing a very useful bump in the shop's profits. She'd been at a trade fair in York the previous weekend, and had nearly bought the entire stock of a rugmaker who created beautiful bedside rugs from recycled remnants. Something like that would be easy enough to slip past Anna's eagle eye. She could put some down on the sanded boards, maybe a basket of them by the counter.

The display table of poetry would have to go. Michelle tried to think about how she could justify that to Anna, then made the executive decision to do it herself. Then and there. Anna might not even notice.

She scooped off the books and was preparing to move the table, when she heard a noise in the back room and stopped. It sounded like a book falling off a shelf.

Michelle put the table down and looked round for signs of an embarrassed customer. Only one customer had entered since she'd been in, and they'd left obviously disappointed that she wasn't Anna with a series of recommendations, but that didn't mean there wasn't someone lingering in the back. That was the thing about having those comfy chairs in the back room – they encouraged people to sink in and stay there for ages, reading.

Michelle wasn't normally a nervy person, and often stayed in Home Sweet Home after closing for hours on end, rearranging displays, but the idea of someone lurking in *this* shop with her was unsettling. Something about the books, maybe. Next door was so clean and calming, like her own house, but the bookshop had a different atmosphere. More thoughtful, more . . . layered, somehow. Less hers. More likely to have shelves with lives of their own, tipping books out at her to catch her attention.

Michelle told herself not to be so ridiculous and walked slowly towards the children's section, letting her heels click on the wooden floorboards to give whoever it was a chance to hear her. The last thing she wanted was to give some poor old dear a shock. Dusk had fallen quickly in the last few minutes and suddenly the shop was quite dark.

But when she peered into the back room there was no one there. The two battered leather armchairs were empty, the Union Jack cushions flat and a few big picture books scattered on the table between them.

Must have been the pipes, she decided, tidying the books back into the fruit crates and plumping up the cushions with quick, fierce thumps. Something falling down the chimney: a bird's nest, maybe. Michelle made a mental note to talk to Rory about the last survey. That was the trouble about taking over a place like this, you were never as confident about the building as you were when you'd bought it and renovated it yourself.

In fact, she argued, it was probably just *him*, making a noise upstairs. Maybe he'd got the abandoned wife hidden in a cupboard up there. Like Bluebeard.

Pleased with this selection of rational responses, Michelle went back to the desk and got her notebook out of her bag to review the day's to-do list, and jot down her thoughts about lambswool blankets.

The noise came again. Something falling, clattering onto the floor, and then scratching.

Michelle's heart gave an undeniable thump in her chest, and her skin crawled. That was definitely coming from the back room. That wasn't upstairs.

And there was nothing in the back room. Just as Kelsey had said.

'Oh, come on,' she said aloud. Who was she going to call? Ghostbusters? Rentokil?

Michelle got up again and clomped across the floor, hoping to send whatever it was scuttling back into the woodwork. As she went, she hit the switch and flooded the back room with light, but that only emphasised the very unsettling fact that it was totally empty.

Lying on the floor, though, face up, was a book. *Tom's Midnight Garden.*

Michelle felt a chill run through her and adrenalin flooded her bloodstream.

Behind her, the doorbell jangled and she nearly cricked her neck spinning round to see who it was. When she saw a figure standing in the doorway, her throat closed up in panic, but then the shape coughed and an irrational relief swept over her. Ghosts didn't cough.

But before the relief died down, a second, more visceral panic clutched her stomach. Was it Harvey? Had he been watching outside the shop, waiting until it was empty? Waiting until she was on her own?

'I'm sorry, I'm going to be closing in a few moments,' she said, her voice rather higher than normal as she strode towards the door, ready to slam it in his face if she had to. He wasn't coming into her house, and he wasn't coming into her shop either.

'Closing? I thought you were of the "Stay Open Till They've Bought Something" persuasion,' said a Scottish voice. 'Mind if I come in?'

As he stepped into the light, she saw that it was Rory, his scarf wound round his neck in a college-y fashion and his battered briefcase in one hand. He was smiling at her hopefully. Probably after a free coffee, she thought. Probably run out of milk.

'I'm still about to shut,' she said. Her voice wobbled. 'Did you want something in particular?'

He browsed the nearest table, as if he had all the time in the world. 'I'm looking for something to read to the old folk up at the residential home, something humorous and relatively short. What'd you recommend?'

'The *Radio Times*?'

'Maybe I'm asking the wrong person . . . I thought I might get a discount, in return for some reviews?' He raised an eyebrow, in a junior professor-ish manner. 'Cash for criticism?'

'It's only cash for compliments round here.' Michelle's heart was still thumping with unwanted adrenalin, and although she was itching to shut up shop, Rory's pragmatic presence was quite reassuring. How could there be ghosts in the back room when Rory was standing there in his tweed jacket, making terrible jokes? 'Are you going to be long?'

'That depends on how good you are at selling me something. Any coffee on the go? Anna usually makes me a cup. Helps the selection process no end.'

'I thought as much,' said Michelle. 'Only here for the free coffee.' She poured two cups from the filter jug, her hand wobbling slightly, spilling a few drops of coffee onto the table she'd just wiped clean.

'You've sussed me. Biscuit?' He looked up from a vintage Agatha Christie, his hair falling into his eyes.

The cheek of the man, thought Michelle.

'The café is next door,' she said.

'I meant, would you like a biscuit?' Rory opened his briefcase and produced a packet of ginger cookies from its depths. 'I've had so many free coffees in here, I thought it was only fair to reciprocate with some decent biccies. Since you're the owner, I thought I should give them to you.'

'Um, thanks.' Michelle felt churlish; they were expensive 'home-baked' ones from Waitrose, not the digestives they handed out. Although she didn't normally eat biscuits, she took one and nibbled it.

The biscuits would go on Anna's 'Rory's not a bastard' list, she thought, watching him as he read the back of a Dorothy L. Sayers novel, his brows beetled in concentration. How can a man who spends a fiver on gourmet biscuits to cancel out his coffee debt abandon a pregnant woman?

A companionable calm descended; she tidied while Rory browsed, but then the CD of quiet choral music came to an end. Michelle was walking over to restart it when she heard the noise from the back room.

'Didn't you hear that?'

'Hear what?' Rory looked up from the crime table.

'That noise.' As she spoke there was another rustling noise, like someone brushing against the woodwork.

'Don't look so scared,' said Rory. 'It's an old building, they creak all the time. I expect you live in some fabulous modern home with brand new double glazing, don't you?'

'I live down by the canal, thank you very much,' hissed Michelle. 'And I'm not scared.'

'You look a bit scared.'

'I'm not.'

'Want me to go and take a look?' He made a 'brave soldier' face.

'If you want.'

'I *do* want. I've often hoped this place might be haunted.' Rory rubbed his hands together with glee. 'Maybe it's Agnes, come back to keep an eye on you? A ghost would be such a feature. You could do haunted Hallowe'en nights in October, or *Christmas Carol* readings in—'

'Just go and have a look and tell me it's a bird stuck in the chimney,' said Michelle impatiently.

'Come with me,' said Rory. He beckoned with a long finger, then held out his hand. 'I'll need a corroborating witness if we're going to be on *Central Tonight* with the Midlands' first haunted bookshop.'

Michelle ignored the hand but followed him towards the back, trying to suppress the part of her brain that *was* suddenly considering the advantages of a haunted bookshop.

At the end of the main room, where the doorway had been knocked through to create one long space, she hesitated. Rory, though, strode on.

'It's not . . .' Michelle began, and then, as she spoke, something black darted across the room, and she let out a shriek.

It was huge. A huge black . . . rat? She almost wished it had been a ghost now, because whatever it was, it was massive – it looked like the sort of mega-rat that was meant to be breeding in the London sewage system. Michelle felt sick. The whole point of moving out of the big city was supposed to be getting away from things like that.

To her horror, Rory was on his knees, crawling towards it.

'I'll get a box,' she called, from a safe distance. 'We can trap it under there and get someone from the council to come and zap it.'

'No need,' said Rory. He sat up and reached into his jacket pockets, patting them down until he found what he was looking for. 'Ah. Good.'

'What the hell are you doing?' Michelle was frantically tipping paperbacks out of a nearby cardboard display box. 'Should I get gloves from next door? It's probably riddled with fleas.'

'Possible, but I doubt it.' Rory peeled off the top two Polo mints and offered them to the bottom shelf of boarding-school books in the children's section.

Michelle stared at his long fingers with horror, waiting for whatever it was to leap out and gnaw them with its sharp teeth.

'Come on,' said Rory, in a soothing, sing-song tone. 'It's OK, it's just me. Come on.'

Slowly, very slowly, a black nose appeared from under the shelf. A mass of black hair followed it and Michelle's stomach turned because it was filthy and dirty and still looking pretty mega-rat-like to her and . . .

'Don't *touch* it!' she blurted out, as Rory's hand deposited the Polos in the thing's mouth and then fondled its black ears.

'He's not an it,' said Rory. 'He's a he, thank you very much.'

Michelle put a table of local maps between it and herself. 'What the hell is *he*?'

'Charming. Tavish, this is Michelle Nightingale, your new landlady. Michelle, this is Tavish, your shop dog.'

'*My* shop dog?'

'Well, not yours, technically.' Rory reached out and grabbed hold of the collar buried under the matted coat. 'Cyril's.'

'There was nothing about a dog in the lease. How long's he been here?' She racked her brains. 'We've been open nearly two months, don't tell me he's been hiding under the floorboards all that time? What's he been eating?'

'I doubt he's been here that long. He's been living up at Four Oaks kennels since before Christmas, I do know that.' The dog was now snuffling about Rory's jacket pockets, in between licking his hand gratefully. Its tongue darted out from the matted fur, a shock of pink against the black. Michelle couldn't even make out any eyes.

'You're in a bit of a state, aren't you, laddie?' he crooned, more Scottish than ever. 'Ye couldn't get him a biscuit, could ye, Michelle? Poor wee lad's awful peckish.'

For a moment, Michelle considered telling Rory what to do with his dog, and his biscuit, but it was late, and she was tired, and spooked. Despite herself, relief was pounding through her system that it wasn't a ghost or a super-rat, neither of which would do her business any good.

And although the voice in her head was wailing in irritation, she couldn't help feeling sorry for the poor bedraggled mutt. He looked exhausted, and more scared than she was.

'Take him through to the staff room in the back,' she said. 'And stop doing that awful Braveheart voice.'

Rory straightened up, hoisted the little dog under his arm and smiled crookedly at it. He didn't seem to care that the dog was depositing dust and drool on his wool coat. In fact, he seemed quite pleased to see it, and Tavish seemed relatively sanguine about being tucked under his arm like a camp handbag.

'Shouldn't Scottish terriers be more trimmed than that?' she asked, before she could stop herself.

Rory turned his crooked grin in her direction. 'Bit of a personal question. He is, normally. Bit of a doggy expert, are we?'

'No,' said Michelle and marched out to the front of the shop to close up.

By the time she went back to the kitchen, both Rory and Tavish had got stuck in to a packet of digestives. She put a fresh cup of coffee in front of him, having made one for herself, and he slurped from it, setting Michelle's teeth on edge. She added to her own list of Rory's irritating tics, to counter the good biscuits.

'So, how come he's here and not up at the kennels?' she said, nodding at the dog. 'This would be a good time to come clean, you know. Have you been keeping him in the flat? As well as your occasional child?'

'I beg your pardon?' Rory stared at her, surprised.

'Anna mentioned you had a son. The buggy, the other day. Upstairs. You never said it was *your* child when you told us to move the books.'

It had sounded a lot less rude in her head. Michelle wished it hadn't slipped out, but now it had, she couldn't take it back. Living alone had made her very witty on email, but not so good on non-edited, real-time conversation.

'Should I have done?' Rory carried on staring at her, and she found his expression hard to read. He wasn't embarrassed, but he was clearly ticked off at being discussed. 'I do have a son, yes, with my ex. And what else did Anna say?'

'Nothing. Well . . .' Michelle realised that she was annoyed he wasn't embarrassed. Walking out on a pregnant woman was about as low as it got. It was cowardly. 'She didn't say anything else. Just that you and the mother split up before the baby was born.'

'We did. I ended it, as a matter of fact.' He sipped his coffee and regarded her squarely over the top of the mug. 'Sorry, should I have issued you with some kind of press release about it? I didn't realise you were running some kind of relationship drop-in centre as well as a bookshop.'

It hung between them, along with Michelle's bubbling sense of outrage and his defensiveness. Hot air and cold air, mingling. Michelle couldn't put her finger on why she felt so furious on behalf of a woman she'd never met, but she did. She fizzed with it.

'Life is complicated,' he said, in response to her glower. 'I'm sure there are things in your life that haven't worked out the way you hoped.'

Michelle opened her mouth to argue back, but something knowing in his tone stopped her. Was it so obvious, her failed marriage? Did he know? Was her mother right – that women who walk out on perfectly good marriages, looking for greener grass, 'have that desperate air about them'?

'You're right,' she said stiffly. 'It's none of my business.'

Rory looked surprised, as if he'd expected more of a fight from her.

'What?' She lifted her hands. Refusing to argue always wrongfooted Harvey; it was a tactic that had taken her a long time to learn. 'I'm sure you had very good reasons.'

He left a thoughtful pause, then said sadly, 'I did.'

'Good. So did I.'

'For what?' The grey eyes were right on her face, at once, reading her.

Michelle couldn't believe he'd lulled her into that. 'For . . . the things that haven't worked out,' she said. Even that was more than she'd intended to say.

Rory said nothing, but let the tension slowly dissolve, which was helped by the dog's curious snuffling.

'So this was Cyril's dog?' asked Michelle, for something to say. 'I didn't notice it in the park. Did he walk him?'

Rory had brushed Tavish's coat and now Michelle could make out a pair of shiny boot-button eyes above the black beard. He was staring at her with the same unnerving directness that Rory had.

'Not since Agnes died. She had a little West Highland White terrier called Morag. You must have seen them. They used to go to the dog café on the high street.'

'Oh,' said Michelle, remembering. 'Anna used to call them

the salt and pepper dogs. Did they have matching coats?'

'They did. Agnes and Morag died about the same time, then Tavish just stayed in with Cyril. I used to give him a quick trot round the block every so often, when I moved in upstairs. You'd be amazed how fast he could shift when he got near that café; I used to wonder if maybe he thought they'd be there, waiting for him.'

As he spoke, Rory stroked the dog's long upright ears and it leaned in towards him, comforted. Michelle felt her heart-strings being tugged, but she resisted. She knew from experience how easy it was to let dogs sneak under your defences, and she had no room for one right now. Her heart still ached for Flash every time she spotted a spaniel in the park, and more than once, lonely in the middle of the night, she'd come up with a wild plan to kidnap him from the house when Harvey was at work.

Maybe in Phase Two, when she'd established both businesses, sold Swan's Row for a profit and met an attractive silver-fox type man, she'd go back and get him. When she wasn't scared of Harvey turning up, demanding access.

'Did you run back here looking for your master?' Rory asked the terrier, tickling his beard. 'Have you been looking all over the town for him?'

'Don't!' That had kept her awake for months, the heart-breaking image of Flash escaping to look for her, getting lost, starving, alone. 'He's fine now,' she said, when Rory looked at her, startled at her outburst. 'Can't we just take him up to Cyril, if he's such a quiet dog?'

'Nope. They've got a strict no-pets policy at Butterfields. That's why we had to take him to the rescue centre on the hill. Well, *I* had to take him.'

'You did? Is that something you offer all your clients?'

Rory looked properly cross. 'His son didn't have time, and Cyril couldn't face handing Tavish in – abandoning him, as he put it – so I said I'd do it. Not a fun experience.' Tavish licked Rory's hand. 'I'd hoped someone would had given him a nice retirement home by now. I'd have taken him in myself, but we can't have dogs in the office. Litigation risk. Shame, really, because he'd just sleep under the desk all day. They'd never know he was there.'

'All dog owners say that,' said Michelle darkly. 'You *always* know they're there. They have ways of making their presence felt.'

Rory snapped a biscuit in two, offered half to Tavish, and raised his eyebrow.

'And that doesn't help,' she said without thinking. 'He'll get plaque.'

Rory gave Tavish the biscuit. 'We've got to take our small pleasures where we can, at his age.'

Michelle's heartstrings gave a mighty twang and she steeled herself. 'Give the rescue a call, let them know we've got him,' she said. 'He can sleep down here tonight if they can't come and get him till tomorrow.'

Clearly anxious at being left again, the little dog followed Rory as he tried to go, but he bent down and picked him up, plopping him on Michelle's knee.

'There,' he said. 'You might want to try to make friends with the wicked witch. She's your new landlady for tonight.'

'Just for tonight,' said Michelle, raising a finger at them both.

12

'*Charlotte's Web is a brave, beautiful story about true friendship, life, death and writing. I never ate a bacon sandwich afterwards or killed a spider.*'   Anna McQueen

When Anna arrived at the shop in the morning, having dropped Lily at school with a promise to talk to Pongo about whether he wanted to read *The Starlight Barking* next, she was surprised to see Michelle and Rory standing by the front desk, apparently engaged in quite an animated discussion.

Rory was definitely talking while Michelle kept trying to interrupt him by waving her arms about and pointing at things. Particularly something by the lower crime shelves.

Anna was intrigued. What could they be talking about? Not books, surely. More likely it was something to do with the shop. Michelle had her business face on. Her stern one.

Don't glare like that, Michelle, thought Anna, with a rush of matchmaking excitement. Be nice to him! Rory was single – despite the child complication – and there weren't many nice single men under fifty in Longhampton. Not many that were smart enough for Michelle, anyway. She'd despatched most of them over the starters round at the McQueens, just for liking football or short-sleeved shirts.

Rory's body language was a lot more encouraging than

Michelle's: he was really trying to engage her attention. Not only was he smiling and pulling amused faces, he reached into his briefcase and offered her a book. Michelle, predictably, did her best not to take it.

Then Michelle glanced up, responding to a question, and although Anna ducked, it was too late. Michelle caught sight of her and pointed through the window display, then pointed to the desk, then at her watch.

Anna pushed open the door and went in, all casual smiles.

'Good, you're here,' said Michelle, rubbing her hands together briskly as if she'd been caught doing something she shouldn't. 'Just to let you know, Rachel from the kennels will be coming in before ten to collect Tavish . . .'

'Tavish!'

Anna crouched down, delighted, as the stubby black terrier skittered across the floor towards her, his pink tongue sticking out from his square head. She kept her fingers at a wary distance; her memories of Tavish were of a 'characterful' elderly emperor, rather than a love-sponge like Pongo, who'd been trained from an early age to endure endless cuddles. 'What are *you* doing here?'

'He tunnelled out of the camp and came home,' said Rory. 'Like Greyfriars Bobby.'

'Oh, don't. We read that at school when I was little and I never got over it. Mum says I cuddled every statue of a dog for miles.' Anna cautiously stroked Tavish's ears. 'Where's Tavish living now? Don't tell me he made his way back from wherever Mr Quentin's son lives?'

'No, he was dropped off at the rescue like an unwanted sofa,' said Michelle. 'And don't look so droopy, Barbara Woodhouse – if Mr Quentin cared so much about his dog he'd have put some kind of legal protection order on him, like he did with his precious bookshop.' She shot a pointed glance at Rory, but didn't give him the chance to reply. 'So the dog should be out of here by lunchtime, and I've marked up that list of orders you left last night. I've authorised payment at the warehouse, so go ahead and arrange delivery of the ones I've actioned. I don't want to go overboard,' she added, raising her hands against Anna's protest, 'I know we're doing all right, but we need to focus on selling what's here, first.'

Anna glanced at the list and winced. Michelle had been busy; every page was covered in her direct handwriting – notes and suggestions everywhere. For someone who didn't read, she had very specific ideas about which books should be in the shop. Or not.

'Right, then, I'm off next door. See you later.' She wrapped her scarf round her neck and gave Tavish a last beady look. 'Give the floor a sweep once he's gone,' she added to Anna. 'Hairs. They get everywhere.'

'And you'll read the book?' Rory prompted.

'It can join the queue behind all the ones I've told her to read,' said Anna, before Michelle could make something up.

'Ha ha,' said Michelle, and swept out in a jingle of bells.

'What's the book?' Anna asked casually, as she dumped her satchel on the chair and checked the diary.

'*The Bookshop* by Penelope Fitzgerald. It's short. It even has a poltergeist – I was reminded of it, last night.' Rory looked faintly annoyed. 'Is she always so touchy about people offering her reading material? Don't bookshop owners have to come into contact with books now and again?'

'Don't take it personally,' said Anna. 'She thinks we're forming a conspiracy of bookworms to undermine her non-reading stance.'

'How can someone as smart as Michelle not like reading?'

'Don't ask me. I think she's got a bit of a chip on her shoulder about not having gone to university, which hardly matters when you look at what she's achieved.' Anna realised she might be straying into indiscreet waters. 'So, you found Tavish last night?' She leaned against the wall as the coffee machine spluttered into life.

'Yup. You're not haunted, I'm sorry to have to tell you,' said Rory. 'We think he must have been hiding in the back for a day or two. Took a while to get the dust out of his coat. Tavish doesn't care too much for grooming. You be good for Anna now, wee man.'

Anna watched as Rory hitched up his trousers and folded his lanky frame down to give Tavish a goodbye scratch, revealing a sudden, unexpected flash of bright yellow sock between his trouser-leg and brogue. Tavish raised his head to accept the attention with a dignified pride, and Anna's heart softened like ice cream.

There was something reassuring about a man who got on well with dogs, she thought. Phil pretended that Pongo was the most stupid thing Sarah had ever given the girls, and that he was more trouble than an extra child, but Anna had caught him more than once, asleep with Pongo's big head draped over his shoulder, the two of them snoring on alternate breaths.

'I'm going up to Butterfields this lunchtime,' she said impulsively. 'Should I tell Mr Quentin about Tavish turning up here looking for him? Do you reckon that I might persuade them to bend the "no pets" rule?'

Rory looked up at her, obviously wanting to agree but struggling with lawyerly reason. 'I don't know. It might upset him if they said no. And he keeps asking me if I know whether he's been re-homed or not yet, so if he's running away that's just more to worry about.'

'You're right,' said Anna. 'Best not.'

'No more running away, Tavish,' he said, then stood up. 'Right, off to the coalface of justice. Bye now, Anna.'

Rory smiled, but Anna thought his sardonic eyes had lost their usual sparkle. Not quite as sad as Tavish's, but close.

Tavish stayed so quietly under the front desk that Anna almost forgot he was there. She'd only had a couple of customers – one lady coming in to collect an overnight order that had arrived, and another browser, who didn't come in for anything in particular, but left with a set of Sherlock Holmes mysteries, after a long conversation about why it was that everyone seemed to discover Sherlock Holmes while they were in bed sick with something.

Tavish pricked up his ears each time the bell jangled, but settled back to a doze soon after, settling himself eventually on Anna's foot like a warm cushion.

He finished the shop off perfectly, Anna thought, as she flipped through her counter copy of *The Jungle Book* and ate her early lunch sandwich while Tavish chased rabbits in his sleep. A shop dog. Michelle might be furious about the hairs, but he added a quirky charm to the place, like the bunting pinned above the novels. Only Tavish had been there long before them.

She peered under the desk and watched him sleeping. The silver hairs around his eyes and nose gave him a bespectacled, learned look, like a grumpy Scottish professor.

Rachel hadn't arrived by the time Kelsey came in to cover her lunch break, and Anna ran through the instructions, while Kelsey and Tavish eyed each other warily. Kelsey, by her own admission, 'wasn't good with animals'.

'He's not going to chew any books, is he?' Kelsey asked. 'Or attack anyone for coming in?'

'What do you think?' asked Anna, slinging her bag of reading books over her shoulder. 'He's worked here longer than we have. Call me if Michelle has any problems and don't forget to let him out for a pee.'

Mr Quentin was one of the residents already gathered in the circle of chairs for the story session when Anna walked into the big day room with Joyce and two of her daycare assistants.

She smiled at him but he didn't smile back immediately. There was a slight delay with all his reactions now, as if he had to think before each one. The crisp bookseller's mind that had once had entire libraries of novels and reference books, tank details and Longhampton Cricket Club, lined up in neat cross-referenced rows was now messy, the facts all still there but in loose leaves, blowing around, disordered, like the back room of the shop, before they'd tidied it up.

He'd been neat, too, in the bookshop, with a red hanky square in his top pocket and a Homburg hat for walking out with the dogs and his wife. Anna realised she'd forgotten that image until this moment – Mr and Mrs Quentin walking their two freshly clipped dogs past the town hall like something from an Ealing comedy. Two matching pairs like ghosts from a different Longhampton time, superimposed on a messier, less stylish street.

Anna's throat swelled, seeing the rumpled collar of Mr Quentin's shirt beneath the lumpy jumper, but Joyce bustled her along with her brisk instructions to 'get everyone's hearing aids turned up and listening ears on'.

'Lovely, everyone's here. Apart from your mum-in-law,' she added to Anna when they were ready.

'Don't call her mum,' she muttered back. 'She hates that.'

'Does she? Well, she has some funny ways, bless her . . . Ah,

Mrs McQueen!' Joyce called across the room, as the door opened and Evelyn entered.

'Am I late?' said Evelyn, sounding more hopeful than sorry. She had finally discarded the hated Zimmer frame, and was walking with a stick that gave her a faintly menacing, regal air. 'The stupid girl who does the hairdressing – is she on work experience? I had to tell her what to do myself. And you should speak to her about her language.'

'Your hair looks lovely,' said Anna. Chloe's obsession with her hair was a genetic bequest from Evelyn, along with her need for constant attention.

'No, it doesn't,' snapped Evelyn. 'I look as if I've been set upon by apes. Apes with hairspray.'

Joyce giggled, which was not Evelyn's desired reaction.

'I realise that hairdressing is probably wasted on most of the women in here, if you can still call them women,' she began, without bothering to lower her voice, but fortunately for Joyce, someone's hearing aid started to whistle and Anna seized the chance to begin while she was sorting it out.

Evelyn stalked off to the furthest chair and pouted. Her lips, outlined today in lurid coral lipstick, looked deadly.

'I thought I'd read some P. G. Wodehouse,' said Anna, ignoring Evelyn's bored sigh. 'We've had a request.'

'Makes a change from all those *women's* books,' said an elderly man, with feeling. He and Mr Quentin were the only men there, surrounded by old women like two droopy cockerels in a barn of hens.

Mr Quentin finally smiled at her, and she smiled back, and began.

Anna's voice lifted and wound around the circle of chairs as she read the story – yet another one about Bertie's troubles with his 'least favourite aunt', Agatha – but it was only when she reached the part about Aunt Agatha's West Highland White dog, Mackintosh, that she noticed Mr Quentin's expression change from quiet enjoyment to sadness.

Anna kicked herself. Now she'd begun it was impossible to turn back. She carried on, getting a few quiet chuckles out of the audience, and when she finished, Joyce immediately leaped in with her discussion questions, designed to keep their minds active for a little longer, while the memories were still freshly shuffled.

Mr Quentin, Anna noticed, stayed where he was, gazing into space.

'Ooh, I bet that brought back memories?' Joyce prompted. 'Who had an aunt like that? Florence? Didn't you have a funny old stick of an auntie who was a nippy in a Lyons Cornerhouse?'

'I still do!' insisted Florence, and the conversation kicked off in that strange dimension between past and present, a mixture of half memories and startling comments, some of which, when they popped out of the speaker's mouth, left them as surprised as the person next to them.

Anna usually liked to stay and listen to the stories, but she was worried about leaving Kelsey in charge for too long. She stuffed the book back into her bag and hurried over to where Mr Quentin was sitting, not quite knowing what she was going to say, but wanting to say something.

'Mr Quentin,' she began, 'I'm sorry, I didn't mean to . . .'

He beat her to it, lifting his watery eyes with a sad smile. 'That brought back memories, my dear. Do you remember our Morag? Our Westie? She was quite a lady.'

'She was a poppet,' Anna managed, already feeling her eyes go hot.

'Agnes was always much better with the dogs than I was,

fussing about with boiled chicken and what have you, but you do miss them when they're gone. I still look around expecting to see old Tavish.' He sighed, and the sound said more than words could have done. It was the regret of a man who wasn't supposed to miss a dumb animal quite as much as he did.

'I . . .' Anna's voice stuck in her throat.

'Will you do something for me, dear?' he asked, and she knew it wasn't going to be a query about the bookshop.

She nodded.

'Will you ask that nice lady at the rescue if she couldn't keep Tavish herself? I've been thinking about him, you see, in that lonely place, being passed over for younger dogs who can run about and play, and such like. I don't mind paying for his food and board, just so long as I know he's with someone kind. Not having to try to get used to strangers, who don't know his habits.' His voice cracked. 'He's a grumpy old thing, like me, you see, and I can't stand the thought of anyone being impatient with the daft old mutt. At his age.'

Anna blinked. She'd seen some of the older rescue dogs waiting in the runs when she'd taken Pongo up for his holidays. Some of them looked up so hopefully each time a human entered the kennel block, then sank back down again, despondent, when they were passed over. Some didn't even look up any more. Anna nearly left with an extra dog every time.

Anna grabbed his hand and squeezed her lips together, trying not to cry. 'Leave it with me,' she said, and when Mr Quentin turned his face away, she had to hurry out of the room before he saw the tears rolling down her face.

Her eyes were still blurry when she marched down the high street, en route to the bookshop, and bumped into Rory outside his office.

'Steady on,' he said, catching her arms. 'Are you all right?'

She shook her head. 'Has Rachel been for Tavish yet?'

'I don't know. I've just nipped out for some lunch. What's up?'

Anna didn't bother hiding her smudged eyeliner as he peered at her. Rory had a kind face, an old-fashioned one, with his clean-shaven jaw. He should be wearing a hat, she thought; he had that rather period drama sort of air.

'Rory, we *have* to do something about Tavish,' she gabbled. 'We have to keep him somehow, I don't know how, but poor Mr Quentin . . . he actually offered me money to make sure Tavish got a good home. And he's already run away looking for his master once, and I've seen how far it is from the rescue. He's old. He must be exhausted, sleeping rough and not being fed . . .'

Anna was vaguely aware that she was now mingling *One Hundred and One Dalmatians* with the real story of Tavish, but she didn't care.

'You've been reading too many books,' said Rory, but he squeezed her shoulders. 'Look, I don't want to see the old mutt passed from pillar to post either. Let's think logically. Can *you* take him?'

'I wish I could, but I don't know if he'd get on with Pongo. He's a ball of energy at the best of times. It would be like moving Prince Philip in with Jedward.'

'Well, I'd have him, but I'm out all day.'

Anna shook her head. 'Rachel would never let you take him if you work full time.'

'Fair enough. What about Michelle?'

'No,' she said at once. 'She hates dog hair in her house. She won't even let Pongo into the house unless he's in his dog bag.'

'Dog bag. Why am I not surprised?' Rory pinched his

eyebrows together as if he was thinking, then said, 'Why don't we go and have a chat with Michelle, anyway?'

'She'll just say no.'

'Where there's a lawyer, there's a plan.' He grinned, and his funny *Brief Encounter* face seemed boyish. 'Maybe I can persuade her.'

Michelle knew she shouldn't start tempting herself until she had her shop plan fully thought out, but a supplier had sent her a preview email of the most gorgeous merino wool blankets she'd ever seen, and it was very hard not to whip out her business credit card and place a sizeable order then and there.

I could get a few for Home Sweet Home, see how they go, she thought, scrolling through the email and mentally piling the cherry-blossom-pink blankets on the dresser where she currently had hand-knitted hot-water-bottle covers.

The image shifted in her head to the big brass-framed bed she planned to have where the children's section currently was next door, whereupon it turned into a much more lavish display, with matching hand-stitched quilts from the Pennsylvania craft co-operative she'd found online, and sheepskin booties from Cornwall arranged on the shelves behind. The bookshelves could stay: they'd be perfectly sized for nets of beeswax soap and a few cosily appropriate paperbacks. Lilac- and cream-coloured ones, ideally. Maybe a few of those vintage orange Penguins.

Michelle jotted down 'A Book at Bedtime?' on her notepad and poked a fork into the remains of her pasta salad from the deli.

Her New Year's resolution not to work through her lunch break had slipped by mid January, but there was so much to do with two shops that she had no choice. Currently she was in the whitewashed office at the back of Home Sweet Home because she didn't want to leave Gillian alone in the shop now Kelsey was next door covering for Anna.

Anna, who – she checked her watch – should be back from her mission of reading mercy any minute now.

She jotted down some more bedlinen thoughts, one ear cocked for sounds of retail emergency from the shop, then heard footsteps approaching the back office.

Please not Owen, she thought. He'd already started making noises about needing a 'temporary loan' to cover some expenses. She wasn't sure what they could be, either, since he seemed to turn up at her house for supper at least every other night and spent more time than she'd bargained for lounging around her sitting room. She didn't mind that; since the fright she'd had in the shop, she was secretly relieved to have someone there, in case Harvey did turn up. But still there was no sign of a new website, despite her frequent prompts.

She circled 'Website – Owen!' on her to-do list, then underlined it.

'Michelle?'

She looked up. Anna was standing in the doorway, looking flushed and excited, strands of blond hair escaping from her knitted beret. Her eyes were shining as if she'd been crying, but she seemed happy, not upset.

Anna's face was like a plate-glass shop window into her soul, thought Michelle. No curtains, nothing. No wonder those girls ran rings around her.

'What?'

'Um, can you come next door? There's something I need to talk to you about.'

'To do with the shop?'

'Sort of.' Anna hopped from foot to foot. 'And no, I can't do it here.'

Michelle sighed and put the remains of her lunch back into the paper takeaway bag for later.

It didn't take Rory and Anna long to set out their suggestion and it took Michelle even less time to say no.

'I don't want a dog,' she repeated, in case it hadn't yet broken through their wall of pleading.

'But why not? It's not like you're jetting off on minibreaks every weekend.' Anna's soft-as-butter heart was right out on display. 'You said it yourself, you *like* staying in. Tavish could stay in with you.'

'I might want to *go* on minibreaks.' Michelle cast a sideways look at Rory, in case he was sniggering at her. 'And anyway, I'm away most weekends, at trade fairs.'

'You could take him with you. He's small. You could get him a carrycase!'

'I don't want a dog who goes in a handbag,' said Michelle. 'That's not what dogs do.'

'He's lived in a shop all his life,' said Rory. 'You and he are soulmates. You're retail trained. You're his ideal owner, even if you didn't lease his old house. Which you do.'

Michelle struggled against the feelings of tightness that were compressing her chest. It wasn't just the sense of being ganged up on by two people who'd read one too many *Lassie* books, or even guilt that she was betraying Flash somehow, but a darker panic that filled up inside her like an inflating balloon. She didn't like other people, other *things*, impinging on the calm order she'd built around herself. It was too hard to explain without sounding like a nutcase, so maybe it was easier to let them think it was about her carpets.

'A dog is a tie I don't need right now,' she snapped, her voice suddenly sharp. 'I mean, having to think about something else all the time. Feeding it, training it . . . And before you even suggest it, no, that dog *cannot* go and live with Owen in the flat. It's bad enough worrying about what *he's* doing to the carpet.'

'Tavish doesn't need training,' said Rory. 'He's nearly eleven – he's as trained as he's ever going to get. That's like eighty in human years.'

Michelle raised an eyebrow. 'That's not selling it to me either. I know what elderly dogs are like. *Unreliable.* Anna, how often do you hoover?' She pointed accusingly at her. 'And don't pretend it isn't twice a day.'

'*Twice* a . . . ?' Anna looked guilty. 'Er, right, yeah. But he won't shed as much as Pongo. I've had a look on the internet.'

'No.'

'But, Michelle . . .' She pointed to where Tavish was sitting in an empty orange crate, his bearded head regarding the shop with an imperial air. 'Look at him. Look at him. No one's going to adopt a dog his age. He's been loved all his life, and now he'll probably die in a concrete run. All alone. No wonder he's desperate to come home.'

'No.'

'What about a dog share?' said Rory.

'Give me a break.' Michelle turned her attention to him. 'I thought you were the logical side of this.'

'I am. Tavish would be fine in the shop during the day. And I'd have him at night. Or some weekends, because I've never been on a minibreak in my life.' He put the word 'minibreak' into air apostrophes, which irritated Michelle. 'I didn't think anyone had minibreaks outside *Bridget Jones.*'

'I'm not Bridget bloody Jones,' she snapped.

'You have read *Bridget Jones' Diary*?' asked Anna hopefully.

'No, I saw the film,' said Michelle. 'Customer,' she added, glad of the distraction as a woman struggled in through the door with a pushchair.

Anna rushed over to hold the door, and immediately started chatting about whatever it was that bookish people chatted about, which usually led to them buying something from her.

Rory took Michelle's elbow and steered her discreetly into the Local Interest section.

'Don't start,' she said, in a warning tone. 'I thought you'd realised by now that when I say no I mean no.'

'Like when you said you didn't want to run this as a book-shop, then changed your mind?' Rory fixed her with his unsettling half-smile. 'Look, Mr Quentin is very fond of that little dog. Very fond.'

Michelle stared back at him. She didn't like the faint note of reproach in his tone. 'There's nothing in the lease that says I have to house his pets as well as his unsellable collection of military history books.'

'Not in so many words.' Rory cast a sideways look to make sure Anna was occupied with the customer. 'But surely a busi-nesswoman like you can see that there might be significant advantages to doing a personal favour for your landlord. It might perhaps lead him to do you a return favour somewhere down the line?'

Michelle's brain raced, trying all the possible explanations like locks. She didn't want to pick the wrong one.

Was he saying that if she took in the dog, Mr Quentin might drop his ridiculous insistence on the premises remaining as a loss-making bookshop rather than a profitable linen heaven?

Was that really it? Rory was almost as much of an evangelical paperback worshipper as Anna and Mr Quentin. Was this dog really that important? Or was Rory just unable to pass over a deal?

Michelle's opinion of him dropped again, irrational as that seemed.

Her gaze strayed across to where Tavish was patiently receiving the attentions of Anna and the woman who'd just come in; Anna had put a cushion in the crate for him, and he already looked like he'd been there since about 1954. Michelle had to admit it – he added a certain bookish ambience to the place. He was a canine Kelsey.

She thought hard. It was already March. Even if the bookshop carried on making the tiny profit it was currently making she still had to carry it for another nine months; there was no money here to cover any emergency repairs, or more wages. She could just about juggle the numbers to give Anna enough to order a constant basic level of stock, but if Mr Quentin could be persuaded that A Book at Bedtime was pretty much the same thing as a bookshop, just with added beds . . .

Michelle felt a flash of guilt, but she tamped it down quickly. Books and beds. They went together well enough – it would just be a case of . . . proportion. There wouldn't be quite so many books as there were now.

'Are you thinking yes?' Rory pressed her.

'Weekends or weeknights?'

'Either. We can rotate.'

'And who'll walk him?'

'He won't need much. I can do alternate lunchtimes.'

'Food?'

'Doubt he eats that much. We can do a monthly kitty contribution. Say, twenty quid?'

Rory's responses were quick and professional, unlike the bumbling manner he'd had in his offices. It gave a sleek confidence to his face, which she had to admit was quite attractive. For a baby-abandoning love rat.

'And you'll work on lifting the bookshop clause earlier if possible?'

'I will speak to Mr Quentin both in my capacity as his executor and as co-guardian of his dog.'

Michelle wondered if he'd been so accommodating or enthusiastic when it came to custody of his kid.

'Done,' she said.

Anna came rushing over. 'Michelle,' she hissed. 'It's Rachel, from the rescue kennels. She's come for Tavish. What should I tell her?'

Rory and Anna stared at her expectantly. Between Rory's stupid floppy hair and Anna's appley blondeness, they looked like two of the Secret Seven, thought Michelle. How did this happen?

Was it the shop? In which case, she didn't want to know what she was turning into.

'Tell her . . . Tavish can stay,' she said, and hoped she wasn't making a big mistake.

13

'There's something refreshingly honest about the
Malory Towers *and* Chalet School *books; being*
rich or beautiful is never as important as being
kind or brave. And there's always comeuppance!
And midnight feasts.' Rachel Fenwick

'You know, I never thought I'd say this to a potential new owner,' said Rachel from the kennels, gazing around Michelle's elegant sitting room, her face soft with envy, 'but I think your house is almost *too nice* to bring a dog into.'

'Thank you,' said Michelle with a proud smile.

Though Rachel was technically part of the mafia-like Longhampton dog set, since she owned the kennels and was married to the town vet, she didn't wear a quilted gilet or match her winter coat to her dog's. She was one of Michelle's best customers at Home Sweet Home, and was the only person Michelle knew who didn't talk about London as if it was some imaginary destination like Narnia, or Heaven.

Had Michelle had more free time to be sociable, or had Rachel been a jogger, they'd probably have got on really well, thought Michelle.

'I can't believe you didn't have some interior designer in to do it.' Rachel looked around, taking in the restored floorboards and mouldings. Her clipboard checklist dangled from her hands, all the boxes ticked and most additional space filled with jotted websites and decorating tips Michelle had passed on as they'd walked around.

'Oh, it's just all things I like.' Michelle shrugged modestly, but she knew the sitting room was looking particularly good today, with the spring sunshine reflecting off the canal water, sending ripples of light onto the china blue walls. There were splashy bunches of bright yellow daffodils everywhere, and she'd brought a whole box of scented candles home, as preparation for serious dog-odour masking.

Tavish had gone back to the kennels for a night or two of pampering – really, Rachel confided, because the staff up there wanted to say goodbye – and in the meantime, she and Rory had equipped themselves for his arrival in their houses.

Michelle wasn't sure what Rory had done, but she'd designated an area at the far end of her kitchen for Tavish and bought the only half-stylish bed she could find in the pet superstore. She'd resisted the temptation to go mad with cushions and toys; Tavish was a lodger, not a tenant.

Rachel picked up a blown-glass dove and sighed. 'I wish I had time to do things to my house. I used to read all the magazines – you know, *Elle Decor* and *House Beautiful* . . .' She laughed. 'Those days of minimalist white carpets are gone, gone, gone.'

'Why? What happened?' Privately, Michelle didn't understand people who let their houses get into a state. All it took was a routine, and some discipline and proper storage. 'I don't see you living in a tip,' she went on, noting Rachel's perfectly messed haircut and dark red nails. 'I see you with a scrubbed kitchen table and lots of Irish linen.'

Rachel laughed aloud, a generous noise tinged with just a little regret. 'I wish! No, I moved out of a chic studio flat into a massive old house, and I had a baby, and a dog, and I ended up living with a man who thinks tidiness is a sign of not enough to do . . . Your priorities change, don't they?' She put the glass dove down. 'Luckily for me, most of the time home checks reassure me I'm not the only one with a pile of stuff in every corner. Not today, though!'

Michelle smiled tightly, but she felt a pinch of resentment at the 'priorities' comment, more so because up till then, she'd been feeling a sort of camaraderie with Rachel, as stylish-offcomers-in-arms. Why did having kids provide you with some kind of moral trump card that turned an elegant house into a sign of 'not enough to do'? Making your living environment as relaxing as possible wasn't some kind of failure.

'But anyway, you've motivated me to go home and tidy up,' Rachel went on with a final glance at Michelle's built-in cupboards. 'Shall we have a look at your back garden?'

Once the garden had been approved ('Fences, great – not that Tavish will want to go far . . .') and admired ('Those pots! Where did you find them?'), Rachel handed over a stapled set of pages to Michelle.

'It's our standard set of guidelines for first-time owners,' she explained. 'My husband, the world's bossiest vet, wrote them, and he does go on, but it's better than having the lecture directly from him.'

'I've had dogs before,' said Michelle. 'I had . . .' She paused, conscious that even Anna didn't know what she was about to tell Rachel. She hadn't mentioned it because she was ashamed at having left Flash behind, at not having fought harder for him when Anna had struggled so much to love Pongo along with the girls. It would also have led to awkward questions about Harvey, and she didn't want to have to answer those either.

'I had a spaniel with my ex,' she confessed. 'Flash. He's a lovely dog, a working cocker, black and white. Speckly nose.'

'Aw.' Rachel looked sympathetic. 'The ex got custody?'

'Sort of. I wanted to move out here for a fresh start, and Flash spent a lot of time with my parents' dogs, so . . .' Michelle shrugged. 'My ex suggested weekend access but I didn't want to confuse him.'

Him meaning Flash *and* Harvey.

'That's tough,' said Rachel. 'I bet you miss him.'

Michelle nodded, but didn't say anything, and Rachel interpreted her silence as regret, carrying on with comforting briskness.

'Still, it's brilliant that you're giving Tavish a home now. It's a bit unconventional, this dog sharing, but I think it's better than him being in kennels. Speaking of which . . .' She checked her watch. 'I need to get round to Rory's flat, give it the once over.'

'I'll give you a lift,' said Michelle. 'He's left a set of keys at the shop to let you in if he's not already there. Do you need to interview him?'

'Rory? No.' Rachel grinned. 'We know Rory up at the kennels. He's one of our weekend walking volunteers. He used to come with Mrs Quentin when she got a bit doddery and couldn't quite manage. Nice guy.'

Michelle's business brain suddenly wondered what a concerned neighbour like Rory might stand to inherit when Mr Quentin died. He was already the executor of the estate. Maybe there'd been method in his dog-walking. Or rather, a long-term strategy.

'Yeah,' she said. 'Nice guy.'

In the bookshop, Anna put her bag down on the desk and stared at Kelsey, but Kelsey had the phone tucked between her ear and her shoulder and was pushing back her cuticles. From the tone of her voice, Anna intuited that she was on the phone to her very patient best friend Shannon, who worked across the road in the deli.

'No Michelle?' she said, but got no reply.

Anna wondered if she could find a book about sign language, so Kelsey and Shannon could just sit in the front of their respective shops and sign at each other through the windows. Their hands would be blurs, she thought. Never stopping, like those French women who used to knit by the guillotines.

'. . . and I was like, I can see Ethan if I want to, Jake, it's not like you own me or anything, and he was like, listen, Kelsey, I am so not cool with that . . .'

Anna coughed and stared at Kelsey until she turned round and said, 'Listen, Shannon, I'll have to call you back, yeah, I'm at work,' and hung up.

'No Michelle?' Anna repeated. It was nearly quarter past ten, and she was late herself.

'No, she's being home-checked by the dog woman.' Kelsey looked as if she'd either been crying or had had a late night. Maybe both. Her big blue eyes looked shiny and there were bags under them the colour of mushrooms. Anna didn't know if it was Ethan or Jake who'd caused them. It was too hard to keep up.

Thank God I don't have to go through this with Becca, thought Anna, with a surge of relief for studious stepdaughters. And fingers crossed Chloe stays completely fixated on impressing Simon Cowell, rather than any of the boys in her class.

'Are you OK?' she asked.

'I'm fine.' Kelsey sniffed.

'Good. Well, listen, you can do something for me.' Anna pulled a set of cards out of her bag and some silver pens. 'I don't think you've done any book recommendations yet, have you?'

'I don't read books,' said Kelsey, alarmed.

'I bet you do. What about *Harry Potter*? Or something funny, like *Shopaholic*? I want comfort reads. Books that make you feel warm, books to read when it's raining outside.'

'I could do *Harry Potter*, I suppose,' said Kelsey dubiously. 'That first one was a short one, wasn't it?'

'Yay! That's the spirit. You only have to fill up this card. I don't need a dissertation.'

Kelsey looked uncertainly at the postcard. 'How big can I write?'

'Big as you want. Here's a silver pen. Go on!' said Anna encouragingly.

The shop bell jangled and Michelle walked in, followed by Rachel. They were both on their mobiles, although Rachel hung up when she came near the desk and smiled.

Kelsey took one look at Michelle, who was having a very terse conversation with someone, and scuttled into the back room.

'Hello!' said Anna to both of them. She'd tidied the shop to make it look as doggy-friendly as possible and put some of Pongo's Bonios in the drawer, just in case.

'Morning,' said Rachel. 'If you've got the keys, we're just going upstairs, so I can check Rory's flat's not full of small furry animals and mantraps.'

'What do you think it *is* full of?' wondered Anna, out loud. 'What's in Rory's flat?' was another game they played in the shop when it was quiet. Even Becca joined in with that one.

'Claymores and chess sets? Or crystal radios and life-size Daleks?'

'Law textbooks and back issues of *Model Railways Monthly*, I should think.' Rachel smiled and started flipping through the 'four for the price of three' box of kids' books.

'I imagine it like Lord Peter Wimsey's apartment,' said Anna. 'Books and bachelor artefacts.'

Michelle had finished her call, and gave her a boggly 'I don't think so' look.

Anna frowned back. She couldn't work out why Michelle was so down on Rory. Was it all to do with his son? She'd tried explaining that families were complicated, but Michelle just seemed to cling on to it, like she needed a reason to distrust him.

'Rory can't make it,' said Michelle, pocketing her phone. 'But he's happy for me to show you round. Shall we?' She gestured upstairs.

Anna watched Rachel and Michelle head out with the keys, then her natural curiosity got the better of her, and she called through to the back room.

'Can you mind the desk, Kelsey? I'm just popping upstairs too.'

Rory's flat was the same size and shape as the one Owen was currently sprawling out in, but there the resemblance ended.

Every wall was lined with bookshelves, and what wasn't crowded with books was painted shabby magnolia. It obviously hadn't been decorated for years and in some spots, Anna could make out Wallpaper Through the Ages – garish 70s patterns in the bathroom, spriggy 50s florals in the hall.

There was a mounted *Star Wars* light sabre along one wall,

and a bicycle wheel in the hall, and two big boxes of assorted Man Junk that had obviously got stuck there when he moved in. The air smelled of washing drying on radiators; not an unpleasant smell, but a disorganised one. This was very clearly The Post-Relationship Emergency Move Flat that Rory had never settled into. Anna's sympathies for him grew when she saw the brand new cot still in its flatpack, leaning up against the door. Bought, but never used.

She flashed Michelle a sidelong glance and could tell from her wrinkled nose that not only had she seen the cot, but she was dying to tidy up and slap a few coats of emulsion over the loud wallpaper for good measure.

'God, this takes me back,' said Rachel. 'My husband's house looked exactly like this when I first met him. Single men just silt up the place with . . . stuff. Every corridor is like an ox-bow lake, ready to cut off whole rooms.'

Out of the corner of her eye Anna saw Michelle pick a tea towel up off the floor, then, finding no hook to put it on, tut and hang it on the door handle.

'Have you known Rory a long time?' she asked Rachel.

'Quite a long time,' said Rachel, ticking off some boxes. 'He used to walk dogs with his girlfriend, then after he and Esther split up, he carried on coming with Agnes. She and Cyril let him move in here. Probably his dream flat, I should think, above a bookshop.'

'But not Esther's?'

Rachel looked up. 'I take it you've never met Esther?'

Anna shook her head.

'This is not Esther's dream flat,' said Rachel firmly. 'Believe me.'

'Does she still live in the town?' Annoyingly, Rory's flat, like Michelle's, had no photos for her to supply a face to the name.

'With Zachary?' she added, in case the detail might make Rachel open up more.

It had the desired effect. 'No, they've moved. She married someone else, quite soon after she and Rory split up. Poor Rory.'

Anna glanced at Michelle to see if she was taking this in, but she was too busy peering disgustedly into Rory's box of cracked CD cases.

'Poor Rory why?' she asked. 'Was it a messy break-up?'

Rachel made a face. 'You could say that. Isn't it always, with kids involved? But they seem to have found a way through it, so probably best to let him put it behind him.' She paused. 'Sorry, I don't mean to sound pious but I know what it's like when an old relationship follows you round. This is such a small town.'

'He needs a fresh start,' said Anna.

'Yes!' Rachel tapped her clipboard. 'Let's hope Tavish is part of that. It's amazing what a catalyst for romance a dog can be.'

Anna nodded, thinking of the way Rory had been looking at Michelle in the shop, and wondered if he'd said anything to Rachel. Michelle was quite a challenge for a fresh start, but she and Rory had a lot in common. They were both single, a bit wounded, professional . . . Maybe not a shared interest in interior decoration, though.

'Looks like he's started making preparations,' she said, gesturing towards the small kitchen.

Rory had put two metal dog bowls on a newspaper, written 'FOR EATING!' in black marker capitals next to it, and placed a big sack of premium dog food by the washing machine. There was also a lead, a tartan collar and a Santa hat from the pet supermarket, with the fifty per cent off sticker still on, and a tartan dog bed, 'FOR SLEEPING!'.

Rachel laughed and ticked a few more boxes on her checklist.

Anna turned round to see Michelle staring at a pile of *Top Gear* magazines with a Thunderbird puppet balanced on top, and muttering to herself. She coughed and drew her attention instead to a big watercolour painting of a sea storm propped up against the wall.

Michelle made a 'Yes? And?' face and started plumping up Rory's flat cushions.

'There's some outdoor access for this flat, isn't there?' asked Rachel, pen poised.

'Yes, he's got a shared yard space with the shop.' She decided not to tell Rachel that Michelle had been talking about turning it into a café area. 'But he'll be taken out to the park at lunchtime and after we close. Most of the time Tavish'll be where he always used to be, under the counter.'

'Perfect.' Rachel finished her checklist with a flourish. 'Sounds like he's fallen on his paws.' She paused, then said, 'And it'll be nice for Rory to have some company.'

'Funny,' said Anna. 'That's just what I said to Michelle.'

They looked at each other for a moment, then Michelle appeared behind them.

'Is everything in order?' Her eyes ranged around the small kitchen, which was much tidier than the rest of the flat.

'Yes,' said Anna. 'All great. Ooh! Is that a pasta maker? He must be really into his food.' She looked sideways at Michelle to see if she'd taken the hint. 'And I love these big photos of . . . um, clocks. I wonder if he did them himself?'

'Probably. He's quite arty,' agreed Rachel, nodding a bit too hard. 'Rory did the photos for my last open day at the rescue.'

Michelle turned and looked at the pair of them as if they were mad. 'Arty in a Tracey Emin "Look at my messy bed" way, maybe,' she said. 'Are we done? Because I think my jacket's about to sprout elbow patches.'

Downstairs, Rachel made a beeline for the table of boarding-school stories Anna had set up in a corner of the front room, Anna's favourite table, and easily the most popular with adults and children alike. She'd added rulers and apples and prefect badges to the piles of thin books, and made 'report cards' for various familiar characters – Pat and Isabel O'Sullivan, Mary-Lou Trelawny, Marmalade Atkins.

'These are the covers I remember!' Rachel held up a second-hand *First Term at Malory Towers*, next to one of the modern editions that Anna had just re-ordered. '*This* is how I remember Darrell Rivers, not like that. Darrell would never have worn lipgloss.'

'Certainly not! Although Gwendolyn would have done.'

'Gwendolyn would have been one of those lip-salve girls,' said Rachel. 'You know the ones, always dabbing.'

'Wasn't there an American girl who came to Malory Towers all glamorous with rolled hair and rouge? I had to ask my mum what rouge was.' Anna sighed nostalgically. 'It sounded so exotic. I still wanted to go there. I think what I really wanted was to go back in time.'

'I wanted to have a pony at school,' said Rachel. 'And midnight feasts and two French teachers and magic chalk. I cried when my parents refused to send me to boarding school. I *cried* when they said they loved me too much to send me away.'

'Didn't you go to boarding school, Michelle?' asked Anna. 'Did they have ponies?'

Michelle was pointedly straightening the rolled-up rugs in the basket by the till. Anna thought for a moment she was actually ignoring them.

'Michelle?' she repeated.

She looked up, her face a blank mask of indifference. 'No ponies at my school. No.'

'Where did you go?' Rachel turned round, interested. 'I *refuse* to believe you didn't have an open-air swimming pool built into the rocks.'

'It wasn't a famous one. No open-air pools. No midnight feasts. They only let girls into the sixth form, in case we put the boys off their Latin.'

Anna wondered if Michelle was being shy, not wanting to show off about her posh upbringing. Putting two and two together from the little Michelle had said about her family – and the story Owen had told her and Becca about learning to drive in a Jaguar – there'd clearly been plenty of money around. She wanted to tell Michelle it didn't matter, but couldn't think of a way to do it without drawing even more attention to it.

'Michelle,' she said, lifting a different title and then waggling it accusingly. 'Were you "The Naughtiest Girl in the School"? I bet you were. Were you expelled for running the tuck shop at a profit and pocketing the difference?'

'Ooh,' said Rachel, joining in, 'did you cut off someone's plait to teach them a lesson? Were you caught making moonlit trips along the cliff path to the post office . . . but with *boys*?'

Two bright red spots appeared on Michelle's cheekbones under her flawless foundation. 'Actually,' she said, 'I was expelled. Wasn't quite the jolly jape it is in the books. Especially not with parents like mine. My mother still hasn't really forgiven me.'

'You're kidding!' said Rachel. 'Sorry. Obviously hasn't done you any harm, though, has it? Local businesswoman of the year?'

Anna didn't share Rachel's easy recovery; she was feeling a

painful wash of retrospective guilt about all the stupid things she must have said. Being expelled would *totally* explain why Michelle had such a chip on her shoulder about university and books – Anna had just assumed she'd chosen to start working for her dad's business. She cringed inwardly.

But Michelle had already plastered a rather forced smile on her face and was swinging her bag onto her shoulder. 'My dad reckons it was the making of me. He's the one who gave me a job, though, so he'd have to say that. Lovely to meet you, Rachel,' she concluded, holding out her hand. 'You'll let me know if there are any problems with Tavish, won't you? I'll put the adoption donation in the post.'

'Oh, we don't charge a donation for oldies.'

'No, really,' said Michelle. 'I'd like to.'

'And I thought we could have a special corner of the shop for animal books, like "Tavish's pick",' said Anna. 'Michael Morpurgo, and Dodie Smith, and Dick King-Smith . . .'

Michelle flashed her tight smile again. It didn't make her face shine like her real smile did, thought Anna. It was more like a mask, so you couldn't see what she was really thinking. 'Great. Whatever. Put a dog bowl out. Anyway, ladies, got to dash!'

And she was gone.

Rachel glanced at Anna and grimaced apologetically. 'Oops. Did I put my foot in it? I thought she was joking.'

'I had no idea.' Anna stared at the door, where the bell was still vibrating. 'I knew Michelle went to boarding school but I had no idea she was expelled. She's never mentioned it.'

'We've all got our sore points,' said Rachel. 'Maybe it's more about the mum than the expulsion?'

'Maybe,' said Anna. She was starting to think Rachel was pretty perceptive. Or had she herself just been too busy to notice this stuff?

'I should go and collect my son from the minder.' Rachel put down the Enid Blytons with a show of reluctance. 'But I really want to stay and flick through these and talk to you about tinned sardines and condensed milk . . .'

'Pop in any time you want,' said Anna. 'Bring friends. We have chairs, we have coffee, we have many, many books. We don't make you discuss their literary significance.'

'That sounds like my kind of book club,' said Rachel. She waggled *Changes for the Chalet School* at her. 'Be warned. The nostalgia-hungry mummies are coming.'

14

'Harry Potter and the Philosopher's Stone is
much better than I thought it was going to be, only I
never worked out why he didn't just magic himself
test results and lottery tickets.' Kelsey Maguire

As the spring mornings became lighter and the air turned softer, Michelle noticed signs of early summer creeping in on her running circuit of the town. Her sharp eyes weren't peeled for the buds on the rosebushes in the parks, or the frothing cherry-blossom brightening the canal towpath, but for the first recycled barbecues appearing in front gardens, and the crop of her super-lightweight foldable umbrellas blooming like poppies at the bus stop. Seeing them cheered her up, sending her onto the homeward lap with a bounce in her step.

Michelle had to pick up a bit of speed on her loop because if she wasn't back within forty minutes, Tavish let her know about it. He showed his displeasure at being kept waiting for his breakfast by climbing up onto the windowsill and barking at everything that passed by, his long grey beard trembling with outrage. His eyesight not being what it had been, he'd already dispatched one potted orchid down the back of her cream sofa, and as a result, Michelle's lap times were improving daily for fear of what she might find on her return.

Tavish loved routines as much as Michelle did. He snoozed happily until she came back from her morning run, then he went for a pee and a sniff round the garden while she showered, and they ate breakfast together while she edited her to-do list. Then it was off to the shop, where he supervised Anna and the customers until six, when, after a hard day of being patted and fed sly Bonios, he came home with Michelle and settled into his basket under the table while she browsed the internet for new suppliers and adjusted her battle-plan for the year.

Neither of them was big on cuddles. Most of the time, Tavish maintained an aloof independence, bordering on grumpiness, apart from one brief nap-on-lap moment while Michelle watched the last news bulletin before bed. Then his head rested against her hand for a few minutes, but as soon as the weather came on, he slithered off to his basket. Tavish had his dignity – he bared his teeth when Owen tried to patronise him with a chew – and Michelle respected him for that. In any case, she decided, babying Tavish would be disloyal to Flash. She and Tavish had an arrangement, and it rather suited them both.

Rory had Tavish at the weekends, and after the fuss she'd made about how her own weekends were packed with buying trips and potential minibreaks, it was Sod's Law that for the first few weekends, Michelle was stuck at home on her own.

She had to pretend to be out when Anna called her mobile ('Oh, just nipped out for lunch with friends in . . . um, Oxford'), and again when Rory called to check what time to drop Tavish off ('No, I'm in, um, London. Earls Court. You can't hear the traffic because I'm not near a road'). She took herself off to lunch once or twice, but she didn't have any real friends apart from Anna, and she didn't want to intrude on Anna's family time. In the end, she spent most of her dog-less weekends stalking around both shops, ironing upstairs where no passer-by could see her, and rearranging her wardrobe into seasonal sections.

It was the first time since she'd left Harvey that Michelle had a routine that involved someone other than herself, and almost without noticing she adjusted her internal clock to Tavish's schedule, slipping extra cans of steak stew into her shopping basket and watching the clock at six thirty for Tavish's Sunday night return. Secretly, she quite liked it. Everyone loved Tavish in the shop, and she was the one who got to take him home. It made her feel part of a team, or like being back at school. She couldn't quite put her finger on it, but it was nicer than she'd expected.

On the last Sunday in April, Michelle had a gourmet lasagne heating up in the oven and a can of chicken supreme ready to go for Tavish when her front doorbell pealed at the usual drop-off time.

'Don't panic,' warned Rory as she opened the door. 'It's not as bad as it looks.'

Michelle's heart lurched. Tavish was wrapped in an old sweatshirt over Rory's long arm, his grizzled snout drooping sadly from beneath one sleeve, his greying beard stuck together with dribble and – urgh – dried blood.

'What happened?' she gasped. 'Is he OK?'

'He's fine. Went off his food on Friday night, so I took him to the vet's on Saturday morning and George took one look at his teeth and booked him in for immediate surgery.' Rory peered under the sweatshirt and moved the sleeve out of Tavish's eyes with a gentle gesture. 'Had to have quite a few out, didn't you, Gummy?'

Tavish drooled and Rory mopped it up with the sweatshirt, then looked back at Michelle. 'He's been dribbling most of the weekend, so you'll have to get your protective sheeting out for your soft furnishings. Keep him away from anything beige. So maybe the garden's the best bet?'

Michelle ignored Rory's attempt at banter – he was always trying to tell her how to look after dogs, as if she didn't know – and reached out to stroke Tavish's long ears. He let her, without grumbling – a sign he wasn't himself. 'Is he all right now?'

Seeing her concern, Rory's expression softened and he dropped his bantering tone. 'George said he'll need to be on mushy foods for a while, but he'll be less grumpy now his teeth aren't giving him gyp. No digestives from now on. Or tea.'

'Poor Tavish.' Michelle felt a nip of guilt. 'I had no idea his teeth were bothering him.'

'Well, I didn't either, so there you go. We're both neglectful parents.'

They were standing at the front door and a chilly draught was blowing through from the canal. Tavish shivered, and Michelle held out her arms instinctively to take him inside.

Rory manoeuvred the dog awkwardly into her grip. It was tricky, what with them both trying not to touch each other, and Tavish unhelpfully making himself into a floppy dead weight. When she was safely holding the dribbly bundle, Rory lingered as if he wasn't quite ready to leave him. His eyes followed the dog with a concern Michelle hadn't seen in his sardonic face before, and she heard herself say, 'Do you want to come in?'

'I need to know what to feed him, and what meds he's got,' she added as Rory stepped into the porch, but the truth was, Michelle didn't mind putting off her weekly overview list for a bit longer. Not only had she not spoken to a soul all day, but this week contained an anniversary she wasn't looking forward to very much, followed by an unavoidable trip to the Nightingale bosom to celebrate it the next day.

Michelle's thirty-first birthday was on Friday. She didn't want to think what Harvey might be planning for it. Something more dramatic than the weekly flowers that had been arriving in the shop and going home with a different member of staff each time. They weren't in her house, but each time Gillian or Kelsey thanked her, Michelle felt his looming presence. She'd lost four pounds since New Year, just through nerves.

'I'm not interrupting?' asked Rory, reverting to his usual teasing tone. 'You haven't just got back from a weekend in Prague and need to unpack?'

'I've already unpacked,' lied Michelle. 'What about you? Not rushing back to a cocktail soirée with Longhampton's glitterati?'

'I might be.'

'I've seen your flat,' said Michelle.

'Then you'll have seen my collection of sauté pans that have never been washed with water.'

'Funny how many men have one of those. Nothing to do with a fear of washing up.' Michelle walked through into her kitchen, conscious of Rory looking round *her* house. He'd never been past the porch before. She wondered what he was thinking, whether it was how he'd imagined. Did it remind him of the house he'd once shared with Esther? Had she let him put his light sabre up, or had she banned it?

Stop it, she thought, pulling herself up short; you're getting as bad as Anna, imagining stories everywhere. She grabbed her handbag off the sideboard, looking for her purse.

'How much was the surgery?' she asked. 'I'll give you half.'

But Rory waved her away with an airy hand. 'Don't worry about it. Mr Quentin settled the bill. He's got an account with the vets.'

'Yeah, yeah. Let me guess – you paid it yourself because you think if you're the one being nice to Tavish, he'll leave you the flat. I know your game.'

It was a running joke they had – or rather, a sort of joke. Rory delighted in reminding Michelle about her less than pure motives for taking in 'the dog that laid the golden eggs', and Michelle had her own suspicions about Rory's long-term plans to secure his own accommodation. The accusations flew back and forth with lightness, but the feathers had a sharp edge.

'If I were doing that,' countered Rory, 'don't you think I'd have him all the time?'

'Why do all the work, when you can get me to do half of it?'

'I *would* have Tavish all the time,' said Rory, surprised. 'I'm only letting you have him during the week for some company. Rachel said your house was gorgeous, but what it needed was a dog to give it some life. Make it a home.'

While Michelle was still reeling from a barb that dug deeper than he knew, Rory smiled, a wide grin that gave his angular face a boyish light. 'Can I have a cup of tea? What with all the dog-nursing, I didn't get any milk this weekend, so I've been drinking that foul peppermint tea stuff you're supposed to keep for guests.'

Michelle opened her mouth to volley back some comment about how out of date his peppermint tea probably was if he saved it for guests, but what came out was, 'This house *is* a home. It's my home. Just because it isn't messy or filled with kids and animals doesn't mean it isn't a *home*.'

Rory's smile froze. 'What? I didn't mean . . .'

'And I am so sick of people telling me I need company,' Michelle went on, powered by the pent-up stress she'd accrued as she prepared herself for her mother's 'You're not getting any younger' birthday lecture. 'If I needed *company* I would move some hot young language student in here. Or a live-in gardener slash masseur, not a dog who sheds all over my carpet. "Company" is what you offer elderly housebound relatives. Or what businessmen pay for!'

'OK.' Rory held up his hands, looking genuinely mortified. 'I'm sorry. I'm not the greatest at . . . knowing when to stop. It's been pointed out before. Things usually sound better in my head.'

Michelle ground to a halt, embarrassed. That rant about not needing company had been one she'd rehearsed in *her* head, ready to throw at her mother, and though it had sounded good then, she had the uncomfortable feeling it made her sound a bit insane when spoken aloud. *Gardener slash masseur. For God's sake, Michelle, you sound like a sex-crazed pensioner.*

'Start again?' she said, pinching her eyebrows in apology.

'Can we?'

'Course. Come through to the kitchen.'

Michelle turned the radio on and wished Rory had found her listening to some symphony or other, then wondered why on earth she'd wished that when she didn't even like classical music that much. It was the kind of thing she used to do at school, forcing herself to listen to The Pixies in case one of the cool boys came round. And Rory was a cool boy, despite his geekiness.

'Busy weekend?' she asked casually.

She swilled hot water round the teapot and tried to

remember what she'd told Anna she was doing in case Rory cross-checked.

'Not really. Took some of Rachel's rescue dogs out for a walk while Tavish was at the vet's. If you do two laps of the park, she gives you a bacon sandwich, so that was my lunch sorted out.'

'Sounds very charitable.'

'It's good fun. And the sarnies are excellent.' Rory picked up a baking timer Michelle had never used, in the shape of a perfect peach. 'You should come,' he said casually. 'When you're not off on a minibreak one weekend.'

'You spend your weekends walking dogs for a bacon sarnie? Surely there's more in it for you than that?' said Michelle. She wanted to say, 'What a sweet thing to do', like Anna would have done, but their relationship seemed rooted in this bantering mood, and she couldn't stop herself.

He put the peach-shaped timer down and gave her a half-annoyed, half-amused look. 'You're very cynical, aren't you? No, as it happens, I go there because it makes me feel like I've done something useful at the end of a week, when usually all I've done is shuffle a pile of paper from my desk to someone else's. If you'd seen how grateful the dogs looked today, just for a quick chuck of a ball in a field . . . maybe you'd come out too. It's really not a lot to do.'

It was Michelle's turn to feel as if she'd hit a nerve. 'Have you ever had a dog of your own?'

'No. Esther always wanted to get one, but we couldn't commit to . . .' He paused, and self-consciously corrected himself, '*I* didn't want to commit to one, so we used to volunteer up there instead. I got to know Cyril and Agnes through Four Oaks, and they took pity on me and offered me their flat when Esther and I split up, and so I guess if you *want* to be cynical you could say I did quite well out of it. If you want to be more philosophical you could say it was a karmic reward. Anyway,' he finished, 'I like a stroll and a coffee on a Saturday, it's not a big deal to walk a dog or two at the same time.'

Rory picked the timer up again and twisted it round to thirty minutes. 'Really, you should come up some time. You might meet some new people. New customers, even. Get Tavish to model some designer collars.'

Michelle put the teapot on the table trivet. Was he suggesting she go with him? Was that a date? She couldn't tell. Something curled away inside her, reluctant and keen at the same time. 'What are you setting that timer for? You know it'll make an unholy racket when it goes off.'

'Good. That's how long I'm staying. When it goes off, so will I.'

She pushed a mug and the milk jug towards him. 'You think you're staying that long?'

'Depends how rude you're going to be to me.' He sipped his tea, not slurping this time. 'While I'm here, I've had an idea for the bookshop – one of my mates has written a novel and I suggested he have a launch party at the shop . . .'

Michelle steeled herself not to agree immediately to Rory's friend's book launch, but grudgingly found herself listening, then trying not to smile at Rory's outrage at the way his mate had dragged every single one of his friends into the writing of his dreadful novel, the phone calls at all hours of the night to get their views on ever more ludicrous murder methods, the list of scores his friend had decided to settle with character names. His eyebrows went up and down as he spoke and his hands flew round, nearly knocking things off the table as he moved jugs and sugar bowls to illustrate how close they'd come to murdering him themselves.

When Rory got to the part where his friend made him lie down in the pub to draw round him with chalk to check how he'd have to fall to leave an 'intriguing outline', Michelle let out an involuntary laugh so loud Tavish jerked awake in his basket and barked. Or rather, it wasn't a bark so much as a scared croak. The pathetic sound made them both stop.

'It's where he was intubated,' Rory explained. 'Might be a bit scratchy for a while.'

Michelle checked her watch, and as she did, the timer went off with an ear-splitting peal and Rory slammed his hand over it, muffling the sound. How could half an hour have passed so fast, she wondered? It felt like, well, not that long. No wonder Tavish was looking peeved, being made to wait for his dinner.

'Is this thing accurate?' he asked, with a smile that caught her unawares. 'That can't be thirty minutes.'

'Are you saying my merchandise is faulty?' she countered.

Ask him to stay for supper, yelled a voice in her head, but she couldn't. What if he said no? Or said yes and then thought she was an awful cook? Harvey had always complained about her cooking, and insisted on taking friends out for meals 'so we can all stay friends'.

Before she could think what to say, Rory was standing up and shrugging his coat on. The tightness returned to her chest. He obviously wanted to get away, had other plans to attend to. Maybe he had company, unlike her. The impulse shrivelled, and she was glad she hadn't asked.

'Let me know if Tavish doesn't seem himself,' he said. 'I told Cyril we'd keep him up to speed about the old boy.'

'Of course you did,' said Michelle, grabbing the chance to tease him. That was safer ground. 'You hero, you. Did you tell him you'd sacrificed your own tatty sweatshirt?'

'What? Oh, I see what you did there. Back to me doing this for nefarious reasons. I thought we were past that.'

Rory held her gaze, and Michelle felt as if she'd overstepped the mark. She wished she could take it back.

She started to say, 'We are,' but he was speaking, and she bit her tongue.

'Of course I'll let him know that you're letting Tavish dribble on your soft furnishing too,' he said, then added, 'He's glad you're sharing the caring. In fact, he said you needed the company.'

'What?' she began.

'Of course he didn't. Cheerie bye, Tavish,' said Rory pointedly. He waved at the basket. 'Bye, Michelle.'

'I'll see you to the door.' She got up and followed him out, aware of his height. Rory towered over her, especially in her flat indoor shoes. Michelle noted too late that she'd forgotten to ask him to take his off, and he'd trailed mud through her hall.

15

'Alana: The First Adventure showed me that you can do anything you want, so long as you put your mind to it. Alana was strong, gutsy and the type of girl you just wanted to be.' Angie Willocks

Tavish slowly began to perk up over the next few days, and made the most of his recuperation with boiled rice and cod and other gum-friendly delicacies. Michelle had to remind herself of the bigger picture as she squeamishly checked his sore gums every morning and hid his meds in lumps of cream cheese, but it distracted her, and suddenly she was at the end of the week, and face to face with her thirty-first birthday.

Anna was waiting for her at the bookshop when she and Tavish arrived to open up, her face bright with enthusiasm at having remembered Michelle's birthday, despite Michelle's best efforts to pretend it wasn't happening.

'Happy birthday! I wanted to give you a breakfast treat, so Phil did the school run.' Anna pressed a bunch of pearl-white tulips into her hand, followed by a bag of pastries from the bakery and a flat wrapped present that Michelle already knew would be a book. She followed them all with a big hug and kiss. 'I hope you have a wonderful year,' she said, into Michelle's freshly washed hair.

Tavish barked, and Anna promptly released Michelle and gave him an ear tickle.

'I'm sorry it's not more exciting,' she went on, 'but it's just a short book that you might get round to reading.'

'Anna, you're too sweet,' said Michelle, feeling overwhelmed by her thoughtfulness. 'I can't believe you found time with all the stuff you've got going on at home. And you know I *love* white tulips. You shouldn't have . . .' she went on, unwrapping the present.

It was an old copy of *The Starlight Barking* by Dodie Smith. The card read, 'From Anna and Lily and Pongo x'

'The sequel to *One Hundred and One Dalmatians,*' explained Anna eagerly. 'It's about what happens when the dogs take over and start running things. Thought it might make you see Tavish in a new light.'

'I already see him as a small dog who thinks he's running things,' said Michelle.

They both looked over to Tavish's box. He'd made himself comfortable and was peering out, awaiting customers with his ears cocked.

'How is he today?' asked Anna, in the same way that she'd enquire about an elderly relative. 'How are you, Tavish?' she added, in a gruff doggy voice. Anna's bad Scottish accent sounded a bit like Rory.

'He's much better.' Michelle turned on the coffee machine.

'Oh, Michelle. Join in.'

'No,' said Michelle. 'It's a slippery slope. Next thing he'll have his own page on the website . . . Don't!' She raised a finger as a lightbulb went on in Anna's eyes. 'I mean it, Anna.'

The bell jangled as they were tucking into the croissants and gossiping about Kelsey's latest bust-up with Shannon, and a huge bouquet of pink roses, yellow freesias and cerise lilies appeared in the doorway, nearly filling it with a clash of colour.

Michelle's stomach sank. Owen was carrying them, but she knew who they were from.

'Owen, you are the ideal brother!' said Anna joyfully. 'Would you like to go round to Phil's office right now and tell him just how much ladies love to get flowers for their birthdays?'

'Um, I didn't get these.' Owen cast a nervous look between Michelle and Anna. 'I wouldn't *dare*. I still owe her for the phone bill. Happy birthday.' He reached into his back pocket and handed over a packet wrapped in the basic brown paper Home Sweet Home used to roll breakables in. 'It's a Furminator for the dog. Stops your carpet getting so hairy.'

'Thanks,' said Michelle. 'Are you saying I have a hairy carpet?'

Anna sniggered and then looked cross with herself. 'Sorry. Too much time spent with teenagers.'

'The flowers came to the shop first thing,' he went on, handing them to her. 'Gillian said they were spoiling the colour scheme in the new spring display.'

Anna turned to Michelle and raised her eyebrows. 'From an admirer?'

'An admirer with no sense of colour,' said Michelle, searching through the foliage for the card, purely to stop Anna getting there first. The roses were scentless though the lilies more than made up for it with a headache-y, over-strong fragrance.

'I bet they're from Mr Quentin!' Anna reached for the card, but Michelle snatched it away. 'To say thank you for looking after Tavish. Or Rory?'

Michelle ignored Anna's 'innocent' sideways glance. 'He doesn't know it's my birthday. You two are the only ones who do, so kindly keep it to yourselves.'

'Why?' demanded Anna. 'How will anyone know to give you presents?'

'Our family go in for birthdays in a big way.' Owen helped himself to a croissant. 'You only get let off the bumps on your eightieth. Shell's got to go down to Surrey for lunch tomorrow, have everyone give her joke presents . . .'

'And make crap jokes about how I don't look a day over thirty, so my brother can say, "No, you look three hundred and sixty-five days over thirty, ho ho ho . . ."'

Michelle stopped as she opened the card. In the florist's round handwriting were the words, 'Happy Birthday, darling. Looking forward to seeing you at your birthday lunch, lots of love from Harvey xxxxx'

A chill ran across her skin. The handwriting didn't match the voice she could hear in her head: 'Hello, darling' – Harvey called everyone *darling*, part Leslie Phillips, part *EastEnders* – 'how big a bunch can you do me for a hundred quid? Got a lady to impress here.'

'Well?' Anna was looking at her, her eyes bright with romance. 'Who are they from?'

'They're from Harvey,' she said flatly.

'Well, that's really thoughtful of him,' said Owen. 'He's a good guy, Michelle. He doesn't have to send you flowers on your birthday. But he still does.'

'But I don't *want* him to. I told Mum to tell him to stop,' she said, feeling her stomach clench. One, or both of them, was ignoring her.

'Didn't you tell me all women loved flowers?' Owen looked confused. 'God, women are *impossible*.'

'Don't,' snapped Michelle. 'That's the kind of stupid thing Harvey would say.'

'Is it? You're too hard on the guy,' said Owen. 'He's just trying to be friends'

Michelle felt a flicker of frustration that Owen, her one ally at home, didn't have the full story. She could tell him, but that would mean telling him a lot of other things too, and she could still barely bring herself to think about those.

He got up and took the rest of the croissant with him. Michelle thought about calling him back, but he was already out of the shop, jangling the bell behind him.

Michelle slumped in the chair, feeling her shoulders lock with tension.

'Harvey isn't the kind of man who "just wants to be friends",' she said, in answer to Anna's confused expression. 'He wants complete control. Maybe now I've made a bit of money he's decided I'm not the stupid daddy's girl he liked to tell me I was. Maybe he's finally realised I'm serious about getting a divorce. It doesn't really matter. But he won't stop until I'm back in Kingston, and nothing I say or do will make any difference.'

'But if you don't want to go back?' asked Anna. 'Can't you just tell him? Can't your dad put him straight?'

People like Harvey didn't exist in Anna's world. Michelle shook her head, unwilling to bring him into her own new, fresh and shiny world now. Even talking about him in the shop felt like soiling the clean paint on the shelves behind her.

'My parents like him,' she said. 'Everyone who doesn't really know him likes Harvey.'

'Did he hit you?' Anna's voice was nearly a whisper.

'I sometimes wish he had,' said Michelle.

She balled up the bag the croissants had come in and threw it precisely into the bin. The neat dispatch made her feel more in control. 'Anna, I can honestly say that's the best birthday treat I've had in years. Thank you.'

She stood up to give her friend a hug and saw that Anna – caring, sympathetic Anna – had tears in her eyes. 'Come on,' she said, 'don't be like that!'

'Why didn't you say?' Anna hugged her hard. 'Why didn't you *tell* me? I thought . . .'

'Because it's finished. It's in the past. I'm not going back.' Michelle stared over her shoulder. 'I move on from things, OK?'

'Can you?'

'I can,' said Michelle. 'I can, and I have.'

That wasn't her problem. Her problem was that no one else in her family seemed to want her to.

Owen was only fifteen minutes late when he arrived at Swan's Row on Saturday morning, which was a significant improvement on his usual time-keeping, but it still meant that Michelle felt behind as they hit the motorway.

'Stop overtaking everything, Shell,' said Owen, glancing up from his mobile as she passed another lorry. He'd been texting nearly all the way. 'I feel like I'm in a car with Jenson Button.'

'We're going to be late. If we get there early, they can't break out into a chorus of "Happy Birthday" when we walk in and make everyone stare at us.'

'Wouldn't you rather be late? Spend as little time with your adoring family as possible?'

'It's not that.' She indicated and overtook another caravan. 'I've got things to do later on. At home.'

Owen stopped texting and looked at her. 'Mum's worried about you, you know. She asked me if she'd done something recently to upset you, because you never call.'

That was rich, thought Michelle. Using Owen – the child she'd sent off to boarding school at ten because she'd had enough of child-rearing – to make *her* feel bad about her lack of family spirit. 'I don't call because I'm busy with work. If *she* was busy with work, she wouldn't notice me not calling.'

'She's worried about you,' he repeated.

'Owen, she's not. She's just annoyed because she'd got my life nicely arranged, with a husband of her choice, and now it's messy again. Give her another six months and she'll start on you. "Owen, when are you going to get married? Owen, when will you give me grandchildren as lovely as you? Owen, have you had dinner with Jenny Lawson recently?"'

He pulled a face. 'If I wanted to go out with Dad's account-ant's daughter I would have done it when I had that run-in with the Inland Revenue last year.'

'Oh ho, that's fighting talk, Owen. Be careful, we haven't got an accountant in the family yet.'

Owen stared out of the window and drummed his fingers against the side of the door. Then he said suddenly, 'Seriously, Shell, if she does start going on about Jennifer, can you steer her off it?'

'Why? You're seeing someone?'

'Sort of.' He corrected himself. 'Yes. Yes, I am seeing someone.'

Michelle glanced across the car, intrigued. 'Who? Do I know her?'

He didn't meet her eye, but he looked unusually shy. 'It's very early days. I don't want to talk about it.'

She laughed out loud at that. 'You don't want to talk about it? Seriously? That is a first, Owen.'

'Yeah. Maybe.' He fiddled with his phone and Michelle realised he'd had it in his hand for the entire journey, as if he couldn't bear to put it in his pocket in case it rang. It must be serious, she thought. Owen's normal tactic was 'very hard to get', followed by 'impossible to get' and a move to a different country.

'Is she a nice girl? Would I like her?'

'Yes,' he said, then, unable to resist, added, 'It's Becca.'

In one movement Michelle swerved into a lay-by, and the car behind her hooted as it sped past. 'What?' she said, yanking on the handbrake and swivelling round in her seat.

Owen looked terrified. 'What the hell was that for?'

'Becca. You're going out with Becca? Anna's Becca?'

'Yes! I thought you'd be pleased.'

Michelle shoved her hands into her hair. 'Owen, Becca is a sweet, talented, beautiful girl. I *really* like her. I don't want to see her heartbroken and dumped just before her hugely important exams that will decide whether she gets into the university of her dreams. Which is also the university of her parents' dreams.'

'I'm not going to dump her!'

'Aren't you? That'll definitely be a first.' She gave him a clear-eyed look. 'I'm your sister, Owen. I've *made* those phone calls for you. I do not want to have to make one of those calls to my best friend to explain why her much-loved stepchild is weeping into her pillow and refusing to eat just before the most important exams of her life. And have you *seen* the size of Phil? You fancy that coming after you when Becca finds out on Facebook that she's no longer in a relationship?'

'I'm not twelve,' scoffed Owen.

'No, you're not. You're twenty-four, and she's eighteen. *Eighteen.*'

Owen opened his mouth, then shut it, then opened it again.

'Oh God. Tell me you're not sleeping with her,' said Michelle.

'Michelle!'

'Well. Are you?'

'No,' admitted Owen. 'It's not like that. You're making out I'm some kind of serial shagger—'

'Which you are.'

'This is different. I wouldn't even say we were dating yet. It's . . . different. I really like her, I don't want to rush it. I wouldn't have said anything if you hadn't asked.' He actually looked affronted. 'Anyway, you're not exactly a relationship expert yourself, Michelle.'

That hit a nerve, but she tried not to let it show on her face. 'I'm not. But Anna's my friend, she's got enough problems keeping things on track in that family and I really, really don't want her life made more complicated than it already is.'

'Are you telling me to finish it with Becca because your friend's *busy*?' Owen's eyes were sarcastic, but there was something else in there too, thought Michelle. She wasn't sure what it was.

Cars sped past inches away from them, making the car sway.

She took a deep breath. She couldn't tell him to break it off. He wasn't a bad lad, just a thoughtless, free-wheeling one. Two things Becca wasn't. She might be younger than him, but in many ways she was a lot more mature.

'No,' she said. 'But I'm asking you to be careful. And kind.'

'I can do that,' said Owen. 'Why wouldn't I do that?'

'Good,' said Michelle. She put the car back into gear. 'Now, help me get through this nightmare of a birthday party.'

Despite her best efforts on the A3, when she pulled into the car park, Michelle could see from the array of Nightingale dealership cars parked outside that her parents, plus her brothers and their families were there, but there was no sign of Harvey's personalised plate, which gave her a small moment of relief.

She plastered on a smile for the loud round of 'Happy Birthday' that rang out when she entered – making heads turn all round the gastropub – then they were shown into the family room, booked especially to accommodate all the Nightingales, including six children and their bits and pieces.

Michelle's stress headache started soon after the menus arrived and built steadily through the endless banter about her age, Ben's bald patch and the pauses for various nieces and nephews to demonstrate their latest party trick. She'd sat as far away from her mother as she could, between her sister-in-law, Emma, and her dad, but such was Carole's close relationship with my 'darling extra daughters', as she called her daughters-in-law, that she spent the whole meal leaning down the table to offer her opinions on whatever they were discussing, and Michelle could hardly escape the sighs and glances that swung her way every time the topic of children and families came up.

Even Emma seemed embarrassed, and tried to change the subject as much as she could.

'Michelle,' she said, after they'd been discussing her son's new piano teacher for what felt to Michelle like nine years, 'you went straight to work from school, didn't you?'

'Um, yes,' she replied, defences rising automatically.

'My best employee ever,' said her dad Charles, straight away, with a proud look. 'Wish I still had her on my team.'

'My best teacher,' said Michelle. Not because it was expected but because it was true. She and her dad didn't talk much about emotional matters but they could chat for hours about minimising overheads, and that made her feel closer to him than an hour's lecture from her mother about everyone else's kids.

'It's just that my sister's going through a bit of a rebellious phase,' Emma went on, blushing, 'and we've been warned she might not pass her exams, so I was wondering . . .'

'She could take the Michelle Nightingale route – get expelled, have a summer off, then get a job polishing cars,' her brother Ben butted in, from two seats down. 'From public school drop-out to mug-tree mogul. Like Richard Branson with jute bags.'

Ben had a very carrying voice. Michelle saw Carole's lips had turned white and she was actually looking round to see if the waiters had heard.

For God's sake, Mum, she thought angrily. *Still?* That had been her sole concern at the time: 'Oh, Michelle, what will people say? They all think you're such a sensible girl.' Carole had stayed indoors for a whole week, and had refused to discuss the reason for Michelle's unexpected arrival home, so crushing was the burden of shame. Michelle had been grateful at the time, because she didn't want to talk about the gory details either, but now she suspected that was more to do with Carole's determination to wipe the whole incident from the collective family memory than from a desire to help.

'Always looks intriguing on the CV, an expulsion,' Ben went on, oblivious to the sudden blankness of his sister's face. 'Shows you're a party girl under the business suit, eh?'

'Shut up, Ben,' said Michelle. 'Do you want us to get onto the topic of hair transplants? Or vasectomy reversals?'

Charles coughed uncomfortably. 'Isn't it time for the . . . thing, Carole?' he asked, flapping his napkin.

'What? What did I say?' Ben demanded of no one in particular.

Carole jiggled her eyebrows reproachfully at her husband. 'No, not yet, Charlie. We're not all here.'

'We *are*,' said Michelle.

As she spoke, three waiters walked in with a glossy chocolate cake, covered with fizzing indoor sparklers. Michelle recognised them from Home Sweet Home and wondered if they'd ordered from her website.

She felt a profound urge to be back in the stylish quiet of her shop, or on her sofa at home, or even in the bookshop with dribbly Tavish and Rory lecturing her on the right way to mash up dog food. Anywhere but here.

'*Happy Birthday to you . . .*' the waiters started, but one loud voice cut through them, a little bit flat, and her mother turned to her with a triumphant smile, as if she'd pulled off the biggest and best surprise of all.

Michelle flinched. A huge cloud of metallic birthday balloons appeared over the top of the waiters and Carole clapped with undisguised delight, her tennis bracelets jingling as a figure stepped out from behind them.

A broad figure in a sharp pin-stripe suit, the sort someone might wear if they had a lifelong fixation on Al Capone and the Prohibition gangsters, despite having gone to an expensive public school. The hand clutching the balloons had a big signet ring on the little finger, and the arm attached to it displayed a chunky gold Rolex, and fine golden hair that was occasionally waxed off in secret by a very discreet woman called Wendy in Cobham.

Michelle focused on those bits because she didn't want to look at the face just yet. Not till the last polite moment.

'Harvey!' her mother called out. 'You made it! Oh, what

sweet balloons! Look at the lovely balloons, Bella! Would you like one?'

'Why did Mum invite Harvey?' Michelle asked her dad under her breath, trying not to let it come out as an accusation. 'We're *separated*. Why does she think she can force us back together?'

Her father looked uncomfortable. 'He *is* my senior manager, love. Your mother asked him. She wants everyone to be friends.'

Not for the first time, Michelle wondered queasily if her mother harboured more than a little crush on Harvey herself.

'Does she invite all your staff to family birthdays?' she demanded, her voice rising hysterically.

She stopped as Ben turned round to see what the problem was. Harvey was coming towards her with the balloons, and she had no option but to look at him now.

Michelle's mother had gone through an annoying phase of calling Harvey 'Bear', on account of 'his lovely big bear face. Like Winnie the Pooh!' His features were very affable; he had a shock of blond hair, a large mouth that gaped open and big ears. But his eyes weren't quite as bear-ish as the rest of him; they were pale blue, and small, like his hands and feet, and they took everything in with the quick assessing stare of a rattlesnake.

Harvey had those eyes trained on Michelle now, and she felt herself go cold as he approached.

'Happy birthday, darling,' he said, planting a wet kiss on her cheek. Michelle recoiled at the intimacy of his hand resting on her hip. Harvey still smelled of too much aftershave and car wax, his hair was still thick and meticulously gelled, his nose was still red and his tie was still patterned with amusing turtles.

She made a non-committal noise in response. It sounded like a squeak.

'Look at you!' he said, squeezing her waist as she tried to wriggle out of his reach. 'You don't look a day over thirty!'

'No, she looks three hundred and sixty-five days over thirty!' roared Ben right on cue, stopping just short of slapping his own thigh.

'She looks a million dollars,' said Harvey gallantly, then added, just loud enough for her to hear, 'Especially now you've lost a pound or two. Must be all that running around at work. Keep it up!'

Michelle felt as if someone had yanked down her dress. Ashamed, self-conscious. Feelings she hadn't had about herself in ages. As she turned her head, she saw her mother look at them both with an expression of supreme smugness, then nudge her husband as if to say, 'Look what I did!'

When she and Harvey had met ten years earlier – or when she'd finally given in and allowed her mother to set her up on a blind date with her dad's star manager – she'd been twenty years old, and still struggling with what no one had wanted to call clinical depression. Michelle wasn't a natural drop-out. In the parallel world where things *hadn't* gone wrong, she was two years into her degree course as planned, making friends, eating Pot Noodles, having close encounters with Natural Scientists and other carefree fun.

Instead of which, she'd been in Kingston, hiding from the world. Harvey had made her his personal project, and she couldn't believe someone as handsome (her standards had been spectacularly low at that point) and successful could want a failure like her. Harvey tended to agree, but with his support she'd stopped running ten miles a day and inched back into something approaching normality – if watching someone else play golf and going to regional launches of new Fords was normal. She was happy to let Harvey take charge of conversations, happy to let him march her to Selfridges with his credit card, and dress her 'appropriately'. He was an adult. He understood these things. And his attention was balm to Michelle's very raw self-confidence.

Michelle was a quick learner, and her dad was touchingly keen to teach her all he knew, since his university-educated sons showed no interest in his dealership empire. She was good at guessing what people wanted and then giving it to them, for a price. She also developed a confident persona when she was in her sales mode, miles away from who she was at home. But as she started to rebuild herself, she began to realise that Harvey wasn't that keen on her recovering. He preferred her when she did what she was told. By then, it was too late. The marquee was booked. Her family were blatantly relieved that the awkward episode was finally over; the black sheep had been safely tinted blond and was back on track to more family success.

Michelle watched as Harvey kissed her mother and shook hands with her brothers and kissed their wives and made faces at their kids, and felt the familiar twisting sensation inside. She'd let the wedding happen because, in her still-numb heart, she couldn't come up with one convincing reason not to marry him, other than he just didn't feel right, and that felt outrageously ungrateful – and he would refuse to believe it – so she said nothing. In the years that followed, she came up with a whole series of very convincing reasons.

'Pull up a chair, fella,' said Ben, trying to sound matey. He was a chartered surveyor and had never come to terms with his lack of cool compared to Harvey and Owen's natural charisma. 'What can I get you to drink? You'll need it with this lot!'

'I'll sit here,' said Harvey easily. 'Next to my lady – if she's left me enough room. Move up, Shelley.'

He was already pushing his way into the tiny gap between her and Emma, and Michelle knew that not moving would mean he'd sit her on his knee. She moved. She had no choice.

Owen glanced at her, and she knew his sharp eyes had taken it all in. His expression was a mixture of confusion and sympathy, but for whom, she couldn't tell.

Sometimes, like now, Michelle really wanted to take Owen aside and tell him everything, bring him right up to speed on why everyone was the way they were. He'd missed so much. But she worried it would alter his opinion of her, and she couldn't stand that.

The rest of the meal passed in an atmosphere of forced good humour, though Michelle was sure she was the only one who felt the artifice. Harvey kept getting nearer, and at three thirty, after the cake and presents (a pedicure set, and a toy cat that purred when you stroked it, 'to keep you company'), Michelle escaped to the loo with her mobile, ready to text Anna to call her with a shop emergency.

'Going so soon?'

Harvey appeared behind her chair the second she pushed it back, and she knew they had to have a short conversation. Better to concede that much. Her breath sped up and she fought to sound normal.

''Fraid so. I've got to get back,' she said, waving her phone. 'Stock emergency.'

'What kind of emergency do bookshops have? Let me see.' He made to take her phone playfully, but she pulled it away. They were out of sight of her family, so he grabbed her wrist hard to get it, but a waiter passed by, and while Harvey was smiling at him, Michelle yanked her arm back and stepped away. Her heart really was hammering now.

'Owen says it's going really well.' He raised his eyebrows, emphasising his ski tan. 'Never had you down for a reader. But then you always could sell anything. I know you like to give people what they want.'

'I'm a good saleswoman, yes.' Michelle knew that wasn't what he'd been insinuating. 'Thanks for the flowers,' she went on politely. 'But please don't send any more.' She dragged up her last bit of bravado. 'I'm sorry but it really is over between us. I've moved on. I hope you can too.'

'Is this how you want to play it? OK, fine. I'm an old romantic, you know that.' He smiled indulgently; the smile didn't reach his eyes. 'But don't do it for too long. You're not getting any younger, you know. Have you been pestered for dates?'

Michelle couldn't answer. Her throat was tight.

Harvey smiled, triumphant. 'Thought not.'

'Sorry to butt in.' Charles put one hand on her shoulder and one on Harvey's, subtly steering them apart. 'We've been clearing out the loft for this extension your mother's organising, and I've got some boxes of your stuff in the back of the car. If you give me your keys I'll pop it in your boot.'

Normally Michelle resisted junk entering her house, but now she was glad of the chance to get away. 'I'll, er, I'll come with you. Bye, Harvey.'

'Bye, darling. See you soon.'

It wasn't a question. He leaned forward to kiss her goodbye, and she made herself stand still while he pressed his lips against her cheek, hoping he couldn't feel her flinch.

I've told him, she thought. I've told him. I just have to keep on telling him.

Over his bulky shoulder, Michelle caught sight of her mother watching them with beady eyes and knew with a miserable sense of claustrophobia that Carole was seeing something totally different.

Outside in the car park, Michelle waited until her dad had loaded two big packing cases into the back of her Golf before she took a deep breath and broached a subject she knew he wanted to discuss about as much as she did.

'Dad,' she said, 'I know you and Mum like Harvey, but I'm not going to get back together with him. It's over. I don't want to be married to him. The only reason I haven't divorced him is because . . . I'd rather be separated for five years and let people think we drifted apart as friends than have anyone be to blame.' That was as close to the truth as she could bear to get.

Charles looked embarrassed, his pink cheeks pinker from the effort of lifting the boxes. 'Your mum just thinks you make a lovely couple. And you do. She can't see why you had to split up, if you weren't fighting.'

'You don't always know what goes on in a marriage.' Michelle rubbed her forehead. That showed how well her family knew her, or wanted to. 'Dad, I thought I was doing the right thing, getting out while we were still young enough to start again. That's why I moved away, to get a fresh start. If Mum's encouraging Harvey, it's not going to help him move on either.'

'There's, ah, no chap on the horizon at the moment, then?'

For a moment, Michelle thought about making one up, to get them off her case, but there was no point lying to her father. He saw through better liars than her every day. 'No, there isn't. I'm not looking for one. I've got my plan, and my shop to run, and that's what I'm focusing on for the next couple of years. I'm only thirty-one and I'm all stocked up with anti-ageing creams,' she added with a grimace. 'I've a few years yet before I have to worry about being left on the shelf.'

Why did I say that, she wondered. It never even occurred to her in Longhampton. Anna's baby panic was as alien to her as Gillian's obsession with quilting.

You said it because Harvey put it into your mind, a voice inside her head replied, and she knew it was right.

Charles rested the last box on the edge of the boot. He regarded his daughter over the top of it, and seemed to brace himself to say something he wasn't too sure about, the same way he did in French *hypermarchés*.

Michelle steeled herself too.

'Michelle, love,' he said. 'Will you take a bit of advice from your old dad?'

'Do I have any choice?'

He acknowledged her with a wry shake of the head. 'Not really. Listen, don't let work be the only thing in your life. I'm proud as Punch of everything you've done with that shop of yours, but no one wishes they'd spent more time in the office on their deathbed.'

'That's good, coming from you,' she said. 'Who gave me this work ethic, eh? Not Mum.'

'I know. And I know it's not the done thing to say, but I'd be as proud of you for having a nice little family as I would if you took over the whole dealer network. Ideally, of course, you'd have both.' He tried a smile, to soften his words. 'You'd make a great mum, Michelle – I've always thought that, the way you took Owen under your wing when ... when your mother didn't have enough time. Don't plough yourself into the ground to please me, love. I already know you're smarter than all your brothers put together. But you've never been as happy as them, and that's all your mum and I really want, to see you happy.'

Michelle blinked back a tear at the anxiety in his face. Anxiety for her, and anxiety not to upset her at the same time. Although there was a lot her dad didn't know about her marriage, and probably even more he didn't want to know, she knew he must have been worried to have said what he'd just said. The difference between him and her mother, though, was that he'd be prepared to hear she was *un*happy, and would want to do something about it.

Maybe I should tell him, she thought, but then shied away from that at once. Harvey was too firmly embedded in her dad's world. She couldn't risk him not believing her.

'I'm fine, Dad,' she managed.

He looked at her for a long moment, just the two of them, in the car park, and years of unaired thoughts hung between them.

'I'll be glad to see the back of these,' he said, heaving the last box into her car. 'We can finally get that loft conversion started.'

'What's in there?'

'All sorts. From your old room, I think. We just packed it all up. Didn't want to throw it out in case it was important.'

'If I've lived without it for the past ten years, it can't be that important,' said Michelle. 'I should probably just dump it.'

Charles laid a hand on her arm. 'No,' he said. 'Don't do that. Have a sort through first.'

She looked at him and impulsively wrapped her arms around him, surprised at how easily they encircled him now.

Once she'd barely been able to touch her fingertips behind her dad's broad back. Now she could almost feel his bones.

He's getting old, she thought with a start. So am I.

'Happy birthday, pumpernickel,' he said, when she let him go. 'Thirty's the new twenty-one!'

Michelle contemplated telling him he was a year out, but decided not to.

16

'The Twilight *trilogy is first love times a million; I feel
sorry for the generation of boys who have to live up to the
broody magnificence of Edward Cullen.'* Anna McQueen

One of the things Anna looked forward to most about the girls'
trips to America – apart from the chance to be alone with Phil,
and not have to do so much laundry, and to get more than thirty
seconds' worth of hot water – was the chance to read in peace.

Parenthood had really cut into her reading time. Before she
was married, Anna's diary revolved around her holidays and
the books she planned to take with her, and if she had enough
baggage allowance to allow for everything she'd stockpiled.

She'd only taken a tiny reading bag on honeymoon to
Venice (four books, two wedding-themed, two Italian-set) and
by then Phil had known her well enough to appreciate that
four books meant almost total concentration on him. In the
holidays they'd shared afterwards, they'd arrived at a compromise; she'd read, while he swam in the pool. The fact that he
let her do that made her confident she'd chosen the right man.

Now the holidays had had to be scaled back, but Anna
didn't mind having a stay-cation. Even as she was folding up
a pile of T-shirts for Becca's suitcase, Anna was feverishly
planning her escapist reading list for the Easter holiday like a

foodie planning a massive nine-course blow-out. For once she wasn't scouring the Sunday papers for reviews, she was cherrypicking books off the shop shelves. Rediscovering how dark Roald Dahl really was had given her an urge to re-read all her childhood favourites, especially now Lily was showing an interest in reading more together.

The whole of the Narnia series, maybe, she thought, as the paperback covers flashed into her mind's eye. That was topical, with Aslan and Easter and all that. Her imagination immediately threw up the snow scenes – the Turkish Delight and the magical drink in the goblet that tasted of something delicious. In Anna's head, it was hot Ribena.

Or Miss Marple? That would be nice if the weather was good. In the garden, with a plate of hot cross buns and a pot of tea, working her way round St Mary Mead's homicidal vicars and parlourmaids. Miss Marple talking like Joan Hickson. Everyone being terribly English. Bliss.

She knew she should probably spend the week thrashing out the baby issue with Phil, while they had some privacy, but something was stopping her. Fear. Weariness. She couldn't bear to think about it.

Becca and Chloe were in Becca's bedroom with her, bickering about something while they packed their suitcases with the pile of clean clothes Anna was decanting from the laundry basket, but Anna wasn't listening. She'd developed a method of tuning them both out until the bickering reached a certain pitch at which she'd have to step in. Or if there was a pause.

Like now.

She looked up from the basket, now nearly empty, and saw that Becca and Chloe were glaring at each other. Neither of them was holding a disputed item of clothing, so it couldn't be the usual argument.

'What?' she said.

Chloe widened her eyes at Anna. 'I should be on the website, not her.'

'No, you shouldn't.' Becca went back to her make-up bag, which she was meticulously repacking to be as small as possible. She had a lot of revision to take, too, and had already been weighing her bags on her home-luggage-checker. 'I've been doing all the reviews, and the blog comments. What have you done?'

Chloe tossed her hair. 'Shut up. I did a review.'

'Did you?' said Anna, surprised, but pleased. Her target was to have a gold-edged 'We Love' card on each shelf in the shop; Becca had contributed about half the total so far, each neatly filled in with her uniform cursive. 'I didn't see that. Did you put it up? If we've run out of stock of what you reviewed, let me know and I'll re-order some.'

Chloe fidgeted. 'Not for the shop. For the website. I emailed it to Owen.'

'Well, I haven't seen it,' said Becca. 'He never mentioned it.'

Something snagged in Anna's mental alert system. Why would Becca have seen Owen's emails? Had things gone beyond a bit of Saturday job flirtation? She'd noticed a frisson between them, but since Owen could generate a frisson between inanimate objects she hadn't taken it too seriously.

This would be a good time to ask Becca, she thought. As soon as Chloe gets bored and slopes off to phone Tyra about her braces, I'll ask then. Getting information out of the girls without the other two overhearing and cackling was like one of those brainteasers involving boats and chickens and foxes.

'So, how's the website going?' she asked, hoping to bore Chloe away.

'It's going really well,' said Becca at once. 'Owen's doing

this really clever thing where you can put in a book you like, then get two or three more recommendations based on that. It's called the New Favourite Read Generator.' She turned pink. 'Working title, obviously.'

'I would hope so,' said Chloe sarcastically. 'It sounds like a really crap band. The sort you'd like.'

'He's done all that by himself? I thought Owen would be more into music than books. I could have had him writing reviews.'

'I've been helping him. A bit.' Becca's blush deepened, and Chloe rolled her eyes.

'Like, *more* than a bit. Are you going to *charge* Michelle for all the work you've done on the website? Which is, basically telling Owen what to write?'

'I don't mind,' said Becca hastily. 'It's not been that much,' she added, before Anna could say anything. 'Mainly when I'm there working anyway.'

'You don't mind because you get to sit up there in his flat with him in all your free periods, going "Oooh, Owen, let me tell you about F. Scott Fitzgerald,"' muttered Chloe, with a sly glance at Anna to make sure she'd caught what she'd said.

'Have you been spending your free periods there?' Anna asked. This was starting to add up. Becca never left the library if she didn't have to.

'No!' Becca glared daggers at Chloe. 'One. *One* free period last week, when Owen texted me to ask something about a review I'd written and it was easier to go there and explain it myself, since I was on the high street anyway, getting some lunch. From the deli. We get a ten per cent school discount, so it's cheaper than the canteen.'

That sounded a bit too complicated to Anna, and she noted

that Becca's ears were now going red. She addressed a question to Chloe, to be sure of getting an honest answer. 'Are you allowed to be off the school site during the day?'

Chloe scowled. 'Year thirteen are. It's just us that have to stay in the stupid library. Most of her emo friends go to the bookshop – I can't believe you haven't noticed.'

'Well, I walk the dog round the block at lunchtime most days. So all those Goths in the back room are from the school?' said Anna. Kelsey had taken particular offence at their habit of drinking all the coffee and then leaving after buying one paperback between the four or five of them, always second-hand and usually featuring vampires.

'Duh,' said Chloe. 'Can't you tell by the smell of hairspray? And tragedy?'

Anna gave her a warning eyebrow-raise.

'Anyway, you're in charge of the bookshop, you should be able to decide who's the face of the website,' Chloe went on, in more ingratiating tones. She blossomed visibly under the warmth of direct attention, even when it was of the warning kind. 'I need the exposure more than Becca. And then when I'm famous, and I'm on the television, they can show the bookshop website as a funny flashback to *before* I was famous, and that'll be more publicity for you.'

She added an instant dazzling beam that Anna found half charming, half scary.

'That's going to be funnier than even you realise,' scoffed Becca. 'The shop assistant who needs to be told that *Moby Dick* is a book, not an author.'

'And you think the website's going to do better with some frumpy geek advertising it in her frumpy geek glasses?'

'Stop it!' said Anna. There was too much information here to process all at once. She had the unsettling feeling that she'd

missed something vital. Miss Marple wouldn't have missed it.
Or Michelle.

'Are those my jeans?' demanded Becca suddenly. 'Chloe?
Don't even try to sneak those out of the basket, those are
mine!'

She went to grab them and Chloe snatched them out of her
way.

'Stop it!' Anna put a hand out to prevent a tug-of-war
developing.

'Does it matter who takes them?' Chloe demanded. 'I'm
saving you some precious grams on your baggage allowance.
I'm doing you a *favour.*'

'You can't get even get your calves in them,' Becca pointed
out. 'They're a size ten.'

'I am a size ten,' howled Chloe.

'In *America.*'

Chloe drew in a breath so loud and dramatic Anna was
surprised the contents of the washing basket weren't sucked
up like a tornado.

'Actually, you know what, Becca? Chloe's right,' said Anna
quickly, seeing a way to get Becca on her own. 'I'd let her take
them for you.'

Becca released them as if they were red-hot, and immediately Chloe switched off the shriek of outrage before it began.

'You're going to have to be smarter than that if you're going
to be a hotshot Cambridge lawyer.' Chloe made a smug 'score
one to me' gesture in the air and flounced out.

Some seconds later, Becca and Anna heard the opening
bars of 'I Kissed a Girl' being bellowed through the karaoke
machine in Chloe's room. Only she was singing, 'I Stole Some
Jeans (and I Liked It)'.

'. . . the jeans of *MY SAD SISTER . . .*'

'Becca,' said Anna, kicking the door shut, 'is there anything going on with you and Owen? You can tell me.'

Becca inspected her ragged revision nails. 'No,' she said. 'We're just hanging out.'

'Really?'

Anna didn't want to push too hard, but nor did she want to embarrass Becca if the crush was a bit one-sided. She knew that feeling too.

'. . . I stole some jeans *AND THEY FIT ME . . .*'

Becca stared into space, unable to hide the smile that had nothing to do with Chloe's singing, then she looked back at Anna, her eyes sparkling with the need to share it with someone. 'We've had a picnic in the park. He's taken me out for lunch. We talk a lot about everything. He's such an interesting guy – he's spent time in India, and Ireland, and he wants to work in New York . . .'

'He's a bit older than you,' said Anna.

'There's a bigger gap between you and Dad,' said Becca, with a speed that suggested she'd pre-prepared that particular argument.

'There's a difference between twenty-four and eighteen, and thirty-three and twenty-four.' As Anna said it, she knew – and Becca knew – that they were arguing about maths; she'd been much more naive than Becca, even at twenty-four with a degree *and* a job.

'But I've got more in common with Owen than with the lads at school,' said Becca. 'They're so fixated on stupid stuff. Owen's done things. He's got his own ideas, not just a load of band T-shirts. I could lie there and just talk to him for hours and hours.'

Lie there. The dreamy way she said it made one question flash into Anna's mind, and she couldn't not ask. Men like Owen didn't lie around for hours just talking. Not for long.

'Becca, are you . . . ?' This wasn't in the parenting books either. But Owen had a flat of his own and no revision timetable, unlike Josh the oboe boy. Phil wouldn't ask. She had to struggle on. 'Are you sleeping together?'

Becca turned red. '*Anna!* No.'

'Right,' said Anna. That sounded more like a 'not yet' than a 'no'. Becca's body language was more forthcoming. Now she had the information she'd wanted, Anna wasn't sure it made her feel any happier.

'Are you going to tell Dad?' Becca asked, and the blissful look left her face. 'It's just . . . You remember what he was like with Josh. That horrendous dinner. I don't want Owen to get the "What are your intentions?" speech. Not yet. Not until he isn't going to go off me because my family are a bunch of loons.'

'No,' said Anna. 'No one wants that.' She struggled internally, trying to balance the trust Becca had just put in her with her own responsibility to Phil. The trouble was, it was so tempting to promise that, yes, she'd keep their secret. It felt like the first proper stepmother thing she'd done.

'Please don't tell him yet,' Becca begged, seeing her waver.

'OK.' She was going to have to talk to Michelle, though. Like that conversation was going to be any less awkward. 'How about *you* tell him, once you're sure Owen won't mind coming to dinner? You can ask him over. Maybe Michelle can come too, make it seem less of an interview?' If Owen was nice, and he liked talking as much as Becca said he did, that wouldn't be too long, she argued to herself.

Becca seemed happy. 'Fair enough.'

'But soon, Becca,' Anna warned her. 'It'd be awful if he found out from someone else.'

There was another blast of singing from across the landing, as if someone had opened a bedroom door to make a loud point.

'. . . I stole her jeans *AND THEY'RE STRETCHY*, hope her *BOYFRIEND* don't mind it . . . A baggy *ARSE*, a baggy *KNEE* . . .'

Becca narrowed her eyes. 'Promise me you'll cut the plug off that thing while we're away?'

'Bring me some Whitestrips from Duane Reade,' said Anna, 'and it can be arranged.'

They shook on it.

Later that night, when Anna was going through her diary at the kitchen table, blocking out the next few weeks with work and Reading Aloud sessions, she noticed something she'd been too busy to notice before.

Her period should have started two days ago.

She flicked backwards through the squares of dance classes, bookshop shifts and supermarket deliveries, and frowned. No, she'd definitely had her last period on the fifth – she'd taken so many painkillers for her terrible cramps that she'd read the same page of *Right Ho, Jeeves* three times over at Butterfields before one of the old dears had pointed it out to her.

'This is rubbish,' Chloe announced from the sofa. The girls and Phil were watching *Britain's Got Talent*, and marking everyone harshly out of ten. 'I cannot *believe* these morons got through the auditions and we didn't.'

'You should have trained Pongo to dance with you,' said Lily, who was allowed to stay up to join in the criticism. Pongo was on the sofa next to her, draping himself equally over her and Chloe, his head resting lovingly in Lily's lap. 'Then you'd have won.'

'They'd have put Pongo through and not the Apricotz,' said Becca. 'That's if they could have told the singing apart.'

'Anna? Don't you think they're crap?' demanded Chloe, over her shoulder.

'At least you can hear what they're singing. And don't say "crap",' admonished Phil. 'Say something more intelligent.'

'Don't you think they're *bollocks*? What? That's Chaucer. Anna, tell him how bad they are. He's too old to realise, poor old man.'

Anna carried on staring at her diary. Was this real? Had she got it wrong? No, it added up. Her heart hammered in her chest. Was she actually pregnant? Without noticing? Was that even possible?

'Er, they're not very good,' she said, without thinking. 'Definitely not as good as the Apricotz.'

Pregnant. For once words seemed inadequate, too detached from what was happening right now inside her. Anna had never been pregnant before. She had no idea what it was supposed to feel like, beyond the swooning, rampant vomiting, or luminous blooming of fictional mothers-to-be, which she presumed was a bit exaggerated.

Although, now she thought about it, she did feel faintly . . . nauseous. Nauseous, and excited.

'Vote them off!' roared Chloe from the sofa. 'It's a NNNGGGHHH from me!'

'And it's a NNNGGGHHH from me too!' said Lily.

'Anna, why don't you come and watch this with us?' Phil looked round from his La-Z-Boy chair, one of the pair he'd bought when it was just the two of them. 'I need some intellectual commentary to counterbalance this honking.'

'Um, yeah, in a minute.'

Anna checked the dates again, and again, and when the pages started swimming in front of her eyes she made herself walk over to the sofa. It felt like walking on clouds, or on the moon, her knees light and insubstantial in her legs.

I'm pregnant, she kept thinking. Over and over. I'm pregnant.

She managed to get through bath and bedtime, and a chapter of Lily's new story, and then chivvying Chloe upstairs, before she finally got Phil on his own.

'Phil, there's something we need to talk about,' she said, watching his back as he loaded the dishwasher.

'If it's letting Chloe audition for *Britain's Got Talent*, the answer's still no. Not even if she trains Pongo to do the paso doble with her.'

'No, it's . . . ' Anna swallowed, watching him ram the pasta pan in the wrong section of the rack. What was the right way to do this? In her imagination over the years she'd gone for all sorts of cutesy tactics: the bootee in the cake box, the positive pregnancy test under his pillow. When it came to it now, she just wanted to blurt it out. 'It's not Chloe. It's me.'

Phil seemed to sense her jitteriness, and put down the tea towel. 'What? Is it something the girls have done?'

'No! No, they're fine. It's . . .'

Phil looked up, then saw the strain mingling with excitement on her face. 'Anna?'

'Sit down,' she said, gesturing at the table. 'I know, it's an awful cliché, but I'd prefer it if we were sitting down.'

He pulled out a chair and slid onto it. The crease between his brows had deepened now. 'OK,' he said. 'Please don't tell me you want to leave. I have literally no idea how anything works in this house. I'm sorry, whatever it is I've done.'

'What? No!' Anna nearly laughed at how wrong he was. She sat down and reached for his hands, and when he curled his fingers round hers, she said quietly, 'Phil, my period's late. It's never late.'

'How late?'

'Two days.'

He said nothing for a few long seconds, then asked, 'Have you done a test?' A muscle in his neck twitched.

'Not yet,' said Anna. She smiled, she couldn't help it. 'I didn't want to tempt fate.'

'How? It's not really up to fate, is it? I mean, you're either pregnant or you're not, it's not like you can . . . Sorry.' He wiped a hand across his face. 'Sorry, that's not the right thing to say.'

'No,' said Anna. 'It's not.' She sat back in her chair and looked at him.

This wasn't the reaction she'd expected. She hadn't been banking on euphoria, given the things he'd said the other day about babies being stinky and exhausting. But excitement, definitely. Pretend disappointment that the shed was off the agenda for a while, possibly. Not this. Not . . . *annoyance*.

'Are you sure?' he said, starting again. 'It's just that two days is quite early. You've been pretty stressed lately, that can affect your period.'

'I know I'm not as expert as you, but I can count,' Anna began, but he held up his hands to stop her.

'Sorry. It's just that . . . well, I've been through a few false alarms, let's say.'

'Well, I haven't,' she said, hurt. 'So bear with me if I'm feeling a bit excited. Phil, I might be having a baby. Doesn't that make you feel . . . thrilled?' She paused. He didn't look very thrilled. 'How *do* you feel?'

'Well, half of me would be pretty impressed that everything was still working,' Phil replied, with a half-laugh. 'But then the other half of me would be a bit scared.' He raised an eyebrow. 'And I'd be on the phone to the surgery, wondering who we could sue about the Pill. Isn't it meant to be ninety-nine per cent effective? What happened? Were you sick? Did you miss one?'

This was it. The point on the tracks where their marriage could go one way or another. Anna couldn't understand how it had gone from fizzy excitement to panic in a matter of seconds.

'It is pretty reliable, yes,' she said. 'If you're taking it. But I'm not.'

'What?' He stared at her. 'You're joking, right?'

'No. You *knew* I'd stopped. I stopped after our anniversary, like we agreed when we got married. Don't pretend you'd forgotten that?'

Phil said nothing, and Anna's heart hung in her chest. Everything felt like it was hanging – for this second, he was still her handsome, reliable husband, her dream man, her complicated-but-worth-it family. In the next moment, all that could be crushed. She knew it sounded melodramatic – she could hear the screechiness of her inner voice – but that was how tightly wound she was. So tightly she hadn't even considered any other reactions.

'I hadn't forgotten,' said Phil slowly, his voice low, 'but I didn't think you'd go ahead and do something as serious *for all of us* as stop using contraception without discussing it first.'

'We discussed it in the car,' said Anna. 'On the way to the airport.'

'That wasn't a discussion, that was just a general chat about families! Did you actually say, oh by the way, just so you know, from now on every time we have sex, you might get an early Christmas present? No!' Phil barked, then swallowed to control his temper. 'Anna. Did you listen to anything I said about the girls being unsettled by Sarah buggering off and leaving them here? Or about how I'd quite like some time to ourselves? Some time off from parenting?'

'I heard all that.' Anna was struggling to keep the tears out of her own voice. 'But did you hear me telling you how much I want a baby? Not just then, but for the last four years? I don't see why this *is* such a bad time. Sarah's coming back in a year, and the longer we leave it, the bigger the gap will be between Lily and another baby, and the older *we'll* be.'

'And the exams that the kids have got coming up?'

'We don't have to tell them yet. When are pregnancies supposed to be safe to announce? Three months? That's *way* after their exams finish.'

'You've got it all worked out, haven't you?' he said, and there was a forced levity in his voice that made Anna flinch. 'How long have you been thinking about this, without bothering to talk to me?'

'This isn't something I did on a *whim*,' she said, angry that he seemed to be making out she'd tricked him into it. 'You knew I wanted a big family. It's all I've been thinking about for the past year. Our baby. Our family.' Anna could feel the tears coming up her throat, a tidal wave of hormones running riot through her body, soaking the tiny bundle of cells in all the essential emotions. Stress. Family politics. Her own all-embracing love for it.

Somewhere deep inside herself she knew she was being irrational and unfair, that she'd let the powerful cocktail of hormones and fermenting broodiness sweep over her usual common sense. She was ashamed of her selfishness but at the same time she wasn't. This wasn't about her, it was about someone else. Something else that relied on *her* to make it happen.

Phil had his head in his hands. 'I, I, I . . . For God's sake, Anna. The whole point about being a parent is that *nothing* is about you any more,' he spluttered unhappily, but then he looked up and saw how shell-shocked she was at his reaction.

Anna was finding it hard to breathe.

At once he pushed his chair away from the table and was kneeling by her side in an instant, his arms around her. 'I didn't mean it like that. It's not that I don't want us to have a baby, it's just that . . .'

'Don't say it.'

He was silent for a few moments, rocking her backwards and forwards in his arms while Anna tried to sort out what she thought.

It doesn't matter what you think, said a voice in her head. *Or what he thinks. If the baby's here, it's here.*

'We'll be OK,' she said, stroking Phil's head. 'It's going to be OK.'

Anna wasn't sure who she was talking to – Phil, the swirling cells inside her, or herself, but Phil's only response was to squeeze her tightly and to say nothing, and that wasn't the reaction she was after either.

17

*'Poor Mrs Pepperpot has an unfortunate habit of
shrinking at the most inconvenient times – and then
has to puzzle her way out of her scrapes using only her
considerable wits. We've all been there.'* Anna McQueen

Anna woke up the next morning expecting the world to feel
different, but she felt disappointingly normal. Pongo still
barked at exactly twenty to seven to be let out; and Chloe still
took twenty-five minutes in the bathroom while everyone
stacked up outside like circling planes. The only real hum of
excitement was that it was the beginning of the girls' holiday,
and the start of her own week off.

This time, the girls were taking a night flight out to New
York to see Sarah, so instead of the usual bleary-eyed rush to
the airport with Becca hustling and panicking all the way, it
was a semi-normal Saturday. Phil took Lily to her swimming
lesson, and Chloe went off to get shopping lists from Tyra and
Paige, now reinstated as an Apricot, thanks to her family's
investment in a Powerplate. Becca insisted on doing her shift
at the bookshop, even though Anna had assumed she'd be
taking the morning off.

'I don't mind, honestly,' she said, already at the door with
her denim jacket on when Anna grabbed her own bag to go.

'But you've got the house to yourself.' Anna couldn't believe that Becca would pass up the chance of a quiet hour or two. 'Stay in. Watch telly. Get your stuff out of Chloe's bag while she's not here. You need to relax, Becca. You've been revising so hard.'

Becca didn't deny that; she'd been working late every night. 'If I stay here I'll just feel I should be revising.' She paused and gave Anna a nudge. 'I *like* your shop. I'd be hanging out there even if I didn't have a job. Come on, let's walk over via the mobile coffee van and get a pastry.'

'OK,' said Anna, touched that Becca was choosing to spend some time with her of her own volition. She'd been planning to go to the shop via Boots to get a pregnancy test, but it could wait. She didn't mind spinning out that excitement a little longer; she wanted to give herself as much chance of a positive as possible.

They set off towards the town centre, chatting about Becca's exam timetable and Chloe's irritating new habit of talking about herself in the third person as if she was narrating her own reality show. Becca was interested in Lily's bedtime reading, and offered to keep it up while they were in New York, something that made Anna's heart glow with happiness. It was a warm spring day, and her whole body felt light and full of possibilities. She could almost feel the hormones surging through her system like the multi-coloured chocolate pipes on the old Willy Wonka book jacket.

'It's funny how one thing leads to another, isn't it?' said Becca, running her hands through the honeysuckle climbing along the park railings. 'If you hadn't met Michelle in the café with Pongo, you wouldn't have been friends, and she wouldn't have asked you to run the bookshop, and you wouldn't have got me a job, and I wouldn't have met Owen . . .'

'Yes,' said Anna ironically. 'It's all down to me.'

'I mean it,' replied Becca. She looked happy, and it struck Anna that she hadn't seen Becca this happy in a while. Revision stress had put a crease between her eyes that was still visible even now. 'I think I've already got my ideal job.'

'Well, you can put it on hold for a while when the exams really get going,' said Anna. 'You'll need that time off for relaxation.'

Becca didn't say anything. She bounced her palm along the railing tops.

'And just tell me if there's anything I can do to help, won't you?' Anna went on. Even now she felt a flood of relief that she'd never have to sit another exam; she still had anxiety dreams about writing essays about Hamlet's inner demons in the nude, under a giant clock. 'My mum used to bring me tea every ninety minutes to stop my brain dehydrating. By the time I sat my exams I practically had tannin poisoning.'

'Did your parents go to university?' asked Becca.

Anna shook her head. 'No, I was the first one in the family. My dad was a builder like his dad, and Mum was a nurse. She went straight to training college, but these days she'd probably have been encouraged to do a proper medical degree.'

'So it was quite a big deal, you going.'

'I suppose so.' Anna remembered the look on her parents' faces when her results arrived. As if they were proud and scared of her at the same time. Five As. Their daughter, 'the brainbox'. 'They wanted me to do all the things they didn't. But that's what parents do – they want the world for you.'

'Did you *want* to go?'

'Oh, definitely. I always wanted to be surrounded by books. If I'd been a bit cleverer, I'd have liked to have stayed at uni forever, doing research.' Anna sighed. 'But I think the job I've got now is almost as good. Better, maybe. I don't think they'd have let me do a doctorate in children's stories. Unless that's what you call a Mickey Mouse degree?'

Becca half laughed, half groaned. 'Anna, that's the kind of crap joke Dad would make. You're catching it off him.'

'Am I?' Anna pretended to look horrified.

This is *really* nice, she thought, slipping her heavy book bag onto the opposite shoulder. This was a proper, sharing conversation, the kind she'd always hoped they'd eventually have. Maybe that confession about Owen meant they had crossed a bridge.

'Where did you go to university?' Becca asked her.

'Manchester. I'd have loved to go to Cambridge,' said Anna. 'No one at my school was really encouraged to apply, so I never bothered. If I had my time again, I would. Definitely. Just to warn you, I *will* be coming to visit.'

Becca chewed her lip, then said in a rush, 'I know everyone thinks I'm going to walk in but what if I get there and everyone's way cleverer than me? I mean, it's not hard to look clever at Longhampton, not when half the sixth form's hungover on Monday morning – don't tell Dad that, by the way – but Cambridge . . . everyone's going to be a genius. What if I get the grades, but I can't do it? What if I get there and I don't *want* to do it?'

Anna had never heard Becca say anything remotely negative about her plans for law school, and it surprised her. She wondered how long she'd been worrying about it without letting on.

Becca had stepped up her pace, as if walking was the only way of getting the words out. 'Dad thinks it's easy for me. Just a matter of reading the books and turning up for the exams. What do you think he'd do if I don't get in?'

'He'd still love you,' said Anna. 'Whatever you do.'

Becca didn't reply, and Anna grabbed her arm to stop her walking on.

'Becca?' she said, leaning forward to meet her downcast eye. 'I mean it. Whatever you do, we'll all love you and support you. Your dad's proud of you, but don't let that feel like extra pressure, because it's not. He just wants you to do everything you can. University's not like school. It's about growing up and learning how to set yourself challenges, finding out who you are. You'll meet so many different people, and yes, some will be cleverer than you, some won't be. But you'll be the one there, having the time of your life. Doing amazing things and stupid things and things you'll never do again.'

They were at the top end of the high street now, nearly at the bookshop.

'And we'll always be here,' Anna added. 'Being proud of you. I know you've got your mum and your dad, but you've got me too. As a spare. If you need a different shoulder.' She could only just get the words out past the lump in her throat. 'I'm proud of you too.'

Becca gave Anna a watery smile. 'I know,' she said. Her lip wobbled. 'Thank you.'

'Oh, come here,' said Anna and wrapped her arms around Becca, feeling her slim frame lean into hers, and they hugged in the street, oblivious to passers-by.

When they pushed open the door to the bookshop, Michelle and Owen were leaning on the counter, staring intently at Owen's laptop.

'Hey!' he said, his eyes lighting up when he saw Becca. He stood up, towering over his sister, and Becca straightened her spine too, instead of hunching over as she had tended to when she was with Josh, who barely came up to her ear.

The crackle in the air between them was so obvious, thought Anna. If she knew Owen a bit better she might be happier about it. As it was, she only had one or two of Michelle's indulgent stories about his shenanigans in Ireland to go on, and they weren't inspiring.

She tried to balance that with her own experience of Owen – charming, helpful, friendly, not that punctual. But Becca was a smart girl, she argued. She wouldn't put up with a wrong 'un, surely?

'I've finished the website,' Owen said. 'Come and have a look.'

'It's not bad,' said Michelle, over the top of the laptop. 'Obviously there's some work still to be done . . .'

'Never satisfied,' said Owen. 'That's your problem.'

Anna went over to look, and was suitably impressed. Owen had somehow managed to capture the friendly atmosphere in the bookshop, with the same soft colours, background music and virtual bookshelves decorated with 'We Love . . .' cards in Becca's artistic handwriting. Becca – not Chloe – featured in the background, leading shoppers around the store, and Tavish popped up now and again if you moved the cursor into certain spots.

'I love it,' said Anna. 'That's gorgeous!'

'Apart from me,' said Becca, twisting in adolescent mortification. 'I look *terrible*. Why didn't you tell me you were using those photos? My nose looks *enormous*.'

'You look beautiful,' said Owen with a touch too much enthusiasm, then covered his reaction by turning to Anna. 'Doesn't she?'

Anna gave him a square look that she hoped told him that she knew what was going on. 'She does.'

His confident grin wavered. 'I can, er, put you on there too, if you want?'

'No, it's OK.'

'Right, well, now the cavalry's here, I can get back to next door,' said Michelle. 'Owen, can you get on with that upstairs? I'd like it to go live by the end of today.'

He started to argue but then saw Michelle's expression and closed his laptop. 'No problem. I'll be . . . next door. Upstairs.'

Becca followed him out with her eyes, watching his slender hips in the faded jeans, then seemed to spring back to life when she realised Anna and Michelle were both looking at her. 'Oh. Er, coffee? Shall I put the machine on?'

'Good idea,' said Michelle and sat down at the counter, scribbling some notes in Anna's day book.

Anna waited until Becca had taken the coffee jug into the back kitchen to clean it, then leaned over to murmur in her ear. 'Michelle, I don't know if you know—' she started, but Michelle looked up before she could finish.

'What? That Owen and Becca are seeing each other?'

'Yes.' Anna was surprised. 'How come you didn't tell me?'

'Tell you what?' Michelle glanced back down at the list and crossed out a couple of to-dos. 'I'm his sister, Anna. Not his mum.'

Something about Michelle's nonchalance riled Anna. 'Well, I'm effectively *her* mum. I don't generally go in for spying on the kids but given that he's so much older than her, and you know she's got her exams coming up, I'm surprised you didn't mention it.'

Anna's surging hormones made it come out more dramatically than she had meant it to, and Michelle's head bounced up. She looked defensive.

'I *was* going to say something. I don't think it's been going on long – and before you ask, yes, I've made it really clear to him how important her exams are, and how I'll personally have his balls for tableware if he's anything less than a perfect gentleman. But if I'd come round to you and said, "Ooh, Becca's dating Owen," what would you have done? Stopped her seeing him? Because that always goes over *really* well with teenagers.'

Anna had to concede, rather unwillingly, that Michelle was right. It still didn't make her any less annoyed that she hadn't said anything, though. Whose loyalty was more important here?

'You know Phil will go absolutely nuclear if this gets . . . messy?' she said. She didn't want to think too hard about what she meant by 'messy'.

'How messy can it get? Look, it's not that hard to keep an eye on them if Becca's in school and Gillian's in the shop under the flat from nine till six every day,' said Michelle reasonably. 'And it's easier to do that if they're not sneaking around.' She tried a wan smile. 'I bet you didn't do much sneaking around when you were a teenager, did you?'

'No,' admitted Anna.

'Well, I've had a lot of practice at keeping an eye on Owen and believe me, it's much easier when he thinks he's not being watched.'

Anna looked horrified and sank into a chair. 'Is that supposed to fill me with confidence?'

Michelle let out a groany laugh. 'Sorry. But it's true. Any teenage boy would be the same. You're just lucky you haven't had to deal with it yet. Think of it as practice for Chloe.'

'Becca isn't a sneaking around type,' she said. 'But she was pretty quick to remind me that I'm not in a position to lecture her about older boyfriends.' Anna put her head in her hands. 'Why do I get a bad feeling about this?'

'Are you saying my brother gives you a bad feeling?'
Michelle's tone was jokey, but the words weren't.

'Not exactly.'

She *did* have a bad feeling. Already she could feel a thin
layer of complication settling over the desk between them.
Michelle was usually bracingly honest about Owen's charm
but now she was being defensive. Anna knew she'd be saying
very different things if Owen had started dating Kelsey.

'I have to tell Phil,' she said, realising that she'd made a
mistake in promising Becca she wouldn't. 'Oh *God*. He's only
just come to terms with his princess going out with that spotty
oboe boy.'

'Owen's not exactly a cradle-snatcher. He's got a job,'
Michelle pointed out. 'And a degree.'

'True. And he doesn't have a motorbike. Or a tattoo.'

'Actually, he's got a tattoo. A small one. Maybe two.'

'What? No . . .'

Michelle checked Becca wasn't on her way back and
dropped her voice. 'Listen, Anna, I've been thinking about this
too and the worst case scenario is that they have some kind of
summer fling, then she goes off to university in October and
it fizzles out. Becca's a sensible girl. She knows how important
her exams are.'

'And Owen? You think he can be sensible?' Anna looked
quizzically at Michelle. 'Before you answer, don't forget you've
told me certain things about him and his less-than-reliable
habits with ladies. '

Michelle paused. 'Owen seems pretty smitten, to be honest.'

'You sound surprised.'

Michelle was choosing her words carefully. 'Normally by
now he's practically moved in with them, or he's disappeared
altogether, but he's been here. On his own. Rory says he's seen

him staying in – he went round to borrow some milk the other night.' They both boggled at that domestic detail.

'So when did Becca tell you?' Michelle asked.

It was Anna's turn to hesitate. 'A couple of days ago.'

'Really? And when were you going to tell *me*?' Michelle lifted an eyebrow. 'If you think it's such an issue?

'Just now. I told you just now!' Anna realised that – again – her moral high ground was a bit slipperier than she'd thought it was. She didn't really enjoy Michelle's answering expression. It made her uncomfortable.

They looked at each other in silence.

Fortunately Becca reappeared before either of them had to think of what they could say next without escalating things.

'Who wants coffee?' Becca waved the jug at them, her face fresh and young and excited. 'I've got biscuits too!'

'Me, please,' said Anna. 'A strong one.'

18

'Are You There, God? It's Me, Margaret *answered all the questions I was too shy to ask. Judy Blume makes growing up seem exciting and intriguing, without ever patronising.*' Becca McQueen

Once the girls had been safely packed off on the night flight, armed with fruit and water – and in Lily's case, an actual book – Anna turned to her holiday list.

The first thing on it was to have lunch the following day with her mum and dad, whom she hadn't seen since her fleeting visit to them before Christmas to pick up and collect presents like a demented courier elf.

Anna missed the companionable walks with her dad and his wheezy old Labrador, and her easy chats with her mother in her small kitchen. Though she spoke to her mum on the phone a few times a week, it wasn't the same as seeing them, and the familiar house they'd lived in all her life, full of books and memories. She knew they missed her too, their only child, and worried about her place in Phil's complicated family, although they were far too polite to say so.

Anna glanced across the car. Phil was resting his elbow on the open window and singing along to Blondie on the radio and not getting the lyrics right, and butterflies fluttered in her chest. They'd managed to talk more, and although he still wasn't exactly joyful about the possibility of a baby, he definitely wasn't as panicky as he had been that first night. She reckoned his mood was now at 'tentatively hopeful'.

Her period was now officially four days late. Though she hadn't had a clear positive test, her obsessive internet searching suggested that this wasn't unusual. She hadn't told anyone else, preferring to hug it to herself until it was definite. Her and Phil's secret. It was like the month before Christmas, or the last few days of term. A delicious certainty was bubbling inside her that something new was happening. They were taking a step forward – everyone together, properly, for the first time.

For once Anna wasn't dreading her mother's veiled, anxious questions about her own grandchildren, usually posed while the two of them made sandwiches in the kitchen well out of earshot of Phil and her dad, because now she could smile enigmatically and say, '*Mum*, it's in hand.'

Somewhere in the car a phone beeped with a text message. They were meeting Anna's parents in a hotel just outside Ledbury for lunch, and her dad's new mastery of his mobile meant any rendezvous required multiple progress updates.

'Is that mine?' Anna looked round; her bag was on the back seat. 'Might be my dad, wanting an ETA. You know what he's like, probably wants to get the menu on standby.'

'No, I think it's mine,' Phil said, turning to find his jacket. 'You keep your eyes on the road, please. I hope you won't be teaching Becca to drive like that.'

'I won't be teaching her at all unless you promise to take out a massive life insurance policy for me,' replied Anna happily. 'And get me a better car.'

'Oh God,' said Phil. 'The *car*. Do you know what

six-seaters look like? Minibuses. We'll look like we're running a youth club.'

'Shut up,' said Anna. 'Becca won't be in it, she'll be away. Five seats will be fine.'

When Phil didn't rise to that, she glanced across and saw he was frowning at his phone. 'What?' she asked. 'Please don't tell me it's work. Don't they understand what weekends are?'

'It's Becca,' said Phil. 'She wants us to turn on Skype.'

'Now?' The Skype request wasn't unusual – they Skyped daily with whichever parent they weren't with — or rather Lily did; the other two often just waved in passing while Lily recounted her day in bum-numbing detail. 'I thought they'd be Skype-ing around seven. Weren't we getting back for that?'

'That was the plan, yes. I'll tell her we're out,' said Phil. 'Sarah probably just wants me to tell Chloe she can't do something ridiculous like get her nose pierced. You know what she's like, always asking for something totally outrageous so we'll give in and let her do something plain daft instead. Expectation management. Bet Sarah taught her that too.'

He fiddled with his mobile and Anna carried on driving, pleased that for once she'd taken priority.

But the phone beeped again almost immediately.

'If that's Lily worried about the soft toys in the heatwave, tell her we'll arrange them in the shade,' she said.

Phil muttered under his breath. 'Apparently we *have* to go home *now* and Skype Becca. Right now, in capitals.'

Capitals. That didn't sound like Becca to Anna, and the first ripples of worry began to disturb the surface of her good mood. 'Are you sure it's not Chloe texting on Becca's phone?'

'There are exclamation marks, too. Lots of them.'

Anna flicked on the indicator, her eyes searching the side of the road for a parking space. *Deal with it before you have time to be annoyed by it* was one of her fail-safe step-parenting tactics. Parents wouldn't think, they'd just act. She'd had to learn to do that, or else she knew she'd have dissolved in a ball of fury months ago.

'What are you doing?' demanded Phil.

'I'm parking. Call her. If it's so important, ring her straight back.' Anna pulled into a space, put on the handbrake and looked at him. She tried not to give in to her crossness. 'Go on. Then you can sort it out, whatever it is, and we can get on with lunch.'

Phil's brow creased. Indecision often paralysed him when it came to parenting decisions. That was how Chloe managed to run rings around him so easily. 'Should I? I mean, what if it's just some silly row that she's having with Sarah? You know what they used to be like when they lived with her – winding each other up, then phoning me to referee. I don't want them to start doing that again. I mean, I don't want you to . . .' He paused. 'It's not fair on you. This was meant to be *our* time.'

'Isn't that the whole point about having kids, according to you?' said Anna. 'You never have your own time again?'

'Don't start that,' he said. 'We're having a nice day, so far.'

She took a deep breath. 'If you don't call Becca back, you'll only drive *me* mad worrying that she was ringing from the bottom of a well or something. Then she'll phone us at my mum's, and she'll get that face of hers on again. Do it.' She turned off the engine and folded her arms. 'Or I will.'

Phil looked as if he was thinking about arguing, but then sighed and dialled the number.

Anna stared at her hands clamped round the steering wheel and focused on the diamond rings on her wedding finger. Two beautiful diamond rings – one exquisite engagement ring, the other an eternity band Phil had given her shortly after the girls moved in, as a silent thank you for dealing with everything. Better that they sorted this out now than at her parents', where her mum's eagle eyes would be on her and her dad would be pretending not to notice Phil's hushed phone conversation in the other room.

'Becca, it's Dad,' said Phil. 'What's going on?'

Anna strained her ears to hear what Becca was saying, but Phil had the phone right against his head.

It would be just the same with our kids, she told herself, then immediately knew it wouldn't be. With their kids, *she'd* be allowed to take this call and deal with this problem. She'd want to. She'd be desperate to know what was upsetting Becca so much. It wouldn't be a case of sitting here feeling involved but not needed.

Anna closed her eyes and rested a hand on her stomach. The fact that Phil looked so concerned and fatherly only made her more anxious inside. He would love all his children exactly the same. But a new thought had started to spring tiny insidious shoots – what if she loved her own baby just that little bit more than these three? What if she just couldn't be bothered as much any more, jumping through these endless hoops? Anna knew she'd make herself do it, because she'd never want to let them see, but what if . . . ?

'Just tell me over the phone,' he was saying. 'Anna and I are in the car, we're on our way to see her mum and dad for lunch.' He frowned. 'Becca, don't talk to me like that. Just tell me . . . Sarah! Did you just grab the phone off Becca? What the hell's going on?'

'What?' Anna mouthed at him, intrigued by the squawks coming from the mobile.

He pressed the phone to his chest and turned to Anna, his

brow wrinkled. 'They've all gone mad. I can't hear anything anyone's saying because they're all yelling at the same time. Becca's on the phone, then Sarah's in the background yelling at her, and someone's crying . . .'

'No singing?'

'Not even any singing . . . OK. Chloe. What's happening?'

Phil started to tell Chloe off, but whatever he was saying died in his throat and his face became stony, then concerned.

'Well, that's not going to happen. You're just being dramatic. You know that isn't . . . Chloe, it makes no difference to how . . . Chloe! Put your mother back on. Actually no, put Becca on. *Put Becca on.* Becca, hello. Now just tell me, in plain and simple language – you want to come home tomorrow *why?*'

Anna groaned silently. *Please don't come home yet,* she thought. She had a lot lined up for the next six days: a mixture of all the fun things Phil claimed to miss doing, plus some important baby testing and preparation that, ideally, she'd share with him alone. She couldn't say it aloud, obviously, but the last thing she wanted was for the girls to come back yet, unless something was seriously amiss. Like Sarah's house had burned down.

Although, even then, there were always hotels.

Anna was starting to make 'let me talk to her' gestures to Phil, when he cleared his throat and said something that made the breath in her chest turn to dry ice.

'Becca,' he said slowly and too calmly, 'just because your mother's having another baby doesn't mean she doesn't love you lot any more.'

The girls' flights were exchangeable and the first one they could book themselves on to arrived back in Birmingham at 10 a.m. the following day. Sarah insisted on coming back with them too, 'for a family summit', so Phil took the day off work to deal with it all.

'You don't have to wade into this,' he'd said, when Anna asked what she could do. 'Unless you want to.'

They'd had an awkward moment then, when Anna honestly hadn't known what to say, or whether he wanted her there or not. On the one hand, she felt she probably should be there, to reinforce the fact that she was a bona fide member of the family; on the other, she wasn't sure she could bear the pain of seeing the girls' reaction to their mother's pregnancy, knowing that whatever they were feeling now would only be doubled when they heard her news. Trebled, even.

In the end, the car made the decision for her. There wasn't room for three girls plus Sarah and Anna. It wasn't a journey that she fancied sitting in on, not until the girls had worked through the first round of hysteria: the memory of Chloe 'disappointed' in a closed space was still fresh from the return journey from the *Britain's Got Talent* auditions.

When Phil had left for the airport, unable to eat more than a bit of dry toast after their sleepless night of circular conversation that had trailed off in the dark, Anna took herself and Pongo round to Michelle's for an early morning walk and a dose of common sense.

'I can't believe you're not squeezed in there somehow,' Michelle said as they walked the dogs round the park in the lemony morning light. 'I'd *love* to be a fly on the wall for that. Has Chloe gone into dramatic overdrive? I bet Sarah's wishing she'd told them by Skype.'

Anna pulled Pongo back from the Weimeraner he had a dog crush on. 'Chloe's already run through her Little Orphan

Annie routine on the phone. *No one's going to love her. She never comes first with anyone. No one understands.* By now she'll probably have moved on to fury. I'm telling you, Phil's longing for the days of "I want blue hair and teeth veneers".'

'What's Phil promised to buy her to make up for *this*? A pony?'

'Ha! He's a one-man Argos catalogue of guilt. Although I suppose this is just a delayed reaction to Sarah leaving, rather than the baby,' Anna added gloomily. 'They've been so good up until now. No major tantrums about moving in with us, coping with their mum being away from them . . . I should have known it would all kick off eventually. I knew it was all too easy.'

Just thinking about the girls' reaction made her wince. Were they going to do exactly the same to her when they found out? Was it better or worse that Sarah was their real mum? It wouldn't be about her, though. It would be about Phil.

'You've worked bloody hard, you mean.' Michelle gave her a firm look. 'Fair enough them kicking off about their mum leaving, but not fair enough when they kick off about something that's not really their business. Chloe's sixteen, not six. Did they really think Sarah wouldn't want another baby?'

'They're kids, they don't even like to think of their parents having sex.' Anna's headache throbbed. She'd meant to do another test that morning, but when it came to it, she was too scared to pee on the stick, in case it said no. In case there was only room in the cosmos for one of Phil's wives to be pregnant at any one time. Which was ridiculous. 'I didn't see it coming, either. Sarah only went out there to push her career on as far as she could. Making up for all the time she took off having Chloe and Becca, or so she told me when she dropped all their gear round.'

'How old is she?'

'Nearly forty, same as Phil. Apparently' – Anna made air commas as best she could while holding Pongo's lead – 'it wasn't planned but she and Jeff are both very happy about it. I think she's hoping for a little boy.'

'Good for her.' Michelle pulled Tavish away from the litter bin he was sniffing. Anna noted his black fur was looking a lot neater than normal, almost as if Michelle had taken him to a proper groomer to be trimmed. 'And how about Phil? How's he taken this? Retreated to his imaginary shed yet? Or have you kept him to his promise?'

'How do you mean?' Anna felt her cheeks heat up under Michelle's direct gaze.

'Well, he could have his own little boy, couldn't he? If he got on with it, and stopped putting everyone ahead of his own wife.'

'I don't know,' said Anna honestly. 'He blows hot and cold about the whole thing. I, um . . .' She wondered how much Michelle could tell just from her face. She'd always been able to read her, even when she thought she was being super poker-faced.

'Are you pregnant?' said Michelle, and Anna glanced shyly sideways.

'Maybe. I don't know. I hope so. Don't say anything. It's early days,' she warned. 'Very, very early days. Too early.'

'Congratulations!' Michelle hesitated for a split second, then slipped an arm through hers, squeezing her waist in a side-hug, all they could manage with dog leads. 'Masterstroke timing. They can hardly complain if it's half-siblings all round.'

'Well, that's one way of looking at it.'

Michelle steered Tavish – and Anna – towards the park

coffee stall, already open and doing business with other dog-walkers.

'Chloe and Becca will be fine, but to be honest I'm more worried about Lily,' Anna went on. 'She's only just got used Sarah being away. She can be really chatty, then she'll go all quiet and you have no idea what's going on in her head until she speaks again, and it's always about something completely different. I told you that she's been letting me read to her at night? I think it's helping us bond. I don't want her to think that she's being pushed out again.'

'Anna,' said Michelle, stopping to get her purse out. 'Why are you acting so guilty? None of this is your fault.'

'But it is, though. I feel like it is. Sarah and Jeff sound really excited about their baby and I just don't know if Phil's . . .' She stopped, then made herself say it. 'I don't know if Phil really wants any more kids. Deep down.'

The words were out in the air and Anna felt shocked by them. Had she meant that? That Phil might ask her not to have the baby? Surely not. But how did she know that? How could you ever know what someone would do, when all the rules were suddenly wiped out like this, and you were the only one sticking to them?

'Really?' Michelle looked stunned. 'What, ever?'

'I don't know. The longer he leaves it, the less he's going to want the upheaval.'

'And if it was a choice between your own kids and Phil? Phil and the children you've already got?' She paused. 'And the child you're already having?'

Anna tried to read Michelle's face but she couldn't. There was an odd sort of neutrality about her expression that she'd seen before when the topic of children came up, as if it was all a bit theoretical.

'I don't know,' she confessed. 'Actually, I probably shouldn't be having coffee.'

Without speaking, Michelle u-turned from the coffee stall where a short queue had formed and directed the two dogs towards the free dog run, where a pair of terriers were already leaping joyously in the sand.

'Did you ever have that conversation with the girls about having sisters? Do you know how they'd react to you and Phil having a baby?'

'Sort of.' There'd been a conversation with Becca, when they'd been discussing *Little Women* in the bookshop, and Becca had joked about them being one sister short of the March family . . . Anna pulled herself up. No, she'd *thought* that it would be a good time to start putting out feelers to find out how Becca would feel about a baby brother or sister, but she hadn't actually mentioned it to her. She'd just thought about doing it, and in her head, that had become a conversation.

Michelle peered over her shades, her sharp eyes squinting against the sun. 'You never know, Lily might like having a kid brother. She can boss him around.'

'I don't think it's going to be as simple as that,' said Anna. 'Phil's the problem. He just wants a quiet life. What if he decides we've got to wait? Or decides that he doesn't want any more? I can't just walk out on the girls when everyone else is letting them down, but . . .'

'But what? Anna, get it off your chest. Stop bottling this stuff up!'

'I'm thirty-one.' She didn't know how to go on from there, and stared out at the flowerbeds full of rosebushes, her lips clamped shut against the tide of panic and bitterness threatening to pour out.

'You're thirty-one,' Michelle prompted her.

'I want this baby,' she said. 'How many chances do you get? Even if I started again now, it could take me a year to find someone else. A year to trust them enough to get pregnant. Another year to get pregnant, if I could. And I *love* Phil. I want his kids. Not someone else's.' She looked up at Michelle and her eyes swam with tears at the unfairness of it. 'I don't want to let anyone down, but what about me? You can't ask someone to choose between the three children they agreed to take on, and their own unborn child.'

'Phil wouldn't ask you to choose like that,' said Michelle, horrified. 'Anna – it won't come to that.'

'I don't want to let them down,' she repeated, but it sounded more as if she were trying to convince herself. Pongo strained at the end of his lead, unable to understand why they'd stopped walking within sniffing distance of the dog run. She closed her eyes and tried not to cry, and a dull ache began in the pit of her stomach. 'I thought this would be the happiest moment of my life, but it's turning into the worst.'

'Anna.' Michelle's voice was gentle but firm. 'They're not your kids. You love them, I know, but they're not yours, at the end of the day. Someone else has the responsibility for loving them.'

Anna didn't open her eyes, but she felt Michelle's hand on her arm. 'They are mine,' she insisted. 'I married Phil, they're mine.'

But she wasn't theirs. Not when it mattered. They weren't running to her because Sarah was pregnant. They weren't crying on the phone to her, needing reassurance.

Michelle gently circled her shoulder in a hug. Anna felt her take Pongo's lead out of her hand, and let herself lean forward, her wet eyes pressed into Michelle's shoulder. She could hear the dogs barking happily as they bounced free in the sand, and she could smell fresh coffee and the lilac bushes and Michelle's familiar fig perfume, and she wished she could stay like this until everything was sorted out.

Only she couldn't. That wasn't what parenthood was about, even when you weren't actually a parent. You had to do the sorting out.

19

'The Hobbit *is a great book to read at bedtime.*
The mysterious, magical worlds spread out of the
page into your own imagination as you drift off to
sleep. The realms and rules of the quest seem to make
sense on the edge of a dream.'   Rory Stirling

The change in the house was obvious from the moment Anna put her key in the door and let herself in that evening. It wasn't just the sound of voices in the kitchen, it was a tension in the atmosphere, the smell of someone else's perfume that made the place suddenly unfamiliar to her.

Pongo held back, sniffing the air as if he knew something was afoot, and then stuck to her heels instead of charging in to see the girls as he usually did.

Anna paused by the hall mirror and checked her reflection, smoothing back the stray wisps of blond hair so she just looked windswept, rather than outright dishevelled.

I'm not putting off going into my own house, I'm just . . . preparing, she told herself, as her ears strained to pick up what was going on in the kitchen. She'd been on tenterhooks in the bookshop all day, but her phone hadn't rung and there'd been no appearances from Phil or the girls. She guessed they had a lot to talk about.

Anna hesitated, then pulled a pale lipgloss out of her bag and hastily applied it. But that's it, she added silently. No point wearing more slap to come home than I did when I left the house. Phil will just wonder what I've been up to.

Sarah was always immaculate and Anna, with her floaty, creative style, had never seen the point in competing with her sharp suits and statement bags. She wondered if Sarah was starting to show yet, whether she had that pregnancy bloom that everyone went on about, or if she was throwing up everywhere.

Stop it.

Anna glanced down to see Pongo lurking by her feet and she nudged him gently. 'Go on,' she said. 'Lily's home! Go say hello!'

But he crouched down on the floor, his tail between his legs and his bright eyes wary. Could he smell Sarah? Was he confused about where he'd be going?

Anna rallied herself, trying to suppress the churning in her stomach. If they've heard the door, they'll wonder why you haven't come in. You don't have to show how you feel. Just . . . show your face.

She took a deep breath, ruffled up her hair and walked down the hall towards the kitchen. Even the concentration of McQueens was unsettling. Normally the girls spread out through the house to get away from each other – Chloe in the cellar 'dance studio', Becca in her room, Lily watching television with Pongo by her side – but it sounded as if they were all standing around the kitchen table yelling, while Phil tried to referee things ineffectually.

Anna could hear him trying to break through the wall of female voices, with the 'now, come on . . . be reasonable' tactics that generally only stoked Chloe's dramatic fires. It wasn't working now, either. He sounded desperate and a bit pathetic.

She could hear Sarah, too, trying to control the meeting as if it was an unfair dismissal tribunal. 'Everyone gets a turn to speak,' she was saying over the top of Phil.

Chloe, meanwhile, was using all her voice projection coaching to drown out Becca, who was yelling for the first time in all the years Anna had known her. 'You're not listening to us . . . you don't care about us!' Chloe and Becca kept saying, then suddenly louder as the door cracked open and Lily slid out like an eel, her face a mask of distress.

Anna held out her arms and Lily ran to her in tears, Pongo trotting over to lick what little of her face he could reach after she'd buried it in Anna's jumper. She half led, half carried Lily away from the kitchen door, not wanting her to hear some of the things Chloe was shrieking, and ended up on the stairs where she held her in her arms and stroked her hair while she shook with sobs and jet-lagged exhaustion.

Anna rested her lips on the top of Lily's rabbit-soft hair and murmured soothingly, rocking her back and forth, wishing she knew the right thing to say. While she sobbed, Anna stared sightlessly at the baby photos of the girls, hanging on the wall up the stairs, starting with Becca, already serious, in a white christening gown, then Chloe beaming like a child star in a headband. Sarah had a matching set in her house; copies were part of the divorce settlement.

Anna first appeared at the second-to-top step, in the Christmas photo four years ago. She'd had the special privilege of holding Pongo in his red Christmas hat. It had been a milestone, hanging that one, but now she felt inadequate, as if she'd been caught out at university with no previous qualifications, which was, by a grim coincidence, also one of her recurrent nightmares.

As Lily's crying slowed to a hiccup, Anna trawled her mind

for the right thing to say, and found nothing. It had been drummed into her that you weren't supposed to lie to children, promise them things you couldn't deliver, especially when you didn't even know the situation yourself, but she couldn't bear to see Lily so distressed.

She wondered how long it would take Phil and Sarah to realise Lily had slipped out of the kitchen.

Lily drew a couple of long shuddery breaths and looked up at Anna, waiting for her to say something, her big eyes wet with tears.

In a rushing instant, desperate to reassure her and take away the pain, Anna heard herself say what was in her heart, not what her head was preparing. 'Whatever happens, it's going to be OK. We all love you, Lily. It's going to be fine.'

'What if Mum stays in America? Does she want a family over there instead of here? Are we going to be left here forever now?'

Anna curled a loop of hair around Lily's ear, trying not to feel hurt by the implication that the girls were waiting out their time in her home like dogs in quarantine. 'I don't know what her plans are, but I know she won't do anything without checking it all out with you and Becca and Chloe first.'

'What if the new baby doesn't like us?'

'Lily?' The kitchen door swung open and Anna saw Sarah standing in the doorframe, backlit by hard lighting. All the spotlights had been turned on at once, instead of the carefully blended ambient combinations she and Michelle had designed. Phil never knew how to put them on properly.

Sarah was dressed in expensive jersey separates that revealed the faintest hint of a baby bump, and she looked tired, her cheekbones sharper than normal in her pointy face. Her hair didn't have its usual bounce, and her face was flushed and tight with frustration; before she saw Anna on the stairs she lifted one hand to her face and squeezed her eyes tight.

Anna heard Phil say, 'Sarah, I'll go to—' but Sarah snapped, 'No, let me,' over her shoulder and, in turning, saw Anna, cuddling up with her little girl, and her face went blank.

Anna knew it must look bad – her comforting Lily, probably saying all sorts, unsupervised by Sarah – but for once she didn't care about what things looked like. She was stinging on Lily's behalf. What sort of mother was too busy shouting the odds to miss the fact that her little girl had run away in tears?

Sarah didn't react with the defensiveness Anna would have done in her place. Instead she let her tiredness show out of Phil's sight, and offered Anna a weary smile.

'Hi, Anna,' she said, more relaxed in Anna's home than Anna was herself. 'I didn't hear you come in.'

'It sounds quite noisy in there,' said Anna, as evenly as she could. 'Is everything OK?'

'Everything's fine.' Sarah's expression softened as she held out her arms to Lily. 'Come here, darling, we need to have a proper talk,' she said. 'On our own. Just you and me.'

Lily didn't move. She didn't cling to Anna harder, but she didn't get up either.

Anna looked down at her small head. Lily's sharp nose was pointed at the banisters as she stared fiercely at the stairs. She knew she should get out of the way, but something made her reluctant to leave Lily, knowing that her carefully ordered world of cuddly toys was about to be turned upside down again.

'Come on, Lilybella,' said Sarah easily, the practised parent. 'What about Mrs Piggle? Why don't we go and tell Piggy-Jo my big news? See what she says?'

That was enough. Lily wriggled out of Anna's arms and ran down the hall to Sarah, wrapping herself round her like a star-fish. 'I love you Mummy I love you Mummy I love you Mummy,' she gabbled, and Sarah bent over to kiss Lily's head, barely able to hide her own tears.

'You'll always be my baby, Lily,' she kept saying, over and over as they fused into one mother-and-daughter shape of messy, instinctive, unconditional love.

Anna felt like an intruder. She slipped off the step and stumbled down the hall, feeling battered by too many different emotions. That was everything she longed for: to be needed so powerfully by one person, someone for whom she was the entire world, for whom she would *move* the entire world, stone by stone. She grabbed Pongo's collar and led him into the kitchen, where Chloe, Becca and Phil were each staring mutely in different directions.

Chloe's mascara was smeared down her cheeks, but Becca's eyes were distant, as if she was computing the effects, process-ing it all with her proto-lawyer's mind. Phil looked up when she came in, his face braced for another round, but seeing it was her, his eyes relaxed into a haunted sort of relief.

He expects me to sort things out, thought Anna suddenly. He's glad I'm here, because he expects *me* to deal with this. It hasn't even occurred to him how this might make me feel, where it leaves me, and us – and our own baby.

She held her breath for a second, suspending her own silent howl of pain in her head, like a conjuror's smoke-ring in a soap bubble.

Then she swallowed it, deliberately, and made herself turn to the shattered, crestfallen faces round the table.

'Shall I put the kettle on?' she said.

★   ★   ★

Much later that night, Anna lay with her head on Phil's chest, listening to him breathe. He was pretending to be on the edge of sleep, but she knew he wasn't, because he wasn't starting to snore.

'How long's she staying?' she whispered.

Sarah was asleep in Becca's double bed, vacated for the night by Becca, who was sharing Chloe's double bed with the fairy lights wrapped round the frame. Pongo was in with Lily and her 300 soft toys, against all official house rules. Lily had insisted on Sarah reading her the bedtime story, with Phil in attendance. No Anna required.

'She's got to fly back tomorrow. Something's come up at work.'

'Shame,' Anna whispered back. 'She could have made a weekend of it. Taken Chloe to some auditions. Tested Becca on her French. Done some laundry.'

Phil rolled over on his side and looked at her. Anna tucked herself into his warm body so she didn't have to meet his eye, because she still wasn't sure what her face was doing when she wasn't concentrating on making it look understanding and calm.

She knew that was what she was supposed to be projecting. Inside she was anything but. After a brief, painful chat with Sarah about folic acid and maternity leave, she'd excused herself for an early bath and worked through shock, fury, frustration and misery as fast as she could in the twenty minutes she had the locked bathroom for. And then she'd come back downstairs and cooked supper for everyone because it got her out of the sitting room while Chloe and Becca expertly shut down Sarah's attempts to start a friendly conversation about their revision timetables. Lily might have forgiven their mother, but they hadn't. Yet.

They'd got through supper without another falling-out

only because Anna had asked every single question she could think of about American life, offices, drugstore cosmetics . . . anything to keep the conversation going. Anything was better than the furious silence coming from the girls. After pushing Anna's crumble round their plates for a bit, they both left 'to revise'.

'I totally fail to see how adults can call teenagers selfish when *they* behave like selfish kids,' Chloe had pronounced, before storming off to her room in a huff.

Becca had followed without speaking, her arms full of books.

Once or twice Anna had lifted up the phone to see if they were moaning away to their mates, but since they both had mobiles and laptops, they had no reason to open up their displeasure to inspection – unlike all the times when Chloe had 'accidentally' let her overhear conversations with Sarah about how unfair Anna was being about bedtimes.

This was serious fury. Private, family, flesh and blood fury. It made Anna feel even more peripheral than she'd done before. The girls loved Sarah so much they could afford to be truly livid with her; they were angry because they loved her so much. That was why Sarah was so annoyingly calm about it; she was their mother and nothing could change it.

'Anna?' Phil pulled her round so she had to look at his face. It was the first time they'd been alone since the oestrogen maelstrom had flattened the house. Was it only this morning that he'd gone to the airport? Anna wondered. It seemed days ago.

'What?'

'At least she's here and we've been able to have a family chat about it, face to face,' he whispered.

'I am *in* this family, Phil.' She struggled to keep her voice down. 'This will affect me too. Affect us.'

He tried to hug her tightly to him. Anna resisted, wanting to punish herself more than him.

'Do you think they'll be OK with it? Having a half-brother or -sister?'

Phil didn't answer. His face said more than he could, and Anna was scared by how unfamiliar he suddenly seemed. They lay looking at each other, too afraid to make their thoughts real by saying them out loud.

Despair washed over her. He hadn't said anything, but she could sense a change in him, and she cursed her own naivety in thinking that it was all so easy. She'd just been lucky, up till now.

The talk radio station burbled on in the background, the twenty minutes of noise that drowned out the sounds of the house and let Anna fall asleep over Phil's snoring each night. She never really listened, but tonight there was a call-in about 'dealbreakers' in relationships, and some woman from Droitwich was railing hard against men who refused to commit and messed women around till their options were closed.

Anna tried to shut her ears, but she couldn't. The radio was on Phil's side of the bed, so she'd have to lean over him to turn it off, attracting his attention to it. He never listened to lyrics, or background noise, whereas she couldn't stop her brain catching words in a net, like butterflies.

I don't want to be one of those mad, bitter women, she thought. How long can I give the girls to get over this? And even if the girls get over this, will Phil?

She closed her eyes, trying to push down the strange yearning impulses that made her a terrible, selfish stepmother, but still just a normal woman who wanted to create a baby with the man she was in love with. For the first time in her life, Anna's bustling stockroom of words refused to help her, leaving the bare thoughts stark and ugly in her head.

Do I want a baby more than I want Phil?

'How are you feeling?' he whispered. 'You know . . .' He twitched his eyebrows.

He means the baby, but he can't bring himself to say it, she thought.

'Fine.' Anna had actually hoped she'd be feeling a bit more by this stage. She'd felt a bit sick earlier, and a bit crampy, both of which were on her internet symptom list as strong indicators.

'Have you actually done the test yet? That one that says pregnant or not pregnant? In actual writing?'

'It's in the bathroom. It didn't . . . It didn't seem appropriate.'

'Go and do it now,' whispered Phil. 'You're five days late, you should be testing positive by now.'

'Then what?'

'Then . . .' He stopped. 'Then we'll know what we're dealing with.'

They looked at each other in the darkness for a long second.

'I'm just a bloke,' said Phil. 'I need facts.'

'OK.' Anna was dying for a pee – another sign of pregnancy, she knew, although possibly helped by the endless cups of peppermint tea she'd drunk that night. She slipped out of bed and pulled on her dressing-gown, her heart already starting to thud with excitement.

It's going to be OK, she said to herself, finding the test she'd hidden in the cabinet. It's one of those serendipitous things; the timing's so bad it's good. Michelle's right. Get all the drama over at once for the girls.

Anna didn't put the light on because moonlight was flooding the bathroom with a romantic sort of glow, but as she ripped open the test stick, pulled down her knickers and readied herself to pee, she realised there was no need.

Her period had started.

There was still only one mother in the house, after all.

She sank down on the side of the bath and wept.

20

'The Railway Children *is a story of three
Edwardian children growing up quickly. If you
don't want a red petticoat to wave in moments of
crisis, or shed a tear when Daddy comes home, you
must have a heart of marble.'*   Anna McQueen

Michelle's obsession with forward planning and weekly accounts meant that she normally had the year under control, but this year seemed to be slipping past far too quickly.

Maybe it was having to do double the work in keeping two shops bustling, accounted, stocked and staffed, or maybe it was feeling more tied to her routine by the small but authoritative presence of Tavish, who only tolerated half an hour or so of after-hours pottering round the shop before he started nudging her ankles to go home. Each day seemed to pass twice as quickly, hurrying her towards the end of each week before she had time to tick off half the stuff on her ever-growing to-do list. She hadn't cleaned her oven in weeks, and the boxes she'd brought back from her birthday lunch were still in the spare room in the flat, untouched.

If Anna's life revolved around the girls' exam timetables, Michelle's revolved around lead times and stock orders and VAT returns, and they were just as demanding. It was May now, and she was starting to feel anxious about some of the stock she'd planned to introduce into the bookshop as part of her subtle slow change. She'd stumbled across a local dressmaker who was prepared to give her an exclusive supply of baby-soft cotton pyjamas, based on Edwardian bloomers – if she put in an order for autumn delivery, with a sizeable cash deposit.

Michelle knew this was a good thing but it meant finding some more money, which meant juggling the figures, and looking at the figures wasn't quite the comfort it usually was for her on a Sunday night. The bookshop was still ticking over better than expected, and Home Sweet Home had had a good spring, but her business instinct was chafing at every week that went by with a tiny profit where there could be a much bigger one.

She chewed her pen and stared at her Year Plan, open next to the fourth cup of coffee of the evening on her kitchen table. Halfway through the year, nearly, and still not anywhere near her target turnover.

Of course, a voice in her head pointed out, the obvious answer would be get the flat upstairs as well as the shop and have *both*. Books downstairs, beds upstairs. 'Upstairs to Bed', even.

Oh, that was a good name, she thought, scribbling it down. Michelle dangled her pen from her fingers and idly wondered how easy it would be to persuade Mr Quentin to evict Rory.

She told herself not to be so mean. Rory was growing on her, despite his awful socks. Maybe when Owen moved on – and now the website was finished, he should be thinking about moving back to London, where he'd find some proper work – she could offer Rory the flat above the shop, and move him sideways? It wasn't as if he'd done anything with the place; he wouldn't even need to unpack those bachelor boxes.

But Owen didn't seem in any hurry to move on. Michelle

had been watching him and Becca like a hawk, and she knew Anna was watching them too – and watching her, watching them. That was . . . sometimes awkward. Although she'd reassured Anna that Owen was trustworthy (what else could she say?), she couldn't be everywhere at once, and Owen's behaviour wasn't following normal patterns. Sometimes Michelle wondered if he might actually be in love.

In any case, she conceded, she knew Rory well enough by now to know that he wasn't going to move to make way for what he still referred to as knick-knacks, albeit more jokily. Without her realising, Rory had filled in the pockets of emptiness that Anna had left when she had to give her time to the girls. The Sunday afternoons. An occasional Saturday dog walk. Neither of them were over-sharers, but looking after Tavish had brought them in and out of each other's lives like a tide, and each visit washed up a personal detail here and there, almost by accident. Esther had insisted on reading his horoscopes, which he, like Michelle, loathed. He hadn't chosen the name Zachary. They both liked porridge made with water.

There was a knock at the front door and she knew it was him; Rory was always punctual when it came to Tavish. Michelle pushed her chair away from the table and closed her laptop, messing up her hair to make it look as if she'd just got in from somewhere more interesting.

'Hey!' he said, when she opened the door. Tavish was next to him, wagging his tail. Rory had the Sunday papers under his arm, even though it was six in the evening.

Michelle let them in and Tavish trotted down the hall, sniffing the air as if he disapproved of the deep clean she'd done to pass the afternoon. 'Cup of tea?'

'If you're not dashing out?'

'If you don't have somewhere to go?'

Rory pretended to think, then said, 'No, don't think I do.'

'I'll put the kettle on then.'

Michelle could pinpoint the first time Rory had come round with his Sunday papers – it was when he asked if he could read them at her house, as he 'couldn't go back to his flat because they're resurfacing the high street' and she couldn't think of a non-rude way of saying no – but she couldn't remember when it had turned into part of her weekend routine. For the past few weeks he'd brought them over with Tavish and they'd sat and read in silence for an hour before he left on the dot of five to seven and went home. Rory read the news and review sections and grumbled at the articles, and Michelle scanned Property and ripped pages out of the supplements for her mood boards.

The first week Michelle had felt rather invaded by the way Rory kicked off his shoes and flattened her cushions and didn't fold the pages in the papers back the way they had been, but the room had seemed empty when she'd finally straightened it out again. She liked the way he didn't talk much and left exactly when he said he would.

'Aaah,' said Rory, prising off one trainer with the toe of the other as he unfolded the Business section of the *Sunday Times* and sank onto the sofa. 'What an *idiot.*'

She left him spreading out the papers over the floor and watched from the kitchen while the kettle boiled.

When he thought she couldn't see, Rory talked under his breath to Tavish – she could see his lips moving – but quietly enough for her not to hear. Tavish seemed to be listening to him; his black ears were pricked, and his stumpy tail was wagging slowly from side to side, feathering the long hairs of his coat.

How ridiculous is that, thought Michelle, amused. As if I

can't tell how soppy he is about that dog from the way he always comes back combed.

'Why is that dog so neat?' she called through. 'Have you been grooming him?'

'No! Well, just a bit. I took him up to see Mr Quentin this afternoon.'

'Didn't he find it upsetting?' she asked. 'Seeing his old dog with someone else?'

'Nope, they both had a lovely time. Everyone patted Tavish and talked about their own ratty little bastard that loved children and only killed black cats. I've got instructions for Anna to take him along next time she reads to them.'

'Lovely.' Michelle dropped the teabags into the pot and made a mental note to go with her. Maybe with a knee-blanket for Mr Quentin. No harm in getting him on side with the linens.

'You should come up too,' said Rory, reading her mind with unnerving casualness. 'Don't you have a favourite novel you could be sharing with them?'

'No. And don't you start. Anna's been on at me to do one of those reading cards for the bookshop.'

'And why haven't you?'

'Because I don't have time.' Michelle opened and shut her cupboards, looking for the right plate to put the biscuits on. 'I'm already thinking about Christmas.'

'Get out of here. It's barely summer.' Rory had wandered in while her back was turned. 'What's this?'

Michelle glanced over her shoulder to see Rory flicking through her mood board folder for the new shop, with pages ripped from style magazines, and the catalogues and order forms from various companies.

'Bedlinen,' she said. 'My winter project.'

'Looks like nice stuff.' He flicked through some more. 'Warm.'

'It is,' she said. She wasn't sure what she felt about Rory passing opinions on bedrooms. Presumably his was quite bare, monk-like with shelves of literary fiction and a bottle of water by the bed. Was he a sheets and blankets man? Or a duvet lover? The door had been shut the day she'd nosed round his flat with Rachel and Anna, and now she wished she'd peeked in.

'It's gorgeous, especially the quilts. They're real heirloom pieces.' She felt more confident talking about her shop idea; even her dad had thought it was a smart move. 'It's a known fact that when times are tough, people cut back on going out and spend a bit more on their homes instead. Nesting is the next big thing. People always need somewhere to sleep, and women *love* their bedrooms.'

Rory gave her a quizzical look. 'It's very . . . neat.'

'What do you mean by that?'

'Well, I mean, it's very demure, all these cushions on the bed. And pretty virginal lace pillows. It's not exactly sexy, is it? For a bedroom. I can't imagine this being the scene of any crimes of passion.' He pointed at the perfect, cloud-like cocoon on the page. 'It'd take you ten minutes just to get the throw pillows out of the way before you could ravish anyone.'

Michelle stared at him. The mental image of Rory throwing cushions to the floor and tumbling his woman on the bed, struggling to undo buttons and zips, was a troubling one. She'd never pictured him that way, but he was speaking as if crimes of passion were a feature of his life.

He has a *son*, she reminded herself.

'But what would I know,' he went on, seeing her face. 'I'm not your target customer.'

'No.' Michelle swallowed. That was *her* bedroom he was talking about. She had eight pillows, and no crimes of passion, by choice. 'Anyway, I've been doing a bit of market research on my customer base, and lots of people round here get those catalogues for The White Company and Cologne and Cotton, but . . .' She rubbed her fingers together, as if she was touching the finest Egyptian cotton. 'But half the pleasure is *feeling* the sheets, and you can't do that with a catalogue, can you?'

She blinked at the sensuous way she was rubbing her fingers together and stopped.

'Indeed you can't.' Rory turned the page and examined the lambswool blankets. 'And how much of Home Sweet Home are you going to devote to this boudoir-ware?'

'I think bedlinen like this deserves a whole shop of its own, don't you?'

'A whole shop! Blimey.' Rory looked up. 'You don't do things by halves, do you?'

'Well, by the time you've made up a bed or two and put in some shelving for the blankets . . . You need a bit of space. You have to recreate a whole bedroom that the customer wants to buy.' Michelle poured the tea and ignored Tavish, who was begging for a biscuit by her side. 'Have you been feeding him from the table again?'

'No, your honour.'

'How come he's giving me a paw?'

Rory looked up and tsked at Tavish. 'I have no idea. He must have learned it somewhere else. So what have you got your eye on? That old betting shop on the corner that's closing down? Is it like Monopoly – when you've got three shops you can build a hotel on one of them?'

She furrowed her brow at him, surprised he was being

so dense. 'Keep up, Rory. It's going to be next door. The bookshop.'

'The *book*shop?' Rory stopped pouring his tea.

'Oh, don't give me that,' said Michelle. 'You knew all along that's what I wanted to do – wasn't that why you told me I should take in Tavish, to try to persuade Mr Quentin to let me change the shop sooner?'

'That's not really why you took in Tavish,' said Rory in a reprimanding, posh Scottish voice. 'You took in Tavish because you didn't want to see a poor old dog out in the cold. You did it out of the goodness of your heart.'

'That's not why you told me to take him.' She opened her mouth in an O of surprise. 'Don't try to pretend that you weren't the one who came up with the cunning plan.'

Rory sipped his tea, then put the mug down very deliberately. When he spoke, his tone was measured, and reasonable, and Michelle knew that behind it, he was annoyed. 'I thought the bookshop was going so well we'd persuaded you to keep it open.'

We'd persuaded you. We. The book people versus Philistine Michelle.

'I'm going to keep some of the books,' she said, irritated. 'It's going to be called A Book at Bedtime, and there'll be . . .' She edited in her head, not wanting to lie outright. 'There'll still be some books. Just not as many. I mean, going well's a bit different from making a profit. Going well for that bookshop is not actually making a crippling loss.'

'If you count loss and profit purely in financial terms.'

'I do. I'm running a business, not some kind of social outreach project for middle-class readers.'

Rory hadn't raised his voice, or even sounded particularly disapproving, but Michelle felt more defensive than if he'd yelled at her. Harvey hadn't been a yeller either.

'You don't think that it's doing more for you than just turning a profit?'

'In what way?'

'You've got a new customer base. You've got a community-enhancing moral high ground. You're supporting cultural activities in the area with the author visits and the book clubs and children's reading groups. Doesn't that enhance your brand in general? Doesn't that rub off on Home Sweet Home?'

'Maybe.' Michelle reached for a biscuit and snapped it in half. 'Those are Anna's projects, though.' He knew that, she knew that.

She felt a splinter of resentment pierce her warm mood. Rory was part of Anna's Reading Aloud gang now and even Owen had started doing book reviews, under gentle pressure from Becca. Even *Kelsey* had done one. But it was her that was paying the bills, keeping the money moving around.

'Oh, you love that shop, admit it,' said Rory, changing tack. 'It's a success story, and that's as much down to you as it is to Anna.'

'No, it's not.'

'It is. The way you've decorated it, brought it to life. The colours. The . . . stuff in it.' He frowned and reached for a third biscuit. 'I can't put my finger on it, because, as I said, I'm a bloke. I just know that I liked it before, when Mr Quentin had it, but I never lingered. Not like people linger now. They linger for *hours*. They meet there.'

Michelle stared into her coffee, suddenly colder inside. It wasn't the compliment she'd been hoping for, although, rationally, she had no idea what compliment she *had* wanted. 'That's not me, that's Anna.'

'It's you too, dumbo. You make it happen, as they say on television programmes. Look, you could easily find another shop on the cheap.' Rory took another biscuit and Michelle moved the plate away. 'The high street's full of charity shops, waiting for proper leaseholders. I could put my ear to the ground for you.'

'I can't afford another shop.'

'Doesn't that depend on the rent?' He waggled his eyebrows. 'I'm a tough negotiator. For special clients.'

Michelle shook her head. Stubbornness had crept over her now, entrenching her in whatever position she'd taken when it started. She didn't even let herself acknowledge the favour he was offering her. 'No, Rory, I've made a plan. I like to stick to plans.'

'Don't all the best business tycoons just go with the flow?'

'They pretend to. They've really got four or five different contingency plans. All watertight. You should know that, you're a solicitor.'

Rory looked at her as if he was weighing up whether to say something or not. Then he spoke. 'So, when?'

'When what?'

'When are you planning to tell Anna her bookshop's closing?'

'I thought it was my bookshop.'

'Your bookshop, then. *Our* bookshop. I speak on behalf of the middle-class readership of Longhampton.'

'Don't guilt trip me.' Michelle refused to meet his eye. 'I'm monitoring sales. If they dip beneath a reasonable operating level then I'll have no choice but to pull the plug. I thought I'd introduce a few lines in the autumn like the blankets and maybe they'll shore up some profits. But between you and me, I'll be very surprised if it goes the whole year. Which is all I agreed to in the first place.'

'Fine.' Rory pushed his chair back. 'Mind if I read the paper?'

The topic was clearly closed.

'Fine,' said Michelle, equally clipped. 'I'll bring the tea over.'

Rory made himself comfortable in the big chair and Michelle sat, knees together, on the sofa, flicking through the supplements without seeing much. Every so often Rory read something out and she made a grumpy noise, but after a few minutes, weariness crept over her, and she swung her feet up.

'I'm not going to sleep,' she said. 'I'm just closing my eyes. Don't let Tavish on the sofa, because I will know.'

'No problem,' said Rory.

Michelle sank her head into the feather cushions and let her body relax. Swan's Row was peaceful in a way no other house had ever been; no sirens, no cars, just faint birdsong and the hum of her dishwasher. And the huff and puff of Rory reading the paper.

'Ha ha ha!' he said. 'Listen to this. It's a restaurant review of a place in Islington. "We spent so long listening to the waiter describing the organic life cycle of what was on our plates that my lamb had matured into mutton before I was allowed to prod it with my fork."'

'That's very good,' she murmured, fighting off sleep.

Rory carried on reading and Michelle couldn't be bothered to tell him to stop. It was surprisingly soothing, listening to his voice rise and fall. Scottish accents were rather soporific, she thought, as the images danced and retreated in her mind, and the birdsong twittered in the garden.

When Michelle woke up it was dark, and someone was snoring. She also had a chenille throw draped over her.

'What time is it? Rory?' She sat up quickly and pushed away the throw.

Rory had gone, leaving only a trail of messy paper, a half-eaten packet of biscuits from the kitchen that he'd evidently helped himself to, and dents in the chair where he hadn't bothered to replump the cushions. He had, though, drawn the curtains and covered her with the throw that had been carefully arranged on the other chair.

Michelle wrinkled her nose. The throw was actually quite scratchy. She'd never noticed that before. And Tavish had clambered up onto the sofa next to her and was snoring in triumph.

'Why can't men *see* mess?' she said aloud, but she couldn't ignore the unsettling feeling that despite the mess, something had gone from the room. For a yearning second, she wished it hadn't.

She turned on the soft table lamps and began to tidy up.

'You're very quiet,' said Phil as they turned onto the motorway, heading back from the airport.

'Lots to think about,' said Anna shortly.

The sense of déjà vu wasn't a pleasant one. The last time he'd said that, they'd been at the start of a nice fresh year. Full of possibilities. Now, it felt as if everything had gone into reverse. Well, reverse for her. Not for anyone else.

'Sarah seemed sad the girls didn't want to see her off,' Phil went on. 'But it's not surprising, I guess.'

'Sunday nights are busy for them.' Normally Anna would have stayed at home to supervise homework and get ahead on the ironing, but something had snapped and she didn't feel like it. Why be SuperStepMum when SuperMum had just left the building? It already felt too much like a competition she couldn't win.

'I know.'

More silence. More miles flashed by.

'I'm sorry, Anna,' said Phil.

'For what?'

'For this weekend. I know it's been hard. The rows.'

'I don't mind the rows.' She bit her lip. 'What was hard was watching you and Sarah parenting in our house. Like I wasn't there.'

He wiped a hand over his face. 'It wasn't like that. Sarah was trying really hard not to step on your toes. Lily asked her to read her the bedtime story. She'd have said no, if you'd asked.'

'I'm not talking about that.' But she was. She knew it sounded petulant, and she knew it was more to do with the crashing disappointment of realising she wasn't pregnant, but there was no point trying to explain to Phil. He just didn't get it.

More silence. More miles.

'Is everything OK with Becca and, er, Jake?' he asked.

'Josh. And no, they've split up.'

'Have they? When? She didn't tell me. Well, maybe that's not something you tell your dad.'

Anna felt a tiny glimmer of triumph that she knew something personal, something trustworthy.

'I suppose this is the beginning of the unsuitable boyfriend stage,' he sighed, and looked sad. 'What else don't I know?'

Anna considered keeping it to herself, but common sense told her it would only backfire. At least this way she could tell Becca he'd asked, rather than that she'd volunteered the information unbidden. 'She's going out with Michelle's brother, Owen.'

Phil glanced across the car. 'Haven't met the guy. Is he

nice? Should I be worried? How much like Michelle is he? Scary?'

'He's . . . OK,' said Anna.

'OK?' He looked worried. 'But you're keeping an eye on it?'

'She's allowed some privacy, Phil.'

'Not until the chastity belt arrives . . . I'm joking. I'm glad she talks to you. Did she tell Sarah?'

'I don't know. Probably.'

Silence descended again, less tense this time, and the atmosphere had almost warmed back to normal when Phil turned onto the main road into Longhampton and said, 'I'm really sorry you got your hopes up for nothing.'

It was the first time he'd acknowledged her tearful disap-pointment, and Anna's throat tightened. She was expecting him to say, 'Let's try again,' but he didn't.

'Maybe it's for the best,' he went on. 'It's not a good time. We didn't really talk about it enough, did we?'

Anna swung round, lost for words. We? *We?*

He took that as tacit agreement and squeezed her knee. 'I've been thinking – why don't you book a week somewhere really nice for us to go away when Sarah has the girls in the summer? Blow the budget. Somewhere second honeymoon-y, lots of cocktails by the pool, no slides.'

'Somewhere grown-up,' she said sarcastically.

'Exactly!'

She stared ahead at the road, watching the familiar sign-posts of her daily life flash past. School, supermarket, hospital, town centre. Sucking her back in to the parenting routine.

They were going to have to talk about it. Very soon. But not tonight. Tonight, Anna couldn't be sure what might come out of her mouth.

21

'I'd like to tell you how the psychoanalytic subtext of
Where The Wild Things Are *spoke to me, but in*
reality, I just liked the pictures.' Matt Dunn

It was ironic, Anna thought, that the massive stress of Chloe
and Becca's exams ended up being a good thing, in that they
gave the whole family something to moan and wail about
other than Sarah's baby.

It also allowed her to adopt a slightly more pick-and-mix
approach to her non-stop to-do list. Whatever had snapped in
her during Sarah's visit hadn't reconnected when Sarah left,
and although she'd re-read all Becca's set texts so they could
discuss them over dinner, and had agreed to Chloe's special
'brain food' internet diet, Anna hadn't bothered to shove the
girls' socks into individual sock pockets on the back of their
bedroom doors as she normally did, or iron anything worn
below the waist.

No one seemed to mind, apart from Phil, but she'd told
him to add it to the cleaner's list and leave an extra £10.

'I can't believe you're reading that for fun,' said Becca late
one night, when she traipsed down to the kitchen to get a last
glass of milk and found Anna reading *Jane Eyre* instead of
sorting laundry. 'You're doing more revision than I am.'

'It's better when you don't have to write essays on it,' said Anna. 'Honestly. Read it again in about five years' time.'

'Have you checked the attic for mad first wives?' said Becca, opening the fridge. Under the table, Pongo's ears twitched at the sound of the fridge door. 'I hear that's the best place to keep them. Should have mentioned it to Dad.'

'I'm sure your mother would prefer to keep her first husband in an attic too,' said Anna, reaching for the chocolate biscuits she kept hidden during the day. 'Do you want to talk about *Jane Eyre*?'

'Not really.' Becca listlessly moved Chloe's bio yoghurts around in search of some food. She hadn't had any supper, despite Anna's attempts to force something down her. Chloe had finished her fishcakes ('I need the extra omega-3 oils. For my brain.').

'Or . . . anything else?'

Becca shut the fridge door and came over to the table with her glass of milk. Her plaits were hanging either side of her face and she had deep circles under her blue eyes. Her alabaster bare feet sticking out from her baggy 'revision trousers' reminded Anna of a goose girl in some European fairytale book – apart from the green nail varnish.

'Anna,' she said, sitting down at the table. 'Tell me something honestly?'

'If I can.' Anna put the book down and braced herself.

'Me and Owen.' Becca looked uncomfortable, then blurted it out: 'Is it a problem for you and Michelle? Us dating?'

'What?' Anna hadn't been expecting that one. 'Er, no, course not, it's . . . Well . . .'

Becca kept looking at her with the piercing expression Anna suspected would see her do well in a courtroom situation. She couldn't deny it; things hadn't been quite so warm as usual between her and Michelle, but it wasn't just Owen. Anna wasn't sure Michelle quite understood how much the pregnancy disappointment had crushed her, so she'd hugged it to herself. It wasn't normal for her not to share something that had upset her so much.

Not that she could tell Becca that.

'Well,' she amended, 'it's not a *problem*. It's just that he's a bit older than you are, obviously, and Michelle knows what he's got up to in the past, and we're both concerned that—'

'Because I don't want it to affect your friendship,' Becca interrupted. 'It's between me and Owen. I've noticed you getting all tense when he's in the shop with me. And it's ages since Michelle came round here for dinner.'

'That's because we're so busy.'

'When was the last time you two walked Pongo together? You used to do that all the time.' Becca was serious. 'What someone's like when they're your little brother, or your stepdaughter – it's not what they're like *as people*, when they're together. So if you're worried about me, and Michelle's worried about him – don't be.' She frowned, as if she wasn't sure she'd made herself understood. 'It's not like you think.'

'I'm allowed to worry about you,' said Anna. 'If Michelle's offended by me worrying, that's her issue – I'd be worried about you if you were dating . . .' She cast her mind about for someone current but innocuous, and realised she didn't know anyone. 'Justin Bieber?'

'Aw.' Becca reached over and squeezed Anna's hand. Anna wasn't sure if she was 'awing' the sentiment or the hopelessly wrong choice of celebrity. 'But there's no need. I know Owen's a bit older than me, but we're on the same wavelength. I feel like I've known him forever.'

'So when are you going to invite him over for dinner, so we can all meet him?' Anna asked. And so I can brush the fact that I've already told your dad under the carpet, she added to herself, feeling guilty.

'Soon. He's taking me to the prom.'

'The prom,' repeated Anna. 'Are we all in America now?'

Becca looked up. The bags under her eyes were still there, but the eyes themselves were sparkling with an excitement that made Anna's own heart ache with nostalgia. She could remember feeling that disorientating first rush of love, as bright and light as if no one else had ever felt it, as if you were looking down into the ultimate pool of emotional revelation. She also remembered how stupid it made you.

'He's amazing, Anna. He's . . . like I wrote down my ideal man and suddenly, there he is.'

Anna watched Becca drink her milk and told herself that it would be fine. Telling Phil had been the responsible thing to do. And she hadn't betrayed the confidence; all she'd done was pass on the fact that it was happening. She hadn't told him about Becca's expression, or the sweet things she said about Owen, or the way the bookshop website was really one big love letter to each other. She'd kept that to herself, and in return for that confidence she was keeping an eye on things. She was the useful buffer between child and parent that allowed Becca to grow into adulthood.

Under the table, Pongo shifted, laying his head on Anna's foot.

It *was* ages since she and Michelle had walked him together, she thought. I should really rectify that. Just as soon as I can find some space in my diary.

On the other side of town, Michelle was unloading boxes from the back of her car and sweating gently while Tavish watched, his tail sweeping the step, his head cocked to one side.

They weren't books for the shop, but she wondered if they could be, once she'd sorted through them. She certainly wasn't going to read them again herself: they were the contents of her old room at home, plus a couple of boxes that been delivered straight from school to their attic after her shameful expulsion, and now from the attic into her spare room, unopened in thirteen years.

Michelle sorted the contents of the first three into bags for the shop, for the charity shop next door, for recycling and for the tip, then stopped when she came to the boxes that were still wrapped in tape with her school crest on.

She took a deep breath, then cut the tape and pulled open the flaps. As she looked inside, her past came rushing up in a wave.

On top were her sixth-form schoolbooks, instantly familiar by their colours and texture, if not their contents. *The Color Purple*, her pale blue Shakespeares, the stone-grey *Story of Art*, wedged into this box in the order they'd been on her study bookshelf. She didn't remember packing but whoever it was had just grabbed and dumped, grabbed and dumped, until all traces of Michelle Nightingale, Upper Sixth Arts, had been removed from the room and taped up in the box.

She'd never unpacked because she'd never needed to revise. '*We regret that it will be impossible for Michelle to return to sit her A-level examinations. Arrangements may be made for her to sit the examinations elsewhere.*' Except arrangements hadn't been made. Michelle had been well away by then, first staying with her aunt in New Zealand, then back home in Surrey – anywhere but in a gym hall, recalling three key dramatic themes of *Othello*.

She pulled the flap back further and saw the pencil cases stuffed in the gaps, the postcards yanked off her study wall with the Blu-Tack still globbed on the back, the revision calendar to her exams with only three days crossed off. The CDs shoved in the spaces; Blur, Pulp, Nick Drake, music she'd never listened to again but which she could hear now in her head, like a jukebox suddenly springing into life.

1999 in a box. Her eighteenth year, frozen and waiting for her to unpack, the breaths and whispers of those months ready to be released from the pages of the books. Even now – was it her imagination? – she could smell the throat-burning scent of Lynx that had permeated every corner of the dormitories.

Michelle slammed the flap down, pushing it back into the sealed position with fumbling fingers.

She would take the other bags to the dump and to the shops, but these boxes were going straight into the attic. There were some things she didn't want to unpack.

22

'I devoured the Sweet Valley High *books as a teen. I'd imagine I had a twin sister who was a more outrageous version of me, and a driving licence at 16, and a prom and a hot date in a Miami Vice jacket.'* Natalie Hodge

Michelle wasn't used to running up against opposition from her Business Relationship Manager at the bank, so it took her a while to realise that Martin Leonard, who'd always insisted she was his favourite client, was telling her, albeit in a very roundabout way, that she couldn't extend her overdraft facility, and that they were very unlikely to approve a mortgage for 'a possible further property'.

Longhampton was enjoying a June heatwave, but the beads of perspiration on Martin's brow had nothing to do with the efficacy of the bank's air-con, and everything to do with Michelle's direct gaze, and the presentation she'd prepared. He kept shuffling and reshuffling her pages but he wasn't saying yes.

When it finally did sink in, somewhere around the nine-minute mark, a dull weight settled in the pit of her stomach. Money wasn't going to be the answer to the unpleasant choices she was now facing.

The bookshop was no longer breaking even now the novelty

value had worn off and the summer had begun. They'd shifted some holiday paperbacks but not as many as she'd hoped; as Anna explained in her generous way, most of their budget-conscious customers stockpiled their holiday reading at the supermarket, 'and you can hardly blame them'. Anna's solution was to push 'classic deckchair reads', not new titles, but that wasn't making much money. Michelle had lain awake for several sticky nights, thinking about what Rory had said about Anna and reflected brand value, and had tried to come up with a different solution that would keep everyone happy. Her last, maybe maddest, idea had been to take Rory up on his offer to find another premises and rent that as well, but Martin Leonard was very firm about the bank's new 'cautious financial overview'.

'If it was up to myself, Michelle, you know I'd invest the money in your venture yesterday,' he'd said, with a new bead of sweat appearing on his forehead. 'But the bank's clamping down. Come back next year, see what's happening then.'

Michelle had smiled tightly, agreed to put aside one of the limited-edition glass Pimm's jugs for his wife, and marched down the high street so hard she lost the heel cap off one of her stilettos. When she reached the bookshop, the fizzing in her stomach hadn't subsided and her brain was still blank, so to Anna's surprise, she'd grabbed Tavish and her trainers and taken him for an impromptu walk. She didn't want any of her staff to see her like this.

They only got as far as the park, where Michelle sat on a bench and stared into the middle distance. If she could get a decent night's sleep it would help but she hadn't had more than a couple of hours a night in weeks, tossing and turning until 4 a.m. She couldn't take the same pleasure in her own cloud-white bedlinen mood board – or even her own bedroom – after what Rory had said about the pillows. Not only was it *wrong* and *irrelevant*, it was also outrageously *rude* coming from a man with a light sabre, and she wished she'd had the presence of mind to tell him that when he'd come out with it.

Rory was much easier to be outraged by in theory than he was in the flesh. In the flesh he seemed strangely reasonable.

Michelle stared across the park, which was dotted with slow-walking senior couples being towed along by their dogs, and mums steering buggies with toddlers and patient Labradors around the path towards the play area.

Beside her – not on the bench, that would be unhygienic – Tavish belched and didn't look remotely embarrassed. Since he'd had his teeth out, he'd taken on a sprightly new lease of life, and ate the most disgusting things when her back was turned. God knew what he found to scoff at Rory's bachelor sty.

I'm thirty-one, she thought, and for the first time, she felt a pang of loneliness. I'm thirty-one and I feel bloody fifty. When's this ever going to get better?

Michelle knew what the answer was: when she summoned up the courage to cut herself free from Harvey. The papers had sat in their thick legal envelope on her kitchen table for a week now, but in that week, she'd suffered the worst nightmares she'd had in years, culminating in a terrible, vivid flashback to her twenty-sixth birthday party, where Harvey had flown into an incoherent rage about the 'tarty' outfit she'd bought from the only boutique he approved of, and locked her in the garage for seven hours, telling their friends waiting at the restaurant that she'd had a disastrous haircut and was too vain to show her face. Michelle only found that bit out later, when Harvey came home, wreathed in their sympathy for his stupid child-wife, and chopped off her long black hair himself – 'So your story's straight.'

Michelle didn't know what he'd do when he got the forms. Although the flowers had stopped, Rachel from the rescue had called to 'thank her' for a friend of hers sponsoring a dog in her name.

'He asked us which dog had been in there the longest, so I suggested Minty, that Staffy girl with one eye,' she'd explained. 'He said he wanted to sponsor whichever one no one seemed to want. Really thoughtful. Most people just want the cute puppies.'

It *wasn't* thoughtful. Michelle knew it was Harvey's way of telling her she was damaged goods, that no one else would give her a second look. But as usual, it was dressed up as a kind act that she could hardly take offence at, and it made her feel like a rat in a trap.

She stared out into the park, feeling more alone than ever.

Normally she'd have turned to Anna, who'd have been by her side wrestling Pongo away from a passing spaniel, and they'd have laughed about it. Anna would have told her she was single for a reason – so Mr Right would know she was available. Then they'd have dragged the dogs to the dog café for carrot cake.

Anna wasn't there, though. She was with her family.

'Time to go, Tavish,' she said and stood up.

Back in the shop, there was a hum of conversation coming from the back room and two folded buggies by the door. Anna wasn't at the counter, and when Michelle stepped inside, she saw Anna in the back room, deep in conversation with a few other women, two of whom had babies on their lap and a book in their hand. Two other toddlers were sitting on the floor, playing with the toys from the toy box. It was rather a charming scene, Michelle had to admit – not least because of the piles of soon-to-be-bought books the women were holding.

Anna was chatting away happily, which pleased Michelle, but as she turned to go back to the till, one of the babies let out a waking mewl and stretched its tiny hands into starfish. Michelle watched as Anna's eyes squeezed shut and her own hands clenched into fists, which only tightened when the mother soothed and shushed it back to quietness. The naked anguish on Anna's face made Michelle's breath catch in her throat.

Anna stopped at once when she saw Michelle and adjusted her expression too quickly, like someone caught with their trousers down in a bad sitcom. But it was too late. She'd revealed a flash of something raw, something hidden.

Michelle felt hurt. She knew Anna was a bit broody, but not wild, like that. Why hasn't she told me? she wondered. Does she think I won't understand?

'Are you OK?' she asked when Anna came over.

Anna started to pretend that she was, then made a 'not really' face. 'Love babies. Can't bear to be with babies. Madness.'

Michelle wasn't sure what the right thing to say was, given the sadness and anger mingling in Anna's face.

'It doesn't always happen at once,' she tried, repeating something she'd read in one of Rory's Sunday supplements. 'Don't get disappointed if it takes a few months.'

Anna's mouth hardened into a line that didn't sit well on her soft face. 'It's very unlikely to happen at all, unless the Angel Gabriel pops in. I've never seen Phil so keen to buy condoms. And if someone's terrified of getting their wife pregnant, Mother Nature likes to step in and help out, just to be on the safe side.' She glanced down, clearly angry at her own indiscretion but unable to stop herself blurting it out.

'But the girls are fine about Sarah now, aren't they? I had Chloe in the shop the other day buying something for the baby.'

'Yes, they're fine about Sarah, but us? Off the agenda. Indefinitely. That's Phil, by the way. The girls haven't been consulted.'

'Anna, that's unfair. And selfish.' Michelle felt on safer ground when it came to Phil's failings. 'He can't make decisions about your fertility for you like that.'

She waved a hand. 'No, it's fine. It makes me feel less guilty about everything else. I binned a load of Chloe's dead strawberry plants last night. I'm not a market gardener. And if he wants Piggy-Jo's ears sewn back on, he can do it himself.'

'I have no idea what you're talking about, but I'm right behind you cutting yourself some slack at home,' said Michelle.

She made a fist of solidarity and Anna managed a weak smile.

'What are the Malory Towers Mums discussing this week?' Michelle asked, pleased to have got some reaction out of her.

'*The Secret Garden* and how much better it is when you read it again and see all the beautiful symbolism about locked gardens and unwanted children being nurtured with love just like the flowers and . . .' She tailed off, seeing Michelle's blank face. 'I loved it.'

'Good,' said Michelle, easing her stilettos back on. 'Have you got lots of copies for them to buy?'

'Yes. I found three in the back, and they're ready on the shelves. Did you get the email?' Anna went on. 'From Nicky Oliphant at the *Longhampton Gazette*? About interviewing us for the Leisure pages?'

'I thought you could do that. You're the manager.'

'They want us both, for the friends angle. You've got to say what your favourite book is.' Anna gave her a resigned look. 'I mean, I can make something up for you if you want. I guess it's not that important.'

'No,' said Michelle, suddenly feeling bad. If Anna was abandoning her attempts to get her to read now, it was a really bad sign. 'It is important. We run this shop together, don't we? It's just that I don't have time.'

'How about putting an audiobook on your iPod?' Anna brightened up. 'And you could listen to it while you were running?'

'Good idea.' An hour or so would do it. Michelle was an expert blagger.

'What would you like? Something you read as a teenager? Jilly Cooper? Shirley Conran? I can ask Becca to download something.'

'Jilly Cooper,' said Michelle automatically. 'Here's my iPod. Tell Becca to knock herself out. But not if she's busy. Obviously.'

Anna picked it up and Michelle sensed a slight tension.

'Is everything going OK ... with the exams?' she asked carefully.

'I think so.' Anna fiddled with the controls. 'I'm trying to make sure she does her revision at home and not round at ... Well, you know what I mean.' She paused and looked up. 'I think we've both been teenage girls. And I can remember what twenty-four-year-old men are like.'

Michelle felt torn. 'I have told him that Becca's special, and that he needs to respect her, or face the wrath of you and Phil. And me.'

'*And* Sarah. This isn't an easy time for them, any of them. I don't want . . .' Anna seemed embarrassed but determined, in a mother hen-ish way that Michelle would have admired under other circumstances, but now struck her as painful. 'I don't want her to think she needs to find affection somewhere else. I'm bloody mad with Phil right now, but as far as the girls go, I'm doing what I can to keep things on an even keel at home. I just want her to get the results she deserves.'

'Believe me, Anna, if anyone's aware of how easy it is to mess up A-levels, it's me,' said Michelle tightly.

'She's not going to mess them up,' said Anna. 'I just think you could talk to Owen. Make sure he realises that. Did he go to university?'

Michelle raised her hands. 'Fine. I'll start calling round at the flat more,' she said. 'I'll give *you* the keys if you want, to make some surprise visits to pick up stock? Call in at shag-worthy times? Shall I try to get a timetable? At least this business with Sarah might make them realise how possible a baby is, and what a headfuck it can be. I can't think of anything more likely to put me off reckless sex with my boyfriend than the thought of my forty-year-old mother doing it, frankly.'

Anna's face registered horror, then weariness. 'God. I hope so.'

'Anyway, if he is taking her back there, at least it's forcing him to tidy up. I've never seen any room of his so clean.'

'Becca's very realistic,' said Anna, as if she was reassuring herself. 'They're so much more . . . blasé about things these days than we were. Maybe talking *is* the new sex. Maybe they're just having passionate discussions about the EU.'

'Sensible girls are the ones who need looking after most.'

It slipped out, and Anna looked at her quizzically. 'Meaning?'

'Meaning . . .' Normally she'd have left it, but for Becca's sake, she said, 'It can get boring being sensible. But I'll talk to Owen again. Lay it on the line about Phil's rugby-playing background.' She scooped up her bag. 'Listen, let me know if there's anything I can do – for Becca, I mean. I was going to give her a bonus for all the extra work she's done for the website.'

'Actually,' said Anna, 'there *is* something. It's her prom coming up at the end of June, and I wondered if you had any contacts in the flashy car department? Phil refuses to hire her a limo. He says he doesn't want her looking like she's in a reality show.'

'Leave it with me,' said Michelle, glad it was something as easy as that.

'Thanks,' said Anna, and touched her arm.

Michelle felt a bittersweet warmth. The fact that she was noticing how nice this moment was, just her and Anna, in their bookshop, was a sad reflection of how few and far between those moments had got lately.

Anna hoped the weather would break to make revision less of a struggle for Chloe and Becca, but it seemed to get hotter every day. The incessant hum of fans didn't do much to help the bad mood already hanging over the McQueen house, and Sarah's announcement that she and Jeff would be getting married in the summer holidays, with the girls as bridesmaids in Las Vegas as part of a big family holiday, only stoked things to volcanic levels.

'She can get lost if she thinks I'm going to stand there like something off of Jeremy Kyle, being a bridesmaid to my pregnant mother,' Chloe announced over dinner, flicking her new extensions so hard she whipped them in Lily's eye.

Lily howled and stormed out, knocking over her glass and sending Pongo leaping from the sofa, barking in alarm.

'Stop crying, you crybaby!' yelled Chloe spitefully. 'You're just doing it for attention!'

Anna looked to Phil to tell Chloe off, but he was already pushing back his chair and going after Lily, before she could. 'I'll go.'

She pressed her lips together with annoyance. Phil had run out of ways to deal with Chloe's simmering fury and now passed all responsibility for tamping it down to her. Meanwhile, he insisted on taking over Lily's bedtime story – the one enjoyable part of her day – so she could deal with Chloe's revision. What Phil didn't know was that Anna was giving Chloe one iTunes download for every hour studied, from his account.

'What?' Chloe demanded. 'What did I say that you're not all thinking? It's disgusting.'

'Nothing,' said Becca. 'You keep going on like that. But you're starting to make Mum look like the reasonable one.'

'It'll be a fab holiday, driving across California,' said Anna. Sticking to the facts was her only tactic; if she thought too hard about the unfairness of everything, her head would explode. 'You could all do with a break after your exams. And your granny and granddad will be going too – won't it be nice to spend time with them?'

'I'm only going for the first week,' said Becca. She turned over a page in her book, and Anna was surprised to see it was Lily's copy of *Ballet Shoes*. Becca had a French exam the next afternoon. She should have been reading *La Peste*.

'What?' demanded Chloe. She raised a finger. 'No way.'

'I totally can. I'm only going for a week. I've got reading to do, and I need to do some extra hours in the shop, and—'

'I can't stand being away from Ooooweeeeeen,' Chloe sing-songed.

'Shut up, tubby. Ow!'

'Chloe, don't kick,' said Anna automatically. 'You're not eight. Becca, you can't just go for a week. Your mum will be hurt.'

'She didn't think of whether we'd be hurt when she totally got pregnant without talking to us about it,' retorted Chloe with another head toss. 'Or if we'd want to be in her embarrassing wedding. I wish I could just leave this dump and go to London and . . . get a proper life.'

Anna wondered if there was a full orchestra in Chloe's head that burst out into song and dance numbers whenever she made pronouncements like that. She watched a lot of *Glee*.

'Get your A-levels, and you can go wherever you want,' she said instead.

'You should read this book, Chloe,' said Becca. 'It's all about stage-school girls who get too big for their boots. Only they learn about Shakespeare and are nice to their wise old foster parents and don't demand hair extensions or leave their moustache bleach in the shower.'

'Shut up, Becca, you don't understand.' Chloe's face was bright red; Anna knew she was trying to look dramatic, but beneath the eyeliner, she had the same overwhelmed tiredness in her eyes that Lily got when school became too much. '*None* of you understand, and I wish I didn't have to live in this house!'

And with a mighty blare of invisible trumpets, she stormed out too.

The cellar door slammed and Becca and Anna looked at each other over the kitchen table. After ten seconds, the opening bars of 'Toxic' began, the Wii turned up to maximum volume.

'She's dancing away the pain,' said Becca. 'Just like the actor playing her will in the film about her life, at this point.'

Anna fought back a smile. 'So that's two girls down. What would you like to storm off about?'

'Me? I'm fine,' said Becca. 'I'm cool with Mum's wedding. If she wants to look back on her wedding photos and cringe, that's up to her. I'm just not going to hang around for the honeymoon.'

'OK, I'll risk it, then,' sighed Anna. 'Have you told your dad that you're going to the prom with Owen yet? Because you haven't arranged that dinner, like I asked, and he wants to know what's happening.'

That was a neat filleting around the truth.

'Did you tell him?' Becca asked.

'I just gave him a name. What? I had to, he asked about Josh!' Anna protested. 'I don't like keeping secrets in this house, from anyone. Becca, come on.'

Becca put the book down, gave Anna a reproachful look, then without saying anything, picked up her school bag and went upstairs. Pongo slunk out from under the coffee table and followed her.

Great, thought Anna, refilling her wine glass. My parenting job here is done.

As Sarah's wedding approached and one exam after another was crossed off, the weather got even hotter, tempers got shorter, and only Lily seemed oblivious to the tension criss-crossing the dinner table. That was because she was lost in her own little world, something else that Anna felt she should be worrying about. Eventually, after hours of sulking, sudden tears, midnight panics and endless chocolate supplied by Anna to the bedroom door each night, Chloe's final exam, then Becca's came and went, and Becca's Year 13 prom night arrived.

Phil's concerns about Owen finally surfaced properly the night before.

'Is he trustworthy?' he whispered over the hum of the electric fan, which was moving the hot air around the bed, not cooling them. 'Does he have his own car? And what kind of car is it? Has Becca been in it?'

'This obsession with his car is saying more about you than it is about Owen,' Anna hissed back. 'What kind of teenager *were* you?'

'An opportunist one with a Mini Clubman. It was my secret weapon.' He lay back glumly on the pillows. 'My little girl. Leaving school. Can you tell Michelle to tell Owen to keep his hands to himself?'

'And how exactly do you propose I frame that request to my boss?' Anna asked crossly, and Phil shushed her.

She rolled over onto her side of the bed, and he rolled over onto his. The coolest part of the bed, thought Anna, as she tried to plump the heat out of her pillow, was the ever-increasing trench in the middle.

To his credit, when Owen arrived at the front door of the McQueen house, he played the role of dashing-but-reliable escort to a point just short of self-parody.

His dark hair was neater than Anna had seen it before, though still tousled, and he'd found a forest green velvet dinner jacket that gave him a 70s era James Bond panache, far beyond what the Longhampton youth in their dad's old dinner jackets would be pulling off. He'd shaved, and although one or two leather bracelets were still visible under the crisp white shirt cuff, he smelled clean and fresh, and exuded a handsome eagerness that made Anna wistful for her own university life, where everyone's scrubbed-up finery was a fairytale transformation from their artfully scruffy daytime looks.

He'd also brought flowers for Becca to pin on her dress, and some for Anna, which he gave her with a shameless smile.

'Thought I'd err on the safe side,' he said, following her into the kitchen where she'd chilled a bottle of champagne to toast them. 'Michelle always told me it's best to give flowers for no reason.'

'She was right.' Anna eyed him, hoping Michelle had given him other advice too. Owen was being charming. Too charming?

Phil appeared behind Anna, with Becca following behind him, suddenly shy, and watching Owen's face for his reaction.

Anna knew Becca looked beautiful in her simple red column dress, bought from eBay and adjusted by Michelle's secret tailor, but the expression on Owen's face was better than a mirror. His eyes widened in admiration, but then blinked rapidly, presumably as he clocked Phil's reaction to his reaction.

'You look amazing,' he said, quietly, and Becca beamed. Anna had to wipe away a sneaky tear.

'Getting Becca ready' had been a happy afternoon for Anna and the girls, with lots of make-up and Diet Coke and pop music and nail varnish for all. Chloe had generously offered a loan of her spare hair extensions and bronzing pearls, but Becca had politely demurred – without hurting her little sister's feelings, for once – and had instead gone for a very simple elegance. Her shiny brown hair was pinned up in a messy bun, and she wore the Tiffany heart necklace Phil had given her for her eighteenth birthday. Becca moved carefully in her high heels and long dress, as if she was feeling her way around an unfamiliar side of herself as much as the unfamiliar outfit, and Anna's heart burst with pride when Becca asked if she could do her make-up for her. They were sharing something new, the four of them, and she was touched to be part of it.

'Now, Owen,' said Phil as Anna handed round flutes of champagne. 'You're going to take care of her, aren't you? I'm her dad. She might have mentioned me. And my black belt in karate.'

'Daaaad,' groaned Becca.

Owen's eyes flicked nervously towards her – Anna hadn't seen him nervous before – but Becca shook her head.

'He's winding you up,' she said. 'He doesn't even have a black belt in . . . in his *jeans*.'

'Good.' Owen held out a hand. Phil shook it, looking slightly taken aback by the firm enthusiasm of Owen's handshake and the appearance of a leather bracelet. 'Don't worry, I'll have her back before the car turns into a pumpkin.'

'And what time's that?' asked Phil. 'Midnight?'

'One thirty,' said Becca.

'One o'clock,' said Anna.

'But it doesn't finish until one . . .'

'One o'clock,' said Owen, with a swift glance at Anna.

'Cheers! To your first ball, Becca!' she said, lifting her flute, but the moment was immediately broken by the arrival of Chloe and Lily, both clamouring for their own glasses 'to try'.

Chloe was also singing 'My Heart Will Go On', but with rather suspect lyrics.

'Now, Owen, what kind of car are you taking her in?' asked Phil, as if this was the most important element of the night.

A horn honking outside prevented Owen from answering.

'I'll go,' said Chloe, who, Anna noticed suddenly, was also dressed up to go out.

'Chloe, where are you . . . ?' she started, but Chloe was gone. Phil didn't meet her eye when she looked at him, and she knew permission had been granted already. She was annoyed; Chloe going out meant that she'd have to be collected from somewhere. Phil could have checked with her first.

Owen, Becca, Phil and Anna stood looking at each other, not quite sure what to say.

'I'm having a prom tonight,' Lily announced. 'It's very exclusive. Everyone's had to find a partner, and Mrs Piggle has two dates because she doesn't want to let anyone down.' She turned to Anna. 'It's OK for her to have two dates, isn't it?'

'Yes,' said Anna. 'Maybe one is her first husband. And the second is her handsome lover.'

Becca laughed and turned it into a cough when Phil looked askance.

'Oh my God,' screeched Chloe from the front door. 'Oh my actual God, you are not going to believe what's outside!'

'What is it?' Phil looked straight at Owen. 'I hope it's suitable . . .'

'Michelle arranged the transport for tonight,' said Owen. 'She said it's her treat. She spoke to Dad and he said he'd find something appropriate, so I honestly don't know what's going to be out there.'

'I trust it's not a stretch Hummer,' said Phil darkly. 'Or anything with blacked-out windows. Or a minibar.'

He made to reach for Owen's glass but Anna stopped him as discreetly as she could.

Chloe came running in, her eyes round with excitement.

'Anna, you have so got to come and see this! They are *so* going to make everyone die with jealousy when they see what they're going in. They'll think Cheryl Cole's arrived.'

Owen held out his arm to Becca and she took it, only looking at him very quickly. Anna couldn't help it; despite every misgiving in her head, her heart was yelling that they made a beautiful couple.

Parked outside their house, the engine idling with a throaty rumble, was a long sleek sports car, dark green with blood red seats. Between their Espace and next door's old Land Rover, it looked like a cheetah in the dog park.

Anna heard Phil make a faint noise of schoolboy longing.

'You'd better tell me what it is,' she said. 'Because I have no idea.'

'It's an Aston Martin Rapide,' he moaned. 'I didn't even know you could buy them. I thought they were like unicorns or something.'

'Who's driving it?' Chloe demanded, as the driver's door opened and a man in a peaked cap got out. 'Is he, like, the chauffeur?'

'I suppose so,' said Anna. 'That's very responsible. So you can drink, I mean – not excessively, of course . . .'

'Oh, very good!' roared Owen. 'I know who that is! Harvey, you joker!' He strode forward with his hand already extended and clapped the chauffeur on the back. 'I can't believe it! This is so good of you!'

'Well, I had a look at what Charlie was going to send up, and I thought, no, no, no. Can't have my favourite brother-in-law turning up in anything less than an Aston.' The man's voice was rich and confident, with a London edge. He swept the hat off to reveal a thick head of blond hair and an affable sort of face, albeit with a red band where the hat had been.

Anna stared, trying to take in as many details as she could without looking obvious. So this was Harvey? He wasn't how she'd imagined. She'd assumed, for some reason, that Harvey would be lean and hungry, a car salesman with ambition and a sharp suit, all jargon and sexy money talk. This man looked like a regular at the rugby club, the guy who always drank the yard of ale in under two minutes. He didn't seem the type of man you'd be scared of. Not the way Michelle seemed to shrink whenever she mentioned him.

Anna couldn't imagine him with Michelle at all. And yet how long had they been together? Seven years? It gave her a strange, tilting feeling, that maybe she didn't know her friend as well as she'd thought.

Phil was looking at her too, with a 'This is *him*?' look, which he wiped off his face when Owen turned back, grinning.

'Phil, Anna, this is Harvey, my brother-in-law. Harvey,' he continued, 'this is Phil, Anna, and my beautiful date for the evening, Rebecca.'

'Lucky chap! Pleased to meet you.' Harvey shook hands with an extra over-the-top-hand-clasp, the mark of a car salesman, thought Anna. 'My own car, by the way,' he added, as if it didn't really need an explanation. 'I love this chap like a brother but there's no way I'd let him drive my Rapide!'

'Why? Is he dangerous behind the wheel?' Phil demanded.

'No, no. She's just my pride and joy. Fancy a spin later?'

'Well, we're not going out . . .'

Phil's protective father act was wilting very fast in the presence of the car. Anna gave him a nudge. 'Shall we let them get away?' she said. 'Time's getting on.'

'What? Oh, er, yes. Be back by one. Give me a call if there are any problems. And I mean *any*. *Problems*.' He directed a meaningful glare at Owen, who smiled his charming smile and put an arm around Becca's slender waist.

Becca smiled too, her face radiant enough without the special expensive compact Anna had lent her for the evening. Well, given. 'We will. See you later.'

'Have a good night,' said Anna. 'You've earned it.'

'Thanks.' She leaned forward and gave Anna a kiss on the cheek that nearly made Anna cry. Becca *had* earned tonight, she thought – the hours of revision, the help in the shop, the general patience when everyone else had been a pain. She deserved a Cinderella moment.

Chloe and Lily watched as their big sister drove off.

'She looked like a princess,' said Lily. 'A happy one.' Then she turned on her heel and ran into the house, Pongo chasing after her.

23

Michelle sat at her kitchen table with the accounts all around her, but she couldn't concentrate on the figures. She was thinking about Becca and Owen at the prom, and it was dredging up some unwelcome memories of her own.

Owen had looked nervous and excited when she'd seen him that morning, not the usual peacock swagger he displayed on dates. He'd even asked her opinion about his outfit, and had his hair cut.

At least he'd had a prom. She hadn't been able to offer any advice, having been excluded from her own. I hope he's being sensible, she thought.

Somewhere, back in her parents' house, there was a white ballgown with accompanying strappy silver sandals. Often tried on, never actually worn. In a different dimension, one in which things had worked out properly, she and Ed Pryce had had the romantic evening she'd painstaking planned in daydreams; then started dating, gone to university together, probably had a few years apart after that, but then bumped into each other in a London bar and realised they were meant to be; got married, had two children called Ivo and Clare, and—

The doorbell rang and Michelle jumped, as if Ed might be there now.

'Don't be ridiculous,' she said aloud. It was much more likely to be Rory, needing some milk or wanting to read the paper at her.

Still, she put on a slick of lipstick to make it look as if she was on her way somewhere more interesting when she opened the door. But the person outside was almost as much of a shock as Ed Pryce would have been: it was Harvey, in a suit and a peaked cap.

'What are you doing here?' she blurted out, her fingers clenching.

'Charming,' said Harvey. His eyes glittered in the light of the solar lamp hanging from her door. 'I drive all this way to whisk you out for dinner and that's the thanks I get?'

'You haven't driven a hundred and fifty miles to take me out for dinner,' she said, taking in his outfit. 'Why are you wearing a hat?'

'OK, I'll come clean,' he said, stepping inside even though she hadn't invited him in. 'Nice place you've got here, by the way. Still just you, is it? No, I've been on chauffeur duty tonight, ferrying your little brother and his date to the "prom", as I believe we're supposed to call it now. Had a couple of hours to kill, so thought I'd come over here, see if you'd eaten. Have a chat. Since you seem so reluctant to come back to the big city.'

Michelle's skin prickled as Harvey's broad frame brushed against her fragile glass wall art. His tone was affable but already she was tense. She put aside the matter of him not asking if she *wanted* to go out for dinner, and focused on the part of the plan she had been informed about.

'Why did you come, though? I asked Dad if Owen could borrow his E-type for the night. He was going to let Owen drive it up and then I was going to drive it back to—'

'I know, I know. Very sweet idea, but come on, Shelley, in the great Top Trumps of cars, I think you'll find my Aston Martin beats your dad's knackered old Jag hands down. Surely a car connoisseur like you would know that. And I thought you might like to see it.'

'Becca doesn't know anything about cars. She wouldn't care.'

'All girls like a powerful car,' said Harvey with a lascivious smile, and she felt ill.

This wasn't about Becca, or Owen. This was about her mum saying to Harvey, 'Ooh, here's a chance to go and get in Michelle's good books,' the interfering old bag, and he knew it.

'Plus, I'll admit it, I wanted to see my wife,' he said, and smiled. 'Is that so bad?'

Michelle stared at him and fought the urge to scream. This had to stop. All she wanted right now was to get Harvey out of her house.

'I'll get my coat,' she said.

Rory could talk for Scotland but at least some of what he had to say was interesting, Michelle thought, as Harvey ordered another mineral water for himself, summoning the waiter in a rare break from his narrative about the state of the pre-loved car market in outer London. He went on and on, ignoring her attempts to interject, until she gave up and watched his teeth instead. He'd had veneers. He was vain like that.

Harvey's loud voice, gold watch and attitude stood out in Ferrari's. The waiter had definitely perked up when he ordered a Barolo from the lower part of the list, even though she was the only one drinking it.

'So, how are things going with your shop?' he asked. 'Or should I say, shops?'

'Up and down,' she said, guarded. There was always a right answer with Harvey, and not always the obvious one. 'What's Mum said?'

'Just that you're so busy you don't have time for them. Which is a shame. Funny that's what you've ended up doing. I never saw you read a book in all the time we were married,' he mused, as if he himself were Jeremy Paxman and she was illiterate. 'Have you got someone doing the actual book part for you, while you concentrate on the paintwork and so on?'

'No,' said Michelle. 'I'm very involved in the bookshop. My manager and I run it together. We arrange reading groups and local activities and author appearances. I get a lot out of it. It's a community thing.'

'Good for you. Good. For. You. Is it making any money, though?'

'It's doing all right,' said Michelle, then bit her lip. Don't give him any details, she told herself. That was how he worked, wriggling in on the details then storing them up.

The main course arrived and Michelle was glad of the break. Her muscles were aching with tension even though she'd done nothing but sit on a fashionably uncomfortable seat for half an hour. She never noticed the chairs when she was in here with Anna.

'It sounds as if you're seeing a lot of my mum and dad,' she said, as Harvey began to dissect his fish, surgically removing the flesh with a bit too much relish.

'Well, someone has to.' He said it lightly, but clearly he meant it. 'You know your dad's not so well?'

'No. I didn't know that.' Michelle put down her knife and fork, her appetite gone. 'Mum didn't say anything.'

'Oh, he's had a few check-ups. I'm sure Carole didn't want to worry you, when you're so busy.' His mouth twisted. 'In fact, I'm not sure Carole knows everything. Charlie doesn't want her fussing.'

'She might *want* to fuss. What kind of check-ups?' Dad had looked a little tired at her birthday lunch, but not ill. Thinner than normal, maybe. Michelle tried to think back for any clues, guilt washing through her for not realising something was wrong. 'Is it his asthma?'

'No, they think it's just stress. He's still doing six days a week at the dealership. Too much for a chap his age, but you know what he's like, Shelley. We can't keep him away. Checking for fingerprints on the cars, moving in to poach sales where he can, the old bugger. You were the only salesperson he didn't pinch clients from. And that was only because he didn't dare get between you and a sale.'

Harvey spoke with real affection for her dad and Michelle smiled back, caught off guard by the flashes of good nature he sometimes showed.

'Mind you, none of us dared,' he added. 'And it had nothing to do with you being the boss's daughter.'

'So that's why you married me,' she joked. 'Protecting your sales target.'

'That was definitely a factor. That and the key to the executive bathroom.'

He paused, suddenly looking crestfallen, and Michelle

paused too. Crestfallen wasn't a natural state for him; it didn't sit well with his confident suit and manner. Harvey wasn't completely evil. Maybe she *was* being touchy. That happened when you were on your own.

Or it could be the third glass of wine she'd started.

'You'll let me know . . . if there's anything I should know,' she said. 'About Dad? I know he tells you things he doesn't tell Mum about the business. He'd never tell me he was ill. It's like a badge of honour with him, never a day off sick.'

'Sometimes it's easier when you're not related,' said Harvey. 'Your brothers . . .'

'Don't start me on them.' Michelle rolled her eyes. 'Well, apart from Owen.'

'He's not going to be a car dealer though, is he?' said Harvey. 'I've never met a bloke with less spatial awareness. I hope you haven't put him on your insurance?'

'I haven't,' said Michelle. 'I need my car for work.'

'What are you driving now?' Harvey sipped his water and looked at her over the top of the glass, his blue eyes fixed attentively on her, as if she was the most fascinating thing in the room.

'Golf.' She wasn't going to go into details, but couldn't help adding, 'FSI engine.'

'Ah, the turbo/supercharger combo. Interesting.' He nodded. 'Economical, yet punchy in the lower range, with that extra kick of turbo at the upper range. You haven't run into problems with turbo lag at all?'

'It isn't interesting, Harvey,' Michelle interrupted, before he went off on a lecture about modern engine technology. She tried not to be amused at his expression of surprise when she stopped him. 'Only to car saddos.'

He raised a hand solemnly. 'That's me. Guilty as charged.

And women who know the difference between a turbo and a supercharger are super-hot in my book.'

The compliment resonated inside her even though it was worse than cheesy. It was so long since anyone had flirted with her; she usually nipped anything like that in the bud. Harvey, though, ignored any warning signs.

Michelle put her glass down. She was already feeling vulnerable. Stupid, she told herself. Stupid for still finding him . . .

She didn't let her brain finish the sentence, even in her head.

'Can I tell you something in confidence?' Harvey said softly.

'As long as it's nothing personal.' Michelle knew her voice sounded brittle. She gripped the stem of her wine glass.

'Your dad floated a business proposal by me,' said Harvey. He lined up his cutlery, fussily arranging the tines of the fork at the same level as the knife blade. 'Your brothers aren't interested in the dealerships.'

It was a fact. 'No,' said Michelle.

'And he's very keen to keep it in the family. You can understand that.'

'I can. But no. I don't want to run a car dealership – if that's your next question.'

Harvey looked up. 'You're the best salesperson he's employed in the past twenty-five years, and I include myself in that, Shelley. I think it would make your dad very happy if you and I could take over the business from him. A gradual handover, say, over the course of a few years.'

'You and I?' she repeated.

Harvey nodded. 'You and me. We're a good team. You know we are. We could double the profits. And it would mean your dad could relax into retirement, look after himself a bit.'

Michelle felt ill and her mind raced. Harvey's twisty

Machiavellian ways were so hard to unpick. What did he want? Her or the business? Had he manipulated her dad to make this offer, so she'd come back? Or was it just the money he was after, and he needed her by his side to do it?

'And your mum could stop worrying about you,' he added, failing to read her expression. 'You know she'd love us to put this behind us and get on with giving her some more grand-children. As would I, if you want to know.' He winked at her, his face all cosy teddy-bear affability. 'Come on, Shelley. We're grown-ups. You can admit when you've made a mistake, right? You've had your time out to spread your wings. The shop's nice enough but it's not giving you the same opportunities as a dealership network would. Come home.'

Michelle suddenly saw it all: Harvey in her dad's office, in an even more expensive suit, ordering everyone around; her back at home in a pinny, being nagged to lose the baby weight 'because I hate to see you let yourself go'.

'And where would I fit into this?' she asked, her voice tight. Testing him out. 'Co-director? Co-owner?'

Harvey's smile faltered. 'Are you negotiating? Same old Shelley, eh?'

'Not same old Shelley,' said Michelle. 'New Michelle.'

She licked her lips, dredging up all her self-control. This wasn't the moment she'd planned to do it, but she had to do it now, while she felt this surge of outrage.

'Was that what all the flowers were about, getting me to come back, so you could get your hands on Dad's business?' she demanded. 'And the dog at the rescue? That was a low blow, Harvey. You adopted a *dog*, when you know how much I miss Flash?'

As usual, he pretended that she'd deliberately misread him. 'You're talking about Flash? I wanted you to come back because you're my wife and I love you!' he retorted angrily. 'And because I care about your family – who, by the way, worry about your mental health, the way you act. Jesus, you're unbelievable.'

Michelle stared at him; he was breathing through his nose like a bull.

A little voice in her head had whispered that from the start – that a man like Harvey, handsome and successful, could only have been interested in someone like her because of her family. Not because of who *she* was.

'I think it's time we drew a line,' she said, in someone else's voice. 'I'd like to get a divorce under way.'

'What?' The affability left his face and was replaced by amazement. Cold amazement.

'I'm not coming back, Harvey. It's time we faced that, while we're still young enough to start again with people we suit better.' Her mouth had gone dry.

'Are you shagging someone else?'

'No!' She recoiled at the coarseness of his tone after his earlier gentleness.

He leaned forward and hissed, 'Because you're still my wife.'

'You keep saying that.' Michelle felt the old fear return, but she made herself keep talking. In this restaurant, *she* was the local. There were no waiters ready to ignore any awkward behaviour from 'good old Harvey' who tipped so generously every time he sent his wife's plate back before she had time to finish. 'I haven't been your wife for years. There's no shame in divorce. It just means we've grown apart. It happens. No one's fault. We were too young.'

She wanted to add, 'Well, I was,' but didn't dare.

Harvey looked away, as if he couldn't bear to see her face,

and she wondered if she'd gone too far and hurt him; but then he turned back and said nastily, 'If you're imagining that men will be queueing round the block to date you, then think again. Decent men, I mean. Men who care about what sort of woman they're with.'

Michelle flinched.

'Have you thought about that?' he went on. 'Having to fill them in about your past history? Because you'll have to. You'll have to go through all that again, all the details.'

'I won't. It's irrelevant. It's nothing to do with who I am now.' She knew her voice was wobbling and she dug her nails into her palms.

'Ah, but it's not.' Harvey put his hands together, gloating now he'd regained control of the situation. 'Women are like cars, Michelle. They've got a service history that men want to have a look at before they buy. Neat stamps, everything checked out. Nice and clean. Who wants some old banger that's been round the block? Been in some backstreet garage?'

His eyes were fixed on hers and she'd never seen them so malicious.

'You can skip over the details if you like,' he continued remorselessly, 'but men can tell. They can tell a cut-and-shut a mile off. And that's what you are. I didn't mind, because I loved you. I was prepared to overlook your madness and your dirty little secrets. But will anyone else?'

He raised his hands and gave her a cold, 'sad' smile. 'I don't think so. Especially not at your age.'

The waiter passed by, and from the approving look he gave them, Michelle guessed he thought they were out on a date. Two good-looking people. Having a romantic meal.

She felt as if she'd never want to eat again. She'd certainly never eat here again. Sorry, Silvio.

'I would rather be alone for the rest of my life than live with you,' said Michelle. She didn't know where the strength came from, but all she could see was her dad, hugging her outside the pub, wanting his little girl to be happy, confused as to why she wasn't. And this bastard, spinning him some tale about how lovelorn he was. It made her more angry than any of Harvey's bruiseless taunts had done over the years.

She pushed her chair back and dropped her napkin on the table. 'Thanks for supper. I'm going home now.'

'Sit down,' he snapped.

'No,' said Michelle. She stared at him. Inside she was terrified but she couldn't let it show. 'Leave me alone. I have a very good solicitor these days. You'll be hearing from him.'

She left her coat and walked straight outside where, for once, there was a taxi idling in the rank. Michelle didn't breathe properly till she was at home, then she raced round, locking all the doors, bolting the windows and drawing all the curtains, until finally, she curled up on the sofa in a tight ball.

I wish Tavish was here, she thought. Sometimes the silent unquestioning company of a dog was all you needed.

Anna lay awake in bed, listening to Phil snore two feet away from her as the fan whirred hot stale air from one side of the room to the other.

She couldn't sleep. She hadn't had a decent night's sleep since before Sarah had announced her pregnancy. If there were a spare room in the house she'd have subtly crept there when everyone was asleep but even then, the girls would notice. They noticed everything. Part of Anna didn't care, but the soft, motherly side didn't want to add another silent worry to Lily's already overloaded shoulders.

Anna didn't know how Phil could lie there, snoring like a

rhino with chest congestion, when Becca and Owen still weren't back, and it was now two o'clock. He was the one who'd made all the fuss about them coming home at one, but then he'd wandered off for a bath and nodded off on the bed, listening to the radio.

She rolled over and looked at the clock, on the other side of Phil's wide-open mouth.

Two thirteen.

Should I call Michelle, she wondered? Or the police? Or just do a dawn raid on Owen's flat?

Or there was always the computer. Anna had registered on Mumsnet in the three days she thought she was pregnant, and had been unable to tear herself away since. Most nights, when everyone was asleep or otherwise occupied, she crept up to her old laptop in the bedroom and gorged herself on other people's pregnancies, symptoms, stepchildren, sometimes arguing in a voice that wasn't hers, behind the safe screen of her username.

She knew it wasn't healthy. But it was the only place where she could confess just how much she thought about the baby waiting for her out there, and how angry she got with every period that came and went, another egg wasted.

As Anna was rolling the possibilities round in her mind she heard a noise outside, and slipped out of bed to see what it was.

A minicab – probably unlicenced, *oh, Becca* – was pulling away from the front of the house, and Owen and Becca were standing by the postbox, kissing.

She caught her breath. They were beautiful in the moonlight, like something from a film, unconscious of their youthful smoothness, the softness of their faces. Becca was wearing Owen's velvet jacket over her long dress, and her hair had come loose, streaming down her back and shining like water. He'd undone his bow tie and some shirt buttons and had confetti in his curls from some end-of-night celebration. They were kissing in a slow, quite reverential way – more romantic than sordid end-of-night snogging – and then Owen pulled back to look into Becca's eyes, smiling as if he couldn't believe his luck.

Anna leaned back from the bedroom window, in case they could see her, but she couldn't tear her eyes away.

With a courtly gesture, Owen lifted Becca's right hand high, slipped his arm around her waist, and silently, to some tune maybe they were humming to each other, they started to swing down the deserted pavement in a slow, looping sort of waltz. Becca tipped her head backwards, letting her hair fall in a glossy curtain, and smiled up at the stars, her eyes closed, tipsy and blissed-out with love.

Then Owen leaned forward and kissed her long white throat, and Anna let the curtain fall back.

She felt weird inside – bad for spying but happy and jealous and wistful all at the same time.

In bed, Phil gave a massive snore and turned over.

Anna looked at him for a long, long moment, then went downstairs, turning on all the lights so Becca would know someone had waited up for her.

24

*'Little Women is quite accurate about what it's like
to have sisters – they can wind you up, nick your best
gloves, and make you wish you could swap them for a
brother. But in the end, you love them more than anything.
Even if they are totally annoying.'*   Chloe McQueen

Neither Becca nor Chloe wrote Results Day on the kitchen calendar, but the whole house knew exactly when they were due.

Becca's would arrive first, in the third week of August, and Chloe's the following week. To Chloe's bitter disappointment, the three of them were going to be in Las Vegas at Sarah's wedding the day the GCSE results were announced, which 'totally ruined' Chloe and Tyra's plan to get all four Apricotz in the *Longhampton Gazette*, leaping photogenically in the air and waving their envelopes.

'If the cheerleading squad gets in instead of us, I am never speaking to Paige again,' she pouted, when the Apricotz reject Paige revealed her counter scheme via Facebook.

Anna dragged herself into the bookshop as normal the morning of Becca's results, even though it took every ounce of self-control not to stay at home waiting for news. She and Phil had agreed to keep everything as low-key as possible, despite their own fizzing nerves; even Sarah had agreed to wait for Becca to Skype her.

Becca herself was playing it very cool, eating a calm breakfast while Anna and Phil picked nervously at toast and coffee, before heading up to the sixth form centre on her own.

She was still trying to look cool when she pushed open the bookshop door just before lunch, but her bright eyes gave her away.

'Well?' squeaked Anna, unable to stop herself.

Becca smiled and handed her the piece of paper. She'd got As in everything. Her Head of Year had even stuck a jokey gold star on it. She'd done it. Becca was going to Cambridge.

'I'm so proud of you!' Anna gasped, flinging her arms around her step-daughter. 'I'm so proud!'

'You're the first person I've told.' Becca's voice was muffled against her neck. 'I thought, you know, after everything you've done this year.'

Her voice trailed off, but Anna did know. It was a tiny little thing, and it meant the world to her.

'Thank you.' She hugged Becca tighter, trying not to cry too obviously. 'I'll always remember today.'

The door bell jangled and Michelle popped her head round, her eyebrows raised in tactful query. She had something behind her back, and when she saw Anna's happy tears, she grinned and brandished a bottle of champagne. 'So it's OK to open this then?'

Anna nodded mistily, and Michelle signalled to someone out of sight. Owen, Kelsey and Gillian streamed into the bookshop with glasses and party poppers, plus Tavish, who had tinsel around his collar.

As the afternoon wore on and the regulars joined in with the celebrations – everyone liked Becca – Anna felt a warmth spread through her that had nothing to do with Michelle's magic refilling champagne bottle. Chloe had turned up from her pre-wedding shopping trip for gradual tanning lotion and was flicking through a vintage *Jackie* annual, snorting at the fashion, Lily was under the counter with Tavish, and Becca, perched on Owen's knee, was lit up from the inside with a giddiness that made Anna nostalgic and protective in equal measure.

She caught Michelle's eye, and they shared a cautious smile, the first real smile they'd shared in days. Weeks, even.

Anna's smile broadened. Maybe things were going to be OK.

Chloe's GCSE results arrived the following week, while she was acting as a bridesmaid for her mother in a bright pink prom dress with mint green netting underneath and some wildly unsuitable fake anchor tattoos on her left bicep.

It wasn't the nicest dress Anna had ever seen. Even Phil had struggled to find something positive to say about it, and he could normally be relied on for a cheesy compliment. Chloe had nearly refused to wear it, claiming that the dresses made the three of them 'look like a Sheila's Wheels advert', but since Sarah's whole wedding was themed around Elvis Presley, Anna tried to convince her it could be a lot worse. No quiffs were involved. The tattoo would wash off.

Chloe was still wearing the Sheila's Wheels dress when she logged onto Skype for the big results reveal, which she was treating like an *X Factor* final. Lily and Becca were in the background – or at least, swathes of more pink satin kept moving around behind Chloe – and Sarah and Jeff were flitting in and out of shot.

Anna could see Sarah's bump, encased in a baby-doll lace wedding dress. It made her heart pinch with an unpleasant envy, especially since Sarah didn't seem to have put an ounce of weight on her gym-toned legs. The heels, Anna noted, had the all-important red soles and looked nearly impossible to walk in.

'She looks like a toffee apple stuck to a tissue,' Phil whispered, passing Anna the envelope with the results inside. He'd been up to the school to get it, and, as promised to Chloe, hadn't looked.

Anna smiled, grateful for the solidarity, but less grateful that he hadn't said, 'Your turn soon, darling.' Phil wasn't even talking about babies now, and it felt as if there'd been a spiteful baby boom in Longhampton, just as her broodiness had reached new peaks. Anna had started to make excuses to check in the stockroom when the Malory Towers Mummies came in to talk about Enid Blyton because she couldn't hide the sudden tide of despair and sorrow that overwhelmed her. Even Michelle had noticed, and Michelle was so weirdly preoccupied these days she barely even noticed when Anna came in late.

'What?' Chloe yelled into the laptop. 'What did Dad say?'

'Nothing. Right, are you ready?'

Chloe had insisted that Anna read her results, not as a gentle compliment for the revision aids and emergency chocolate she'd provided, but because she was 'less likely to go spare than Dad'.

'Oh my God, I'm really nervous now.' Chloe put a hand to her mouth; she had fuschia false nails. 'I don't wanna know. I don't wanna know. Have you got a nice holiday booked without us?' she asked, prolonging the tension like a pro. 'Are you looking forward to it?'

'Yes,' lied Anna. As instructed by Phil, she *had* blown the budget and had booked a week in the Maldives, flying out the following morning to a luxury hotel that would probably be filled with honeymooning couples. He hadn't bothered to look up from his phone when she'd told him about it, just grunted. What Anna was really looking forward to was the seven books she'd packed, none of which were romances.

'Don't keep us in suspense,' said Sarah's disembodied voice. 'I can't cross my fingers much longer. My nails are coming off.'

'Shut up, Mum,' wailed Chloe. 'This is only my whole life! I feel like there should be music playing . . . that, like, atmosphere music?'

'Der dum,' said Phil, doing the *Jaws* theme. 'Der dum. Der dum . . .'

'Daaad. OK, tell me,' she said, closing her eyes and holding out her hands so her sisters could grab one each side.

'OK, here we go,' said Anna. 'The results for Chloe McQueen are in, and . . .' She unfolded the paper and her heart sank.

Oh, shit, she thought. What to start with, the good news or the bad news?

Phil looked over her shoulder and his intake of breath gave the game away. Chloe's eyes snapped open.

'Well,' said Anna quickly, 'you got a B in Drama!'

'Re-mark,' said Phil. 'She can't just have got a B. That's impossible.'

'. . . and a B in English Literature. And a C in French. And a D in Music, an E in English Language, E in History . . .'

Chloe's face was falling with every word Anna spoke and now she looked outright distressed.

Why am I the one who has to pass on the bad news? Anna thought helplessly. Isn't this Phil's job? But it was too late. She had to plough on.

'And an E in Maths, an E in German. And Science was . . . U.' She folded up the paper.

'It must be a mistake, we'll get them re-marked, Chloe,' said Sarah's voice, and Anna saw Chloe turn away from the laptop and run out of the room. Sarah's legs followed her.

Becca appeared in the space Chloe had vacated. Her hair had been backcombed into a huge beehive and the winged black eyeliner only made her eyes look more cynical. 'Just to say, I'm coming home the day after tomorrow. Don't worry about collecting me from the airport, Owen's coming to meet me.'

'Hi, Anna!' Lily's face made a sideways entry into shot. 'Hi, Daddy! I'm getting my hair half white, half black like Cruella de Vil! Mum's taking me to her hairdresser! And I've got my eeeeeears pierced!'

Anna looked at Phil, and she knew before he spoke that he had nothing useful to say.

Since her dinner with Harvey, Michelle was finding it even more difficult to sleep, despite refurnishing her bedroom with some of her new bedlinen, transforming it into a marshmallow-white oasis of calm and soft serenity.

It wasn't just the hot weather that was unsettling her. For several days in a row, Anna had come into the shop with bags under her eyes, and wouldn't say what the problem was. Michelle knew it had to be a family issue, and felt hurt that Anna clearly didn't expect her to understand. Their chats seemed shorter and more work-orientated every day, and Michelle was irrationally jealous of whoever it was that Anna was talking to now.

And then there was the bookshop. Anna had displayed a surprising new lease of confidence about her 'Deckchair Classics' campaign, but with most locals on holiday or cutting back it was a losing battle, and Michelle was finding it hard to come up with reasons to carry on. She knew she should listen to her Jilly Cooper audiobook so they could do their 'summer reading' interview in the paper, but all Michelle's instincts were telling her to stop rearranging the deckchairs on the *Titanic* and ring for the *Carpathia* asap.

Tavish was off his food. She'd tried all kinds of tempting nibbles, but he was eating less and looking as morose as a dog that looked like a black car-wash brush could. Rory hadn't mentioned it, so either he hadn't noticed or Tavish preferred living with Rory – which would be the final bloody straw.

And Harvey. God. He'd gone quiet, which didn't mean a thing. It just meant he was thinking. He wouldn't have given up, she knew that. He was waiting for her to follow through on her threat and send the papers. What would be unleashed if she did that? What would he say to her dad? How far would Harvey go?

There were other darker thoughts he'd churned up too, about herself and who she was. Harvey was right when he said no one really knew her. Even Anna didn't, not really. Michelle had done such a meticulous job of building her new life, refurbishing herself just like she'd done up her house and shop, that she sometimes forgot too. Harvey coming back like that had disturbed the layers of dust and something was moving inside her that scared her.

Her mind skirted around the worst thought, then touched it, tentatively. How could she still have felt that shiver of attraction to him, when he looked at her like that? She *loathed* Harvey, but he *did* know her. And still wanted her.

The only small consolation was that her dad wasn't ill. As far as she could tell, anyway. She'd got in her car one morning and made a surprise visit home, catching him and her mother on their own before Harvey could sniff out her presence.

When her mother had gone out to answer a call from one of her brothers, Michelle had asked her dad in a roundabout way what he'd been up to, how he was feeling – he'd seemed surprised, and told her about the track day he was planning for his birthday. That didn't sound like a man who was 'fragile'.

More to the point, when she'd brought the conversation round to the business, he hadn't mentioned anything about her and Harvey taking over the dealership network. The thought of Harvey playing her father, who trusted him, as well as her, made Michelle angry and sick.

She looked at the perfectly plastered ceiling rose above her bed. It was gone five. She wasn't going to sleep now.

What can I achieve in the next few hours? she thought.

When in doubt, run.

Michelle turned on her iPod and headed out of the house, along the canal path, feeling her way into her running rhythm as her heart began to pump in her chest. Running made her feel better, more connected to things. It occurred to her that this might be a good time to listen to the audiobook for her and Anna's interview, and she clicked her way into it without breaking stride.

To begin with, Michelle wasn't really listening to the words, hoping they'd sink into her subconscious on their own, but as she left the yellow arrows of the riverside footpath and headed up the poet streets towards the centre of town, the story started to catch her attention and her brain engaged.

The names were as familiar as friends on her old school register. Rupert Campbell-Black. Jake Lovell. Helen. As each character appeared, swimming into focus in her mind's eye, Michelle began to get odd flashbacks to school, to the places she'd been when she'd first read *Riders* and these characters had first sauntered across her imagination, with their jodhpurs and Jack Russells and their cruel mouths that bruised girls with Marlboro-tinged kisses.

Michelle never thought about her past life, but now it came back to her in pin-sharp detail.

The library. She had a sudden, almost physical memory of the cool, green smell of the oak-panelled school library in summer, where she'd snatched a few chapters when she should have been revising. The too-sweet perfume of the tiger lilies that sat in the Gothic alcove above her usual place. The moment the narrator's voice caressingly described Rupert's horse's flanks, and then his, Michelle could smell the flowers again, and knew where the rest of her English set would be sitting, in their usual places too. She remembered the disorientating but delicious embarrassment at reading something so sexy so close to other people.

She shook her head and missed a few steps, nearly tripping over her own feet as she tried to get her stride back.

But now she was listening to the book it started to come back in twin streams – the story, with its passionate crushes and twists and yearning love triangles and sweating horses; and the memory of her reading of it for the first time, in a place she'd pushed so far to the back of her mind she'd almost forgotten it had been real.

By the time she got to the park, deserted at this time on a Sunday morning, the narrative had moved relentlessly on and she had no way of escaping it. A tidal wave of emotion swept over Michelle, so fierce that she felt as if she were choking under the weight of her own need.

I wanted to be loved like that, she thought. *That's how I thought it would be when I was grown-up. And it's not. It's not.*

She stumbled to a halt and held on to the railings,

pretending to be stretching her hamstrings, but really bending her head so she could fight back the tears. She yanked the ear buds out of her ears, but the voice carried on in her own head; Michelle remembered now how the story ended, and something scraped inside her chest with longing for a happy ending like that.

Once upon a time, she'd actually believed it was round the corner. She could remember believing it, sitting in the library, confident that that sort of jolly, easy, vigorous love was about to arrive in her life.

She stared unseeing at the park railings, the black paint flaking away in chunks, exposing the Victorian iron beneath. Why hadn't it come? How had she got to thirty-one, been married and nearly divorced, and never felt the knee-weakening passion even frumpy, mousy Tory Maxwell had enjoyed?

Michelle knew herself well enough to know the answer. Because she hadn't let it come. It was easier to keep everything at arm's length, under control, because this new Michelle, the bright tough Michelle, was not the sort of girl who let things happen to her, not like hopeless romantic Tory.

The old Michelle, the girl who'd sat in the library with her shoes off, reading when she should have been revising, reading when she should have been training, reading when she should have been listening to good advice and not believing in easy happy ever afters . . . That Michelle let things happen to her, not the other way round.

Her heart contracted as if an invisible hand were trying to squeeze it dry. I *want* to be loved, she thought in one sudden clear pang. I *want* to be held. I *want* to be swept away by someone. When was the last time someone kissed me and I felt like that?

Thirteen years ago. The last time she'd felt her whole body go light with lust was thirteen long years ago. Ed Pryce.

Michelle bent her head and let the pain rush through her, clinging to the railings as her chest throbbed. She had no idea where all this pain was coming from, but her body was aching as much as her heart, and big sobs were racking her chest, the sort of gulping child-like sobs she hadn't had in years, the sort that wouldn't stop until they'd blown themselves out.

She pulled herself nearer the railings, trying to make herself invisible in the clipped box hedge.

'Are you all right?'

She felt a hand on her shoulder, and spun round.

Rory, of all the people in Longhampton, was standing right behind her, too close as usual, with Tavish by his side, not on the lead. Tavish looked pleased to see her, Rory less so.

To her mortification, Michelle couldn't stop the sobs. 'I'm fine,' she hiccupped, trying to hide her face.

'No, you're not.' He peered at her. 'Are you hurt? Have you pulled a hamstring?'

'No!' The hiccups made it almost unintelligible, but she couldn't stop them. Her chest was aching doubly now with a sobbing stitch.

'Do you want me to look at it?' he persisted, as if he was actually keen to investigate her injuries. 'I'm the first-aid officer at work. I've been on a course for—'

'Fuck off,' gasped Michelle. 'Please!'

Rory took a step back, apparently realising she was crying, rather than moaning in pain. Michelle flapped her hand, hoping he'd take it as a sign to go away, and for a second, she thought he might.

Then he took a step nearer again and put his hand on her

shoulder, with a gentleness that nearly set her off again. 'You're not all right. Please let me take you home.'

It wasn't an order, like Harvey would have issued. It was concern, and for a moment, Michelle thought about letting Rory lead her home like a lost dog. Then she grappled her dignity back under control.

'I'm fine,' she hiccuped, and wiped her face with her hand, amazed at how wet it was. She dragged a breath into her lungs. The only thing to do was to run it out, to run away from Rory and force her body to start doing something else.

To run away from yourself, you mean, said a cool voice in her head; but she ignored it, pushed herself off the railings and set off in the opposite direction without turning back.

Crying and running was hard, but it distracted her mind and by the time Michelle turned back down towards the canal, it was nearly eight, and her face was normal enough not to raise concern from the early morning dog-walkers she encountered on her route.

She jogged slowly down Swan's Row, lining up a whole morning's worth of tasks to blot out the lingering embarrassment, and slowed even more when she saw a figure sitting on her front step.

Rory, and Tavish. Rory was eating a croissant from a paper bag and Tavish was waiting patiently for crumbs. A thick wodge of Sunday papers was on the step next to him, along with a Sainsbury's bag of breakfast ingredients.

'Oh God,' breathed Michelle out loud, as he got up to welcome her.

'Morning,' said Rory, brushing pastry flakes off his trousers with a flick of his hand. 'I've got to bring Tavish back early today so I thought we could do brunch and papers . . .'

'You didn't think I might want to be on my own?'

'What could I do?' Rory pointed at the dog. 'I'm at his beck and call. We're merely his hand-maidens.'

Grudgingly, Michelle reached under the terracotta dove-cote, withdrew the house key and let them in.

Rory insisted on making breakfast while she showered, and when she came downstairs in fresh jeans, her hair damp and unblowdried, the smell of a full English was filling the house and Rory was busy at the hob, a tea towel over one shoulder.

Michelle assessed the damage to her clean kitchen. He'd used four pans, five bowls, several plates and had still managed to get crumbs over the countertop. Tavish was also sitting right underneath his feet, wearing the guilty but triumphant air of a dog who's been fed from the kitchen work surfaces.

Michelle looked more closely and saw that Tavish had crumbs in his straggly black beard. 'Rory,' she began, 'has Tavish had—'

'Sit down,' said Rory, without looking round. 'I'm bringing it all to a precision finish. Timing is crucial.'

Reluctantly, Michelle sat down at the table and poured herself a cup of tea from the pot. Then she put the pot on a trivet and coasters under the mugs in advance.

'There. Eat that.' Rory slid a full plate in front of her and one in front of himself, and proceeded to cover his bacon in tomato sauce, then brown sauce. 'Dig in,' he added, when she didn't start immediately.

Michelle ate a bit of sausage and had to admit that Rory could make good scrambled eggs. Her churning stomach began to feel better the more bacon she shovelled into it.

When Rory had cleared his plate, and Michelle was halfway

through hers, he pushed back his chair and regarded her with his cool, clear gaze.

'Well, while we're both here, I want to tell you about me and Esther and Zachary,' he said.

'Why?' She carried on eating to hide her surprise. 'It's none of my business.'

'Yes, it is. You're judging me all the time about being a selfish absentee dad. Don't deny it. All that stuff you keep implying, like I only volunteer at the old people's home to drum up business, you don't think I can take care of Tavish properly . . .'

'That's not true.'

He raised an eyebrow. 'Yes it is. Anyway, 1 want to tell you, not because I like a gossip or want sympathy but because it's not what you think. I can see why you'd think I was a bit of a shit, but believe it or not, I'm not. If you still think I'm a shit after I've told you, then fair enough, but let's get this out of the way.'

Michelle shrugged. Rory's privateness was something she liked about him; it went both ways. This changed things, and she wasn't quite sure how. 'Go on then, if it makes you feel better.'

Rory leaned on the table, steepling his fingers, and looked her in the eye. 'Esther Wiseman was my first girlfriend. She was a clerk in the Magistrates' Court – we met when I was had up for armed robbery and arson. No, of course I wasn't,' he said, as Michelle's head jerked up in surprise. 'I met her during a very dull morning prosecuting television licence-fee avoiders when I was a trainee. We bought a house not far from here, in Milton Road.'

'Poet streets,' said Michelle. 'Very nice.'

'Is it?' Rory looked as if he wasn't quite sure what she was getting at, but carried on. 'Anyway, we'd been together for a while when Esther started talking about getting married and having a family – not necessarily in that order – but I wasn't ready. I worried about money, wanted to get promoted first, bigger house, usual sort of thing. Like the dog – she wanted a dog, I wasn't sure, hence the volunteering at the rescue that you think is so sinister. It was a compromise. Long story short, Esther got sick of waiting and she ended up having an affair with a friend of ours from the pub quiz team – Adam, nice guy, I liked him – and she got pregnant.'

'Oh,' said Michelle, in surprise. This wasn't turning out quite the way she'd expected. She'd been guessing something more along the lines of *Rory* being caught cheating – although the more she got to know him, the less probable that seemed.

'Esther decided, since she was thirty-seven, that she wanted to keep the baby, but she didn't know whether it was Adam's or mine. That was a bit of an issue, so I told her I wanted to sell the house, and moved into the flat above the bookshop.' He rubbed his chin. 'I'm not particularly proud of that bit, but . . . you can imagine things were a bit turbulent on both sides.'

'How long had you been together when this happened?'

Rory fiddled with the teapot. 'Um, nine years.'

'Nine years?' Michelle widened her eyes. 'You'd been living together for *nine years* and you weren't sure whether you wanted to get married or not?'

'She didn't *have* to have an affair,' he pointed out.

'I'm not saying either of you did the right thing. But *nine years* . . .'

Rory mimed someone banging a gavel. 'Both guilty. Bam. Next. Is that your final decision?'

She ignored that. 'And so whose was it? I mean, *he*, Zachary? Who's the daddy?'

'Well, Esther was fairly confident he was Adam's, and she was in a relationship with him by the time Zachary was born, so she wouldn't do a DNA test for a long time. But we found out earlier this year that he's mine. Hence the visits. I've seen him three times since he was born. He's very sweet, as little children go. I'm no expert. Obviously.'

Michelle bit her lip. Just three times since he was born. No wonder he'd been so arsey the day the buggy got stuck; what kind of day had *that* been? A whole world of awkwardness.

'How do you feel about that?' she asked.

'I don't really know what I'm supposed to feel about it, to be honest,' he said warily. 'We're still feeling our way around what the right thing to do is.'

The initial spiel had sounded rehearsed but these words sounded hesitant, as if he hadn't actually spoken them aloud before. He looked at her as if he wanted her opinion, but was reluctant to ask.

It occurred to Michelle that maybe he didn't *have* anyone to ask. That maybe all that hanging around he did in the book-shop – talking to Becca about law school, discussing Norwegian children's stories with Anna – was not because he wanted to air his extensive knowledge, but because he didn't have many friends. Maybe he was trying to learn about women and parenting by osmosis.

She felt a sudden sympathy for Rory. Off duty in his jeans and weekend shirt he didn't look so middle-aged as he did in his weekday suit. She felt a tug of something, but immediately pushed it down.

'That's all you can do,' she said. Hadn't Anna said some-thing very similar to her, when they first met? That she was still feeling her way around? 'Most families now have some kind of complication. It doesn't mean you can't build a relationship with Zachary. The more people kids have around them who love them, the better, no?'

'I don't know,' Rory admitted. 'I keep reading about how mothers have this powerful love-urge thing when they see their baby. I've seen Zachary three times. I'm not totally convinced I could pick him out of a baby line-up.' He looked mortified. 'You know, you're the only person in the world I could say that to. It's parental sacrilege.'

'Thanks,' said Michelle. 'So I'm a child-unfriendly monster too? Joking,' she added when Rory started to apologise.

They were silent for a moment.

'Do you regret it?' Michelle asked. 'Losing Esther?'

'No.' Rory looked sad, then buttered another slice of cold toast, dipping the knife into the marmalade. 'I think we both knew things had run their course well before she had the affair. Neither of us wanted to call it a day – you know, it was just . . . over? Esther wanted a fresh start and I thought it was better to let her go, and yes, she is with Adam now, and yes, they are very happy, and yes, Zachary calls Adam "Daddy".'

'Are you happy with that?'

A long pause. 'Not really,' he said slowly. 'Well, I don't know. It's messy. I don't like mess. We're discussing what appropriate maintenance should be, given that she's marrying Adam. I think Esther would really like to pretend none of this ever happened. I don't know whether pretending it never happened is the kindest thing for Zachary, or whether that would be a mistake.'

'Maybe,' said Michelle. 'But what about when he's twenty-one, and he finds out his dad walked away without a backward glance? That's major league therapy. I suppose the best thing you can do is to keep things civil. Like Anna and Sarah and Phil. Well,' she amended, 'as far as you can. It's hard.'

'It is.'

Rory chomped down on his toast and regarded Michelle carefully. 'Still think I'm a baby-abandoning bastard?'

'No. A messy, bossy one, maybe.' She helped herself to a slice of toast and cut it in half. 'Are you wanting me to perform some kind of absolution? Ten Hail Marys and a Dan Brown novel?'

'I could have handled it better,' said Rory. 'I should have been brave and ended it, instead of putting her in a position where we both behaved badly. But it's like my old landlady once said, God rest her soul – nice people sometimes do terrible things because they don't want to do one small mean thing. It doesn't automatically make them a bad person forever.'

'That's very true,' said Michelle. 'Even if it does sound like something you've said more than once in court.'

'Ha. Very good. So,' he said. 'Your turn. How about you tell me the real story of your divorce.'

'What do you mean, "the real story"?' Michelle reeled. 'I don't even recall telling you I *was* divorced.'

Rory waved his toast dismissively. 'It's common knowledge. Don't remember who told me – Anna, or Rachel? I sort of assumed that you drove him away with your endless nitpicking about scatter cushions and obsession with lists, but you can tell me different, and dispel *my* misapprehensions.'

Michelle opened her mouth to protest, but closed it again. Was that how she came across? Was this how Rory had felt, knowing she and Anna and Kelsey were discussing his buggy issues?

Rory was looking at her and she thought about telling him

to sod off, but he'd just been very honest with her. And her anger with Harvey was still tingling enough to override her shame.

She took a deep breath. 'Well, there's not much to tell. I got married very young – too young, probably – to a guy who worked with my dad. *Unlike* you, I worked out reasonably quickly that we didn't have much in common, and when I started lying to the doctor that I needed anti-depressants again because my grandmother had died, I realised maybe I should leave instead.'

Rory was staring at her and Michelle felt uncomfortable. Well, she hadn't really explained herself. What bits could she tell him without revealing the worst stuff?

'He made me give up my job,' she went on. 'Harvey wasn't very keen on me working, because he thought all the male customers were hitting on me, so eventually I stopped and stayed at home. And that wasn't ideal, for either of us, because I'm not really the housewife type. I got into decorating because I was bored. He used to come home and mess things up "to give me something to do". And move things in the night, and joke that I was losing my marbles.'

Rory said nothing. Were these examples bad enough? Maybe they were just normal married couple things. She gripped her mug. 'He used to weigh me, too, which I didn't like, considering he was three times my size. And he told me he didn't want kids, then he'd tell my parents that I was the one who refused to lose my figure. When actually it was him who didn't want my . . .' Michelle swallowed the rest. Too much.

'So why did you marry him in the first place?'

'It seemed like the right thing to do. Harvey was always really lovely to everyone else.' Michelle gripped her mug harder; this was stuff she hadn't even told Anna, for fear of Anna feeling so sorry for her that she'd never like her again. Harvey was right when he told her pity ruined friendships. 'Plus, Mum wanted the excuse to arrange the big fat royal wedding she didn't have, thanks to what she calls her gymslip motherhood. She had my older brothers when she was just twenty. There's a big gap between them and me and then Owen.'

'Forgive me for saying this,' said Rory, 'I don't want to sound out of line, but what was an independent, professional woman like you doing with a manipulative bully like that?'

'I wasn't always independent,' she said. 'When I met Harvey he dragged me out of a big depression and I think he felt he'd made me into what I was after that. As if he owned me.'

'What depression can be worth *that*?' demanded Rory. He seemed angry – for her.

Michelle looked across the table at him and without pausing to think, she said, 'I was expelled from school when I was seventeen and I ended up having a breakdown. It took me years to get myself back together, because my mum refused to talk about anything, and I let a lot of things happen, because I didn't know who I was any more. I'd gone from being a top-stream swot to a drop-out with no future. I put up with Harvey controlling me because everyone else kept telling me how happy I was. I thought he was doing it for me. He always said he was, anyway.'

'So what was your breakdown about?' Rory asked.

Michelle's hand wobbled. 'That's not really the point. It's all in the past.'

'Well, you brought it up. Was it to do with the boarding school? Did you fail some exams? Was it something at home?'

'It's irrelevant.' Michelle started to tidy up the table and

Tavish appeared from under Rory's chair, obviously hoping for toast. 'It's something I got over, and put behind me.'

She knew Rory was looking at her but she refused to meet his eye, stacking the plates and collecting the crumbs.

'Do you always cry when you're out jogging?' he asked. 'Or has something happened today? I'll come clean – you looked so upset I thought something had happened with your ex. I didn't mean to come round and make things worse. I just hated to think of you running round like that on your own.'

Michelle stopped clearing up and shoved her hand through her hair, trying to swallow the lump that had appeared in her throat.

'I'm not actually divorced,' she said. 'But I'm going to be. Soon.'

Before he could respond, she walked through to the kitchen and stacked the plates in the dishwasher systematically. She glared at her reflection in the kitchen window, trying to make herself see the straight-nosed, clear-skinned, independent, successful thirty-one-year-old woman, but a different Michelle had escaped from that box of schoolbooks and was floating around the back of her mind like a ghost blown off course: a hopeful teenager with glasses and dreams about polo players. A version of her that existed even before Harvey. One that even he hadn't known.

She could see in the reflection that Rory was still watching her, his usual self-assured expression replaced by nervousness. He wasn't sure whether he'd upset her or not. And he'd been so honest with her about Zachary, in the hope of trading a confession, so he could legitimately comfort her. There was something chivalrous about it.

Something from the Jilly Cooper echoed inside Michelle. If

Rory was as nice a guy as he seemed, that was even more reason not to tell him the whole tacky story. She preferred it when he just felt sorry for her, married to a bully.

'Divorce is hard, but if it means a fresh start . . .' Rory began.

Michelle turned round. 'I wasn't crying about that. I'm worried about the shop, too,' she said, because that was true. 'I'm worried about my best friend and her stepfamily, and how I'm going to keep everyone happy. I'm worried that you're not quite the arse I thought you were, because that means my arse detector needs recalibrating.'

Rory looked relieved. 'Good,' he said. 'Now you just have to prove to me that you're not the uptight control freak I think you are by sitting down and reading the papers with me without picking up the scatter cushions when I move them off the sofa.'

Michelle smiled tightly. 'One step at a time.'

When he was gone, she flicked through the supplements, but she couldn't settle. Her mind kept wandering back to Jilly Cooper and the packed boxes upstairs. Her original copy of *Riders* was probably still in there – she could skip ahead with it this afternoon, quicker than waiting to listen to it on her next run. But even though part of her wanted to unpack them and see what was in there, a bigger part wished they'd just disappear without her having to touch them again.

Michelle put the magazine down with a slap that made Tavish jolt awake next to her on the sofa. This was crazy. They were only books. Books and pencils and junk. This was why she never allowed clutter in her home. It bred dust and regrets and mess.

Before she could think any more, Michelle forced herself off the sofa and up the stairs to her spare room.

The boxes were stacked against her wardrobe, the flaps bent where she'd hurriedly rammed them shut. Michelle opened the first one and started unpacking the books inside.

'Surprise, surprise,' she said aloud, as a dog-eared copy of *Riders* came out, sandwiched between *The Color Purple* and *Othello*.

It was the smell that came back to her most powerfully, along with the order in which the books had been stacked – the exact left-to-right order of her bookshelf. Her books smelled of the Anaïs Anaïs that her study-mate Katherine had applied liberally every time she had a cigarette out of the bathroom window, and coffee.

These could go into the shop, she thought. Anna could sell them as vintage editions.

Michelle lifted out three books at once, and in the middle was a fabric-bound notebook, with leather ties wrapped around it. As she touched it, another memory leaped up in her chest; this was a book she'd forgotten about entirely until now, but it was so familiar she felt jerked backwards into a different time, as if she'd never left it.

She stared at it. How could that be there? Hadn't she got rid of it? More to the point, who'd packed it? Had her dad swept all this stuff into boxes when he came for her? Had he read it? The thought made her feel nauseous.

Michelle put the surrounding dictionaries down and held the notebook in shaking hands, remembering the feel of the paisley-patterned Indian covering. A present from a school friend who'd gone travelling in the summer. Handmade pages, perfect for miserable outpourings of teenage angst.

Of all the books in the box, this was the one she'd written herself. My diary, she thought. Still hidden between the books on her shelf, sandwiched spine in so no one would spot it.

Her stomach began to sink as she opened the pages and saw her rounded teenage handwriting, the purple ink, and although she didn't want to read, she couldn't stop herself.

15 September
  My first day at school and I feel like I've gone to some boys' version of Malory Towers ...

25

'My romance-o-meter was set ridiculously high by reading
The Thorn Birds *when I was twelve. I fell madly in love*
with Father Ralph but more with the idea that one day I'd
meet someone and time would stand still.' Anna McQueen

Michelle's diaries began when she started the Black Monk School in the lower sixth, and initially detailed – quite obsessively – the daily routines, how often she could call her parents, Owen's homesickness in the prep school attached to her secondary school, then Owen's complete conquest of his entire year, and so on.

Until then, she'd gone to the local school in Kingston, but an upswing in her father's business, combined with her mother's determination to carve out some more 'me time', had meant she and Owen had moved up in the world. Owen, a natural athlete, had settled in quickly; for Michelle it had been harder, since the school only took girls in the sixth form, and those that were there seemed much more worldly than her, more skilled in playing off the constant jostles of male attention.

Romance entered the picture early on. Her crush on Ed Pryce started from the first day she had to do a lunchtime queue supervision with him. Her handwriting scrawled in awe as each detail of their conversation was forensically recorded, and it came back to her at once – the hot-chips smell of the dining hall and the musty reek of 200 teenage boys queueing outside. Ed put two fourth years in detention for being cheeky to her, and her heart was gone.

I don't remember being this soppy, she thought, her eye skimming her lovelorn notes on every detail of his 'thoughtful expression' while trying to translate French texts, and his 'gorgeous long lashes'. She couldn't really remember Ed's face that well, just the feeling she got when she looked at him sideways. But the metallic pang of longing leapt from the page, of afternoons spent chewing a pencil and staring out of her study window, hoping to see the flash of blond hair over the hedge that meant he was coming to visit someone in her boarding house.

Even in Michelle's elaborately 'theoretical' lists of her ideal man, written because Katherine had read in *Company* magazine that if you visualised your ideal man, he'd appear in your life, she was clearly describing Ed.

'My ideal man would be tall,' she wrote, 'probably a rugby player or cricketer, with blond hair and green eyes, with his own car (not Vauxhall).'

She sank back onto her heels, as her lower sixth year unfolded in a series of tests, and petty arguments with the other girls, and agonies about her weight, and the triumphs and failures of the rugby team, in which Ed Pryce was a key player. Reliving it all wasn't quite as traumatic as she'd expected when she first saw the notebook, and she found herself smiling at some of her cattier comments.

I was so dull, thought Michelle, amused at the way she measured her thighs daily to see if the cabbage soup diet was taking effect. And quite a cow.

She was brought up short against one entry, towards the end of her first year. '*Mum's away again for half term, so Owen*

*and I are staying with Ben in London. I don't know if Dad's going
with her. He didn't know anything about it when I phoned.'*

Michelle remembered staying with Ben, and trailing round
the Planetarium with Owen, but she didn't remember it being
because her mum wasn't around. Funny how she had blanked
that bit out; it was such an obvious palming-off. I should ask
Ben about that, she thought. If he even remembers.

Come on, come on, she thought, skimming through endless
reports of classroom bitchery in search of juicier observations
about Ed Pryce. Hadn't she managed a single snog? But then,
as she turned into her upper sixth form, the words started
getting more familiar, and she slowed down, feeling a sudden
dread in the pit of her stomach when she reached the spring
term.

15 March
  *Will Taylor is having a party after the exams, so we've
  got to put the date in our diaries and get as much booze as
  we can in half term before the exams. It's either going to be
  on the beach or at his dad's house, if we can persuade
  Danno to let us all go out for the weekend. I've asked Ed if
  he's going and he said—'*

Michelle slammed the diary shut, her face suddenly hot. A weird
sense of déjà vu filled her head, like being at the top of a rollercoaster and already feeling the plunge though it hadn't started,
and she felt caught between a need to read on, and a need to
throw the book so far away that she'd never have to look at it again.

She held the diary in her hand for a moment and then, without
even thinking, shoved it between the mattress and the base of her
spare bed, and began piling the books back into the box.

                        *   *   *

The shockwaves from Chloe's exam disaster took a long time to disperse in the McQueen house. Chloe was distraught but defiant, and kept insisting that she 'might as well' leave school to become an international pop star now. Phil was furious with the teachers, with the exam board, with Sarah, with himself – everyone apart from Chloe and Anna. He didn't dare be furious with Anna, since she was only just holding things together as it was, mainly by taking Pongo for extended walks while listening to audiobooks. Superwoman had gone by the wayside: she hadn't done a deep clean on the house since May, and she didn't care. If Phil cared, he was too scared to point it out. Chloe's general mood was one of operatic fury in every direction, interspersed with some breathtaking displays of meanness that reminded Anna of Evelyn. The school wasn't being as sympathetic as they'd all hoped about her grades, despite Anna and Phil's desperate conversations with the staff, and even when they persuaded the school to let her continue into the sixth form, she accused them of 'making the school treat me like a freak'.

It didn't help that Becca's Law reading list books were now sitting in a box by the stairs waiting to be opened. Becca herself was very quiet on the topic of Cambridge, as if she didn't want to rub her sister's nose in it, but Lily guilelessly triggered at least one spectacular row every day by asking if she could have Becca's room 'when she went to university'.

Phil's response to the roiling tension in his family was to order the shed he'd dreamed of for so long. It arrived in the garden the same day that Chloe was brought back by Tyra's mother, giggling hysterically and drunk on cider, and it took all Anna's strength not to lock herself in it.

*   *   *

Evelyn's birthday at the end of August was an annual trial for all the family, but particularly Anna, who had to find a present as well as arrange a lunch and guilt-trip the girls into being nice to their granny, who celebrated her birthday by being twice as rude to everyone, as if it was some kind of special treat.

'Michelle, I need your help,' she said, popping next door during a lunch break. 'What do you get a seventy-nine-year-old woman who not only has everything but also hates everything?'

'Budget?' Michelle stopped flipping through a catalogue. She couldn't resist a present challenge, just as Anna couldn't resist recommending books.

Anna smacked Phil's credit card down on the counter. 'Whatever it takes. Plus fifty quid danger money for me, since I'll have to bear the brunt of the sarcasm when she hates it.'

Michelle laughed. 'When for?'

'It's her birthday on Sunday. We're taking her out for a meal, and I've got to organise that, and the present. Obviously.'

'And Phil can't do it because . . . ?'

'Because he's more scared of her than I am. She blames him for Chloe's grades, Becca's height and Lily's braces.' Anna rolled her eyes. 'And she is in no way genetically responsible for any of that, the cantankerous old bag.'

'Woah! You're not scared of anyone any more, are you?'

'Nope. Clearly I'm a terrible stepmother, so what can she tell me that I don't know already?' said Anna recklessly. 'I might as well just spend the weekend in bed with Lily reading *Anne of Green Gables*. At least two of us would be happy then. Three, if I let Pongo up.'

'Anna, you know you're not a terrible stepmother.'

She fiddled with the card. 'It feels like it. I should have checked up on Chloe more. I should have tested her.'

'How? She's old enough to know when she's not putting the hours in. Look, if you were such a bad stepmother then Becca would have failed everything too, wouldn't she? And,' Michelle added, more tersely, 'kindly tell Phil to stop making out that the world ends if you fail some exams. It's not true, and it's pretty offensive to those of us who've managed to drag ourselves out of the gutter without a degree.'

Anna looked at her. 'That's a good point. I will mention it.'

'Thank you,' said Michelle. 'Now, how about a silk Liberty scarf? You can always throttle her with it if she winds you up. A very stylish way to go.'

It took ages to get the girls ready on Sunday. Chloe had to be dragged out of bed, and Becca had already vanished to Owen's and had to be called back. While Phil took Pongo round the block to wear him out, Anna checked the contents of the fridge to see if they needed to call in at the supermarket while they were out.

She peered into the depths and frowned. The big Sainsbury's order had come on Friday as usual, but there didn't seem to be as much in there as she remembered unpacking.

'Chloe, have you eaten the mascarpone?' she asked as Chloe wafted in, furious in her one appropriate dress.

'No. Why's it always *me* who gets accused of things?' She looked outraged. 'It's so unfair!'

'It's not unfair, it's a reasonable assumption based on fact,' said Anna. She adopted Becca's courtroom style, since it got such instant results with Chloe. 'Where did the two tubs of Ben and Jerry's go last weekend?'

'That's not fair either!' roared Chloe. 'The band were here! You didn't give us enough supper!'

'Well, on that basis, did you eat the mascarpone?'

'Oh my God. It's like a police state.' Chloe boggled her eyes and said in a deliberately slow voice, 'I don't even know what mascarpone is.'

'White cream cheese stuff. I was going to make a tiramisu for later, so it's your loss.' Anna peered more closely at her. Was that evidence of secret scoffing on her top lip? Or moustache bleach?

Chloe flounced her hair. 'I have literally no idea what you're talking about. Are you sure Pongo didn't have it? He likes cheese.'

'There were two whole tubs of it. And now there's no sign of either of them.'

'Are you sure you put them in your shopping bag? You've been under a lot of stress recently, Anna. Perhaps you're forgetting things.'

Anna started to inform Chloe that in that case maybe she should forget her pocket money, but Phil swept in, jangling his car keys anxiously.

'Come on,' he said, flapping them into the car. 'I don't want to be late. You know what Mum's like when we're late.'

'Just the same as when we're early but slightly ruder?'

Phil and Chloe stared at Anna. Normally she was the one who told them off for being mean about Evelyn.

'Anna!' said Chloe admiringly. 'Are you on HRT or something?'

Phil gave her a tetchy look. 'We're not that old. Look, go and get Lily. I'll load everyone in.'

Anna went upstairs to find Lily sitting on her bed with Mrs Piggle, Piggy-Jo and an assortment of other toys in order of height. She looked pleased when Anna walked in.

'Anna, Anna,' she said. 'We're playing Malory Towers.

Mrs Piggle and Piggy-Jo are the French teachers and they're going to expel someone. Who should it be? Who looks naughtiest?'

'That's not a very nice game,' said Anna, thinking uncomfortably of Michelle.

'They're very sad.' Lily pulled a sad face. 'Darrell's going to plead for them to stay.'

'That's nice of Darrell. What a nice friend. Come on, we need to leave. Gran's waiting.' She held out her hand.

Lily looked at her from the bed, surrounded by her army of fluff. 'Anna. I've been thinking about you and Daddy.'

'Have you?' Anna started to get Lily's pink rucksack; the prospect of packing it usually speeded her up. 'Do you want to take Mrs Piggle out for lunch?'

'Yes. Anna . . . You know when Becca and Chloe and me go away, do you miss us?'

'Course I do. Daddy says it's so quiet he can hear Pongo . . .' She was about to say farting, then changed it to '. . . thinking.'

'It'll be *really* quiet when we go back to live with Mummy, won't it? And you'll probably be quite lonely.'

Anna stung inside at the reminder that, for Lily, this wasn't really their home, but she pushed it aside in her head. 'Well, that's still a little bit away, isn't it?'

'I think you should have a baby too.'

She stopped, then turned round slowly, her heart beating fast. She tried to keep her face very neutral. 'Do you?'

'Yes. You're going to be so bored when Becca and Chloe and me go back to Mummy's. You'll be here on your own with Daddy. You won't even have Pongo to cuddle. It's only fair.'

Lily was big on fair at the moment. About as much as Chloe was big on unfair.

'And you wouldn't mind, if Daddy and I had another baby

brother or sister?' said Anna cautiously. 'I thought you were a bit upset about Mummy's baby?'

'I was upset, but then I thought she was lonely too, without us in America.' Lily looked pleased at her own logic. 'So that was fair. Maybe you could have a boy. Or a pig.' She smiled, the sudden sun-through-rainclouds smile that made Anna's ovaries twang.

'Well, we'll see,' said Anna, and her mood lifted as if someone had deposited an unexpected million in her bank account.

Evelyn had already arrived at the restaurant by taxi, and had decided that she didn't like the menu, the water she'd been served, or the table they'd booked. Anna could tell all that just from the expression on her face as they were shown to their seats, but even that couldn't dampen her spirits.

'Happy Birthday, Evelyn!' she said, kissing her hollow cheek and ushering the girls round her.

Evelyn ignored her and focused her disapproval on her son first.

'Philip, you're just like your father,' she informed Phil. 'Always late.'

'My late father, in fact,' said Phil, trying to joke his way out of the awkwardness.

Anna passed the present to Lily, since she was wriggling with excitement to hand it over; Michelle had gone to town, deploying every gift wrap option.

'A scarf,' said Evelyn, brushing aside the tissue and curled ribbons. 'Next time I'm in my open-topped sports car or lunching with Princess Anne I'll be sure to wear it. Did you girls pick this?'

'Anna did,' said Lily, missing the sarcasm. 'She's good at colours.'

'How useful,' said Evelyn. But Anna didn't care. She had something to hug inside that sugared every acid drop Evelyn could throw at her today.

Later that night, in bed, Anna curled up against Phil's back while he lay on his side and checked his phone for emails.

'I really liked that restaurant,' she said happily. 'That was a good lunch.'

'Yeah. I thought Mum was on reasonable form, considering.'

'I spoke to Joyce about her forgetfulness last time I was reading up there. The doctor thinks it's just stress rather than actual dementia symptoms. They try to keep them as active as possible so he's pleased that she's reading, and joining in with the discussions afterwards. It's when she stops being foul to everyone we should worry, apparently.'

'Good.'

'It's more than good!'

Phil looked up from his phone. 'Yes, it is. You're right. Thanks for talking to Joyce. And for getting the present, and for stopping everyone kicking off at lunch.' He sighed. 'That's done for another year. Well, until Christmas.'

'My pleasure. Do you know what Lily said to me today?' She snuggled into his back.

He put his phone down, pulled up the duvet and turned off the bedside light. 'Something about Mrs Piggle having super-powers? That was the last thing I heard. I wonder about her imagination sometimes. I mean, is there such a thing as too much imagination?'

'No!' Anna nudged him. 'She said she thought we should have a baby. You and me.'

'What?'

'Just that.' She leaned forward and nibbled his shoulder

playfully. 'I went upstairs to get her, and we were just chatting, and she said, I think you and Daddy should have a baby, because you'll miss us when we go home.'

'And what did you say?' Phil didn't turn round, but Anna didn't care. She was too lost in her happiness.

'I said we'll see. I didn't want to promise anything, obviously, but isn't that sweet? She said she was upset at first about Sarah's baby, but now she's had a chance to get used to the idea, she's looking forward to it . . .'

Phil rolled over and she stopped when she saw the stormy expression in his eyes.

'I can't believe you did that,' he hissed.

'Did what?'

'Put words into a little girl's mouth. Honestly, Anna, I know you want a baby, but getting the kids involved isn't on. It's really not on.'

'I did nothing of the sort!' Anna squinted at him in the half darkness. 'And that's an *offensive* thing to accuse me of.'

'Lily's only saying what she thinks you want to hear because she's scared that you'll leave her as well,' he whispered angrily. 'She's eight. The only people who should be talking about whether you and I should have a baby are you and me. No one else. And definitely not my kids.'

They lay very close and she could smell his toothpaste-y breath, quick and angry. Part of her knew he was right, but she hadn't coerced Lily to say what she had. Phil was using that as a moral shield for his own reluctance.

'So talk,' said Anna. She sat up and put on the bedside lamp, blinking in the light. 'Come on. Whether you like it or not, the girls *are* getting used to the idea. Sarah's showing them her scan photos over Skype – and by the way, how do you think that makes me feel?'

'She's not the most sensitive woman . . .'

'Give me a time frame,' she whispered, trying hard to stop herself yelling. Anna could feel her mad broody self bargaining, trying to pin down her incoherent emotion into rational language. 'You were happy to talk about waiting four years when we got married. OK. I'll wait a bit longer, I understand it's hard for them. But how long? Six months? A year?'

Phil didn't rise from his curled-up position. He didn't even meet her eye.

'Phil? I don't mind waiting, but I want to know that I'm waiting *for* something,' she said desperately.

'I don't know if I can put a time frame on it,' he said, towards the pillow.

'What? Ever?'

A long silence stretched out and Anna felt sick, wanting to turn back time so she could start this differently.

'Phil?'

'I don't know if I can go through babies again,' he said. 'It might be different when the kids aren't here with us full time. I don't know. But I miss my space. I don't want to have another twenty years of this, when I could have more time alone with you. I barely see you as it is. I miss the way things were. Can't you take that as a compliment?'

'No, I can't,' said Anna. 'When I got married, it was with the understanding that we'd have a family together. Now you're telling me we're not?'

'This isn't a good time to talk about it,' said Phil. 'Lunch with the world's worst mother and all that . . .'

Anna smacked her pillow, unable to believe what she was hearing. 'You're telling me I can't have a baby? Ever?'

'Not . . . ever. I don't know. Stop being so selfish!'

'Me?!'

'Yes, you! You say you want to be a mother – well, there are three kids here already who apparently need more parenting than they're currently getting.'

Anna stared at him. 'That is the most appalling, unfair, *unreasonable* thing anyone has ever said to me.'

'Lucky you.' He rolled over so he didn't have to look at her, but Anna knew he wasn't asleep. He was staring at the wall.

She wanted to punch him, but Chloe's room was next to theirs and she was a light sleeper.

Goosebumps of humiliation and rage sprang up along her bare arms. She reached over and pulled her dressing gown off the bedside chair and got out of bed. Phil didn't even ask where she was going.

Anna didn't let the tears flow down her face properly until she was on the sofa, with Pongo, and no one could hear.

26

*'Winnie the Pooh is as charming for the adult reading
as it is for the child listening, though it seems more
poignant to a grown-up ear. Pooh's misadventures are an
amusing but thoughtful introduction to the silliness and
greed and forgiveness of adult life.'* Evelyn McQueen

The August heatwave that had sent Longhampton into an
unsavoury display of long shorts and hairy sandal-feet blew
itself out in a two-day thunderstorm at the beginning of
September. Any dreams of an Indian summer – and for
Anna, dreams of reading E. Nesbit into the warm evenings
under the sweet peas – were drenched by dark afternoons of
sticky air and driving rain that flattened the grass and drove
the remaining rose petals off the bushes in the municipal
gardens.

By the time the rain stopped, a night chill had set in, and
Anna felt as if the gloom had penetrated the town's soul, as
well as its leaky windows and roofs. Macs and boots reappeared on the dog-walkers, Pongo blagged a new jacket from
Auntie Michelle, and customers' umbrellas dripped over the
wooden floor of the bookshop.

All Anna's energy was now being channelled into the bookshop, since the atmosphere at home was bleak and silent. She

and Phil moved around the house like chess pieces, dropping the girls off, collecting them, taking Becca shopping for university stuff, running Lily to ballet, fitting in as much as possible to avoid each other. She felt like a cog in a well-oiled machine; too valuable to the smooth running of the McQueen engine to leave, but invisible and unimportant. Trapped, in other words. She couldn't even contemplate upsetting the girls any more; her only hope was that Phil might change his mind.

Tidying the shop and updating the website and pinning the customer recommendations on the shelves almost made up for her inner sadness. The little community around the shop was blooming, and her regulars increased each week, popping in to collect their 'book box' or order more book bouquets. She learned to avoid the children's section whenever her broodiness threatened to engulf her. And the rain reflected her mood.

'That's the end of our summer trade,' she sighed to Michelle, packing away the deckchair display she'd replenished daily when the weather was glorious. The buckets of beach reads around it had been snapped up, but most of them were second-hand favourites, so the mark-ups hadn't been quite as big as the sales figures.

'End of the summer, start of the winter,' said Michelle. 'Time to get that fire lit in the back, I reckon. I was thinking we could start selling hot chocolate? Unless there's a book-related hot beverage we could specialise in? Oh, and clear one of the tables to put these out.'

She piled a soft stack of chenille throws on the counter.

'What are these?' asked Anna. 'Shouldn't they be next door?'

'They're for people's knees,' Michelle explained, taking one off the top and draping it over the side of the leather armchair that had appeared overnight. 'Cosy. People like cosy. Hot chocolate, plus cosy, plus books. It's a winner.'

'But we've already got those blankets by the shelf,' said Anna. 'And you keep bringing more and more cushions in. And those teacups on the crime display – there are more teacups than books now.'

She said it lightly, but it was starting to bother her. Every day Michelle moved things before she came in, to make more room for merchandise that belonged in Home Sweet Home, not here. The front part of the shop, in particular, was starting to look less like a bookshop and more like an extension of next door. There was a velvet-covered chair near the window that actually had a 'Please do not sit on this' note on it, something Anna had removed when Michelle wasn't looking.

'That's the reality of selling. We've got to keep the profit margins up.' Michelle was arranging the throws while she spoke and moving Anna's books out of the way to do it. 'You know how nice those blankets are. You've got one yourself.'

'I know, they're lovely but . . . they're not *books*. And this is a bookshop!'

'Fine. You can have just books, and you can close next month. Do you want this shop to stay open or not?'

Anna was startled by the snappiness in Michelle's tone but she stood her ground. 'Of course I don't. But if you put too much other stuff in here people won't think it's a bookshop. Everyone says how much they love it now. We can do other stuff. I can do more promotions, get the library involved again . . .'

'Listen, I know what I'm doing.' Michelle didn't sound

like herself at all; she sounded tight and stressed. 'Don't start all that "books are precious" bollocks. You've been doing this for eight months. I've worked in retail since I was nineteen.'

'What is *wrong* with you?' Anna burst out.

They stared at each other, then Michelle rubbed her face. She looked on the verge of tears. Normally Anna would have been the first to apologise but today she didn't want to. The bookshop was her baby and she was going to defend it. It was the only thing she had left.

'I've had a horrible morning,' said Michelle. 'I had a meeting with my solicitor.'

'Rory?'

'No. My real solicitor.' Michelle sank onto the 'Do not sit' chair. 'I'm getting a divorce.'

'You've finally filed papers?' Anna's concern swept away her anger and she crouched by Michelle's side. 'Well done. Well done, Michelle. You're doing the right thing.'

Michelle looked up and her eyes were hunted. It was nothing like her usual confident expression. Even her liner flicks seemed subdued. 'It doesn't feel like it. I'm terrified of what Harvey's going to do when he gets the letter. I'm worried he'll tell my parents I've had some kind of breakdown. They'll believe him.'

'You're the bravest woman I know,' said Anna, meaning it. 'And the toughest.'

Michelle managed a short, sad laugh. 'Well, I'm not exactly the person you think I am. I'm a lot of window dressing.'

'I don't think so,' Anna said. This was going some way to explaining Michelle's bad mood; if her divorce was out of her control, at least her shop wasn't. She tried to be positive for her. 'It'll be grim, but it'll be over in a few months. Then you're free. Focus on that. You don't have children to sort out, and the assets should be easy enough to split.'

'I don't want any money,' said Michelle.

'Come on,' said Anna. 'What's the worst thing he can do?'

Michelle shook her head slowly. 'What if he's right? What if he really is the only man in the world who'd put up with me? What if I am making a big mistake?'

'You're not. And if you believe that, then you're better off on your own,' said Anna. 'And I can think of at least one other man who'd—'

Michelle held up a hand. 'Don't.'

Anna had thought about telling Michelle about her row with Phil but when she saw the fearful expression on Michelle's face, she decided not to. It wasn't so much that her news wasn't as bad, but that Michelle just didn't seem capable of hearing anything else.

Anna realised she'd left her mobile phone at home just before she had to go up to Butterfields to do her Reading Aloud session, so she drove back to pick it up, taking Tavish with her for his weekly visit to the old people.

He waited patiently in the car while she dashed into the kitchen to get it. There she found Becca standing in front of the fridge, eating mascarpone straight from the tub and staring into the chilled depths as if to see what she fancied next, with no thought to the cold air escaping from it.

'Oh, it's you,' said Anna. 'That's a relief. I thought Chloe had developed some kind of eating disorder.'

Becca looked guilt-stricken. 'Why did you think that?'

'I can't seem to keep the fridge full, and I knew it wasn't Lily, or me, or your dad. I didn't think it was you, because you only eat cottage cheese, so I assumed it was Chloe. And she wasn't getting any fatter, so I . . .' Anna stopped. She didn't need to go into her insane Googling of bulimia symptoms, or her spirals of guilt that ended with Chloe on a drip in a treatment centre blaming Anna for not spotting her dairy product cries for help. 'I don't mind you lot *eating*, it's just when no one will admit to it I wonder if I'm going mad and leaving unpacked bags of shopping to rot behind the sofa or something.'

Becca looked down at the pot of mascarpone. 'Sorry. I didn't think about it like that.'

'You'll think about it soon enough when you're having to fill your own fridge,' said Anna. 'Have you got your marker pen ready for putting lines on the orange juice? Would you like your own lockable tuckbox? It can be arranged.'

'I'll borrow Lily's.'

Lily had been going through a Chalet School phase now she'd despatched Malory Towers; so far she had a tuckbox, a washbag with a flannel, and two bottles of ginger beer in the fridge, which would be there for years since everyone hated it.

Becca hesitated, then went back to eating the mascarpone, spooning it into her mouth with a rhythmic compulsion, as if she wasn't even tasting it.

'You're not comfort-eating because you're unhappy, are you?' Anna asked, paranoid that maybe Becca had picked up on the coldness between her and Phil. 'You'd tell me if you were? It's better to talk about stuff, Becca. Don't bottle it up.'

'I don't want to worry anyone.'

'You won't worry us! I'll only worry if you don't say anything!' protested Anna. 'I'll miss you, you know. You're the voice of reason round here. You neither sing everything nor express your inner thoughts through the medium of a velour pig.'

'I'll miss you too,' said Becca. 'I can stay if you like.'

'No, you've got to go,' said Anna. 'You've worked hard. You deserve it all.'

Becca looked at her with big eyes that forecast rain. 'Anna . . .'

Anna didn't wait for her to say any more. She opened her arms and pulled Becca into a big hug.

'It's going to be fine,' she said, stroking her hair. 'Just remember, you can always come home. That's what my dad said to me, when he drove me to Manchester. "If it gets too awful and you can't bear it any more, you can always come home." And you know what? I phoned home on the third night and begged them to come and get me, and he said, "Of course, Annie, we'll come at the weekend." And what happened at the weekend?'

'I don't know,' said Becca in a dull voice.

'I was at a party and I missed them arriving.' Anna unwound her arms and looked into Becca's face. 'Call me if you want to come home,' she said. 'Call me if you need *anything*.'

Becca smiled, keeping her lips together.

'Listen, I'm going up to Butterfields to read to the old folk,' said Anna. 'Want to come with me?'

'Not really.'

'Go on. It'll be a chance to see your gran before you go. And I'd like to hear you read,' Anna went on. 'I could do with half an hour of relaxation myself.'

'OK,' said Becca. 'But no set texts, please.'

★   ★   ★

If Anna had hoped there'd be some tender grandmotherly behaviour from Evelyn on the eve of Becca's departure, she was disappointed.

She and Becca were waiting in the day room, talking to Mr Quentin, who had Tavish tucked happily on his knee, when Evelyn stalked into the Reading Aloud session as if it were a verruca clinic. She swept the room with her gaze and sighed with disappointment to see Anna. She managed a wintry smile for Becca.

'Hello, Evelyn,' said Anna. 'Not wearing your new scarf?'

'When I find something in my wardrobe that it goes with, it'll be the first thing I'll reach for,' she said witheringly, and focused her attention instead on Becca. 'You're looking very peaky,' she informed her. 'Too many late nights?'

'I've been working on my reading list,' said Becca. 'I've got loads to do before I go away.'

'Too much studying isn't attractive. No one likes a smarty-pants. Especially men.'

'Wrong,' said Mr Quentin from his wing chair. 'Nothing more interesting than a lady you can discuss a good book with. Even better if she has some smarty-pants too.'

He winked at Anna and Becca, who smiled back. Mr Quentin always seemed to perk up when Tavish arrived, thought Anna, as if his dog and a story reminded him of happier times.

Evelyn raised her eyebrows. 'Is that thing staying during our literary hour?' she demanded, enunciating each word. She liked to imply that everyone but her was deaf or mentally impaired. 'Is it *hygienic* to have animals on the furniture?'

'No more *unhygienic* than having incontinent old women around the place,' said Mr Quentin.

'Do you mean me?' Evelyn began furiously, but Anna interrupted her.

'Becca's going to read for us today,' she said. 'It'll be her last reading session before she goes to university, so I know you'll want to wish her luck!'

There was a ripple of applause and murmurs from the assembled residents, and Becca rounded her shoulders shyly under the attention.

'What do you want to read?' Anna asked. 'I don't think we had any requests in Joyce's book.' She handed her the anthology they'd been using and Becca flicked through the index, then stopped.

'I'll read this,' she said, glancing at Anna. 'For you. It's one of your favourites. *Little Women.*'

Anna settled back into her chair as Becca began to speak. She had a confident reading voice, with the long local vowels and rolling intonation. Anna wondered how much of that would still be there when she came back to them in a term's time.

She had chosen the chapter about Beth creeping into the Palace Beautiful, as the Marches called the Laurences' big house, to play their piano – one of Anna's favourites. There was something about unassuming but talented Beth, with her big shy eyes, that reminded her of Lily – she could imagine Lily playing to herself in an empty house and not noticing the staff watching her in secret.

She could imagine her own grandfather, too, ordering complete silence so Beth would believe she was on her own, so she could play freely. Anna loved stern but gentle Mr Laurence, and this chapter often brought her to tears, thinking how good a grandfather her own dad would be. When she was Lily's age he used to wait until she was playing the

piano, clumping away badly at her exercises, then walk in
and say, in pretend amazement, 'Isn't the radio on? I thought
I could hear a record!'

Anna's eyes misted over and she nearly missed the murmur
that ran around the room. She blinked. Becca had stopped
reading and tears were running down her face. With one look
at Anna, she pushed the book into her hands and ran out of
the room.

'It wasn't *that* emotional,' said Evelyn dismissively. 'It wasn't
even the chapter where the child nearly dies.'

It took Anna a while to find Becca, but when she pushed open
the door of the staff lavatories she heard sobbing coming from
inside the disabled cubicle.

She knocked softly on the locked door. 'Becca? It's me.
Come on out, sweetheart.'

The sobbing stopped momentarily, then started again,
harder.

'Becca? Is it college?' Anna didn't want to put more worries
in Becca's mind, but she wanted her to know she understood. 'Is it leaving Owen? Because terms aren't very long.
They fly by before you know it.' She paused, then added,
'And if he moves back to London he'll only be an hour or so
away.'

There was no response. 'Is that not it?'

Anna leaned her forehead against the door, trying to
remember what it felt like to be eighteen, and the first person
in the world to fall in love. 'I know it's hard to leave him. I
know. But the next few years are going to be so wonderful. So
many opportunities and new things. The people, and the
lectures, and the parties . . .'

Slowly the door opened and Becca's tear-stained face

appeared. She looked about twelve years old, exhausted and scared. Anna's heart ached for her; surely this wasn't about leaving Longhampton to go to the university she'd been looking forward to for so long. This had to be the aftermath of all that exam stress, and Sarah's news, and exhaustion. Becca had coped so well. Too well. She knew that feeling too.

She held out her arms and Becca flung herself into them.

'What was it that upset you?' she asked, as Becca, nearly a head taller than she was, clung to her. 'Was it thinking about your granddad?'

'It was thinking about . . . *Dad.*'

Anna couldn't see Becca's face, but she could picture it. Becca adored Phil and he adored her, his uncomplicated, high-achieving first-born. He didn't hug Becca as much as the other two, limpet-like, girls, but his intense love for her radiated around them in other ways, in their private jokes, and his near-bewildered pride in everything she did.

'You'll always be his little girl,' she said, stroking Becca's hair. 'Even now you're grown-up and ready to make your own way in the world. He's so proud of you.'

That provoked another flurry of hiccuppy sobbing. Anna was congratulating herself on correctly diagnosing the cause of Becca's distress when she pulled away from her shoulder and looked her in the eye, then looked straight down at the cubicle floor.

'Anna.' Becca's voice was barely a whisper and she seemed to be testing each word carefully, as if she was scared to hear them come out of her mouth. 'Anna, I've got to tell you something, but you can't tell Dad.'

Anna's heart sank. 'You know I can't promise that,' she started, but Becca was insistent.

'You have to,' she said wildly. 'You have to *promise*.'

Anna held her by her arms, trying to look calmer than she felt. 'You haven't got engaged to Owen?'

Becca shook her head, and relief washed over Anna's chest.

'Thank God. I mean, he's a nice guy, a lovely guy, but you're very young and . . .'

Shut up, Anna.

'So what? What's so bad that you can't tell your dad, eh?'

Becca lifted her wet eyes, beseeching her to understand. 'I can't take up my place.'

'Why not? Is it the course? Because you can always change after a year if you really don't enjoy it. I'm sure with the grades you've got they'd be fine about letting you read something else. What about English?'

Becca's lip wobbled. 'Dad'll be so disappointed.'

'No, he won't! He only wants what you want and he thought you always wanted to do Law. Don't tell him, but *I'd* be thrilled if you did English. I'd love it! It'd be our secret that I made you change courses by letting you work in the bookshop. Eh?' Anna smiled encouragingly.

Becca managed a broken half-smile, then her face collapsed again. Anna put her arms round her again, feeling more confident now.

'Things change,' she said into her hair. 'That's life. We're all allowed to change our minds, and you're not letting anyone down by wanting something different. I mean, it's not like there's a ten-year-old in your old house stamping her foot because she's not going to grow up to be Judge Judy. Hmm? But you've earned that place, and it's yours to take. And you should take it.'

'I can't go,' said Becca, more emphatically this time, and she pulled away, staring at the floor now as if she was dragging up all her reserves.

'Owen will understand,' Anna began, but Becca stopped her.

'No,' she said firmly. 'Anna, I can't go to Cambridge next week.' She swallowed, then looked her in the eye and said, 'I'm pregnant.'

27

'Reading my old favourite Ballet Shoes *again to my grandchildren, it struck me how those three girls coped with rejection and success, all with a commendable resilience. They just stiffened their upper lips and got on with it.'* Gillian Knight

Later, when Anna replayed the moment in her head, she really hoped that her first reaction hadn't shown on her face, because she wasn't proud of it. It was going straight into the box of terrible things that she kept locked at the back of her mind, to pick over masochistically on sleepless nights.

The bitter, white-hot thought that flashed across Anna's brain like a streak of sheet lightning was: *How come everyone else gets to have a baby except me?*

She slammed it down instantly, ashamed of herself for even thinking it, but she had the awful feeling that Becca had caught a brief glimpse of it as it crossed behind her eyes, and Anna hated herself.

But there it was. Another baby. Another unarguable reason for Phil to say no to theirs.

She started talking immediately to wash the thought away – 'How many weeks? Are you sure? Have you done a test? Does Owen know?' – but the questions were too much for both of them. Becca started crying again and Anna felt a dam burst in her own heart, and they cried and hugged each other until a sharp voice cut through the air behind them.

'For heaven's sake, what's going on? This is a public place, anyone could walk in! Have some dignity!'

Anna spun round. Evelyn was standing by the cubicle door with an expression of curiosity mixed with disapproval, pinching her mouth into a scarlet crimp. She had to press her hands against her sides, so strong was the impulse to slap her.

'Becca's upset,' she said tightly. 'Isn't it obvious?'

'It's very obvious. It's obvious all the way down the corridor. What is it this time?' Evelyn tipped her head like a bird. 'Something to do with Sarah again? She always was a troublemaker, right from the time she got herself pregnant when she was barely out of school. I did tell Philip that – a mother can always see when a girl has no moral fibre, but—'

'It's got nothing to do with Sarah,' snapped Anna, feeling Becca flinch under her arm.

'Rebecca?' Evelyn peered at her beadily. 'Cat got your tongue? Aren't you a bit old for this sort of carry-on? This is behaviour I'd expect from that silly little sister of yours, running out of rooms like a drama queen. Come on, what's this about? They're all talking, you know,' she went on, as if it was a personal slight. 'It's going to be the *only* topic of conversation at dinner . . .'

'Stop it!' Anna was startled by her own anger. How Phil – thoughtful, easy-going, loving Phil – could possibly be related to this self-absorbed old bag was beyond her. Evelyn didn't *deserve* family. She didn't deserve grandchildren.

'Evelyn,' she said, her voice shaking, 'I'm no relation of yours, so I have absolutely no compunction in telling you to mind your own bloody business.'

'She's my granddaughter, and as you say, you're no relation,' Evelyn retorted. 'So in the circumstances, as her only *real* family member present, I think I've got every right to ask what's going on.'

'Becca, come on,' said Anna, before she lost her temper properly. She put her arm around Becca and started to usher her out.

'I really thought more of you,' said Evelyn, as Anna passed. 'I really did.'

Anna couldn't work out whether she was talking to her or to Becca, but she was too furious to ask.

Anna called Phil at work and by the time she and Becca pulled up outside the house, they could see him in the kitchen, staring anxiously out of the window.

'Oh my God,' said Becca under her breath. She shrank back in her seat. 'He's going to be so disappointed with me.' The last word vanished in a new hiccupping sob.

Anna turned round and grabbed Becca's hand. 'Listen, just remember that whatever he says first, he loves you,' she said urgently. 'He will always love you, whatever you do. He might say some things first that he'll regret, but—'

'Can't you tell him? Can you go in first and tell him?'

'No.' Anna's voice was firm. 'I'll be right behind you, but if you want him to treat you like an adult, then you've got to do this yourself. We'll do it together.'

Becca nodded as if it hurt her head to move it.

'And I'll help you make all the calls you need to, and I promise I won't lecture you, and . . .' She stopped, close to tears herself. These were calls *she'd* hoped to make, with happier news than this. 'Becca, I know it's not the same as having your mum here, but till she gets here I'll do everything I can. I promise that. You mean the world to me. If I could take some of the pain away for you, you know I would.'

Becca looked up at Anna. 'I know. And I need you here *because* you're not my mum,' she said. 'That sounds wrong. But I mean it in a good way.'

She gave Anna a brief, awkward hug, then got out of the car with a determined set to her jaw, before she could change her mind.

Anna watched as she marched down the path, her biker boots huge on the end of her slender legs, Owen's leather jacket slung over her shoulders. Already she looked like a different person.

That's the end of her childhood, thought Anna, watching the buckles on Becca's boots flash in the cool autumn sun as she made the short journey from car to kitchen. That's the beginning of the end of Phil's parenthood; and I'm going to be a step-granny before I get the chance to be a mother in my own right. And there's no way Phil will agree to us trying for a baby now.

She closed her eyes against the stab of bitterness that nearly stopped her heart beating. It was so unfair, she couldn't see the whole unfairness at once – just the middle of it, the tiny baby in Becca and Owen's arms part.

Then, just as quickly as Becca had left the car, Anna pushed her own door open and hurried up the path after her.

She was just in time to see Phil's face as Becca said, '. . . pregnant.'

He looked confused at first, then horrified. And then, when

Becca sank against his chest, sobbing and wrapping her arms around him like a child, his own eyes filled with tears and he lifted his chin as high as he could over her head so she wouldn't hear any stray gulps.

'Becca,' he kept saying, 'my little girl. My little girl.'

'Don't be angry,' Becca sobbed. 'Please don't be angry with me.'

'I'm not angry. How could I be angry?'

Anna hesitated at the door, unsure whether he wanted to be left on his own with her, but his eyes told her that she should come in. She found it unbearable, the sight of Phil crying. She'd never seen him cry before, not like this.

Slowly she went over to the pair of them and put her arms around Becca too, wrapping her up in what comfort she could offer. And Phil seemed as grateful for her hug as Becca did.

Michelle watched Owen shovelling back his supper at her kitchen table as if he hadn't been fed for a week, and wondered when he'd started looking so . . . ironed.

'Owen, have you had your hair cut?' she asked curiously.

'Yeah. I had a meeting with the gym about doing their website support, and Becca said I had to go to the hairdresser.' He stopped shovelling and looked sheepish. 'Rory said it might be a good idea too, so, you know . . .'

'*Rory* said?'

'Yeah. I'm going to do the new website for Flint and Cook. Had to go and meet the head honcho and Rory reckoned he's got a thing against guys with long hair.' Owen touched his new, somewhat shorter but still shaggy hair. 'It'll grow back. Becca likes it. And the suit.'

Michelle marvelled at how she'd managed to miss all this.

What suit? Since when had Rory been helping Owen find work? Since when, in fact, had Owen been motivated enough to seek out new contacts, without her nagging him from a great height?

Maybe they'd been wrong to worry about Owen being a bad influence on Becca. She seemed to be having a much more significant influence on *him*. He'd be reading books next.

'When did Rory put that your way?' she asked, trying not to sound nosy.

'I saw him in the bookshop. He's often in there, browsing. Telling Anna how to do her displays better.' Owen looked cheeky. 'Passing comments about what you're feeding Tavish.'

'What?' Michelle started but Owen's phone beeped by his plate and his eyes swung to it at once.

'Sorry, can I just get this?' he said, already reaching for it. His generous lips curved into an automatic smile, and Michelle knew the text must be from Becca as he pushed the button with a practised thumb.

'Don't tell me, you're supposed to be having dinner with her tonight?' Michelle tried not to be jealous at the way a cloud of cartoon stars practically appeared round Owen's head whenever he texted Becca. It *was* real for some people. It seemed to be happening for Owen.

He didn't reply, and Michelle started to clear the plates to distract herself. Much as she loved Owen, and liked Becca, this wasn't the best time for her to watch the cutesy texting back and forth. Now she'd unleashed it, Michelle's grief for her lost twenties had sharpened over the past few days, and only close study of her accounts could take her mind off it.

'Owen, can you come and help me?' she asked. When he

didn't reply she looked over to the table. He was staring at the phone. 'What's up?'

Owen said nothing, but pushed his phone over the table. His expression was oddly blank, and she wondered for a second if Becca had dumped him.

It'd be a bit mean to do it by text, she thought – not Becca's style. Maybe it was some other girl, the Dublin fling coming over and wanting to hook up? Awkward.

Michelle picked up the phone. The text was from Becca, but it read, 'I'm pregnant. Can you come round to mine tonight at 7pm?'

'Oh my God,' said Michelle.

It was perfectly punctuated, no txtspk for Becca. And yet the tiny message was explosive. It changed the direction of everything, in just enough characters to fill a mobile phone screen. She had to read it three times just to absorb what Becca had said.

Michelle felt her head go light with adrenalin. 'Oh my God, Owen. What were you thinking?'

He shook his head, unable to speak.

'She's only just eighteen! She's a child! Why in the name of all that's holy weren't you using any kind of *protection*?' Michelle's voice was rising, as the knot in her stomach tightened. 'You stupid, stupid, feckless idiot! What's Becca going to do now? What about her university place? That poor girl, you're old enough to know better than to—'

'Shut up!' Owen shoved his chair back and leaned on the table, glaring at her with shell-shocked eyes. 'Give me a chance!'

'Oh my God, poor Becca,' said Michelle, covering her mouth as the full extent of it all sank in. 'She's only ever wanted to do what everyone else wanted. Poor Anna. Oh God, poor Anna . . . And Phil, he'll be devastated . . .'

'Stop going on about everyone else,' Owen yelled. 'What am *I* supposed to do?'

'You do whatever she asks you to do.'

'And don't I have a say?'

'To be honest?' Michelle's eyes flashed. 'No. No, you don't. This is about Becca, not you. Whether she goes ahead and has a baby, or decides not to, her life has *changed*. You'll be the same person whether she has a baby or not, you can walk away from this, but Becca's going to have to live with this forever, one way or another. So you do whatever she wants.'

Michelle barely knew what she was saying; the words were tumbling out of her faster than she could think them. Even the voice didn't sound like hers; it was higher and shriller. She was talking about Becca, but a small voice underneath the stream of words warned her that this was coming from somewhere else. These were words she'd been thinking a long time, storing them up in a locked box in her head, and suddenly they were coming out, in full sentences.

Owen stared at her, uncomprehending.

'My life would change too!' he objected, slapping his chest. 'There's no way I'd walk away from Becca. What kind of person do you think I am?'

'Someone I've had to bail out loads of times?'

'That was rent! We're talking about a human life! I can't believe you think I'd do that.'

Michelle brushed his protests aside. 'It's not the same for men. You have no idea the *weird* things she'll be thinking, either – not just, oh no, I've let down my family, and I've screwed up my career, and everyone at school's going to be talking about me. They're bad enough. She'll be thinking, how did I let this happen? What kind of *woman* will it make me if I choose not to have this baby? And everyone will be offering her solutions and advice whether she wants it or not, and telling her what to think, as if she's now a different person, and *your* job, the most important thing you can do, is to make her feel that she's still *her*. Still her.'

She drew a deep breath as an awful thought occurred to her. That text had been very blunt. 'Owen, this isn't the point where you tell me you've already broken up?'

'No.' He paused for a long, long second. 'I love her, Michelle. I've never met anyone like Becca. I'll marry her if that's what Phil wants.'

'If he'll let you, more like. Getting married isn't always the answer. Sometimes it makes everything worse.'

Michelle sank down onto the sofa. Her fierce words hung in the air between them like the smoke after fireworks, and she knew she'd said too much, just from the stunned but curious way Owen was staring at her, afraid she might explode again at any moment.

That's not his fault, she told herself. This is about him, not me.

Owen sat down next to her and the pair of them stared at the carefully restored Victorian fireplace that Michelle had never lit. It was full of identically sized pine cones, sprayed gold.

Silence stretched out between them, broken only by the sound of Tavish, who had just appeared, waddling to the sofa and clambering up next to Michelle. She let him. Then Owen said, 'Michelle, did I say something to upset you personally? I don't know if there's something I missed?'

She shook her head. 'No. No.'

'You and Harvey didn't have children. Was there some sort of . . . ?'

'It's nothing to do with Harvey,' said Michelle. She struggled to express herself when dark thoughts were flying around inside her head, too fast to catch. 'I've been eighteen. I thought I knew everything, then when I got expelled it was as if I woke up one morning in someone else's life. I know how Becca feels, that's all. And I promised Anna this wouldn't happen. She was terrified something like this *would* happen, and I promised her you were responsible.'

'I have been,' said Owen glumly. 'I swear to you, it was only twice.'

'Don't they do scary sex education in schools any more? It only needs to be once.'

'I know. And hello, it's not just up to the bloke.' Owen looked hurt. 'You're making out I forced this on her, and I didn't. At *all*. I keep telling you, I've never felt like this about anyone before. I was prepared to wait as long as it—'

'Well, clearly you didn't,' said Michelle.

Oh God. Poor Anna. Her heart ached for Anna. Where was her own baby going to come now? It would be just like Anna to insist on helping to raise Becca's baby instead of having her own. And Phil would probably go for that.

Owen pushed himself off the sofa.

'Where are you going?' Michelle demanded. 'We haven't finished talking.' She could hardly bar the door, but rational as he was being on the surface, the temptation to do a runner must be overwhelming right now.

And Owen had form, she reminded herself; he always meant well, but didn't always follow through. This was a massive thing.

'For a walk. Then I'm going to see Becca and tell her everything's going to be fine. Whatever she wants.' He paused, then looked at her with an angry sadness. 'I don't know what happened to you that you're not telling me, but not all men are total bastards, you know. You always jump to the worst conclusions. You do it with me, with Rory, with Harvey, with everyone. You're never going to be happy if you expect the worst all the time. Think about it, Michelle.'

He turned and left, leaving Michelle staring at the fireplace, her hand resting on Tavish's wiry coat.

She knew she should be thinking about Becca, but Owen's voice refused to leave her head.

28

'I loved the Greek Myths as a child. I liked the brutal logic of the divine punishments, and the clever explanation of natural phenomena. Quite reassuring.'   Rory Stirling

Sarah came back on the first available flight, a 'permission to fly' note wrestled out of the hands of her expensive gynaecologist. Her reaction to Becca's phone call could have powered her halfway across the Atlantic on its own. In an hour she went from disbelief, to disappointment, to fury (with Owen, who she 'hadn't even met!'), to happiness (of sorts), to anguished self-blame, to fury again (this time with Phil), to encouragement, and finally a lot of tears.

As it turned out, Becca's panic about what to say wasn't necessary, since she only managed to get about five per cent of the available airtime, anyway. When the call finished, her notebook of things she wanted to say was still open in front of her, covered in anxious doodles of circles within circles.

'At least you know what she's going to say when she gets here now,' Anna reassured her, pressing a cup of tea into her trembling hands.

'She'll think of more on the plane,' said Becca miserably. 'You were the only person she didn't lay into, Anna.'

'And she needn't start when she gets here,' said Phil,

speaking for the first time. 'Because if she does, I'll give her the last remaining piece of my mind.'

Phil and Anna had sat next to Becca while she made the phone call, using the old-fashioned telephone rather than Skype, 'because I don't want to see her face when she realises I'm not going to Cambridge after all'. Phil hadn't been a huge amount of help so far – his initial shock had moved into a silent sort of despair that Anna suspected hid feelings he didn't dare give voice to – and it had been Anna who'd taken charge, fumbling her way through the etiquette of a family crisis. Who to tell, in what order, and how much.

'Thanks,' said Becca. She rubbed her face. 'I'm going to my room.'

'Sure you don't want any supper?'

Becca shook her head. 'Don't feel like eating, to be honest. Feel a bit sick. Apparently morning sickness can go on right until the third trimester.'

'Of course.' Anna kicked herself. Of course. There was so much she didn't know. Her ignorance of motherhood was coming at her from both generations now.

When they got home, she'd discreetly left her secret stash of baby books in Becca's room; if she asked, Anna decided, she'd pretend she'd got them from the shop. Becca hadn't asked. She'd just started studying them with the same intensity with which she'd studied her set texts.

'Give me a shout if Mum calls back,' said Becca and shuffled out without looking back at Phil.

I should have started a conversation there, thought Anna, berating herself for her slow brain. The distance between Phil and Becca was killing her; Becca had barely been able to look at her father since she'd broken the news, and he seemed lost for words. And if it was killing Anna, she had no idea how painful it had to be for them.

She slipped her hand into his and squeezed. 'It'll be all right,' she whispered.

'Will it?' Phil sounded bleak. 'How can you possibly know that?'

'Because things work out.'

'What? Like they worked out for me and Sarah? Pregnant at twenty, married at twenty-one, divorced at thirty-three? It's just what my mother said would happen. History repeating itself. Only I always thought it would be Chloe who went off the rails and—'

'Phil,' said Anna in a low, warning voice, but she was too late.

Chloe stalked into the kitchen, shooting daggers at them both. 'Why stop talking?' she demanded, hands on her hips. The singing had stopped. 'It's not like I *matter* round here. What were you going to say? You always thought *I* would be the one to fail my exams and get pregnant? What a disappointment that must be for you. That I've only failed my exams so far!'

'Chloe, that's not what your father was going to say . . .'

'I hate you,' said Chloe very clearly, looking at Phil and ignoring Anna. 'And as soon as Mum gets here, I'm going to tell her how much I hate living here with you, and I'm going to ask her to take me back to America with her. I've been looking up high schools in her area on the internet, and you can't stop me.'

She turned and stormed out, stifling a sob or a scream, Anna couldn't tell which, but it carried on right down into the cellar where the door slammed hard behind her.

Anna turned to Phil, expecting him to go after his

daughter, but he just raised his hands, then dropped them wearily in his lap.

'Go after her!' she urged.

'What can I say?' he asked. 'I *have* let her down. We've all let her down. It's going to be chaos here, with Becca having the baby . . .' He paused; that conversation hadn't even been properly broached yet. 'Or *not* having the baby, whatever she decides to do. Maybe it would be better for Chloe to have a year in the States with Sarah. Maybe she'll get the attention she needs.'

Anna couldn't believe he thought that, but then lately, she'd started to realise Phil took the path of least resistance a *lot*.

'With Sarah?' she repeated. 'And *her* new baby? You think Sarah's going to want to handle a stroppy teen as well as night feeds and a new routine and Jeff? I mean, yes, I don't doubt she made the offer before she got pregnant, but now . . . You want Chloe to hear from her own mother that she doesn't have time to deal with her right now?'

Phil frowned, then seemed to get her point. 'God, you're right.' He sighed. 'Maybe you could . . . I mean, they seem to take these things better from you.'

Anna bit her tongue. She was pretty sure she hadn't married this spineless man. The one she'd married had been a lot more proactive.

'So I'm useful for some mothering things, then? Just not having our own,' she added, and hated herself the moment the words left her lips because she knew they weren't true.

If she'd got pregnant first, it wouldn't have made the blindest bit of difference to Sarah or Becca, whereas their babies had shoved hers right off the agenda, maybe forever, and what was she left with? A choice between bringing up Becca's baby like a martyr, or abandoning the children she'd taken on willingly, in order to have her own? It was no choice at all.

'Anna,' Phil started, but she was already marching out of the room. She didn't let herself storm off when the girls were around, as a matter of principle, but Anna's patience was hanging by the thinnest of threads, and she didn't trust herself to stay.

She took Pongo's lead down from the hook by the door and he was by her side in an instant, his whippy tail flashing back and forth, always delighted by the chance of spending an hour with her.

'Come on, Pongo,' she said. 'We're going for a walk. A very, very long walk.'

If Anna had started feeling more like a mother to Becca, the illusion was instantly dispelled as soon as Sarah arrived. She was relegated to the background as rows and tears spilled out all over. The only spells of calmness came from Becca, who insisted, with a face like a Renaissance Madonna, that she was having her baby, that she refused to let it down. Her quiet confidence only made the whole thing more heartbreaking.

Anna ran around making sandwiches and keeping Lily and Chloe out of things while Sarah, Phil and Becca argued and wept, and then argued and wept with Owen and Michelle there too. Phil put up some token threats to smack some sense into Owen, but Becca refused to let him do anything of the sort, and his anger subsided back into bewilderment as the two beautiful young people sat holding hands in the kitchen, more composed than anyone.

Anna knew she should be standing up and marking her place in all this, since her life was about to be hijacked, but she couldn't find the right words to express herself. She was over-whelmed by the force of Sarah's pregnant presence, her taut bump only emphasising her position in the house: the mother. Becca's mother, the one person qualified to help her through a pregnancy.

Anna felt disorientated in her own world. The only place she felt completely at home and secure was the bookshop, where she could lose herself, however temporarily, in worlds where there were happy endings, and rewards for self-sacrifice.

'Still here?' said Michelle, when she came to do the last hour in the shop. The light had started to fade into dusk outside and the table lamps in the shop were giving the place a cosy autumnal feel.

Anna moved a pile of Roald Dahl stories off the front desk and hoped Michelle hadn't been watching her reading *James and the Giant Peach* through the window. Even the gulls on the cover were comforting now. The twenty minutes she'd just spent listening to Bach and the crackle of the log fire in the back room, imagining herself in the cosy centre of a giant fruit had been the highlight of her day, even though the shop had been deathly quiet.

At least the Peach got to New York, she kept telling herself. There's always an end. Even if the two evil women were child-less aunts who looked after poor James. Childless wizened aunts were leaping out at her a lot at the moment.

'Go home if you want,' Michelle went on. 'I've got some things I need to do here. Kelsey's covering next door. She needs the overtime.'

'No, it's OK, I can stay until closing today,' she said. 'Sarah's taken the girls shopping, then out to a film. Thought I'd give them some time together.'

'Really?' Michelle's eyebrow hoiked up. 'That's nice of you. Don't you want to grab some time with Phil?'

'And do what? Go over all the reasons Becca's making a huge mistake by keeping the baby? No thanks.'

'He'll come round. When he sees it.'

'I don't know about that,' said Anna. 'Once he's made his mind up he tends to stick to it.'

Michelle started refolding the blankets on the biggest display table. 'How long's Sarah staying? When's she due?'

'She's due at the end of November. She's enormous. I think that's been more of a wake-up call for Becca than when we went to the clinic for her first check-up.'

One of the reasons Anna didn't want to go home was that she couldn't bear looking at Sarah's enormous bump. She stroked it constantly, smoothing out her clinging maternity tops, talking to it, insisting on getting the girls to talk to their 'new baby friend'. She was glad for their sakes that they were getting used to the idea of a new sibling – Lily, in particular, seemed to be fascinated, and had decided Mrs Piggle was also up the duff, father TBA – but that felt like just another thing Anna had to smile her way through, and the strain was getting unbearable.

'Poor you,' said Michelle, seeing her face.

'It's like having the Malory Towers Mummies in my own kitchen, but at least in here, I don't have to join in and pretend I'm fine about it,' Anna said. Michelle was the only person she could tell. 'Sarah's being really cooey about *Becca's* bump, and how she's going to send her weapons-grade cocoa butter for her stretch marks. All they talk about is birth plans, and how Chloe and Lily can be involved so they don't feel left out. It's all positive, which is great, but Phil's retreated to his shed and I just . . .' She bit her lip. 'I just make the meals and nod a lot.'

'And you organise Becca's life for her,' Michelle pointed out. 'You do all the boring admin so she can _be_ a barefoot student mummy.'

Anna had been helping Becca work through the system for deferring her place and applying for childcare at her college, trying to keep her focused and optimistic about the future when she panicked about everything heading her way. Anna didn't let it show, but stacking up facts was equally reassuring for her, a handrail along a mountain road she daren't look down from.

'Yes, well, wasn't it you who told me about the healing power of a good to-do list?' Anna managed a grin, and Michelle smiled back sadly.

'She's flying back tomorrow,' Anna went on. 'She's only allowed to fly for another forty-eight hours on her doctor's note, so she was cutting it fine to begin with.'

'I'll bring in cakes. You've earned them.'

They didn't have many nice moments like this any more, thought Anna. They were both worried about things they didn't want to share: her broodiness, which she knew made Michelle impatient, and Michelle's divorce, which she hadn't mentioned again. She hadn't told Michelle about the scan dates or the midwife Becca had met, feeling those details should come via Owen, but she also got the sense that Michelle wasn't telling her everything about the shop either. She still hadn't got back to her about the orders for their big Christmas promotions, and the bookshop website hadn't been updated for several weeks, even though Anna was getting regular orders through it for the more specialist second-hand stock.

It had been easier when they used to talk about coffee and scarves and _The Apprentice_ and Phil's shed and Anna's book-shop regulars and Pongo. There was no time for that now.

'I miss our chats,' she said suddenly, reaching out for Michelle's hand. 'So does Pongo. Lily says that he tells her Juliet doesn't walk him as well as you do.'

'Does he?' Michelle looked pleased. 'Well, maybe I could take him out for a run one weekend.' She glanced down to Tavish's box, where he lay curled up, his eyes invisible in the coal-black fur. 'It's not like this one demands much athletic input. He's barely walked around my garden for the past few weeks. Even Rory's noticed, and all he does upstairs is sleep anyway.'

'He's been really quiet all day,' said Anna. 'Really quiet.'

'Ill quiet?'

'No, just . . . He reminds me of some of the old folk up at Butterfields. He's just lying there waiting for something.' Anna felt a lump in her throat as Tavish raised his head slightly, then slumped back in his box.

'Mr Quentin noticed when I took him up there the other day,' she added. 'He just sat on his lap, very quiet. Do you think he's on his way out?'

'I don't know.' Michelle bent down and stroked Tavish's head. Tavish bore it with dignity. 'I took him up to the vet's, and George said he was just getting on a bit, couldn't find anything wrong. But when a dog won't eat hand-poached chicken shredded on a bed of steamed rice, then something's up.'

'Michelle! You fed him that?' Anna was amused, despite her sadness. 'Does Rory know you're making gourmet dog meals?'

'No. And don't tell him,' said Michelle. 'I get enough lectures from him about how to look after a dog, as if I'd never had one.'

'I didn't know you did.'

Michelle looked a bit shifty. 'Harvey and I had a spaniel. Called Flash.'

'You never said!' These days there seemed to be more and more about Michelle that she didn't know. These bits of information kept drifting out like stray feathers from a cushion.

'I felt bad about leaving him behind. I missed him for ages. I still do.'

'That's not surprising,' said Anna. 'Sometimes dogs love you more than people. They're easier to love, too.'

Michelle seemed on the verge of saying something else, then picked distractedly at a roll of pink satin ribbon, left over from a recent book bouquet. 'Look, I'm sorry if I haven't been a great friend lately. You know you can always come over for a coffee if things get unbearable. We don't have to talk about babies, or work, or anything. We can talk about books if you want.'

'Oh,' said Anna. 'Can we really talk about books? Did you finish *Riders*?'

'I did, yes.'

'And did you enjoy it?' Anna probed, determined to get Michelle to confess to liking a book. 'Don't deny it. I defy anyone not to love Jilly.'

'It . . . brought back a lot of memories,' said Michelle.

'Brilliant! Then I'll order you some more. In fact, why don't I order in a whole load of Jilly Cooper novels and we can have an Orgasmic October promotion?' Anna's face lit up at the thought of her next display. 'Or . . . Naughty November? We could make the window display look really steamy, and have bonkbusters in stacks – "Who needs central heating?" We haven't got much planned for the autumn. I was going to talk to you about that anyway.'

'I know, I needed to talk to you too,' said Michelle, but

Anna had waited a while to deliver her autumn pitch and she wanted to get it all out before Michelle talked over her. She'd been planning it in her head during her escape walks with Pongo.

'If you move those blankets back into Home Sweet Home and free up my best table,' she went on, 'we could do an amazing display of pony books! Everyone loves pony books in the autumn. Rachel asked me today if we were going to replenish the Pullein-Thompson section . . .'

Michelle was winding the pink ribbon round her fingers, too tightly.

'What?' said Anna. One silver lining of recent events was that she'd lost any fear of bad news. How much worse could it be? 'Go on.'

'The books just aren't making any money. We've had this conversation before. I've tried to balance it out, but it's not going to work, not without some drastic reassessment. I want to be honest with you, I don't think we can carry on like this. I've got to make a decision very soon.'

'A decision? What are you saying?' Anna's stomach sank.

'I'm planning to move some more bedlinen stock in here over the next few weeks.'

'How much? Where's it going to go?' Anna's eyes darted around the shop, alighting on all the corners and shelves she couldn't give up – the colourful children's section, the tatty green Penguins in the vintage crime shelves, the swooning white-gloves-and-cigarettes covers of the 1950s romances someone had given them from a house clearance. The reclaimed Welsh dresser with the coffee machine and cups on it. The rocking horse.

Anna loved all of it. That was the whole point – the bookshop had finally gone back to being the warm, alive place it needed to be, and she felt like flinging her arms around it all. It was the heart of everything she believed in – the happy ever afters and the broken children brought back to life with love. Everything she'd pinned her hopes on. If this went, how was she supposed to keep believing in her own dreams for a family, despite it all?

'I can't believe you want to change this,' she burst out. 'We've got it perfect. Everyone *loves* this shop. You know how many regulars we have these days.'

Michelle sighed. 'I know you love it. I love it. But business isn't about making something for yourself, that's why Cyril went bust. It's about making something for people to *buy*.'

'That's rich, coming from someone whose shop looks exactly like their own house!'

'And this isn't *your* fantasy bookshop?' retorted Michelle. 'Look, you've made the ultimate palace of books, just like I made the ultimate sitting room next door, but you've got to face up to reality, Anna – this isn't some lovely Magic Bookshop. There isn't a big trunk of doubloons in the cellar. There aren't even any convenient priceless first editions! This is business.'

'Why are you being so hard about it all of a sudden?' Anna demanded, shocked at the way Michelle was talking about the dream they'd created together. 'Why now?'

Michelle sighed, as if it were too obvious and annoying to explain; that wound Anna up even more. 'Because there are lead times and orders to place now for Christmas. This is no reflection on what you've done. You've sold more books in the last three months than Cyril did in a year. But it's not enough. It's just the way the bookselling business is going. Bigger and better shops than this have closed. This is my livelihood, and I need to make it work. You've got Phil and the girls. They need your energy right now. Don't get distracted by something you can't fight.'

'And *you're* not using this as a distraction from *your* problems?' Anna snapped.

'No! No, I'm not. Are you? Because you'd be better off persuading Phil to have a baby than trying to make this place turn a profit on books alone. Seriously.'

Anna stared over the counter at her friend, and realised that up until now, she'd never seen the Steamroller Michelle that Gillian and Kelsey were so scared of. This Michelle had a way of speaking that made any sort of resistance seem futile, as if the decisions were already being rolled out around them as they were talking. If blankets had materialised on the shelves behind her, she wouldn't have been surprised.

'Don't tell *me* how to handle my relationships.' She felt a rush of defensive fury that made her speak without thinking. 'Maybe if you'd spent less time thinking about *blankets* and more time keeping an eye on Owen I'd be in a position to *have* a baby! Instead of facing the prospect of looking after my own step-grandchild for the next eighteen years!'

Michelle's mouth dropped open. 'Sorry? Are you saying that because you feel responsible for not telling Becca the facts of life, or do you actually mean it? Because if you do, I hope you never ever let Becca hear you say it.'

'You're in no position to be sanctimonious about relationships, Michelle, and you know it.'

'What's that supposed to mean?'

'It means what it means.' Anna felt white-hot. 'I've shared everything with you. All my worries about Phil, and the girls, and about how much I want a baby. But you keep things back! And not just from me. You keep everyone at arm's length because then you don't have to get involved. You can be all rational about them. Is that why you don't care about the bookshop as much as your own shop? Because customers come in here and talk? They don't just buy a lampshade and go home to their perfect houses, they *share* things. That's why it means more than just money. But that doesn't matter to you because you've never understood.'

There. It was out. The niggles that had been boiling away under the surface for so long. It made Anna feel better for one second to have said them, but already she was feeling a creeping horror at what she might have just done to their friendship.

'You're not listening to anything I've said.' Michelle's expression was cold and detached.

'I've heard *everything*,' said Anna, and stormed out.

There was no text or phone message of apology from Michelle when Anna got home. And none the following morning. She didn't tell Phil about their argument – it sounded too petty, and they'd stopped talking over breakfast anyway – but went into work with a heavy heart, ready to find her P45 on the desk.

When she arrived, Kelsey was doing the early shift Michelle usually covered, and the local interest section had moved into the space where her giant Paddington Bear had been. A cream-painted stepladder covered in lace-trimmed nighties stood by the door.

If she'd seen it in Home Sweet Home, Anna would have wanted to buy the whole lot, but now she felt invaded. Even a note offering her the Paddington Bear for Becca's baby's nursery didn't take the sting out of it.

Throughout the week, other small changes occurred – always at night, when Anna wasn't around. The more esoteric stock vanished into the stockroom upstairs and reappeared in virtual form on the website, and in its place came lavender bags and cashmere bed socks. Some customers loved the new additions – the Malory Towers Mummies especially – but some of the regulars demanded to know what was going on with the sudden influx of sheepskin slippers.

'What next? Duvets in the bloody thriller section?' asked Rory, calling in one lunchtime to pick up some reading matter. He was clutching a pile of old Horatio Hornblowers for reading at Butterfields, and Anna had suggested *The Very Hungry Caterpillar* to him, for Zachary, and he was holding that too, less confidently.

'She says we need to up the profits.'

'Does she indeed?' Rory snorted. 'I think I need to talk to her about that. If she wants to get rid of anything she can do something about that awful cupcake cookery section, but to dispatch the historical fiction . . .'

He shook his head in disgust. It sounded more personal than professional to Anna.

'Can you talk to her?' she asked. 'She listens to you.'

'I'm not sure about that,' he said, and Anna noticed a blush speckle his cheeks.

Anna liked him more now Michelle had confided the truth about Zachary and Esther. She'd always liked Rory, though; he was dry like Michelle, but not so brittle. Kelsey had warmed to him too, and even Gillian had speculated on whether Tavish might bring Rory and Michelle together, since 'they both needed some company'.

Anna had always believed, romantically, that Michelle's wounded heart just needed a tidal wave of real passion to revive it; lately, though, she wondered if she might have been wrong. Maybe Michelle was better off with Tavish. Maybe

Rory and his dry wit and fury at misplaced apostrophes deserved something more.

'Think of the bookshop, Rory,' she said. 'Do it for us.'

He smiled sadly and pushed back his long fringe. 'Six impossible things before breakfast, eh? I'll do what I can. But I can't promise anything.'

'None of us can,' said Anna. 'That's the trouble.'

29

*'From the Mixed Up Files of Mrs. Basil E. Frankweiler
is so smart. I loved the idea of running away to live in a
museum – it always seemed they would be so much more
magical with nobody else around.'* Allison Hunter

A thin, cold wind was whipping around the trees, bending them towards the house like listeners as Anna and Tavish walked over the gravel towards Butterfields on Thursday lunchtime. It was a rather sinister image that she half remembered from some storybook, though she couldn't think which one, and she shuddered, pulling her scarf further round her neck. Tavish was walking even more slowly than normal, his short legs stiff under his curtain of fur, so she picked him up and carried him into the house.

The hall seemed quiet when she went in, with the heating on full blast and a strong smell of stew in the air. Tavish wriggled free and trotted down the hallway towards the day room; since there was no passing Zimmer frame traffic, Anna let him go to find Mr Quentin while she signed the checking-in book.

'Anna?'

Joyce hurried over, her face already set in a warning Bad News mask, one finger raised to her lips. Anna peered more closely and saw that Joyce's cheeks were slippery with tears and her small eyes were red. Joyce wasn't a weeper; she was normally bracingly pragmatic.

'Joyce? Are you all right?' she asked, touching her arm.

'Oh, I'm a bit cut up, to be honest. It's poor Mr Quentin.' She fished a hanky out of her sleeve and wiped under her lower lashes. 'He passed away about an hour ago. He was all ready for you, too, in his usual chair. Couldn't wait to see you and the little laddie. Kept asking when you were coming. If we'd got the Bonio ready for the dog. Then he closed his eyes – for a quick nap, he said, before his story – and . . .' Her voice cracked. 'Didn't wake up.'

'Oh no.' Anna's hand flew to her mouth. 'Oh no.'

'To be honest with you, he'd been poorly for a while. His heart.' Joyce patted her own bolster-like chest, covering a multitude of diagnoses. 'Dr Harper didn't think he needed to go into hospital, but he did warn us that Cyril might go suddenly.'

There was a keening noise from the sitting room and Anna dashed down the hallway. What she saw made the lump in her throat swell.

Tavish had jumped up into Mr Quentin's winged chair and was circling frantically, trying to pick up a smell from the cushions, all the while making a low, heartbreaking sound in his throat while his tail wagged from side to side, swishing at the cushions with slow thumps.

The other residents were watching him in silence, some pressing hankies to their crumpled faces, but not one shooing him off his master's chair.

Anna rushed in and picked him up but he scrambled out of her arms and returned to the chair, circling and sniffing and whining, and all she could do was watch him.

He'd known. Somehow Tavish had known before they did.

Anna sank into the seat next to him and cried out the storm of tears that had been building inside her for days. Some for Mr Quentin, but most of them for the display of simple, unconditional devotion playing out in front of her.

She couldn't help feeling she'd lost something too – with Phil, with Michelle, with her own dreams – but she didn't want to think about exactly what it was.

Michelle called in to the bookshop at half past four, as usual, and found Anna and Becca sitting by the fireplace in the back room with Tavish. He was curled up on Anna's knee and for a split second, what with their red eyes and his still shape, Michelle thought the little dog had died. Her heart thumped with shock.

'Is he OK?' she asked, dropping her bag in the doorway and hurrying through, forgetting that the shop was still open, and that she and Anna were barely talking beyond basic civilities.

'Mr Quentin's died,' sniffed Anna. 'This morning, just before we got there. Poor Tavish was so upset. He ran off and found his body in the bedroom, and then he was howling so much I rang Rachel and she got George the vet, her husband, to come out and give him a tranquilliser.'

She blew her nose on one of the expensive tissues from the basket on the counter. She and Becca had gone through two packets of them, going by the screwed-up pile around them. 'I nearly made him give me one too. It was the saddest thing I've ever seen.'

'And is he all right now?' Michelle bent and stroked Tavish's ears, but he didn't respond. The fine hairs on the tips of his ears that were always such a clear indication of his mood were lifeless.

She hadn't realised till then how much she'd learned to read into his grumpy body language, or how subtle Tavish could be in communicating his feelings. Or how much she would miss his imperious presence around her house if he suddenly wasn't there.

Don't die, little man, she thought fiercely. I've got chicken in the fridge for you. And salmon. And you can sleep on my bed, if it makes you feel better.

'George said if he made it through the next few days he'd probably be OK, but he's an old dog and sometimes they can just go when their owners do.' Anna wiped her face. 'It's like that awful book. *Greyfriars Bobby*.'

'I hate that book,' said Becca suddenly. 'Gran read that to me and Chloe once when she was babysitting and we cried for days. I still can't get the image of that poor dog waiting on his master's grave out of my head ... Oh, *Anna*, you've started me off again,' she added as more tears filled her eyes.

Anna tried to brush her own away with a joke. 'Evelyn read you that? Typical. So sensitive.'

'Before you ask, I haven't read it,' said Michelle. 'And now I don't want to.'

Becca got up and Michelle spotted a small but definite baby bump under her long-sleeved T-shirt. It gave her a start. Time was really passing.

She turned to Anna, wanting to say something, but she didn't know what. There was a painful blank in her brain where the right words should have been – she had no idea what broodiness felt like – and Anna's face was defensive. Michelle realised she was too scared to say anything, to gentle Anna who'd always been there with the right words for her.

'Anna, now Michelle's here, I might go,' said Becca. 'This is going to sound really sad, but I want to take Pongo out for a walk.'

'You go,' said Michelle. 'Take Owen with you too – he's next door.'

'Is that a good idea?' said Anna stiffly. 'Shouldn't he be working?'

'Pongo's strong,' said Michelle. 'You've got to be careful. And Owen needs to learn about routines. And responsibilities. And picking up poo. Start him with the dog. He's got five months to get used to the smell.'

Anna didn't say anything. She started picking up the used tissues.

Becca gave Michelle a sad smile, a 'You tried' smile, and left them alone.

'Anna,' Michelle started, but Anna wasn't interested.

'I've got a few books to sell,' she said. 'While the shop's still open.'

The day passed so slowly that Michelle wondered if the clocks had stopped a few times, and she left the shop at six fifteen, not even bothering to tidy up.

Back home she poured herself a glass of wine and sat down on the sofa with Tavish. By eight o'clock, she still hadn't moved. He'd fallen asleep properly, and seemed so comfortable that she couldn't bear to move him, even though her left leg had started to prickle with pins and needles. Her hand moved automatically along his back, stroking him more for her own comfort than his, feeling the slow up and down of his breathing.

Michelle knew she should be getting on with her to-do list for the week but sadness was pressing down on her, trapping her on the sofa like a steel rollercoaster bar. The things Anna said had wounded her in a way Harvey had never managed to do. They went round in her head, sharpened by Anna's hurt eyes. Did she really think she'd kept her at arm's length so she could be judgemental? How *could* she be judgemental when Anna's life was so warm and welcoming, everything Michelle would have loved to have, if only she'd been lucky enough?

Michelle wasn't a weeper, like Anna, but her whole body ached with a loneliness that made her want to finish the bottle and start another. If she fell out with Anna, then she had no one. Being alone and celibate was wearing and depressing, but being without the only real friend she'd had since school . . . She wasn't sure she could bear it.

When the doorbell rang, both she and Tavish jumped, and Michelle limped to the door to answer it.

Rory was standing on the step, his coat turned up at the collar, his nose a bit red at the tip. He didn't grin as normal when he saw her, and he lifted his shoulders without taking his hands out of his pockets. 'Hello.'

'Hello. Did I miss an arrangement? You're not meant to be collecting Tavish today, are you?'

'No. I just thought I'd pop round. For a coffee and a chat.' Rory raised an eyebrow. 'Sorry, I should have called to make an appointment but I assumed you'd be here. Let me in, it's freezing.'

'A phone call would have done.' Michelle opened the door and found herself wishing she'd bothered to get changed. She was still in her work clothes – a black pencil skirt now covered in dog hairs, and a shirt that was a tiny bit drooly where Tavish's head had been resting against her arm.

'Sad news about Cyril, isn't it?' said Rory, bending down to tickle Tavish's beardy chin. 'I'm really going to miss him. Still, he's left a very complicated will so I reckon he'll get the last laugh on us all.'

'Complicated how?'

Rory strolled into the kitchen, without taking off his shoes. He did his usual thing of picking things up to inspect them, then putting them down in a slightly different place. 'It's a real Agatha Christie one, with individual bequests and bits and pieces going everywhere. He used to love writing his will. Redid it every few years, apparently.'

'Oh.' Michelle started spooning coffee into a cafetière and then changed her mind and opened the fridge. 'Wine all right?'

'Perfect.' Rory sat down next to Tavish and let him clamber onto his knee. 'Of course Cyril's death is going to affect you more than most, isn't it?'

'In what way?' Michelle knew exactly what he was getting at but wanted him to say it.

'You don't have to stick to his year-of-books clause. Although, to be fair, it's a good job Cyril wasn't popping in to check on you. Good job I wasn't holding you to it, either. But then I know when to compromise.'

Rory was looking at her, a challenge in his grey eyes, and she knew he meant the slow creep of bedlinen. She guessed he'd spoken to Anna. They'd probably had one of their 'woe is me' conversations about her and her Philistine ways.

The serenity of her sitting room gave way to a crackling tension; Rory's voice was polite, but she could tell that beneath it was genuine annoyance.

'Don't beat about the bush,' she said stiffly, handing him the glass. They could talk about this like adults, or more to the point, like solicitor and tenant, if that was how he wanted it. 'If it's been bothering you so much, why didn't you say something?'

'Because *technically*, I suppose you're not breaking the letter of agreement, but in a bigger sense, I guess I'm just disappointed.'

'Disappointed?' Michelle repeated. 'Who the hell are you to be disappointed?'

She'd met a lot of men with nerve in her days selling cars, but not one like Rory. Not one powered with turbo-charged self-righteousness the way he was. He ignored the temper in her voice and replied earnestly.

'If you're going to lose Longhampton's one point of warmth and intelligence then at least put something more interesting in there than more of your awful sexless bedding. Anna deserves better, for one. It's insulting, after all she's done. Bloody scatter cushions.'

Michelle's hackles rose. Being lectured about sexless beds by a man with a light sabre on his wall? She wished she hadn't given him the glass of wine. It would have been nice to pour it over him.

'I beg your pardon?' she said icily.

'What's the point? What are you giving the town with scatter cushions? I honestly thought you were committed to making the place work, the amount of time you and Anna spent getting it right. I guess I thought it meant something to you, the way it means something to me. And Anna. And the other regular customers.'

Michelle gave herself a moment to control the surge of furious adrenalin running through her body, but found she couldn't. It was too personal.

'Do you have *any* idea how smug and ignorant you sound?' she demanded. 'It's got nothing to do with you what I sell in that shop. The day I take business advice from a small town solicitor who doesn't even own his own *flat* is the day I know I've really run out of ideas.'

That seemed to hit a nerve. He put his glass down on the coffee table, deliberately ignoring the coaster.

'And I suppose you'll be wanting to hand Tavish over to me now he's not needed?' he said, deliberately provoking her.

Michelle narrowed her eyes. 'That's below the belt.'

'Really? It's fine for you to make mean comments. I'd be happy to have him. I expect the hairs have been driving you mad. And you don't need the *tie*, do you? The big scary emotional tie that stops you flying around the country collecting more meaningless *stuff*.'

'How dare you?' she started, but Rory hadn't finished.

'I mean, you could sell anything. Why not sell something that *means* something? Something that matters?'

'Like stories?'

'Books matter. They're an inspiration, an escape. Something bigger than we are . . .'

'Like stories. Great. That's really meaningful, isn't it?' she said sarcastically. 'Escapism. Wow. Because that really helps people. I might as well open an off-licence. Hey, get drunk and in the morning have all your problems to deal with plus a hangover. What is the difference between peddling people some totally unreal version of life, and selling them drugs?'

There was a distant voice in Michelle's head arguing back even as she was speaking, but she ignored it. Even the way Rory was looking at her – those grey eyes scrutinising her face as if he could read something in it, his foot wagging agitatedly where he'd crossed it over one long leg – even that was winding her up. He felt too masculine, too messy, too unpredictable in her house and she wanted him out, *out*, as soon as possible. But not in the same way she wanted Harvey out. She wasn't scared of Rory. She was just *infuriated* by him.

He opened his mouth to argue back, then stopped and wiped his face with one hand.

'Why are you so hard to help?' he demanded from behind it.

Michelle flinched. 'I'm not.'

'You are.' He peered out from between his fingers. The eyes were still fierce, but not hostile. 'I've known some control freaks in my time – I'm a property lawyer, for God's sake – but I've never know anyone so defensive.'

'You don't know me *at all*,' said Michelle.

'I do.' Rory threw a hand out, gesturing at the sitting room. 'Look at this place. You've got a beautiful house with absolutely no personality. No photographs, no art, no books, nothing that tells me anything about you. And that tells me everything! You don't *want* anyone to know you. You just want them to admire your taste. And those are two very different things.'

'That is such bollocks,' scoffed Michelle. 'You're not on *Judge John Deed* now, you know.'

'No, it's not bollocks. You've got a shop full of beautiful, meaningless clutter that encourages women with nothing in their lives to clutter up their own houses with more nothing. I mean, scatter cushions.'

Rory picked up a satin pin-tucked scatter cushion from the sofa and dangled it sarcastically in front of her.

'What is this for? Other than to arrange on your sofa?'

'It's to support your back,' said Michelle.

Rory tossed it on the floor, not letting his eyes drop from her face.

'Oh, very clever,' said Michelle.

He picked up another one, looked at her challengingly, and dropped it too.

'You want me to pick it up,' she said. 'But I'm not going to.'

Rory dropped the third cushion on the floor, and Michelle had to steel herself not to pick it up, but then he cast his eyes around the room until they fell on the flat bowl of shells on the coffee table.

They were a selection of cockle shells, butter-yellow cowries, tiny curly conches that Michelle had spent ages methodically arranging into size order, so they formed stripes of colour, order superimposed onto their natural randomness. Owen had asked her what the point of arranging them like that had been and she hadn't been able to come up with a reason; it had taken her mind off thinking about Harvey and her wasted youth, was the real answer.

'Like these,' said Rory. 'They're shells. They're meant to be scattered on a beach, not lined up in order of preference. Their charm is random and you've—'

'Don't,' said Michelle, knowing what he was about to do.

'Why not? Doesn't make them less lovely. If they were jumbled I'd think, hey, what an interesting souvenir from a holiday. I wonder where she went. I must ask her.' Rory held her gaze and Michelle felt a shiver of something inside her that sent the hairs on the back of her arms right up.

Again, keeping his eyes locked on hers, he reached out a hand and pushed his fingers into the shells, extending them until the lines began to jumble and blur. All that obsessive compulsion undone in one sweep of his pianist's hand. Then he flexed his fingers so they ran back through the shells, making them hush against the bowl. There was something curiously sensual about the movement and Michelle's stomach fluttered.

Then Rory went to tip the bowl over altogether and her resolve snapped.

'No,' she said, lunging forward to stop him emptying it onto the carpet.

She grabbed his arm, her fingers locking around his wrist, and he grabbed hers, to stop her falling onto the glass coffee table. The force of her movement nearly sent her into his lap and they both froze. Although they were only touching by his hand on her wrist, and hers round his, the connection felt much more intimate. The moment wobbled on a knife-edge.

Their mouths were very close together, and Michelle could taste Rory's breath. Her heart was thumping so fast it was making her want to pant, but she held her breath, desperate not to let him think she was panting with unbridled desire like some kind of Jilly Cooper stablegirl.

But the truth was that her insides seemed to have turned to fire, and her knees weren't much better. Blood was charging around her system as if released for the first time in years. She wanted to pant, because she really was breathless, but she kept on holding her breath, worried now about what Rory was tasting.

Did she smell nice? Was her breath fresh? It had been so long since anyone had passed a comment. He wasn't going to kiss her, though. She just had to work out how to get up without making this look embarrassing.

I want him to kiss me, wailed a plaintive voice in her head. *Kiss me!*

Rory's nose brushed hers and she realised he must have moved a fraction closer. Or maybe she had. But now their noses were definitely touching, their lips were open and she could feel his quick breath. He was breathing very hard, struggling to control himself.

And then Rory leaned forward the last, vital inch, and

kissed her. Michelle couldn't remember being kissed like this. His lips felt strange against hers, masculine but soft, and his skin's scent was different but familiar at the same time, and she leaned into him as if she'd been waiting for it for a long time.

Rory's hand cradled her face, barely touching her jaw, then slid into her hair. Michelle was kneeling by the sofa, and there were shells digging into her knees and probably breaking into the carpet, but those thoughts were only at the very back of her mind.

At the front of her mind, pushing everything else away, was Rory.

Michelle thought it was sad that in all the years she'd owned this sofa, she'd never realised how very comfortable it was to lie on. And how it could easily accommodate a six foot three man lying on it with you.

I should tell the manufacturers, she thought dreamily, as Rory's hand continued to stroke the long curve of her waist, dipping hopefully into the gap between her skirt and her shirt. It could be a major selling point.

She trailed her hand along the scratchy slope of his jaw and stopped him. 'No,' she said.

They'd kissed for a long time, but whenever he'd tried to take it further, she'd firmly stopped him, grabbing his wrist again, keeping his hands away from any zips and buttons. After a while he'd stopped trying, concentrating instead on the parts of her body that were exposed, and that had been . . . well, amazing enough.

'Michelle,' he said, 'don't take this the wrong way. But why is someone who kisses like that in a house like this?'

'What do you mean?'

'You know what I mean. You don't have an inner scatter cushion queen. And you said you weren't always so tidy. It was just giving up your job that made you decorate.'

Michelle looked up at the ceiling, although her eyes didn't see anything. She was seeing a different ceiling, the ceiling of her room at home, where she'd lain for a long summer, refusing to come out.

It was amazing that he'd listened to her. And remembered. *At this point I could make something up,* she thought. *This could be the fresh start moment when I step into a new life.*

She thought of Harvey. *When are you going to tell him? When are you going to come clean about what sort of person you are?*

If I tell Rory now, she thought, *he's got the option of not going any further.* It made her feel sick, but Rory was a solicitor. He knew much worse people than her, surely? Even if he thought she was disgusting, she couldn't be worse than some others he'd encountered.

Michelle's stomach lurched as she hoisted herself off the sofa and went upstairs to her spare room. It was pristine, as she'd left it, with a sweetshop sprinkling of bonbon-coloured scatter cushions on the unused double bed.

With one hand she swept them off, then reached under the mattress for her diary. Her hands touched the fabric of the cover and very slowly, she withdrew it, the leather ties still tightly secured.

This is it, she thought, weighing it in her hands. *The book that no one else but me has ever read. And the reason I wrote it was so that I wouldn't have to explain it now – just as if a future me told the past me to do it.*

But still, should she hand it over? Really, she barely knew Rory. But she had a feeling about him that she'd never had with anyone else, a feeling that whatever she told him wouldn't affect his opinion of her. He might ask questions and probe more than she'd like, but underneath that was a steady hum of something positive, trustworthy.

More than that, she wanted to tell someone. She didn't want her and Harvey to be the only people who knew any more.

30

*'The Secret Diary of Adrian Mole Aged 13¾ still
makes me laugh. My teenage diary was just like that.
Looking back, I edited shamelessly, even though I'd have
died if anyone but me had seen them.'* Katie Parkinson

'Here.' She passed the diary to Rory. 'Read this.'

'Read what?' He looked amused, then serious when he saw
her expression. 'What is this?'

'My diary.' Michelle spoke slowly, choosing her words very
carefully. 'I told you I was expelled. Well, it was a big scandal at
the time. It was in the papers. And it wasn't just for drinking,
like they reported. It was . . . worse than that. I tried to forget a
lot of what happened. I was in shock for a long time, and when
I came out of that, my mum made it pretty clear that she didn't
want to hear any of the sordid details, as she called them, and
warned me that if I wanted my dad to carry on loving me, I
should put it behind me and never mention it again.'

'But you wrote it down?'

'I wrote everything down in those days,' she said. 'That
saying about if no one hears a falling tree – that was me, when
I was a teenager. If I didn't write it down, it never happened.'

'So you were a closet writer?' he said, intrigued. 'And a
reader?'

Michelle nodded. It felt like talking about an old friend, not herself. 'Read all the time. I stopped because . . .' She tried to pin down a slippery thought that she'd never quite been able to articulate. 'Because when I came to read my diary again, right from the start, that girl wasn't me any more. The experiences were mine, but I wasn't the same person. I couldn't believe the words. And I'd been through such a nightmare – and it was a nightmare in the real sense of the word, it felt like it was happening to someone else – that reading about anyone else's stupid broken heart or misunderstanding felt pointless. Books felt like a cheat.'

Rory was silent. He looked at the book in his hands. 'You're sure you want me to read this?'

She nodded. 'I want you to know . . .' Michelle's lips had gone very dry and her tongue felt as if it was sticking to the roof of her mouth. 'Why. Why I had to start again, and control everything exactly the way I wanted it. I know I'm a control freak. But it's the only way I could cope.'

'Have you read this recently?'

She shook her head, repulsed by the thought of seeing those facts in her girlish handwriting again. 'Not since the day I wrote it. Well, I flicked through the early stuff, but I stopped. I don't want to read about the party. I know what happened.'

The party. It sounded so innocuous. It was only a word, a word she'd used a million times since, but now she was having a conversation about *the* party, for the first time in thirteen years, it stuck in her throat.

Michelle licked her lips.

Rory undid the ties and opened the book, then stopped.

He handed it back to her. 'I think you need to read this more than me,' he said. 'I don't need the details. I just need to hear what you want to tell me. Here.'

Her hands were shaking as she took it back off him, but she made herself start at the beginning of the Easter term.

It started off well enough, with Michelle getting good results in her mocks, and Ed Pryce taking the seat next to her in their weekly General Studies classes, causing her to spend all of Tuesday lunchtime doing and redoing her make-up in preparation.

There was a blip around February, when her three Valentine's cards turned out not to be from Ed, but from her dad, Owen, and some strange boy in the lower sixth who always had inky fingers, but things had picked up again as plans for Will Taylor's eighteenth birthday party started to thicken.

As usual Michelle noted that she'd skipped any reference to major world events of the time, but recorded in meticulous detail the political machinations of day boys (with access to parental drinks cabinets and venues) versus boarders (the popular, party-starting ringleaders). Ed, being head of house, was a boarder, but not the most popular boy in the set – something she seemed to find reassuring at the time, since the other girls had their sights set on the first rugby team.

3 April

Ate two Crunchies during last revision period. Hate myself, will never get thin. Ed asked me if I'd done something different with my hair when he walked me over to the dining hall, but Katherine said I'd just washed it with her shampoo, which I guess was funny at the time but it meant I only had about three minutes to talk to Ed properly before we went into lunch, so didn't manage to drop any hints about the party.

Daniel says his parents will be away on the Party Weekend, so we could go to their house and have a barbecue in their garden. Anthony keeps going on about us having the party down on the beach, though. He reckons it'll be closer to the school for getting back, so we can stay later, plus he can hide some booze down there beforehand. I like the beach idea. It's romantic. Katherine says the sand dunes are OK, but you need to take a blanket down if you don't want to be shaking sand out of your parts for the next two days. Was a bit shocked by that, to be honest – didn't think she'd done that but she says she has, with Anthony. She swore me to secrecy – he's on a warning already for smoking, and if he gets another suspension, he'll be expelled. Anyway, beach will be absolutely freezing probably so no chance of sand getting anywhere!

10 April – Party!!

Underneath that, in pencil, she'd written something in a hand so different it almost looked like someone else's writing. It shook and distorted on the page, smeared in places and angrily crossed out in others.

Writing this down, so I can get it out of my head, and seal up this diary and destroy it.

Went down to the beach with Katherine, Sophie and Marlene. We drank a bottle of wine in the study before we left. When we got there, Anthony had built a bonfire and half the lads were already pretty pissed. They'd been drinking on the bus back from the Austin Friars game, and kept chucking beer onto the fire.

There was a big cheer when we arrived, and I felt really

popular (ha!). Ed was there, wearing the black shirt that I really fancy him in, and his faded Diesel jeans. He looked so fit I couldn't believe he was even looking at me, let alone talking to me and smiling and being all attentive. God, I am so stupid.

Daniel had got a crate of beer from his dad, and nicked another one from their garage, so we started drinking straight away and eating marshmallows off the bonfire (my idea). It was getting dark, and cold, and we were all sitting close together, and I'd managed to get myself next to Ed. I was snuggled right up to him, and he put his arm round me.

I don't know if someone was putting something in the beer, but I don't remember the bit between starting to drink and being really drunk. I was basically lying in the sand feeling all blissed out and thinking what a lovely bunch of friends I had. Anthony was holding my hand on one side, Ed on the other. Then I remember feeling dizzy but horny, and thinking that maybe I should just grab Ed and kiss him, like in Riders. *As I turned to do that, I realised his arm wasn't round me any more. And he was turned away. He was snogging Katherine next to him. I hadn't even realised she was there. It was dark by now, and I couldn't make out a lot of what was going on, but I think pretty much everyone was snogging by then, and people kept getting up together and going into the dunes. Someone had a CD player and they were playing 'A Girl Like You' by Edwyn Collins. I can't stop hearing it.*

I thought I was going to be sick. My head was spinning, I needed a wee, and I was really, really cold in my stupid impress-Ed shirt. I managed to go off into the dunes, far enough away so no one would see me, and I had my jeans round my ankles when I heard a voice behind me, laughing and calling me a bad girl. Then someone pushed me onto my knees. I got seagrass in my face and in my nose, and I yelled that I was going to throw up, but the voice just said, you'll be fine, and then I felt something being shoved between my legs. I screamed because the sand was scratching inside me but Anthony wouldn't stop. He kept pushing and pushing, gripping me round the waist so I wouldn't move, and I did throw up and I tried to think about that, rather than what was going on between my legs, because that wasn't happening to me.

And then it was all over, and I lay in the sand, listening to the sea coming in and out, in and out, and I wanted to lift out of my body and float away on the tide. Anthony was lying next to me. He had his arm over me and it was really heavy. It felt like that was the only thing stopping me floating up to the stars.

I remember Katherine finding me and pulling my jeans back on. I remember laughing and crying at the same time because the sand scratched me and I told her she'd been right and she said I was weird. I remember Ed carrying me up to the cars, and me thinking it was ironic this was the only time I'd ever get him to do that, and I remember being sick again in my coat rather than on Mrs Nichols' back seat.

I don't remember anything else. And as of now, I don't remember this either.

Michelle closed the notebook. Her face was wet and the words blurred in front of her.

'What happened?' asked Rory gently.

'Someone raped me at a party,' whispered Michelle. 'I

didn't tell anyone about it because that would have made it real. And no one would have believed me anyway, because other people were doing it. A bunch of us got caught and it was pretty clear that there'd been sex going on, as well as drinking and some drugs. The papers called it a public school orgy but obviously they couldn't name names. I didn't tell my parents because being expelled was bad enough, as well as being caught drunk. I wasn't the kind of girl who did that. Let alone anything else. I wanted to forget all about it.' She swallowed. 'Because I didn't want to let one night define the rest of my life. I wanted a new life. A fresh one.'

'But you could have got counselling!'

'I did. For a bit. But I found it easier to pretend it hadn't happened.'

'What about the boy, though?' Rory seemed angry, a reaction Michelle hadn't expected for some reason. 'He should have been prosecuted!'

She shook her head.

'He should!'

'He was a boy. A stupid teenage boy who I'd kissed earlier. One of the popular ones. What was I going to say? That I was a geeky girl who felt flattered by the attention, right up to the point where I decided not to have sex?'

She hadn't written that down, Michelle noted. Editing even then. She'd missed out kissing Anthony, and also Daniel. Overwhelmed with the attention. Unreliable narrator.

'I didn't want to be that girl,' said Michelle. 'But I couldn't be the college student I was going to be either. So I went home and I was Daddy's star salesgirl for a bit. Then I was set up with Harvey and he must have realised he could make me into anything he wanted, and I let him. But he never stopped reminding me that I was the sort of tease who got drunk and led boys on. That I couldn't be trusted. Underneath it all.'

Rory said nothing, but he took the book off her, did the ties up tight, and threw it across the room. Then he put his arms around her and held Michelle while she cried into his shoulder, until her perfect eyeliner smeared all down her face.

He didn't kiss her. He held her in his arms, and he listened to her shame spilling out after so many years, and when he told her, in his soft Scottish voice, that things were going to be all right, that she was brave and clever and beautiful and everything a good woman was, she could almost believe him.

31

'Matilda is very very smart, but her parents are very stupid and don't know she has magic powers, and her teacher is so mean! A good book 10/10.' Lily McQueen

As November turned darker and damper, and the Christmas lights appeared between the street lamps, Anna noticed that the nightly march of bedlinen into the bookshop seemed to have stopped. She didn't take it up with Michelle, assuming this was the last reprieve before the new year, when everything would be swept out – and in any case, she didn't want to ask. Escaping to the bookshop each morning was the only thing she looked forward to any more.

Sarah's due date was approaching, and the incessant Skype calls between Becca and Sarah, as they compared bumps and stretch marks, were unbearable, despite the smile Anna plastered on for the camera. There was nowhere in the house where she couldn't hear the laughs and screeches from downstairs, and her worst fear was that Sarah would take the laptop into the home birthing pool with her and they'd all have to sit round it and watch.

Anna knew she was tormenting herself, but she couldn't get the thought out of her head – that *she'd* let Becca down. To have the shaming evidence of her parenting failure on one side of the screen while the real mother paraded her fecundity on the other felt like a particularly mean punishment.

Anna longed to make it up to Becca somehow, but she couldn't, because Becca wasn't even there any more. Owen had asked her to move into the flat above Home Sweet Home at the beginning of November, and she'd gone, with all her books and her guitar and her dry sense of humour that kept Anna sane. Anna had offered to take her to her scans and midwife appointments, but Becca had insisted, kindly, that Owen would go with her.

'I know Dad's just waiting for him to do a bunk,' she explained. 'He can hardly think that if he's the one learning breathing exercises with me. And anyway, we can't both leave the bookshop, can we?'

Michelle had given Becca a full-time job between the bookshop and Home Sweet Home, fulfilling the Christmas internet orders and taking charge of restocking. Anna was grateful for the practical way Michelle was helping, but she couldn't quite bring herself to have a proper conversation with her about it, not with those angry words still hanging between them. Once upon a time, the idea of the pair of them hovering over a cradle like hopelessly unqualified fairy godmothers would have made them both roar with laughter – how bad could they be? – but now they were polite, and that was about it.

With no one to talk to any more, Anna's sadness flooded her. The slightest emotional nudge and tears spilled out of her like an overfilled glass, sending her into the back room of the shop whenever someone brought in a baby or discussed Michael Morpurgo animal stories. It was bad enough coping with Becca, but with every empty day that passed, she was forced to face the horrible truth that her marriage seemed to be over, too. Phil, cold and distant, seemed oblivious to her misery, and they passed each other like strangers in the house, while Chloe sang louder and Lily begged for more stories to fill up the growing silence.

Anna phoned Becca most nights that she wasn't round at the McQueens, 'just to check she was OK'.

'Where's Owen?' she asked, one Friday night in early December, tucking the phone under her ear while she scooped out Pongo's kibble with one hand and switched on the kettle with the other.

'He's gone to London for a meeting.' Becca sounded more relaxed out of the house than she'd ever done in it. 'He's trying to get some work going so he can move to Cambridge with me after the baby's born – tell Dad he's really trying hard, OK?'

'Are you sure you don't want me to come round?'

'No! I'm looking forward to putting my feet up, actually. I've got a bar of chocolate and my book. Don't ask what though. It's pure trash fiction. This baby wants romance and Dairy Milk.'

Anna smiled sadly. 'As long as you're reading. Give me a shout if you need anything.'

'I will.' Becca's voice changed. 'Why don't you go out? Take Dad to the movies or something?'

Anna blinked hard to stop her voice changing too. 'I can't. He's out tonight with some guys from work. Leaving do, I think. He didn't say, just that he'd be back late.'

'And he didn't take you? Charming. I'll tell him to make it up to you this weekend!'

'There's no need.' Anna didn't want Becca to know how bad things were between her and Phil. Not even bad. Just . . .

nothing. Two people who worked together in a parenting office, but with less chance of an office romance.

She shook herself. 'Listen, you enjoy your night in and I'll see you tomorrow. Chloe's making some kind of baby shower parcel for your mum and she wants your help. By which she means, your twenty quid.'

'As long as she's not recording a song for the baby. Can you imagine her lullaby album? Night, Anna.'

While Anna had been talking, Lily had appeared, snaking her hand round Anna's arm. She looked up at her now, already changed into her pyjamas even though it was just gone six. 'Are you ready for a story? I chose a new book at the shop. I thought it might be good for Chloe.'

'I was humouring you,' came a voice from the sofa. 'But if Anna's making cocoa I might come up and listen for a bit. Until something good's on telly.'

It was moments like this, thought Anna, which kept her in the house, in this family. Only just, though. They were tiny clothes pegs that stopped her blowing away altogether.

Anna lay awake, listening to Phil snoring, and decided that from now on, she was going to start each night in Becca's old bed, instead of creeping in there at 2 a.m. each morning. Who was she fooling, anyway? It wasn't as though either of them were missing anything.

Phil had rolled in at half one, after his leaving do, reeking of beer. He never used to drink beer, priding himself on his preference for wine. It was just in the last few months he'd suddenly overcome his aversion to it.

She swung her feet out of bed and pulled on her dressing gown grumpily. If she was going to be kept awake, then she might as well be reading in peace.

Anna padded quietly down the stairs to make herself a milky drink, and was passing the hall phone when it rang.

She grabbed it almost absent-mindedly, trying to work out what time it was in America. Had Sarah forgotten the time difference?

'Anna!' It was Becca and her voice sounded ragged. 'Anna, I've been trying your mobiles for ages.'

'What's the matter?' Her brain sprang into wakefulness. 'Are you all right?'

'I feel terrible. I've been puking all night and I've hurt my ankle. Owen's in London, and I can't get up. I'm really worried about the baby.' Becca dissolved into tears.

'Don't worry, I'm coming,' said Anna, turning to run back up the stairs. 'I'll be right there.'

She dashed upstairs two at a time, trying not to wake Lily or Chloe.

'Phil.' She shut the bedroom door behind her. She shook his shoulder till he woke. 'Phil.'

'What?' He rolled over, bleary-eyed and annoyed.

'Becca's sick. I've got to go over there.'

He sat up at once. 'Shit. Where's Owen?'

'London.'

'What the hell's he doing in London? He should be looking after her.' He tried to get up but lost his balance and fell back heavily onto the bed.

'Stay here with Lily and Chloe,' said Anna. 'I'll go. I'll call you.'

Phil looked at her resentfully. 'I'm her dad. *I* should go.'

'What difference does that make? And you can't drive in that state. How much did you put away tonight?'

'Don't start.'

He glared at her. He didn't look like the man she'd married, thought Anna, with a stab of misery. He looked like some random middle-aged man who didn't even like her. And if she stayed for Lily, until she left, she had another nine years of this.

'I'll call you,' she said.

Anna drove like a mad thing to the high street and let herself in with the spare key.

'Becca?' she yelled, running up the stairs. 'Becca?'

'Bathroom.'

Anna pushed open the door to the bathroom and found her wedged between the bath and the loo. The air smelled of vomit and Becca's face was grey, with tiny flakes of loo roll stuck to her lip. 'Poor darling!'

'I was throwing up, then I slipped and hurt my ankle and now I'm stuck.' She started to cry.

'How long have you been here?' Anna asked, lifting her up gently.

'Since eleven. I texted everyone but my reception kept fading and I don't think they all went through. Then my phone died and I couldn't move . . .' Becca's hand went to her stomach. 'If I've done something to the bean, I'll never forgive myself,' she hiccupped. 'It's my fault.'

'That's motherhood for you,' said Anna, stroking her hair and wiping her face. 'It's always your fault. Now I'm taking you to the hospital, no arguments.'

Phil joined them in A&E, having left Lily with Chloe under strict instructions to return to bed and not put on her *Glee* DVD – itself tantamount to an invitation and a bribe at the same time.

He looked grey with worry, and when the nurse was showing Becca to the loo, he grabbed Anna's hand.

'Is she OK?' he asked. 'What happened?'

Anna filled him in on the details she'd gathered – a prawn curry Becca thought couldn't hurt, the vomiting, the sprained ankle, the all-clear with the baby – and relief swept his face.

'That's it, she's coming home,' he said. 'There's no way I can leave her in that flat on her own.' Phil had his paterfamilias expression on – a bit late, Anna thought – and had obviously been rehearsing on the way over. 'I won't be happy unless I know she's safe. She's moving back in.'

'You realise Owen's going to want to be with her too?' Anna pointed out.

'Fine!' Phil raised his hands. 'The more the merrier! We've got room.'

'Not really.' Anna's head swam at the thought of all the cooking and cleaning required for Becca and Owen, Lily, Chloe, the various Apricotz who always seemed to need feeding, Pongo, and her and Phil. The house wasn't small but when they'd bought it, they hadn't had a family that big in mind.

'It's family. That's what life's like with a big family.' He didn't add, 'Isn't that what you always wanted?' but the implication was there.

Anna stared at him, and he glared back. Around them, hugely pregnant women were wheeled past by their beaming, dazed husbands; others were carrying pink new babies in their arms.

Anna thought of Becca's baby, only a few months away now. That made seven – seven, and definitely no chance of eight – and she wondered just how much more she was expected to bear.

On 5 December, Sarah had a little boy called Henry Graham Boston Rogers, 8lb 3oz.

Henry after Jeff's father; Graham after hers. No one wanted to think too hard about the Boston part.

Since Sarah left a webcam in the baby's room, Chloe, Becca and Lily were on Skype constantly, staring at their new half-brother as if he and they were on some sort of television programme. Anna developed an immunity to the sound of transatlantic baby crying, but inside it felt as if someone was peeling the skin off her heart. Henry's surprised face and wispy duckling hair were everywhere: on the fridge, on cards, in emails. The house felt crowded. Becca's bump was getting bigger by the day, and there never seemed to be a room that didn't contain a pregnancy magazine or something Sarah had sent from America to help with stretch marks or morning sickness.

Phil said nothing. Now he barely even looked at her, and she spent most evenings on the sofa, or upstairs in Lily's room, reading *What Katy Did* and *The Little Prince*, and flinching at all the messages about love that seemed so clear.

It was while she was packing the girls' bags for their Christmas visit to their mother that Anna made up her mind: while they were away, she would move into the flat above the shop. Just for a few days until she worked out what she wanted to do.

She had Becca's keys already. She knew she should call Michelle, but decided it wasn't worth trying to have a personal conversation with someone in the grip of a new relationship. Michelle and Rory were at the bantering, dewy-eyed stage of first dates, and it added a new edge to Anna's isolation.

Michelle was the only person she could have confided in: it was a dilemma she didn't dare reveal to a parent. How could she leave the stepchildren who needed her, who she'd signed up for from the start, for the sake of a child who didn't even exist? Anna thought about ringing the Samaritans, but she felt ashamed to ask even them.

She knew it was selfish, but she also knew, deep down, that being a second-string mother wasn't enough for her. Especially when their father didn't seem to care. Leaving Phil was easy; leaving his children was the hardest part.

There was no room in the car to the airport for Anna, since Owen was going to Sarah's for Christmas too, so she said her goodbyes in the house, with the usual tears all round. Anna couldn't make hers stop.

'No books this year,' she said, hugging Lily as she handed her the bags she'd packed with presents. 'Don't worry, it's wishlist stuff only.'

'But I wanted books,' said Lily. 'Didn't you see my wishlist?'

Anna wiped her nose. 'Well, there's always the sales.'

'Bye, Anna,' said Chloe. 'Or should I say, *so long, farewell, auf Wiedersehen, good-byeeeeee*?' She added a theatrical flourish and narrowly missed backhanding Becca in the face. Her new ambition for the year was to audition for a West End musical.

'It's going to be very quiet without you,' Anna gulped. 'Bye, Becca.'

'Have a lovely time without us.' Becca hugged her hard and Anna felt the firm pressure of her baby bump against her stomach, and had to squeeze her eyes tightly shut.

'Everyone ready?' Phil jangled his keys and avoided her eye.

When the door closed behind them, Pongo went sadly to his bed in the kitchen, his tail between his long legs, and Anna went upstairs to pack.

32

'The Children of Green Knowe *is a story about a lonely boy who goes to live with his great-grandmother in a mediaeval house in the Fens. It is still one of the most magical, atmospheric and moving books I have ever read.'* Kate Parkin

Michelle was looking forward to Christmas for the first time in years, but she didn't have time to do half of her usual decorating. Normally she set aside two weekends to wind the garlands around the banister, fix pine cones along the mantlepieces and make her Christmas cards, as well as trimming the tree and pinning stars and baubles into place. It took hours and hours, and felt more Christmassy than the lonely day itself, despite what she'd pretended to Anna in the past.

This year, Michelle had only time to get a tree, and that was it. Even the tree was a last-minute panic; things were so busy in both shops she hadn't had time to order her usual majestic pine from the specialist, and her evenings were taken up with Rory and Tavish. In the end, they'd grabbed the last wonky fir in the garden centre on their way back from a country walk and pub lunch, stuffing it unceremoniously into the back of her car, much to Tavish's disgust at the needles in his car crate.

Michelle looked at the lopsided tree, relatively plain with just gold baubles and a big gold star, and decided that she liked it. Minimalist. Like the minimal decor in the house this year. An under-decorated home, she decided, was a busy, happy one.

Her mother had started the guilt trip about where she'd be spending Christmas early in December, but Michelle had got her story straight, thanks to a surprise present from Rory.

'Would you like to go to Paris for Christmas?' he asked, coming into Home Sweet Home one lunchtime. 'It's just that I've always wanted to go to Notre Dame on Christmas Day and if I go on my own, I'll look like a sad man from an E. M. Forster novel.'

'And if you go with me?'

'I'll look like the romantic hero in a Richard Curtis film.'

'Are you saying that because you think I can only do films?' said Michelle, ignoring Gillian's 'wedding hat' face behind Rory. 'I've actually read *The Da Vinci Code*, you know. I know about Paris.'

Rory winked at her, but underneath the teasing, she knew he was thinking about what she'd told him about Harvey, and about her nightmare family Christmases. He'd been horrified by them too, and had obviously been thinking about how he could rescue her.

'I'm going to see Zachary the weekend before,' he added, before she could ask. 'Let's get the family duty done first, then we can enjoy the holiday.'

'Ho ho ho,' said Michelle, and smiled.

The following weekend, she took the bull by the horns, packed her car full of presents and drove down to her parents' to surprise them.

Her mother wasn't that thrilled to be surprised. She was,

she explained, right in the middle of making a complicated trifle, with two kinds of custard and fruit layers, for some dinner party the following night. Michelle looked at the apparatus, arranged on the kitchen counters like a set of operating instruments, and for once she didn't feel like a domestic failure. It just looked like a lot of washing-up. For a trifle.

'Michelle!' Charles looked pleased to see her. He was restricted to a corner of the kitchen, thanks to the freshly mopped floor, but he stood up and opened his arms and mimed a hug.

'Shoes off, please,' snapped Carole as Michelle went to hug him. 'Well, this is an honour. We weren't expecting to see you without at least four phone calls first. Is there something wrong?'

'No. It's just that I won't be here for Christmas Day,' she said, 'so I've brought everyone's presents now.'

'Oh, not again? I thought after last year you might make the effort – to help me, if nothing else.' Her mother looked cross, apparently forgetting that Ben and Jonathan regularly begged to be allowed to have Christmas on their own. 'And please don't tell me you're helping out in an old people's home. At least be honest and say you're spending the day in bed watching films.'

'No, I'm going to Paris,' said Michelle happily. 'Minibreak.'

'Paris?' The crossness turned to sympathy. 'You can't go to Paris on your own, not for *Christmas*. Is it one of those singles' events? Because you could be *here* with—'

'I won't be on my own, Mum,' said Michelle. 'I'm going with a friend.'

'Really? I thought your friend had that complicated family situation? Won't she be with them?'

'No, Carole.' Michelle's father stepped in before Michelle

could reply. 'It'll be a bloke. Paris at Christmas – how romantic, Michelle.'

'We're staying in the Marais. I've never been. Apparently the shops are gorgeous. Although,' she added, 'I've been told I'm not allowed to do much shopping. Even if anything's open.'

'That sounds marvellous,' said Charles. 'Good for you. Any room for a little one?'

'Don't even joke, Charles. I need all hands on deck. Ooh. Is that the phone?' said Carole, tipping her head to one side.

'I don't think so,' said Charles. 'Would you like your hearing aid turned up?'

'I don't have one. As you well know. I think it was the phone. Will you excuse me?'

Michelle knew from the artificial way her mother was pantomiming concern for the phantom missed phone call that she was up to something; it didn't take much to work out what.

'Dad . . .' she said casually, when Carole had scurried out – if her mother was putting in a call to Harvey, she didn't have much time before he appeared at the front door, all smiles and tactics – 'this is a bit awkward, but a friend of mine bought a car from the Kingston dealership, and she had a bit of a problem with the money side of things. She was charged for something she didn't get, or there was some issue with the finance agreement? Anyway, she was worried that something didn't seem quite right about it all, so I said I'd mention it, find out what was going on.'

'I hope you told her we'd put things right,' said Charles. He seemed uneasy. 'That's not the first time someone's mentioned Kingston to me. The accountants weren't very happy with the last quarter, between you and me.'

'Really?' It wasn't a complete fabrication; Michelle had rung one of the girls she used to work with at the main dealership for a chat, on the hunch that Harvey might have something to cover up. You didn't buy new cars like his on commission alone; it must have cost five times what hers had, and she knew what commission she'd been earning.

Michelle hated seeing her dad worried, but it was better than the alternative; letting Harvey get away with scamming him. 'I thought I'd tell you rather than Harvey so there's no embarrassment if someone is ... up to something. I know what a team player he is.'

'That's thoughtful.' Charles was reading her face shrewdly. He knew what she was trying to say; they didn't always have to put things into words. 'I could do with someone like you to oversee all this,' he said, with a hopeful smile. 'No chance of persuading you back, I suppose?'

'Not at the moment.' For an instant Michelle panicked that Harvey had been telling the truth – that her dad *was* ill and *did* want them to take over to let him retire. But his expression was concerned, not exhausted.

'Thought not,' he sighed. 'Had to ask, though. From a selfish point of view, there's no one else I'd rather see running it, but I'm glad you've got your own business. It's good to grow something for yourself. We've been telling everyone about that website of yours. I think your mother must have sent everyone in the golf club a what do you call it? A link.'

'Really?' said Michelle. 'Mum was telling people?'

'She was.' Charles ignored Carole's clean floor and came over to put his arms around his daughter. 'I don't tell you enough, Michelle, but we're so proud of you. I know things weren't easy after that business at school, but the way you've pulled yourself up, and worked so hard ... That means a lot more to an uneducated grafter like your dad than just getting on some corporate escalator. Don't tell your brothers.'

'I won't.' Michelle was moved. It was the first time he'd ever referred directly to her expulsion. She'd never even mentioned it to him after it happened, much less discussed the reason for it. She wondered what had prompted it now. 'But I'm sorry, Dad. For embarrassing you and Mum. For wasting that money and time and . . .'

'What? You're apologising for that? To be perfectly honest, love, we blamed ourselves for years. Your mother and I . . . Well, we had a bit of a falling-out before we sent you there. It doesn't matter now, all water under the bridge, but your mother didn't want you and Owen listening to us arguing. We thought a school like that would be the best place, till we worked things out.' He seemed determined to get it out, though he clearly felt uncomfortable.

'You were arguing?' A door opened in Michelle's head, and suddenly she saw it from an adult's perspective. 'That was why Mum was away a lot?'

'I'm afraid so. But you see, we patched it up. It's probably why your mother's so keen for you to try again with Harvey. She knew how bad things were for us, but we pulled it around.'

'Dad,' said Michelle, only just keeping the tears out of her voice. 'Harvey and I . . . It's not like you and Mum. Please believe me.'

'We shouldn't have sent you away,' he said, his voice crackling.

Charles held her at arm's length. His weathered face, toughened by years in the sun and rain of garage forecourts, tensed with emotion, and she could see tears around the edges of his eyes.

She looked into his familiar old face and wondered if he

knew. He would never have said. But there was something in his eyes that hinted at a sharper pain; that something had happened to his golden girl that he hadn't been allowed to fix. Not even allowed to try.

He pulled her into his chest again and said, sadly and fiercely, into her hair. 'It doesn't matter how old you are, Michelle, you'll always be my little girl. My perfect little girl. There's *nothing* you could do that would stop us loving you. I'd go to the end of the world and back for you.'

She hugged him tight. 'I know. I know.'

For a second, she was eighteen again, when there was nothing her wise, bullish father couldn't sort out with his money or his contacts or his savvy. But Michelle didn't want to go back. Now she was her own fixer and sorter. It had taken a long time to get there.

'What's going on in here?'

Carole appeared at the kitchen island, the cordless phone ostentatiously in her hand. It looked like a prop.

'Bit of seasonal emotion,' said Charles, reaching into his pocket for a spotted hanky. 'Just telling Michelle here how proud we are of her.'

'Of course we are,' said Carole. Her face didn't quite match the words. 'And we'd be even more proud if—'

'Carole!'

'What? You don't know what I'm going to say.'

'I do, Mum,' said Michelle. She tried to temper her words by thinking of what her dad had just told her. 'You say it every time I come here. And the answer is, sometimes things can't be fixed. Sometimes, with the best will in the world, they're just not right.'

'I can say what I think in my own house, Michelle.'

Michelle looked at her mother and wished she could tell

her. But Harvey had spent much longer charming her than she had.

'Anyway, this hanky?' said Charlie, shaking it out to blow his nose. 'The ones you gave me for Christmas last year? Best present I got. You always did know what people needed before they knew themselves. Even when you were little.' He smiled, and Michelle gulped.

'Did you say you'd brought presents for Ben's children?' Carole asked. 'Is it a good idea to leave them in the car?'

'I'll go and get them,' said Michelle. She saw her parents exchange a silent eyebrow raise and frown, and knew that Harvey was probably on his way over to 'drop in'. She was prepared for that, though. She'd rehearsed it with Rory until she was confident she could deliver it calmly.

Although that had been at home, in her lovely ordered house with swans outside and Tavish inside. She scanned the street nervously for signs of Harvey's car, then shook herself. She could do this.

'Oh, Michelle, you've gone a bit overboard,' her mother said reproachfully when she brought in the fourth bag of ribbon-tied gifts. 'What if the boys haven't got as much for you? They'll be embarrassed.'

'I'm sure you can manage it,' Michelle said. 'They always get me the same thing anyway. Space NK voucher from Ben, Argos voucher from Jonathan. Is that meant to be a joke, by the way? Because you can tell him I always end up spending it on printer cartridges.'

Have I caught Anna's reckless tongue syndrome? she wondered. Because it was all coming out now.

Carole sighed. 'It'll be so quiet this year. You won't be here, Owen isn't coming . . .'

'Owen's got his priorities right,' said Charles. 'He's where he should be, spending Christmas with the in-laws. Getting to know his new family.' He beamed at Michelle. 'Very charming, aren't they? Lovely girl, Becca.'

'*If* you think that's the right thing to be getting involved with,' muttered Carole. 'Teenage mothers . . .'

'Mum, you weren't much older when you had Ben,' said Michelle. Another door opened; was that why she and her dad had hit that bump? Had Carole got to her mid-forties with four children and wondered where her life had gone?

'I was *married*. And I wasn't trapping your father into anything – I'm sorry, but it's true. I'm only saying what everyone else is thinking.' Her face was alive with self-righteous disapproval and Michelle felt sorry for Owen. And for Becca. And for Anna. Maybe if her mother was now sharing her disapproval between her and Owen it might lessen the impact for both of them, but she doubted it.

'I don't think Owen is being *trapped* into anything,' she said. 'She's got a place at Cambridge to read law – that's more than Owen managed! And I can think of much worse families to be trapped in than Anna's. Anna's the best mother-in-law anyone could wish for. She's . . .'

Michelle would have said something else if the doorbell hadn't rung.

'I wonder who that is?' said Carole, stopping just short of putting a finger on her chin.

'Oh, for God's sake,' muttered Michelle. She marched through to the door and opened it. 'Merry Christmas, Harvey.'

To no one's surprise Harvey was standing there, carrying a bunch of flowers with the Waitrose sticker still attached. He was wearing a Santa-patterned tie with his expensive shiny Hugo Boss suit, and it made Michelle loathe him a little bit more.

'Hi, all, I was just passing and . . . Shelley!' he said, opening his arms wide. 'Great to see you!'

There was an unpleasantly triumphant gleam in his eyes, but Michelle forced herself to think of Rory, and the kind, logical way he'd helped her put her thoughts in order. Reminding her that those thoughts were, it turned out, important, and not the ramblings of a neurotic woman.

'Shall I go and put the kettle on for a cup of tea and a mince pie?' asked Carole, to no one.

Charles gave Harvey a long look, then said, 'I'll give you a hand. Mince pie, anyone?'

'As long as they're homemade!' Harvey said with an obsequious smile.

He thinks I'm here to roll over, thought Michelle, and she sizzled with a rare moment of advantage.

'For you,' he said, pushing the spiky white bouquet into her hands. Michelle looked down at the aggressive chrysanthemums and wilted foliage and felt sorry for it.

'How did you know I was here?' she asked. 'Aren't they for Mum?'

'Don't tell her, then.' Harvey flashed her a confident smile. 'I think she'd be happy for me to give them to you. If I'd known you were here I'd have brought your Christmas present.'

'I've got yours. You can have it now.' Michelle looked at the flowers in her hand and put them on the sideboard, as if she didn't really care what happened to them, then went into the hall to find the small parcel she'd wrapped for Harvey.

It had the same neatly tied and taped silver ribbon and bow on it as the rest. She wasn't going to make a point that way.

'Shall I open it now, or save it till the big day?' asked Harvey as she handed it over. 'Are you going to be here? Will we have that pleasure?'

''Fraid not, no,' she said. 'I'll be in Paris. You can open it now if you want.'

He hesitated, not sure what to make of her tone.

'Go on,' said Michelle, before he could ask about her trip. 'Open it. It's a book.'

'A book? Well, well, well. Talk about born-again intellectuals.' Harvey started to undo the ribbon and Michelle braced herself for his reaction.

'*How to Lose Friends and Alienate People*?' He looked up.

'Probably not a lot in there that you don't already know, but I thought you might like the ending,' said Michelle.

Harvey's affability evaporated. 'Is this your idea of a joke?'

'Sort of.' Michelle raised her chin to hold his hostile gaze. 'I was going to give you *Divorce for Dummies*, but I thought you might already have that.'

'What?'

'You should be getting the divorce petition in the next day or two. Sorry about the timing but I think a new year, new start's best for both of us. Let's get things moving.'

'And if I don't want to divorce? If I want to try again, with my *wife*? Don't those vows mean anything to you?' Harvey looked martyred but angry at the same time. 'I *love* you, Michelle.' He made it sound more like an accusation.

'Let's drop that. This isn't about love,' said Michelle quietly. 'You don't love me. If you loved me, you'd let me go. I don't know whether you want control of my dad's business, or control of me, or both. You know that's what it comes down to, and so do I. But it's not what I want, and you can't control me any more. I want a divorce.'

'You know it'll all come out if it goes to court?' he said, his tone turning spiteful. 'You'll have to prove I'm unreasonable, and actually, *you're* the one with mental health problems, you're the one who was in therapy all those years. I'm only thinking about you, Shelley. Do you want your private life dragged in front of everyone? Our friends brought in to testify about your unhinged behaviour?'

'Do you want your business arrangements dragged in front of everyone?' she hissed back.

Harvey stepped back as if she'd spat at him. 'I beg your pardon?'

'Your business arrangements. I've been taking legal advice. We'd have to have our joint finances checked out for any settlement, so if you want this to go to court, fine. I'm sure you've got nothing to hide in that department, have you?' She left it hanging.

Harvey didn't flinch, but his eyes weren't as confident as before. They were making tiny movements, as if he was thinking fast.

'I mean, what were you planning to drag out about me?' said Michelle. 'I was *raped* when I was eighteen. I didn't kill anyone, I didn't steal anything, I didn't hurt anyone. I only told you because I loved you and I wanted to share my biggest secret with you, so you'd understand why I was how I was. I didn't think you'd spend the next seven years making sure I stayed that way. Now I realise it should never have been a secret in the first place.'

As soon as she'd told Rory, and watched his face freeze with sympathy and horror, not disgust, it was as if a spell had been broken. Michelle was suddenly flying above the scene, seeing it again as if it had happened to someone else, and her heart broke for different reasons. She'd shaped her life around the one night, like a tree growing crookedly around a wall, growing only to cover it up, never branching outwards. Just inwards.

Harvey wasn't going to give up so easily. 'And how do you

think your dad would react if he found out that his princess had been keeping that secret from him all this time? Eh? Think about it.' He curled his lip. 'Wouldn't take much to tell him. Might make him wonder what else you've been keeping from him all these years. Like why you decided to run away from his business so quickly?'

Michelle steeled herself. 'I should have done this a long time ago, and I'm sorry I didn't,' she said. 'Start again. Find someone else. I don't want money or the house, I just want Flash. You've had him for the last three years. Let me have him now and keep everything else.'

'You're not capable of looking after him,' said Harvey nastily. 'You can't even keep your own legs closed. Little sluts like you never change, but they always get what they deserve. You just watch. Your dad might think you're something special, but your mother doesn't. She knows the real you. Just like I do.'

Michelle heard something clatter to the floor behind her, then roll along the floorboards and crack. It sounded like a plate of mince pies. Harvey's face froze, then flushed a dark red.

'Out,' said a voice behind her, a voice so sharp with rage Michelle barely recognised it. 'Get out of this house *right now* before I throw you out.'

She turned and saw her mother standing in the hall, her eyes furious. She seemed bigger, suddenly. Like a lioness.

Harvey only hesitated a second, then he turned and left.

Carole gazed at Michelle for a long second, her face freezing, then contorting with shame, and then she opened her arms wide.

33

'My favourite Jilly Cooper novel will always be Rivals.
If Rupert Campbell-Black can find true love (after
bonking his way round Britain!), then I reckon anyone
can have a happy ever after…'   Michelle Nightingale

Once she was back in her own home, in her own life, the only thing Michelle really wanted was a hot chocolate and half a slice of cake with Anna to put things right, like the old days, but Anna was impossible to get hold of.

They were both working flat out, Michelle in Home Sweet Home and Anna next door, with Becca and Chloe helping, but instead of hanging around for the daily debrief as they'd done in the early days, Anna was out of the shop before the 'closed' sign stopped swinging. She'd stopped giving Michelle pages of suggestions for community activities, and wasn't even updating the reviews on the website any more. As far as Anna was concerned, it seemed from the rather formal Christmas card Michelle had got in the post – not hand-delivered – that they were work-mates. Not mates.

It wasn't that Anna was actively rude to Michelle, but for someone as warm and interested as she usually was, her civility felt worse than outright insults. The sparkle in her face had gone and her shoulders slumped with a permanent sadness that Michelle couldn't bear. She couldn't share her happy amazement about Rory when Anna was clearly so miserable with Phil, and for the first time she realised how Anna must have felt on the other side of the happiness fence, watching her trudge on, refusing to discuss it. Michelle didn't have Anna's natural way of teasing out a problem, and she was scared of making things worse.

Even Rory had to admit defeat. 'I tried to ask her if she fancied a pre-Christmas sherry with the Reading Aloud team. But she wasn't having it. Too busy,' he told Michelle one evening, bewildered by Anna's unusual lack of enthusiasm.

The manic shopping days to Christmas passed in a blur of Dean Martin and mulled wine and pine-scented candles and beeping tills. Normally Michelle would have stayed in the shop right up to Christmas Eve, getting her lonely Christmas fix from the decorations and Carols from Kings, but this year Rory insisted on her handing the keys to Gillian on the twenty-second and leaving the festive spirit to him.

'She's coming to Paris with me, Gillian,' he said firmly. 'If you need anything, it can wait until the day after Boxing Day.'

'Unless the shop's burning down,' said Michelle. 'Or there's a break-in. Or if Tavish is ill. Or—'

'I'll deal with it,' said Gillian. 'I have my instructions.'

Rory glanced quickly at Michelle. 'If there is a problem with Tavish you can call. But my mobile. Not hers.'

Four days in Paris passed too quickly for Michelle. She and Rory walked through empty starlit streets late at night, holding hands and saying nothing while the church clocks chimed the hour; they ate croissants and drank hot coffee during the day, gobbling up the intricate old churches and the frosted gardens, and behaving more like goofy teenagers on a school trip than thirty-somethings on a first weekend away together.

It was awkward sometimes. Rory seemed determined to pass on every shred of knowledge he had about Parisian architecture whether Michelle wanted to hear it or not, and she couldn't quite undo so many years of physical self-consciousness overnight. But he was patient, and she was determined to step outside the defences she'd built up, and so they inched their way past the scratchy moments. The occasional silences that fell in between the croissants and kisses were comfortable, like the softest cashmere blanket, and she felt safe but adventurous in a way she'd always dreamed grown-up life would be.

She wasn't sure, not having references beyond the works of Jilly Cooper, but Michelle thought she might be falling in love. And from the way Rory looked at her, with the quiet adoration and semi-bewilderment she'd read about, she wondered if he was too.

New Year's Eve was a bright but chilly day, with a whisper of snow in the pale sky. A perfect morning, in other words, for walking a dog. Or, if you were two friends who used to go dog-walking together all the time, two dogs.

Michelle stood on the McQueens' front doorstep with Tavish next to her in his Christmas tartan coat, rehearsing what she was going to say when Anna opened the door.

'*No arguments, we're going for a coffee.*' A bit bullying? She might be busy getting the house ready for the girls coming back.

'*I've got you a present from Paris!*' True. But excuse-y.

'*Hey! Has your phone been off?*' Also true. But a bit pointed.

Michelle frowned. Why did she feel so nervous? Why was she even thinking of excuses – surely she didn't need one?

The door opened and she was surprised to see Phil standing there. He was in his dressing gown, his hair unwashed and flattened, and for a moment Michelle wondered if she'd interrupted a romantic lie-in, but the beaten expression on his face said otherwise. Phil looked as if he had a hangover that extended to every part of his body.

'Merry Christmas,' she said, then stopped. 'Phil, are you all right? You look terrible. Sorry.'

'If you've come to see Anna, she's not here.' He ran a hand over his stubbly chin.

'Oh. Is she at her parents'?'

'No.' He hesitated, then admitted, 'She's in the flat above the shop.'

'What? Owen's flat?'

He nodded.

'Since when?' Michelle couldn't believe she hadn't noticed, but then neither she nor Rory had been spending much time there in the last few days.

'Since the day we took the girls to the airport. Since before Christmas.'

Michelle stared at Phil's Weetabix-encrusted dressing gown and felt an awful dread. 'I think I'd better come in,' she said, stepping over the threshold.

Michelle made a pot of tea – as Anna would have done – and listened with a sinking heart as Phil spilled out the depressing details of their Christmas.

Perfunctory meal, no conversation, film in silence, then Anna clingfilming the leftovers and going back to the flat.

'She says it's for the best,' said Phil, staring at his tea. 'She says it's not about the girls, it's about me and her. She doesn't want to let them down, but she can't see a future with me.'

'And did you try to stop her?'

'I couldn't. She'd made up her mind.'

Michelle smacked the table so Phil had to look up. 'You don't deserve her, you know that? Of *course* you could have stopped her. If she didn't want to be stopped she'd have moved back to her parents'! Why haven't you been round there on your knees begging her to come back?'

Phil's sullenness cracked and he looked desperate. 'Because I don't know what to say! I already feel like I've asked too much of her – first the girls, now Becca's baby . . . maybe she doesn't deserve all this. I can't give her the one thing she wants to make this worthwhile so yes, maybe she should find someone else.'

'Do you honestly believe that?' Michelle stared at him in horror.

'Yes.' He sank his head into his hands. 'No. Of course I don't. She's the best thing that's ever happened to me. Look at me. Even the dog wants to move in with Anna.'

Michelle took his tea away, just as he reached for it. 'Phil. This is a personal question, I know, but what's stopping you having a baby with Anna? You were happy to have one once. What's changed?'

He said nothing for a few moments, then spoke without raising his head. 'I'm not a great dad. I had Becca far too young, and Sarah was just as clueless as me, so we were both making it up as we went along. And then when our marriage fell apart we had Lily to stick it back together – that's how crap we were as parents – and then Sarah divorced me, and between us we ruined the girls' lives.'

'Well, that's not true. People make mistakes,' said Michelle. 'It's not what you've done, it's how you go about fixing it. And presumably you've learned a bit on the job?'

'But would it be what Anna's imagined?' Phil looked up. His eyes were bloodshot. 'She had an idyllic childhood – only child, happy parents. She's been planning this baby since we met, but some of the worst moments of my life were when Becca and Chloe were little.'

'How much of that was down to parenting and how much was down to being married to someone you didn't want to be with?'

'How can I take that risk? I don't think I can do it again, and watch her be disappointed. With parenthood. With me. I love her. I wish I'd met her twenty years ago.'

Michelle said nothing, stirring her tea. She wasn't sure Phil's milk was very fresh, but she tried not to think about it.

'Well?' said Phil. 'Is that a good enough reason?'

'No,' said Michelle. 'It's not. She loves you. She wants *your* baby, not just any old baby. Do you have any idea how lucky you are?'

'But what do I say? I don't want to lose her,' Phil looked close to tears. 'I don't want the girls to lose her. They adore her.'

'Then you've got to get round there and get her back. Today.'

'I can't,' said Phil. 'I've got to collect them all from the airport at three.'

'Then that gives you six hours to come up with some better reasons. She's worth fighting for.'

'And are you going to help?' Phil regained some of his usual spirit. 'You haven't exactly been there for her over the past few months, either.'

'OK,' said Michelle. 'Us.'

Anna sat in the cramped upstairs flat, wrapped in one of the new cashmere dressing gowns Michelle was selling by the armful, and tried to find some comfort in *Charlie and the Chocolate Factory*. Even Charlie Bucket was letting her down, the little prig. His obsession with the rules was annoying her now, not filling her with hope. What sort of child was let loose next to a river of actual chocolate, and thought about *hygiene*?

Following the rules was no guarantee of anything, she thought, taking another slug of wine. He should have dived in, along with Augustus. At least Augustus found out what it was like to drink from the river of chocolate.

She tossed *Charlie and the Chocolate Factory* onto the pile of discarded reading matter next to her.

It had all let her down. There were no happy endings in real life, no miraculous recoveries, no convenient arrivals of legacies or aunts from abroad. She'd been stupid to think that there would be.

Anna concentrated on her anger because it distracted her from the real sadness; all the books reminded her of Lily, and Chloe, and Becca, and the dreams she'd had only twelve months ago. How had things changed so fast? And why hadn't Phil come round?

She jumped when the intercom buzzed, and was going to ignore it when it crackled into life.

'Anna. It's me. Michelle. I know you're up there.'

Anna pushed herself up and shuffled over to the door. 'I'm busy.'

'No, you're not. Come down.'

'Why?'

'There's someone here who wants to see you.'

Her heart thumped. Phil. Maybe he felt as if he needed a bodyguard. Still, it was better than nothing.

Anna pulled on her coat and scarf and went down the stairs, trying to compose a dignified opening gambit in her head. But when she opened the door, there was only Michelle there, with Pongo in a new red coat and Tavish in his tartan winter number. Michelle was holding two paper cups of coffee, the way they used to in the days when they'd walk Pongo before work.

There was no sign of Phil, though. She tried not to let her disappointment show.

Michelle offered her Pongo's lead. 'Pongo asked me if you'd come for a walk with us. He was going to leave you a message on your step,' she added, 'along with some biscuits, but I told him I couldn't wait that long.'

Anna forced out a smile that Michelle seemed pleased with, and they set off down the high street towards the municipal gardens. Pongo seemed thrilled to be out – she was willing to bet Phil hadn't been walking him anywhere near enough while she'd been away – but he was making an effort not to pull, and she felt a sudden burst of affection for him.

Michelle didn't bother with any niceties. 'I've got a business proposition for you,' she said. 'I need a manager for my new shop.'

So this was it. The bookshop was closing. Anna took a deep breath, knowing this was probably the end of their friendship.

'I don't want to manage it if it isn't a bookshop,' she said. 'Sorry. It wouldn't be the same.'

'What if it was a bookshop *and* something else?'

Anna glanced sideways and Michelle carried on. 'What if it was a bookshop downstairs and a bedshop upstairs?' She made a signage gesture with her hand. 'Upstairs to Bed.'

'But you don't have the upstairs.'

'I can, if I want. The new landlord is happy to let it to me.'

Anna gave up her pretence of not being interested. 'And who's that?'

'Rory. Mr Quentin left it to him in his will, on the condition that he let Tavish live there too.'

'Really?' That was so typical of Mr Quentin, she thought. Eccentric, but kind. 'And who owns the shop?'

'You'll love this. The rescue kennels who took Tavish in. So they're happy for me to stay too, but it's only fair that I make enough money to pay the rent. So, my plan is to put my blankets and bedlinens and rag rugs upstairs. And if you're as good at selling them as you are flogging paperbacks, it might just keep the books side of things going downstairs.'

Anna bit her tongue. She didn't want Michelle to see how excited she was. Not yet.

'Oh, come on!' said Michelle. 'I'm totally excited about this. Please say you are.' When Anna didn't reply, she added, 'Because if I can't have you managing it, then I won't do it.'

'You wouldn't.'

'I would. It's your shop as much as mine. It wouldn't work the same without you.'

Michelle stopped walking and slipped Tavish's lead over one wrist, so her hands were free to catch hold of Anna's. 'I'm sorry,' she said. 'I've never been as good a friend to you as you've been to me. I never thought anyone could care about me as much as you have, and if I didn't tell you things, it was only because I was scared I'd spoil whatever lovely version of me you seemed to see.'

'Don't.' Anna's own eyes were filling up at the anxiety in Michelle's face. She looked so young, not her normal, polished, confident self. Anna realised Michelle wasn't wearing any make-up.

'No, really. I've never had a proper friend. Isn't that sad? I only realised what I'd missed out on when I met you. When you came and shared your cake with me, and left me that note on my step – it was like I'd come home, even though I'd never been here in my life. I've missed you so much these last few months. I've . . .' She gulped. 'I've got a lot to tell you. Not here. But soon. I want to tell you all sorts of stuff.'

Anna looked at her for a second, through a wobbly mist of tears, then dropped her coffee on the ground and hugged Michelle tight.

'Stop it!' she said, crying into her hair. 'I've been so worried about you. I wanted to call but I didn't know what to say.'

'Me neither,' said Michelle. 'Just sorry.'

'Don't be sorry. I am.'

'No, I am.'

'Do you want to row about this? Because you *cannot* be sorrier than me.'

Anna half laughed, half cried, and she and Michelle hugged each other while Pongo and Tavish waited patiently beside them.

'You should go home,' said Michelle, as the sun set and the red and green lights around the bandstand began to gleam against the slate sky.

'I don't want to.' Anna's heart broke to hear herself say it. 'It doesn't feel like home.'

'I meant go back to the flat,' said Michelle. 'Isn't that home now?'

Anna turned her head in surprise. 'You're not going to give me some pep talk about going back and working things out with Phil?'

Michelle shrugged. 'If you want my opinion, you've done enough talking. It's about time he did something.'

'He won't.' Anna pulled Pongo back from a smelly litter bin. 'I've tried.'

They walked back up the high street more cheerfully than they'd walked down it, pointing out sales to each other and making lists for the new year, but when they got to Home Sweet Home, Michelle reached into her bag and pulled out a flat present, gorgeously wrapped as usual.

'For you,' she said with a smile. 'Don't bother to save the paper, please. Get it unwrapped.'

'Don't tell me it's a book.' Anna pulled away the ribbon and turned the book over. It was an old hardback copy of *Madeline*, in French.

'It's lovely!' she exclaimed. 'I love *Madeline*.'

'She reminded me of you,' said Michelle. 'She's brave and she cares about people. And dogs love her. I bought it in Paris. Rory translated for me.'

'That's the nicest present anyone's ever given me,' said Anna, touched that Michelle had been thinking of her on her romantic break, and also that she'd gone into a bookshop.

'Want to come in?' she asked.

'I can't.' A look of pure happiness lit up Michelle's face. 'Rory's been to pick up my dog, from my mum's. The big handover – I didn't trust Harvey not to get funny about it, so I said I'd send my solicitor. I've got to get the house ready, haven't I, Tavish? For your new friend.'

'Dog bags for two, is it?' said Anna ironically.

Michelle shook her head. 'No dog bags. Just a much more powerful hoover. There are limits. It's like you said, if you make people keep their shoes on, they won't get hairs on their socks.'

Anna was privately amazed at the turnaround. Michelle seemed looser. Happier than she'd been before. Her hair wasn't quite so straightened, and she was wearing jeans. Jeans!

She looked down at Pongo, scratching at the door. 'Is it OK

if he stays for supper with me?' she asked. 'Now I suppose you're my landlady? I'll hoover . . .'

'No worries. He can't be messier than Owen.' Michelle gave her one last hug, then strode off. When she was halfway down the street, and she thought Anna wasn't looking, she picked Tavish up and tucked him under her arm, so he didn't have to keep up with her.

Anna smiled and put the key in the lock.

Pongo ran up the stairs ahead of her and started barking even before he reached the top.

Anna could hear movement, then she heard a voice say, 'Shhh! Shhh!'

Another voice, very familiar, said, 'Oh my God, it's so typical of that stupid dog to ruin everything!'

Then another voice said, 'Shhh, Pongo, pretend like you're in the van and the baddies are coming, shhh!'

Then another, male, voice said, 'Sssssshhhhhhhh!'

Her chest fluttered and she pushed on upstairs, determined not to think anything until she got there.

When she opened the door to the flat, it was dark. And then someone flicked a switch and the room was lit up with hundreds of tiny lights, pearl-sized glow-worms around the mirror and the walls. Anna could smell pine and realised that there was a Christmas tree in the corner of the flat, decorated rather haphazardly with crimson glass baubles. She could see presents under the tree, and tinsel all over the furniture, and in the soft glow of the candles burning on the shelves were Becca, Lily, Chloe, Owen and Phil.

And Pongo – now happily licking Lily's hand as she tried to keep him quiet.

'Happy Christmas,' said Becca. 'It wasn't Christmas without you.'

'Becca!' Chloe looked furious. 'I was going to do my song.'

'Let her do her song,' said Phil. 'Let's get it out of the way.'

Chloe glared at him, then coughed, and closed her eyes in the approved talent show style, holding out her right hand as if she was pinching an invisible balloon.

'Anna McQueen,' she began, to the tune of 'Silent Night'. '*Anna McQuueeeeen*, You are there when my sisters are mean, You're the one who cooks meals that I'll eat, You care that I'm allergic to dairy and wheat . . .'

'So you say,' muttered Becca, as Chloe gave the line some extra soul diva vibrato and joggled the invisible balloon up and down.

'You're not my mother, that's true-ooo . . .' Chloe tried to hold the note, but it dropped off with a wobble she couldn't help. She opened one eye and finished, 'But we love you 'cos you are you.'

Anna's eyes filled up.

'Don't let her do another verse,' said Phil. 'We'll all go deaf.'

Becca was watching her reaction, her face wreathed with concern as she rested one hand unthinkingly on her bump.

'I don't know what to say,' she managed, trying to smile. 'That's a yes from me. You're going to boot camp!'

Chloe looked very pleased with herself.

'Yay!' said Lily. 'Do you like what we did? Michelle gave us the keys to the shop and said we could have what we liked! It's like an extra Christmas picnic!'

'It's beautiful,' said Anna. 'Thank you!'

'Why don't you go through to the kitchen and put some of that food onto plates,' said Phil. 'I want a word with Anna.'

'Come on,' said Becca, hustling them through. She closed the door behind them with a nervous backwards glance at her dad.

Phil and Anna stood in the fairy lights, each waiting for the other to speak.

He's got to go first, Anna willed herself. He's got to make the first move.

After what felt like an hour, Phil took a deep breath and said, 'I'm sorry.'

'Sorry for what?'

'For not being the husband you thought you were marrying. For not being able to give you your big happy ever after.' He looked desolate.

Anna's heart plunged. 'That sounds like a goodbye, not an apology.'

He reached out and took her hands, and she could feel him trembling. 'You are the most articulate person I've ever met. You always have the right words on the tip of your tongue and I don't. I've spent the last few months trying to find the right way to express how I feel, and hating myself that I can't. I still don't think I've got it.'

'Try.' Her voice sounded thick.

'OK. I love you,' said Phil simply. 'I love you so much I don't have the right words to tell you. I feel like I waited my whole life to meet you, and when I did, I couldn't believe my luck. You're not my second chance, you're my first real love, Anna. My life is a complicated mess but you make it seem straightforward, just as long as you're there with me. Please come home. I need you.'

'For the girls?'

'For all of us.' He looked her straight in the eyes. 'I know I've messed you about this year, about having our own baby. I'm sorry. It's not that I don't want to have one, I just . . . I have a crap track record as a dad. I didn't have a father. I had no idea what dads were meant to do, just my mother going on and on about what they *shouldn't* be like. And then suddenly when I was twenty I *was* one. And again, at twenty-two. You're a much more natural parent than me, and I've got three kids.'

'You're a *great* father.' Anna couldn't believe he was saying this. 'Look at your girls.'

'Do you realise how much of that is down to you?' He held her gaze. 'If it hadn't been for you, putting yourself last for the past couple of years, just so they'd feel they were always coming first, who knows how much worse it could have been? I don't think I realised. And you know who told me?'

'Michelle?'

'No. My mother.'

'Evelyn?' Anna just stopped herself adding, 'That old bag?', as was her mental habit.

Phil rubbed his chin, like a guilty boy. 'I went up to see her on Boxing Day and she told me she'd said something mean to you the day Becca . . . the day Becca told us about the baby. She said she felt bad about it, because you'd done a much better job with them than Sarah was doing.' He raised his eyebrows. 'Well, she *actually* said if they'd been with Sarah, Chloe would probably have been pregnant too, and Lily would have an imaginary friend. But still . . .'

'Is that a compliment? I'm only a semi-negligent stepmother?'

'No,' said Phil. 'You are the *best* stepmother any child could have hoped for. Ask the girls. You make Mary Poppins look like . . . like . . . Oh God, I don't know enough children's books.'

'Try *The Witches*,' said Anna. She could feel something melting inside her, warming her like mulled wine. 'Or Cruella de Vil. You should do more reading with Lily.'

'I should.' He held out his arms and slowly she stepped into them, thinking she could be dignified about it. But then Phil's strong arms were round her, and his nose was pressed into her neck, and she was clinging to him as if she could somehow merge her body with his. He smelled so familiar and safe, and it scared her how close she'd come to losing everything she loved most.

'I love you, Anna,' he said, his breath hot against her skin, whispering so they wouldn't be overheard. 'All I care about is giving you the happy ever after you want. In our own messy, complicated way.'

'You're doing that. And I don't think we're quite at the end yet,' she said.

Out of the corner of her eye, she saw the kitchen door was open, a tiny wedge of yellow light against the darkness of the sitting room. Some of the light was blotted out by bodies, but at the bottom was a black-and-white spotted nose.

'Let's go home,' said Anna, feeling a sudden need to hold her whole family tightly around her and cover them with the love bursting out of her. 'I want to have Christmas all over again.'

Anna McQueen's childhood favourites for recommended bedtime reading★

- ❖ *Charlie and the Chocolate Factory*, Roald Dahl
- ❖ *James and the Giant Peach*, Roald Dahl
- ❖ In fact, everything by Roald Dahl!
- ❖ *Ballet Shoes*, Noel Streatfeild
- ❖ *One Hundred and One Dalmatians* and *The Starlight Barking*, Dodie Smith
- ❖ *What Katy Did*, Susan Coolidge
- ❖ *Charlotte's Web*, E. B. White
- ❖ *Tom's Midnight Garden*, Philippa Pearce
- ❖ *The Sheep-Pig*, Dick King-Smith
- ❖ *Little Women*, Louisa May Alcott
- ❖ *The Famous Five*, Enid Blyton
- ❖ *Anne of Green Gables*, Lucy Maud Montgomery
- ❖ *The Secret Garden* and *The Little Princess*, Frances Hodgson Burnett
- ❖ *Pippi Longstocking*, Astrid Lindgren
- ❖ *Peter Rabbit*, Beatrix Potter
- ❖ *The Worst Witch*, Jill Murphy
- ❖ *Winnie the Pooh*, A. A. Milne
- ❖ *Mary Poppins*, P. L. Travers
- ❖ *First Term at Malory Towers*, Enid Blyton
- ❖ *Harry Potter* 1–7 (all of them, you can't just read one!)
- ❖ *The Railway Children*, Edith Nesbit
- ❖ *The Jungle Book*, Rudyard Kipling
- ❖ Any of the *Chalet School* series, Elinor Brent-Dyer
- ❖ *Mrs Pepperpot*, Alf Prøysen
- ❖ *Madeline*, Ludwig Bemelmans (not necessarily in French, although that adds a certain *je ne sais quoi*!)

★ Children and Dalmatians are optional

Read on for an interview
with Lucy Dillon . . .

The books from our childhoods seem to form very powerful, evocative memories. What are the books you most fondly remember from your childhood, and why?
Looking back now I realise how lucky I was growing up in the 70s and 80s in the middle of a creative boom in children's fiction, and with an English-teacher mother who read a book a day, and also ran the school library. I read, and was read to, all the time, so I probably only spent about 50% of my waking childhood in the real world. As well as the classics like Enid Blyton, E Nesbit and Arthur Ransome (which I gobbled up, living in the Lake District), I have vivid memories of all the Roald Dahl books, *Pippi Longstocking*, the Pullein-Thompson sisters' pony books, Judy Blume (v racy!), *The Worst Witch*, which predated Harry Potter by quite a long time... The ones that stick in the mind most, though, are the Roald Dahl books like *Charlie and the Chocolate Factory* and *Danny, Champion of the World*; I suppose that's partly because they're incredibly vivid narratives, written in Dahl's instantly recognisable style, but partly because they were read to me at bedtime, when words seem to sink in deepest. And also, maybe, because they're classics that engage an adult imagination just as much as a child's.

Is there a character or story that you particularly identified with?
Jo March – I wasn't a tomboy but I had one sister, and loved scribbling away in the attic, like her. I knew exactly how she felt on discovering libraries in her aunt's house - those

bookworm butterflies of excitement at all the different worlds hidden in the shelves. That was the first book I longed to 'go into', button boots and cotillions and all. My lifelong fascination with American baking – grits and muffins, pies and biscuits – started with the Marchs' dinners, and Katy Carr's tuckbox.

Was there a hero you dreamt of running away with and marrying?

I wish I could say Mr Darcy, but my first crush was on sensible Julian from the *Famous Five* series. He probably grew up to be a very sensible accountant with sensible shoes and a Volvo, but at the time I thought his quick thinking and good manners were splendid. Soon after, I went through a Greek mythology phase, and rather fancied Hercules (setting the bar quite high there for future boyfriends), but then I found a tatty copy of *Gone with the Wind* and it's been all about Rhett ever since.

Was storytime an important part of your bedtime ritual as a child? Is it still?

It was always the highlight of the day. My younger sister and I had a bedtime story every single night for years and years – my parents took it in turns to read to us, and I think they enjoyed it as much as we did, although we learned the stories very quickly and knew if they were trying to cut them short by 'abridging'. There's nothing more soothing than dropping off to the sound of someone's voice, letting the pictures bloom in your imagination as sleep rolls in – I think that's why children's books take root so firmly in our memories. Listening to someone read, rather than reading yourself, seems to let even more of your imagination loose, especially when the setting is unfamiliar: I have extremely vivid mental images of the European children's stories like *Mrs Pepperpot* and *Emile and the Detectives*, for that reason. Now I listen to Talk Radio on a sleep timer when I drop off, which isn't always quite so soothing.

Why do you think bedtime storytelling has become such a tradition?

Storytelling has always been an important part of the human cultural instinct, the sharing of stories between one generation and the next, and it's one of the reasons that children's classics endure for so long, because there's real pleasure in revisiting them as an adult. Modern life is busy and also visual; sharing a slower, aural experience, in which imaginations connect by telling stories that the parent or grandparent loved when they were the same age as the child, is special. It's almost like *Tom's Midnight Garden*, in a way – the 'ghost' of the parent's own childhood comes back to life again in the same story. It's lovely to think of all the children who grew up on Harry Potter dusting down their editions in twenty years' time and sharing them with children and grandchildren; I read the Potter books as an adult and a big element of their charm for me was the echoes of so many familiar story traditions hidden inside.

Animals, especially dogs, feature prominently in children's literature – and indeed in your novels. Do you think that animals can sometimes help the human characters in stories express themselves better?

It's an interesting point! I think, looking at it with a grown-up reader's eyes, that often the animals in books are aligned with the children, as co-conspirators in the magical non-human world – the innocent child can see and understand the animal much better than the adults can, and the animals reward the child's honest trust by sharing some secret with them or saving them from the consequences of the adults' stupidity. Animals (OK, dogs and horses) don't have very vested interests beyond being warm and being fed, but in return they give disproportionate amounts of loyalty, courage, and love, something humans usually end up learning from in children's books.

Although, having said that, I'm a real wuss when it comes to animals in books; from Black Beauty onwards, there's a huge pile of stories that I've never been able to finish, thanks to the constant shedding of tears. Even Michael Morpurgo is too hardcore for me. We had to read *White Fang* by Jack London when I was at school, and I never really recovered.

You show that the pleasure of sharing a story isn't exclusive to childhood: Anna's visits to Butterfield's to read aloud bring the resident's great joy. What do you think it is about this activity that so draws people in?
Reading aloud is such a positive community experience – it builds an instant relationship between the listeners, and opens up a whole map of different discussions, such as their interpretation of what everyone's just heard, or their related experiences, or perhaps their memory of reading it themselves for the first time. When I was researching The Secret of Happy Ever After, I found a lot of inspiration in The Reader Organisation, which works to promote reading in communities; they run 'Get into Reading' sessions all over the country, particularly among groups who've lost their connection to literature, either through blindness, or lack of reading skills, or

other social or mental problems. The website is www.thereader.org.uk and it has lots of interesting information about joining or starting a group, as well as glowing testimonials from happy readers!

As the Reader Organisation's work demonstrates, reading aloud has many positive therapeutic effects beyond basic entertainment; for example, it seems to help dementia sufferers to access different areas of their memory, by retreading familiar old narrative ground. It's a gentle way of making a connection with an elderly relative; if you struggle to find the right conversations to engage each other, why not offer to read from a favourite book for half an hour? The Reader Organisation has produced *A Little Aloud,* an anthology of easy-to-read, inspiring-to-listen-to selections from different genres of literature, for all age groups. I really recommend it.